*The*
# CHAMPAGNE WAR

Fiona McIntosh is an internationally bestselling author of novels for adults and children. She co-founded an award-winning travel magazine with her husband, which they ran for fifteen years while raising their twin sons before she became a full-time author. Fiona roams the world researching and drawing inspiration for her novels, and runs a series of highly respected fiction masterclasses. She calls South Australia home.

# PRAISE FOR FIONA McINTOSH'S BESTSELLERS

'A blockbuster of a book that you
won't want to put down.'
BRYCE COURTENAY

'McIntosh's narrative races across oceans and
dances through ballrooms.'
SUN HERALD

'This book is fast-paced, beautifully haunting and filled
with the excruciating pain of war.'
WEST AUSTRALIAN

'A fine read . . . The moral ambiguity McIntosh
builds into the novel gives it a depth that takes it beyond
a sweeping wartime romantic thriller.'
SUNDAY HERALD SUN

'McIntosh weaves a diverse cast together,
and you gain an appreciation for her depth of research.'
BOOKS+PUBLISHING

'A captivating saga of love, loss, and the
triumph of the human spirit . . . Fiona McIntosh
is an extraordinary storyteller.'
BOOK'D OUT

'A perfect blend of romance, action,
mystery and intrigue by one of our best
known and popular authors.'
NOOSA TODAY

# FIONA McINTOSH

## *The* CHAMPAGNE WAR

MICHAEL JOSEPH
*an imprint of*
PENGUIN BOOKS

MICHAEL JOSEPH

UK | USA | Canada | Ireland | Australia
India | New Zealand | South Africa | China

Michael Joseph is part of the Penguin Random House group of companies
whose addresses can be found at global.penguinrandomhouse.com.

Penguin
Random House
Australia

First published by Michael Joseph, 2020

Cover design by Louisa Maggio © Penguin Random House Australia Pty Ltd
Cover photographs: woman by Rekha Garton/Arcangel;
vineyard by Martijn van der Nat/Getty Images
Inside cover image by Champagne Michel Gonet
Internal images by Val_Iva/Shutterstock
Typeset in Sabon by Midland Typesetters, Australia

Printed and bound in Australia by Griffin Press, part of Ovato, an accredited
ISO AS/NZS 14001 Environmental Management Systems printer

A catalogue record for this
book is available from the
National Library of Australia

ISBN 978 0 14379 545 2

penguin.com.au

MIX
Paper from
responsible sources
FSC® C009448

*Was it fate or chance that brought an Australian writer and a French champenoise together, one to inspire the story and the other to write it? Neither of us could know that during the course of this book we would both lose the precious men who were the first to hold our hands and assure their little girls that we could achieve our dreams.*

*To our beautiful fathers, forever sparkling in our hearts: Frederick Richards and Michel Antoine Gonet.*

# PROLOGUE

As the new year of 1910 moved closer to its second month, the world marvelled that there had been so few deaths in Paris when the River Seine rose more than eight metres and flooded the city. The water didn't burst the banks as many presumed; instead it took a more sinister path, rising up through the subway system and over-flowing through sewers and any tunnel that its liquid tendrils could discover. Mother Nature, in her stealth, brought the city to its knees and covered its homes with her waters. And yet she had warned them – winter rainfall had been much higher than usual, and other rivers were showing signs of breach. Makeshift bridges had to be built to allow people to move around Paris, and some chose to row up and down its great avenues, even the Champs Élysées. The atmosphere in the city felt almost carnivalesque. The scenes described and photographed for the rest of the world were surreal.

In its gleeful rush to the sea, the River Seine took with it a restless highway of trees, furniture and shopfronts, amid a parade of possessions and the carcasses of animals caught unawares.

It also took three people from the same family with the surname Delancré.

Sophie, its one member left behind, busy in Épernay while her family was in Paris, and furiously regretting a chance to visit her favourite place on earth – the Opéra Garnier – these days never chose to recall the winter of 1910. Her mind, however, sometimes walked where her thoughts didn't want to travel. It was impossible to clean away her sorrow in the same way Paris had cleansed itself of the flood's repercussions.

It had been four years of sadness since learning that her parents had been hauled dead from the muddy waters but her brother – a gift from heaven, as her mother had called him, because she'd delivered him in her early forties – had vanished into the swirling depths, never to be recovered. The passing of his life was a tiny event among the broadening drama as more than two hundred thousand Parisians were made homeless over the day of the deluge.

She'd never discovered what had actually happened to put her three beloveds in that muddy water, but she had to presume ten-year-old Olivier had perhaps fallen into the water and her father had leapt in to rescue him; presumably her mother had tried to help and they'd all perished with the ferocity of that water. None could swim so their deaths, she knew, would have been panicked but she hoped swift. The horror taunted her for long winters of loneliness until the bright-natured vigneron Jerome Méa caught her elbow as she stumbled and changed her life as swiftly as the flood had changed her family's.

They'd only met by chance, for although their fathers knew each other, the children's lives had never intersected. He'd been born in Avize, about seven and a half miles from where she had been born and raised in Épernay. Four years after her father's death, she received a message from the elder brother, Louis Méa, who wanted to discuss with the champagne house a new technique the family was trialling for winter pruning.

She noted Méa's surprised expression, soon dissolving into a sardonic smile that the daughter had kept the appointment booked with senior winemaker Étienne Doremus. Méa proceeded to give her a tour of their chateau . . . not that she had come for that reason. As he did his best to impress upon her through his boastful facts about which king had slept in which wing down the centuries, and in which room Napoleon had presented Josephine with the rose- and violet-scented gloves he'd had crafted for her by House Galimard in Grasse, she realised how thoroughly bored she was by the somewhat paunchy and flamboyant Méa. He had ten years on her at least, and she noted, as he took the liberty of pressing gently on her back to guide her through a doorway, that his hands were small and well-manicured. Would he even know what a vineyard looked like?

'Ah, now, my dear, do you know what this is?'

Sophie wanted to cut him a withering look and explain that not only could she not know, she certainly couldn't guess, and most of all that she was entirely uninterested to know, but that would be impolite . . . and this was business. Instead she smiled her query, forbidding herself to speak.

He carried on as though the question were rhetorical. 'This is where Victor Hugo, when he regularly visited my forebears, liked to write from. He was born but three or so hours from here at Besançon, near the Swiss border,' he continued. His lightly pitched voice sounded like it enjoyed whispers and gossip. 'I'm told he worshipped the light in this room . . . I rather like to think he might have penned some of *The Hunchback of Notre-Dame* here – perhaps been vaguely inspired by our own cathedral at Reims.'

What a pompous ass he was. She couldn't wait to get away from this ghastly fellow, but diplomacy rode her shoulder and warned her that she needed his grapes, which were unrivalled for quality.

'Now, my dear, do you believe in first impressions?'

She looked back at him, baffled. 'I do,' she said, again forbidding the next truth, which was desperate to come out, from escaping.

'Oh, I do too,' he said, and licked his lips, which he tended to suck on, so they appeared redder than they should. 'And my first impression is that you are a woman of intellect and motivation. You've mentioned opera . . . Only the truly intelligent understand it.'

'And yet opera isn't about intellect; I like to think it's all about the emotional —'

He cut blithely across her remark without even an apology, as though he hadn't heard her beginning to respond to his crass idea, or didn't care. 'I should like to escort you to the opera one day, my dear . . . In fact, let me be transparent in these trying times for you and for your champagne house. I should like to escort you to many fine establishments. I feel I can offer you what you most need.' His pudgy smile made her shudder inwardly.

'And what is that, Monsieur Méa?' She wanted to hear him say it.

He considered his words; chose one. 'Tethering,' he replied, with a slight lift of an eyebrow that looked like a caterpillar moving in a new direction.

Her private shudder turned to revulsion. Of all the words! 'Er, Monsieur Méa, I —'

He raised the hand of hers she'd wanted him to let go of more than a minute ago, held it up and first sniffed it, making a sighing sound before he kissed it. Slightly wet ruby lips lingered far too long on her skin, leaving it damp as he pulled away. 'Call me Louis, please,' he urged. 'We are friends now and no doubt can be more. We must protect what our two families have built. Our fathers have always been close and their children should cleave to that bond, especially now that your dear parents have passed, rest their blessed souls.'

Revolted, she wanted to wipe her hand against her skirts but instead she gave a nervous laugh. 'Er, Louis, what about the vineyards? I think it's important that —'

They were interrupted by the hectic arrival of a tall man, pulling off a cap; his broad face was displaying earnest apology over the panting of someone who had clearly been running. His voice was loud, his huge hands were grubby, and his gaze shifted from Louis to lock on to her from beneath symmetrical heavy eyebrows. If the touch of Louis felt wet, then this man's eyes seemed to scorch her skin as he landed his attention wholly upon her. He was unshaven and didn't seem to care much about his dishevelment, extending a hand he wiped on his stained work trousers as if echoing her own thought of a heartbeat ago.

'I'm sorry I'm late. Louis sent a messenger to fetch me.'

She stared at him, baffled but intrigued. 'Who are you?'

He laughed, loud and free. 'Apologies, Mademoiselle Delancré. As well as being an idiot and late, I am also Jerome Méa, brother to Louis here.'

'My stepbrother has tested my patience with his tardiness since he was born, my dear.'

She blinked, trying to catch up.

'Different mothers,' Jerome explained gently. 'But I don't bother with the remove. Louis and I are brothers as far as I'm concerned; we share everything.'

She looked back at Louis and doubted he felt the same.

'My mother died as I was born. Jerome's mother raised us.' He tried to disguise it in a matter-of-fact tone but she heard the regret.

'Ah,' she said, dawning. 'I had no idea. I'm sorry you lost your mother at such a tender age.'

Louis nodded and continued, seemingly unmoved. 'I've asked Jerome to take you around the vineyards and show you what our family wishes to do with the vines.'

Jerome grinned at her. 'I hope that suits, mademoiselle?'

What luck! 'Perfectly,' she replied as crisp as she dared, delighted to escape the presumptuous elder brother. 'Shall we head out now?'

He bowed as if he was hers to command. She could smell the scents of the land emanating from him: earthy and leafy, his skin slightly shiny from toil rather than lip-licking.

'I've had a spread put out in the morning room,' Louis reminded them. 'That's Victor's room,' he added with a narrow smile that fought its way through his pale, fleshy face. 'Do join us later,' he urged. 'You and I have so much to discuss, Mademoiselle Delancré.'

It took all of her resolve to give him a smile that was not a rebuke but hardly agreement before she followed the bold stride of the brother as he led her out of the chateau into the fresh bright air of the vineyards . . . his vineyards.

'Louis owns the house. I own the vineyards. That's the agreement. We share the spoils.'

She hadn't asked him to explain but she was grateful for his openness. 'That's very . . . er, brotherly.'

He gave her a sideways grin. 'We couldn't be more different, I know.'

She sighed her relief at his remark. 'I would never pick you as brothers. Where do you connect?' Sophie watched him frown and immediately regretted her boldness. 'You must forgive me. I should not have spoken out of turn.'

'You didn't.' He laughed, sounding carefree. 'I have nothing in common with Louis other than our father. And we both did love him enormously. My mother tried to love Louis and I think they were close enough until I came along.' He shrugged. 'Blood will out, they say,' he continued, sounding guilty. 'I was her true son. I suppose she couldn't hide that.'

'Do you get on?'

He shook his head. 'No. But I love him as a brother. I know that sounds odd to love even when we aren't good friends. I stay out of his way. I work the vineyards and I'm happy out here. Louis likes being in Reims or Paris at parties and social events. He comes to Avize mostly to check the books or to entertain when he needs to impress someone.' He picked off a leaf from the closest vine. 'Someone like you,' he added.

'Me? He doesn't know me.'

He nodded, turning serious. 'He does. Since we heard about your father . . . and Louis, he has a plan.'

She made the leap as fast as wildfire. 'Oh no.'

Sophie heard the rasp of his beard as he scratched his face. 'He sees it as the perfect blend of two families begging to be bonded through marriage. You make champagne. He has grapes.'

It was her turn to fix him with a firm gaze. 'Except the vines are yours.'

Historically, the Méa family had made their money from many crops, but it was the grape in particular they excelled at. The three famous women of the Épernay region – meunier, pinot noir and chardonnay – were their specialty . . . but chardonnay was Jerome's.

He met her look with an amused one that gave the impression of being conspiratorial. 'I can refuse to grow them for you . . . would that help?'

She poked the air towards him. 'I am not going to marry Louis, not if he were the last man on this earth, not if he offered me the last grape on this land.'

Jerome let out a wild, generous explosion of laughter. 'I believe you, mademoiselle, but I thought it only fair to let you in on my brother's grand scheme.' He ran his hand through thick hair that showed a reddish tinge in the sunlight, which had bronzed his skin so every laughter line, of which there were plenty, seemed more clearly etched. She recalled how pale his brother was and how few creases there were in that smooth skin that she might attribute to the unreserved joy of laughing. This younger man was broad where his brother was simply enlarged from indulgence; Jerome was hard and muscled from his efforts in the fields, while Louis was soft, his skin plump from the good life and little exertion.

'Is everything all right?' he asked, noting how she watched him.

'Everything is suddenly right,' she answered, more cryptically than she had intended, noting his hooded gaze, which tried so hard to hide the laughing eyes, and how it narrowed further in query. 'Show me more of your vines and your plans. Let us see how you and I can work together.'

If laughter had been the spark, then their shared fascination for chardonnay was the vital breakthrough. Sophie discovered that afternoon how much she enjoyed his manner of telling her a story about his vines. She knew most of what there was to know about the life cycle of the vineyard, but the way Jerome Méa described what he was doing in his rows of vines, and why, charmed her. He spoke about his vines like they were his children, and his respect and love for the land, the flavour it gave to his precious charges, delighted Sophie.

'I wanted to show Étienne how I would be giving a more vigorous pruning this year. I felt it respectful to demonstrate for him what I was doing and explain my reasons, especially as my father – if he were alive – would likely not agree with my actions, not after the catastrophe of the disease that has traumatised France's vines.'

Sophie nodded. 'So, you're a renegade, Monsieur Méa?'

He grinned. 'I'm sure you have your own innovations in mind.'

'I do.' She returned the smile with one that was more secretive.

'As we are both our families' heirs, we must be progressive and not frightened to take risks.'

'*Santé* to that! However, am I to gather that this is a warning we may not get the yield we are used to from your vineyards this year?'

'Yes.' She appreciated his candour. 'Perhaps not as much as usual but by, let's say, the 1915 harvest, I am prepared to gamble all I have that we will be celebrating one of our best yields, and I believe with all my heart that Delancré will proudly offer one of your finest vintages ever.'

'The grapes will be that good?'

He put his hand on his heart and promised, his eyes twinkling with amusement, and she felt a genuine vibration of romantic interest in her heart that she'd not felt for any man before. There had been many who had tried to capture her attention but until now she'd felt almost ashamed at her lack of interest. Her mother had counselled her against pushing so many fine young men away.

'They're all too earnest, too polished, too sophisticated,' Sophie had explained. Her mother had sighed that anyone should complain about such commendable qualities. 'I want someone who makes me laugh. I want someone who is different to me, not from another winemaking family . . . someone who is perhaps my opposite.'

If her parents had felt any despair, they hadn't shown it, but even she had known that turning twenty-five without any leanings towards an engagement was causing tongues to gossip.

And now, without warning, a grape grower had caught her attention. She'd read romantic novels and wondered at the notion of one's heart skipping a beat, a hitch in the breath, one's chest feeling tight when the attraction was strong. They had struck her as clichéd, but to be experiencing all three symptoms both horrified and amused her. So, they were not only the dreamings of novelists; these were real experiences . . . and as that dawning struck, she stumbled in the vineyard. Jerome caught her elbow just as she lost her footing, and in that moment, as she looked up into his open, easily read face, she knew this tall, broad-shouldered man, with his rough stubble of growth, unruly hair and flat cloth cap worn rakishly, was the brother she intended to marry.

As it turned out, his heart and breath were skipping and jumping in tandem with hers. And later that day, as he helped her into her family's car, he kissed her hand and looked into her eyes in such a way that they both knew something special had erupted between them.

'Are you sure you won't stay for Louis's spread?'

She grinned at how he'd loaded the word. 'Will you explain that I had stayed longer in the fields than I intended and was feeling a little weary?'

'Of course. Will you visit again?'

She shook her head. 'I trust you, Jerome. And I do not want to run into your brother if I can help it. Why don't you come to Épernay – mention that I would like you to visit the cellars?' She tried to sound jaunty when all she wanted to do was stay longer . . . and have those large working hands around her waist, pulling her close.

'I shall.' He shrugged. 'Tomorrow?'

Sophie laughed. 'Perfect. Come alone. Stay for dinner.'

He stayed the night. And from thereon, he barely left her side.

The Méa family had always grown vines while her family had always been champenois, so while their union could be viewed by some as strategic, she knew it was one that only the angels could dream up, for theirs was founded on such deep affection that both Sophie and Jerome had admitted to not believing their good fortune.

Their pleasure was counterbalanced by Louis's horror at the news of their engagement, which developed into loathing for the couple that Sophie could feel like a solid entity glaring at her, no matter how much Louis smiled through all the congratulations.

The late summer wedding at the end of harvest, while his grapes matured and her ideas for the next vintage ripened, involved the whole town. The entire population lined the streets to watch the groom escort his bride to the church.

Sophie glided down the stairs of her empty home, now so quiet without the noise of a busy youngster roaming its hallways. This bride had no chattering mother fussing at her veil and no beaming father at the bottom of the stairs. There was Gaston de Saint Just, of course, her cousin and best friend, who would stand in for her father.

'I'll be outside,' he whispered, allowing the groom's first glimpse of the bride to be private.

Her fiancé's bright smile faltered at the sight of her and she hesitated.

'Jerome?'

'You're a vision. Don't move,' he pleaded. And she stopped midway down the stairs as the morning sunlight arced through the landing window to cast a shimmer around her beaded veil. 'Let me commit this moment to my deepest memory. I never want to lose this image of your glowing beauty or the realisation that you said yes to me.'

The guilt at being happy again tried to derail her but she pushed it aside, lifted the buttery silk of her gown and tiptoed carefully down to meet him. They paused again to hold the intimate moment.

'Jerome, I can't remember ever being happier than right now,' she admitted. 'My heart is yours forever.'

'Never let that change.'

Out they stepped. Gaston took her arm to guide her towards the church, as Jerome led the procession up the main street of Épernay to the rousing cheers of the townsfolk. Some worked for House Delancré, others worked for the neighbouring champagne houses, but everyone knew her. She'd grown up around these people and she felt their affection through their applause.

Gaston leaned in. 'I haven't seen you smile like that in an age, Sophie,' he admitted. 'I'm very proud to do this for you. Thank you for asking me.'

'Apart from my father, there is no one else I'd rather walk alongside today, darling Gaston.'

'Jerome's a good man; you are a perfect couple.' Gaston winked.

'I'm glad you approve,' she murmured from beneath her veil, feeling her spirits – although it seemed impossible – lift higher still.

'You need to be careful of his brother, though. I grew up with Louis Méa. He's not a man who takes scorn on any of his several chins easily.'

'He doesn't scare me.'

'It's not about being scared. You've told me he had desires for you. I want you to be aware that although you have married his brother, he will find a way to make up for the humiliation.'

'Don't be ridiculous.'

'It's not ridiculous in his mind. It's a slight.'

'Gaston, he's ignored me since my relationship with Jerome first became obvious.'

'Means nothing. Louis is a spider. He'll wait in the corner.'

'Oh, help me to find him a wife, then! This one's taken.'

Gaston leaned in and kissed her head through the veil. 'Sorry to mention him. And that all this well-deserved happiness is surrounded by so much discontent in Europe.'

'Let's not speak of it on my wedding day. It won't come to anything – we're all just feeling nationalistic,' she said, sounding more confident in her dismissiveness than she felt. The truth was that even to her in tiny Épernay, Europe felt as though it was a tinder-box waiting for some spark to light it up. She read the newspapers from Paris regularly; she paid attention to the shifts and upheavals in Europe and was more politically aware than most men might give her credit for. As an only child for such a long time her father had raised her as his heir, and part of her fundamental education was that she remained conscious of the world and its moods.

'Our world is not Épernay . . . our big city is not Reims. We do not belong to Champagne, or even to the Marne region, my child. No, we belong to Europe. That's your primary focus, and then you must look further to Great Britain and to the United States of America – that's where our product is consumed, so that's where our focus must be.'

He'd drummed this notion into her from when she was still small enough to be carried around the cellars that snaked in narrow tunnels beneath the house, alongside the cellars of the other top houses. She'd barely understood the sentiment as an infant, had no idea of geography as a youngster, but as she grew, her young mind had grasped that her father was reinforcing important information. She'd paid attention, and over the years he had widened her view of the world, taught her about current politics, encouraged her to discuss them with him and to form an opinion even if she didn't share it with her peers.

'As the person who will take over this house, you must know the world of men while moving effortlessly through the world of women,' he'd said. 'Until you take over, most will view you only as a beautiful daughter looking forward to her marriage and starting a family with a wealthy man of Champagne. Only you, your mother and I know that is only the tiniest part of you, my child. The future of House Delancré rests with you. You are its daughter, its lifeblood . . . its heir.'

Thus, as her wedding day approached, Sophie was well aware of the Kaiser's militarisation in Germany, the efforts at diplomacy between Britain, America, France . . . even Russia. She, like anyone else with a vested interest in a peaceful Europe, was relying on the familial relations between the three principal monarchs in Germany, England and Russia to prevent war. But even Sophie held grave fears for the repercussions of the assassination of the Archduke and Duchess in Sarajevo a couple of months ago. Her father's wisdom had never felt more prophetic.

'Whatever is happening in the world is happening to champagne,' he'd counselled.

Her champagne was drunk by the wealthy, and predominantly by the wealthy overseas. Their business couldn't rely solely on Paris. They also needed London, New York, Berlin and other grand cities like St Petersburg and Moscow to be buying their product and drinking it in vast quantities. Should war break out, their product and its earnings would be compromised and their ability to export whatever they might make nullified.

But today was not the day to contemplate nations falling out. Today was the biggest, brightest and happiest of her life. Sophie rallied her thoughts away from all political upheaval.

A young girl, part of the procession of children leading her towards the mayor's office for the formalities, looked back and waved at her, giving her a heartbreaking smile that echoed the dying summer. Today was as warm as that smile and the sun beamed a mellow gold from clear, azure skies. It was perfect for the outdoor feast that would come later. The children skipped ahead, excitedly holding the small rolls of ribbons they would stretch between themselves at the church. Jerome certainly planned to have a large family – it made her laugh each time he began discussing names, often ranging up to half a dozen options for boys and girls.

'We'll have enough children to use all our choices,' he'd promised.

She smiled inwardly knowing they would get busy realising that promise tonight. Jerome was not her first suitor – she had chosen him from a long line that had been queuing since she turned nineteen, but he was her first lover and that was exciting. The town, although understanding her despair of the last few years, could be forgiven for thinking House Delancré would not have an heir. She was late to lose her virginity – no one appreciated that fact more keenly than Sophie – but her circumstances meant she'd had to wait for love and someone worthy of hers and all that came with it.

Gaston patted her hand, breaking into her thoughts. 'Are you enjoying all this attention? I know you never seek it out.'

'I'm enjoying what it means. I'll be glad, though, when all the formalities are over.'

He nodded as they reached the town hall. After the mayor had officiated and pronounced them married, they were permitted to continue their procession to the church for the holy ceremony at Saint-Pierre Saint-Paul. She had always liked its Roman-Byzantine design and its stained-glass depiction of the patron saints of Champagne, especially Vincent from the year 304, and Urban, patron saint of bottlers – she knew them all from early childhood.

Jerome cast her a final grin as he disappeared into its depths to await her at the altar and all the children of the town unravelled their white ribbons.

Someone handed Sophie the scissors and she began to cut a path through the satin lengths that the children raised like streamers. To the villagers it symbolised that Sophie would get past all obstacles in her life, but to her it represented cutting away all ties to her sad past. This was her future she was cutting a path towards, and with each slice of the blades through satin she spoke silent words of optimism.

*Love*
*Happiness*
*Affection*

*Laughter*
*Children*
*Safety*
*Strong vines*
*Strong arms around me*
*Music*
*Dancing*
*Lovemaking*
*Family*

And as she said the final word, *Joy*, as if casting a spell to banish the grief of the years gone, she and Gaston emerged into the church. Its build, funded by the Chandon family, had been completed just two years after her birth; this was the church where she'd been confirmed.

Incense burned, fragrant and spice-laden, lifting up from the charcoal burner to waft notes of frankincense and myrrh along with forest oils like sandalwood and gums. And now as the congregation fell silent, she could hear the soft rustle of her silk gown.

Her rebellious nature showed in the design. She had flouted the corseted era of her mother's time and fallen in love with Paul Poiret's avant-garde *directoire* silhouette. It was both feminine and flattering, its highest, narrowest point highlighting her small waist and elongating her torso. Long, gently curving lines were achieved with the softest of fabric folds and a mix of silk thicknesses. She had even turned away from white, instead choosing an exquisite antique cream, the colour of her champagne. Clear glass seed beads offered a nod to the tiny, chiselled bubbles, while the greyish bugle beads that highlighted the design curtsied to the colour of the earth from which Jerome's grapes grew. She'd insisted on any train being modest and Poiret had respected her wishes with a short, pointed satin train that was given its angular shape via small lead weights sewn in at four separate points.

It was a statuesque look, but when the cutaway back was revealed, showing Sophie's wide, bare shoulder blades and the dip of her spine, it drew soft gasps of surprise from the older women and looks of thrilled approval from the younger ones. Having someone of Sophie's wealth and status wear such a daring design would give unspoken permission to all future brides to cast away the tailored, corseted gowns and voluminous skirts. A bride could now feel free to wear this styling that spoke of freedom and independence, unafraid to show either her skin or her femininity.

As she drew closer to the appreciative and beaming smile of her husband-to-be, she thought of the strong women of Champagne who had gone before her – like Veuve Clicquot or Madame Pommery. She knew they would approve of her determination not to conform, not to be fearful of the champagne world of men she worked with, but perhaps and most especially of her choice in a husband, who was a modern thinker and encouraged her independence.

She allowed herself a moment to ponder how it might have been if she'd become a wife to Louis; she could feel his scowl following her down the aisle like an unpleasant smell. He must move on, and could perhaps take solace in the fact that his grand plan to link their families had come to fruition . . . just with the other brother. Jerome turned and she felt her breath catch as she let Louis slip out of her thoughts, no longer important, no longer able to make any impact on their lives now that the brothers had reached an agreement to allow Jerome his vineyards and all profits from the grapes, while Louis kept the chateau, its contents and the proceeds from their other lucrative farming ventures.

She had her own chateau – several houses, in fact – and more wealth on her own terms than both brothers could muster. She did not need Louis, his advice, his money or his meddling. They were free to be Monsieur et Madame Delancré-Méa. Stepping beneath a silk and lace canopy, a throwback to the days before the veil came into vogue, Sophie took a deep breath of relief that gave clarity to the knowledge that she and Jerome were destined to live happily together until death parted them.

Later, after treading over a path of laurel leaves that had been laid down outside the church to celebrate love and respect, they were showered with rice by gleeful guests harking towards fertility, and the wealthier threw some gold coins in their path so they would always be prosperous. Later still, in the gently sloping gardens behind her house, after all the official duties were complete and even the grand feast had been enjoyed, the guests insisted on the old country tradition of bundling up small cakes into a pyramid and making the newlyweds kiss over the stack without any toppling.

'Now, let's bring out the wedding cake,' she said, and her proud housekeeper and aides carried out a tower of custard-filled pastries with a cloud of spun sugar looking as though it hovered around it. The croque-en-bouche was studded with tiny fresh flowers picked that morning from the surrounding meadows, and the tall, glistening creation drew a collective gasp of pleasure from those gathered.

To accompany the cake, Gaston took obvious pleasure in opening still more bottles of Sophie's champagne but in the traditional way – sabrage, expertly slicing off the collar of the bottles with a sabre. And as Gaston presented the newly married couple with the intact collar and cork, Jerome presented Sophie with a choker of crystals.

'They remind me of those glittering bubbles you strive so hard to achieve,' he whispered as he kissed her gently at the top of her neck, after he'd fastened the clasp.

The look in his eyes of hammered steel told her there was a lot more affection to come later in private.

'It's beautiful, Jerome,' she said, touching her fingertips to the beads.

'They're nothing in comparison to you,' he whispered. 'Tell me again how this man got to be so lucky.'

She gave him a smile that was all his. She would never lay that warmth on any other man than Jerome.

'I feel I must sing my happiness,' he threatened.

'Oh, no, Jerome,' she half pleaded, half laughed.

'I must,' he said in a tone of resignation and burst into a rousing song that soon had all the guests joining in.

This was Jerome's way. Loud, boisterous, affectionate. He loved everyone and everyone loved him . . . except perhaps Louis, who had quietly slipped away from the celebrations. No one missed him, least of all Sophie. She felt blessed. Theirs was truly a union forged in heaven and Épernay would benefit now that one of the pre-eminent growers of the region had unified with one of the most innovative and exciting new winemakers that Champagne had reared in a long time.

'I have one more gift for you, my love,' Jerome said as the song ended, and he returned to her side having woven his way around the tables, encouraging everyone to join in.

Her gaze narrowed, wondering if he was about to say something seductive.

He grinned, guessing where her mind was heading. 'That gift can wait. Will you come with me?'

She frowned. 'Leave our guests?'

'Only briefly.' He didn't wait for her answer, instead bellowing out to all at their wedding feast that he and his bride had somewhere to be and would return shortly.

This was greeted by whistles and cheers.

'Settle down, everyone . . . just a gift for the woman I love. We shall be back.'

'Go on,' Gaston encouraged her. 'I'll keep things bubbling along here.'

Sophie stood, open-mouthed, the silk of her dress creasing in her fists as she held her gown and train clear of the dark, dry earth, and gazed across a vineyard as the sun lowered in a glorious champagne-and-pink sunset.

'Chardonnay,' she whispered. 'Here?'

'An experiment that this goddess of grapes agreed to join me in. She's all yours.'

'Jerome!' She swung to look at him, knowing her expression was struggling to convey her awe, her gratitude, her love for his romantic soul. 'You did this for me?'

He nodded, grinning at her obvious pleasure. 'Everyone was sworn to secrecy. I mean, this field is a few years off producing fruit you can use but I think she's going to flourish for you because from the moment you told me about your dream for an all-chardonnay champagne, I wanted to make it come true. I think one day it will be the style all houses aspire to. But you will be among the first, if not the first.'

Her eyes misted and glittered from being filled with his love and hers for him. 'I don't know what to say other than thank you for believing in me.'

'Make these little vines count. Love them as I love you.'

She reached up to embrace him, wanting to kiss him deeply, to run her hands through his hair, which had been combed straight but wanted to go wild. She had a better idea. 'Let's hurry up and bring our wedding feast to a close so you can carry me up the stairs and shut the world out.'

'That's a lot of stairs,' he mumbled as their lips met and she had a taste of what awaited her at the top of her house . . . their house now.

But the world was not to be shut out. As she flung her arms around her husband, a youth ran over and interrupted them.

'Monsieur, madame!'

'What is it, Stephane?' She watched Jerome's forehead crease, knowing hers was doing the same at the boy's urgent tone.

'You must come, quickly.'

'What's happened?' Sophie asked, feeling tendrils of fear emerge from the place to which she'd banished them.

'Commandant de Saint Just has sent me. You must come immediately.' They both stared at him, bewildered. 'He has received word and had to announce to your guests that Germany has declared war on Russia, monsieur . . . and that France will be next.'

The lad tugged at Jerome's sleeve and, shocked by this revelation, they began to run, Sophie no longer caring about ruining her silk. It was like hearing the news that her family had gone missing all over again; all the same feelings of dread began to crowd in as she held grimly onto Jerome's hand and hurried alongside him.

'Wait!' They all stopped. 'How do we know France is involved?' Jerome demanded, looking as though he'd refuse to take another step until that question had been answered.

The lad shook his head. 'All I know is what the commandant whispered to me, sir. He's received word that German troops have begun to assemble on the frontier of Belgium.' He shrugged. 'I don't know what that means but he said you would.'

Sophie's mouth pursed in private despair. 'Yes, we do.'

# Part One

# 1

*April 1915*

It was the infant at home Dieter thought of as he watched his fellow infantrymen retreat. If his son were old enough to understand, he would surely be proud to know that his father had been chosen among the few for this special task. And if he grew up to have a similar interest in science, he might also be as intrigued to learn how the clever German Jewish chemist, Fritz Haber, had arrived at his cunning plan.

*This will end it*, they had been told, and Dieter believed his superiors, keen to be among those selected to unleash a new weapon on this forsaken salient in Belgium they were all fighting to own. He wanted to be home with his wife and child . . . in time for summer. Perhaps that didn't have to be a dream. Let this war be done during spring; he couldn't think of a better birthday present for his wife than what was about to unfold, and if it did all go to plan, it would be science and not artillery that closed this hellish war. Home to his peaceful hamlet of Kerpen, back to his job as a teacher of science and arithmetic as well as husband, father. Riding a bicycle to the school where he taught no longer seemed unimaginative or unambitious – it was his safe world and he wanted to return to it with all of his heart, for this new world he was moving through was ugly and frightening . . . and nothing could be worth the mass death and suffering.

The men in charge had judged the day perfect: it had broken clear and the evening winds of Flanders tended to blow cool, damp, and tonight they would whisper in the right direction. He was simply obeying orders. He noted it was uncharacteristically quiet for what felt like a momentous time: no guns, no activity. Mostly it felt as though everyone – on his side, anyway – was holding a collective breath.

He cast a glance down the line to where the next soldier, tasked with a similar duty, was looking back at him in similar nervous anticipation. Dieter's rib cage suddenly felt like an anvil, his heart a hammer pounding against it. It was his moment; he was one of the heroes. Dieter was going to be one of the integral parts of a machine that would end this war. Bless Fritz Haber and his big brain.

So it was with a certain amount of righteous pride that Dieter Meyer, from a small hamlet about twenty miles from the grand city of Cologne, pulled the string that opened the valve on the bottles he was responsible for – three of more than five thousand, he'd heard – on this sunny late afternoon in the region north of the large town of Ypres. There were still some bright patches of grass to admire in the distance, beyond the crisscross of trenches that the French occupied, as spring beckoned summer. If the cunning of Fritz Haber was right, there would be no French left breathing in the next hour . . . and as the first hiss told Dieter that the gas was escaping, he wondered about the animals of the region. Would everything in this killing mist's path die? No one he'd spoken to in the army knew what it was capable of, how effective it might be, or how expedient as a weapon.

The vapour was trying to emulate the colour of that bright spring grass of Belgium but instead rose up in a sickly hue that was more chartreuse . . . but even that was being kind. It was more like the colour of the slime one finds in a pond, its dirty tone leaning towards puce spoiling the green. He watched the chlorine gas rise to the top of the trench, where it seemed to hover momentarily on the parapet as though taking stock of its surrounds. Then, as if on a given signal, this twenty-foot wall of green fog began to move, riding on the wind that gave it motion. It wasn't in any hurry, he noted, but it was in constant motion and it felt relentless as it rolled over itself towards the trenches of France and her allies.

———————

As Dieter Meyer was considering himself a hero, in the opposing trench Lieutenant Jerome Méa was thinking how glad he was that his army had finally addressed the dismaying losses of French infantrymen due to their scarlet trousers making them easily visible to the enemy. He had been informed that a new uniform was now being distributed through France and would be in Belgium shortly. He smirked to himself. Ypres should have been first on the distribution list, for here was the fiercest fighting. The cloth, which was to have been made up in patriotic threads of the tricolour – red, blue and white – was apparently now woven from only two threads, forming a new hue termed 'horizon blue'. Ironically, the red thread could only be achieved with a dye available from Germany. He didn't even know why he was pondering such trivia: probably because this tiny patch of land in Flanders was an ancient town known for its cloth trade. Whatever had prompted it, the thought was as useless as their presence here felt hopeless. He didn't regret joining up and doing his duty, but he didn't believe this place was worth his life or the lives of the men under his command, or indeed the Allies who fought alongside them, from the Algerians in their exotic uniforms to the Australians from the other side of the world. It made him stand straighter to know that all these men had enlisted and travelled so far to look after France, but instead they were here in a tiny Flemish place to prevent the Germans sweeping through Belgium.

Yes, he would defend her in spirit, but he reminded himself that the 'she' to whom his heart belonged and for whom he would gladly sacrifice his life was not a nation but his wife, Sophie. They'd barely been married a month before he joined up and left with other men from the Reims and Épernay region to rousing cheers, while they made promises to be home soon, victorious. That was last summer – not yet a year, but it felt like eternity since he'd caressed her oval face, which held so much promise in eyes the colour of the winter vines she prized. She was the first woman he'd met who set no store by her looks and took no pain to highlight them with cosmetics or fancy styling. Churlish rivals had suggested it was easy to be casual about prettiness when one was blessed with a body shaped like a mannequin and features that presented such harmony. And it was true – the mirror could not deny the beauty of her wide gaze, which looked out over a promontory of chiselled cheeks. The defined eyebrows matched the wide bow lips that found their widest smile for him. And he liked her best when she flung off that straw hat she wore in the fields and untied her hair to remind him of burnished oak, which in the right light cast off golden glints. Jerome still couldn't understand how she had not married that dashing cousin of hers, Gaston de Saint Just, who might even be here among the Arab forces he led. Instead, and this prompted a small but genuine grin, she had chosen him. He'd only known her from afar as the child of the Delancré champagne house. Unlike his paunchy brother, he'd not thought himself in the league of the Delancré heiress and had thus never attempted to gain her attention and risk rejection, disappointment or humiliation.

If he was honest, it was only he who liked to think of himself as a simple farmer, and Sophie had called him out on several occasions for a conceit of false modesty. She suffered no fools, this woman. That he farmed was fair enough, but there was no way around the fact that he came from a family of wealthy grape growers who owned great swathes of the finest agricultural land, including vineyards in and around Reims and Épernay.

And now he wanted to go home to continue that marriage. He'd answered his call to duty. He'd carried himself tall and heroically through this last six months certainly, and through some of the most unimaginable fighting that any soldier could be asked to survive. He'd led his men with courage and by example, never asking them to do anything he wouldn't do himself, but Jerome was feeling especially maudlin this bright spring day, which had slipped into a soft afternoon. He had the curiously morbid sense that a bullet had his name inscribed on it, or a mortar shell would single out his trench and his section of it to land upon. Why? Why today of all days did it feel so prophetic? Perhaps because the guns had become quieter; the enemy didn't seem as lively or busy at their role of killing. It was as though, in this last hour or so, the other army wasn't present. The damp winds were, though, and were blowing towards them, bringing that familiar stench of the dead. The German silence felt ominous, especially given that there had been such a robust strafing in the morning with an increase in shelling. So why the quiet now?

As he frowned into this query, his sous-lieutenant sidled up. 'Supper, sir?'

Jerome nodded; he hadn't realised that afternoon had slipped away. Supper used to be his favourite meal in the short month he'd lived with Sophie as man and wife. What he wouldn't give to eat supper in her presence again. He'd give his life for a night with her.

'I'll be right there.' He nodded but his attention was caught and trapped by a strange miasma that he noticed was reaching over the lip of the enemy trench in the distance. Fingers of a sinister green clawed above the top, and then what could only be described as a sheet of mist kept rising until it formed a vast wall that seemed to run the length of the front for as far as he could see. Was this some sort of new gunpowder the Germans were using? He couldn't make sense of what he was seeing and had barely realised he'd called out.

Men ran to his call; orders were given and a hail of bullets began. As if travelling on unseen wheels, the wall of green began to accelerate towards them. Fear gripped them all, including Jerome, who yelled as loud as his neighbour.

'Fall back!' he bellowed, unsure they could make it far enough. Whatever that was, he didn't want to find out what it was going to do to them. 'Run!'

Most of them made it about two miles before it consumed them and they began to founder and fall, a green froth at their mouths. And as men in masks or clutching thick pads to their faces materialised out of the killing mist, all Jerome could hear was the screaming of donkeys and horses along with the screams of men clawing at their throats. He was strong; with two soldiers hanging off his shoulders, he used all his power to drag them along before he himself dropped, a tingling sensation clambering through his body.

Jerome was astonished and somehow deeply saddened that in this moment, as he heaved to get more air into his lungs, he would focus on the tiny mice and voles and other small creatures dying alongside them in the choking chaos.

# 2

*August 1915*

The woman in front of Sophie looked over her shoulder and caught her attention. For over two hours they had been riddling the champagne bottles, angled into the shelves they called pupitres. It needed focused diligence to carefully turn the thousands of bottles one-eighth forwards from yesterday's position. She thought the woman was suggesting they have a break from their toil, but when she followed her neighbour's gaze, she recognised a man waiting.

Sophie straightened, frowning momentarily at the mayor. Had she forgotten a meeting? The smile that began to erupt shrank alongside the sudden bitterness in her throat, as though she'd swallowed aloes. Mayor Maurice Pol-Roger looked as though he too was tasting something unpleasant and his normally tall stature appeared slumped, defeated. She wiped her hands on her apron in a nervous gesture and tried not to hear the sudden heavy silence in the cellar, which had been full of women's chatter just moments earlier. There was only one reason that their fine mayor would arrive unannounced at the Delancré mansion on the avenue and that was to do his sorry duty. She even had a moment in these terrifying seconds to feel sorry for him before the silent pain

31

roared in and consumed her. It was a wave whose one purpose was reaching the shore of her heart, foaming and clawing to hang on before the sea of trauma would claim it back, dragging it shrieking. But the shrieks were hers. They were not histrionic or highly pitched. No, they were formed from sharp and shallow breaths with a lower sound . . . more like a keening animal.

But only Sophie could hear them. She had deliberately trapped them inside her chest: courage was everything in this moment. The country demanded this of its women at present, but her surname especially counted for so much that her bravery, it seemed, was something to which the women of Épernay aspired. They needed her strength to embolden them . . . but also to lean upon. War arriving on French soil almost a year ago meant the women were already adrift on a dark sea; with the arrival of today's news Sophie guessed that she no longer had even hope to shield her from the war's ocean of pain.

Jerome was gone. It was her turn to grieve.

The mayor could tell she already knew, and saved her any preamble. 'Madame Delancré, I am so deeply sorry . . .'

She didn't need to hear any more. She had heard those words time and again as they were spoken to other distraught wives, mothers, fiancées and sisters.

Pol-Roger brought news only of loss. Loss of the future and its potential; loss of the one aspect of her existence that made life bearable through the war. It especially – and perhaps most poignantly – carried news of the loss of love. Love during war was the one shining beacon of survival. When it was stolen, the thieving hands took everything. She'd taken so long to find romantic love and once it was hers it had consumed all corners of her existence. She had felt invincible with it. Love had become her armour and even as she'd stayed strong and smiled as Jerome left, proudly wearing his new uniform with those scarlet trousers, she'd felt as though her mind might just implode from sadness. They'd only just found each other, just understood what it felt like to have a full heart; she'd been swollen with her desire for him and what they were going to achieve together.

War took him from Épernay. And now a few words were about to take him from her . . . forever.

Sophie Delancré wouldn't cry. Tears would come later in private. Now it was brittle shock, as dry as the envelope sounded when the mayor put the telegram in her hands, along with another murmured apology. He could have just allowed the messenger on his bicycle to deliver it, but he'd made it his obligation to visit every woman to deliver the news in person, as much as it pained him. He was a good man, an excellent figurehead for Épernay, and he needed her to be strong now for all of them. She raised her eyes from the paper to meet his gaze and saw he was struggling for composure. Everyone loved Jerome.

'We must be brave,' she heard herself say, appalled at her cool tone. The words sounded meaningless and yet even in their hollowness there was a sense of comfort. Saying them helped simply because it was something to break the dread silence. The tall man – who in spite of his thick, wiry moustache bore a striking resemblance to his clean-shaven father, one of the founders of the industry she was a part of – touched his hat in silent acknowledgement and withdrew as the women workers flocked like hens to each other, making soft sounds. She felt hands on her; they squeezed her arms and hugged her soundlessly to convey their pity and understanding.

'Thank you,' she whispered. 'Excuse me, please,' she appealed to them, hating their looks of sympathy. She knew, as they did, that the pain was only just beginning. Shock would tranquilise her for a while, keeping the agony of despair at bay. But the reality would soon sink its claws in and hold her helpless, before tearing away at even the smallest shreds of resolve. Sophie made it all the way to the second floor before she had to face a smile from a maid who was ignorant of her news. The envelope was buried in her apron pocket, rustling with dark eagerness to be opened.

'Madame?'

'I'm fine, Helene . . . a headache.'

'Rest, madame.' The young woman frowned. 'You work too hard.' And then she was gone, none the wiser, busy at her chores, herself stretched thin, doing the work of several maids. They were all shouldering far more than one person should. No one complained.

Sophie hauled down the timber stepladder that would allow her to escape to the gods of the house. She'd laid boards on the rafters and fashioned a haven for herself in the attic. The other six bedrooms she had turned over for visitors: everyone from political dignitaries to army officers and any one of the many men of note who worked for France and needed a private room. She was happy to extend her hospitality. She wasn't alone – all the major houses were helping wherever they could for France's war effort. She imagined that by moving to the attic and allowing the second floor to be used as visitor rooms, most of the ground floor might soon be turned over entirely to wounded soldiers, recuperating men or simply those being rotated and rested.

Her world had changed in a blink. Yesterday she could plan. Today? Was there any point?

Sophie's shoulders had never felt heavier as she ascended the shallow steps of the ladder before hefting it up and closing the snug-fitting lid of the loft space. Alone. She reached for one of the beams and gripped it until her knuckles were leached of colour. The sobs shuddered through her, still silent, full of private pain. *Hold it in,* she demanded of herself. *Bear it! You must. There is no choice. You are not special. You are bereaved: one of hundreds in Épernay, one of thousands in France, one of tens of thousands in Europe.*

Sophie breathed out softly, made herself inhale immediately, inflate her lungs all the way as she had advised others who had faced this challenge before her. She breathed out again, audibly this time, pursing her lips enough to allow air to come out in a tunnel of control. *Channel the fear*, she said in her mind. *Breathe in and out . . . and again.* She groaned with the final exhalation, at least slightly steadier on her feet, if not calmer within. When she felt her legs were reliable, Sophie moved to the salon chair she'd had carried up and placed by one of the gabled windows. It was one of a few luxuries from the life she had known just a year ago.

If life before the war had been privileged, then life now had few soft edges about it. This chair, however, was one of them, and she sank into its plump cushion to rest a clammy palm on its golden walnut arm, partly padded in the same soft green embroidered fabric of its seat. She adored this chair: a small place to feel safe, or at least loved. It had been her mother's; she used to sew from its embrace using the light flooding in from the tall picture windows downstairs. She would now have to face the telegram with light illuminating it from the dormer window. She wished it was simply sewing and she could wear that soft smile of her mother's contentment. She tried to picture her own expression. Pale and pinched, no doubt, over a skull beginning to show its hollows. Sophie was grateful that neither of her parents had lived to experience this war, or to see her so wasted and unhappy.

But now she would move beyond simply being too thin, too fatigued, too grief-stricken for others and for France. Now it had become deeply personal.

She couldn't put it off any longer and withdrew the envelope from her apron. The inevitable tears arrived. Hot and salty, stinging her eyes and warping the words on the page as she read the official notification. It was crafted with carefully chosen phrasing, but it couldn't deflect or hide the blow.

Jerome was lost in action. She scanned the telegram, not really absorbing it, just confirming what she had suspected. The mayor had been told more, apparently, and that would come in writing soon; witnesses had said they saw him fall. Was that two or three of them? She didn't care. The mayor assured they had described a man, tall and broad, with dark, curling hair. He was a farmer – a grape grower, two recalled – cheerful for others, always full of optimism despite the bleakness of their days. They couldn't have described him better.

And so, just like that . . . in the space of a single heartbeat, the love of her life was gone.

'I'll be home for Christmas,' he'd promised.

Sophie breathed out her agony softly.

'That was eight months ago, my darling,' she whispered to wherever he was buried beneath the mud of France, a German bullet likely embedded in his chest. She hoped it hadn't passed through his heart. That belonged to her.

Sophie stood now to lean against the window and gaze at her favourite view in the hope of anchoring herself. The mayor had made a wise decision. The German soldiers had marched through their silent, cowed city and had only been able to call it theirs for a single week. Brave French fighters on its other side had sent them scuttling, scampering back through the city, this time not nearly as composed or smug. The German soldiers had been chased all the way back to the hills around Chemin des Dames. The ferocious Battle of the Marne the previous year had seen an Allied victory, but it was short-lived as the Germans had dug in deeper. The enemy was still entrenched in all but one of the semicircle of tiny medieval forts that had guarded Paris in centuries past. Sophie sighed. Épernay and Reims were not occupied but they were still prisoners . . . with Reims once more the only city standing between the Germans and the French capital.

She looked beyond the familiar tiny clusters of rooftops pin-pointing the villages of Dizy and Ay. Angling her gaze south, she squinted at the patchwork of misted vineyards that stretched up into the hillsides. Over the hill, Jerome's precious chardonnay grapes were already bursting into bud . . . new life for them as her own life felt as though it was ending. The vines didn't understand war or peace; they knew only the cycle of life. They had fought through the epidemic of disease that had wasted most of Europe's grape stocks. Now, strengthened by the grafting of American vines, they were flourishing once more. They had beaten back the phylloxera virus, and in the first year of the war had known one of their best vintages. She must draw strength from Jerome's proud vines and protect them; without her they would wither and the war – no matter which side one fought on – would win.

In the time she'd stood here, how many men had been hit by bullets? How many men had died from artillery? Or shrapnel wounds? A new battle was now raging in Belgium. Flanders was aflame again, and the French soldiers were bogged in trenches alongside their allies. Listening to the wireless just days earlier she'd heard the horrific news of the Germans using chlorine gas in front of their trenches, waiting for the prevailing north-easterly breeze to carry the hideous greenish-yellow mist, up to four miles wide, towards their enemy's trenches. It had happened at dusk, trapped between day and night, and the men could barely believe what they saw, according to the report. The fingers of scalding green had only had to travel half a mile to take French troops by surprise. So many had died within minutes, and those that didn't were blinded or their lungs burned. Casualties ran into the thousands. She had wept to hear it.

Perhaps Jerome was one of the lucky ones? Dead before he could understand what had happened. No time to contemplate his demise; no opportunity to think about the wife he worshipped and who loved him with the same fervour; no chance to feel agonising pain or sadness like the fellows on that ridge. A swift bullet that stole his heartbeat.

Should she be grateful, then? Had he left his life bravely, honourably and in defence of the France he adored? Had he left his life? The thought kept nagging. She could accuse herself of being overly romantic but Sophie, deep in her bones, didn't want to accept that this was it – their lives together halted. It could be stubbornness or just plain grief that refused to let her believe her husband was dead. Jerome couldn't be found . . . he was missing but he could be injured, lost, wandering. She allowed herself to let this tiny glimmer of hope flicker.

And so, for him and his courage she must find more of her own. He had defended France. She must defend her tiny corner of it. Her vineyards, her family's legacy, her name and the people around her. It was no longer up to anyone else. This is how it had always been destined. Her father had said she was the one. She would have to take on the burden alone.

She was a sixth-generation champenoise. So be it. House Delancré – just like Paris – must endure. And Sophie must proceed on her own terms but not before she was sure that Jerome was dead. And she would only accept that if there was proof he no longer lived. Until then, she would advance in blind hope . . . growing his grapes, tending his vines, making her champagne and, above all, waiting for him to return.

# 3

He recalled being knocked backwards into the filth of his trench and regaining his wits to understand that he was in a casualty clearing station.

'Hello, Captain Nash. I'm Ellen.' She smiled brightly enough to break any man's heart. 'How do you feel?'

'Blurry,' he admitted, gauging her to be in her mid-twenties. Golden hair was tied up beneath her nurse's cap but a lock had come loose. He wanted to touch it.

'That's due to concussion. You can hear properly?'

He lifted a finger to poke in his ear. 'I can still hear guns,' he admitted. Then nodded. 'Just a bit of ringing.'

'To be expected,' she said, cocking her head slightly and looking at him with a gaze the colour of ancient waters trapped in ice. Yet there was nothing cold about it; her eyes spoke only of heat . . . maybe a tropical current had been trapped in that pre-historic glacier. Her eyes were all warmth, like her smile. 'You've got a bad head wound but we stitched you . . . I stitched you, actually.' She shrugged her squarish, narrow shoulders, which spoke of small meals and long hours. 'I was a seamstress before . . . ' She frowned.

'Well, before all of this, so I get the trickier patch-ups around here. You'll have a handsome scar to go with your handsome face.' She paused, but when he didn't reply she gently touched his shoulder. 'Oh, come on, soldier, please smile for me. You didn't get killed out there today.'

He attempted for her, knowing it came out lopsided. 'I am grateful,' he lied.

'But?' *Perceptive.*

'To be honest, Ellen, I'm not convinced that living is worth the trouble right now, but thank you for patching me up so well.'

'You know something, Charlie?' She cocked her head again as she regarded him, and he liked that habit. 'I spent a lot of time on you and I did an exceptionally neat job too.' She grinned but he could see the sadness in it and needed to move her on before she started offering him the predictable wisdom on staying cheerful.

'May I return to my men now?'

'Yes. But may I say one more thing?' She didn't wait for his reply, but he saw something defiant flash in her eyes. The calm, pretty grey of her eyes was an eternity away from the bleak grey world he moved in. '. . . and I've heard soldiers make similar heart-breaking remarks as you just did, and it has a corrosive effect.' He frowned, only just catching up with her words; she was clearly educated, and she was obviously not going to tell him to keep his chin up. 'It infects all of us. We're all in this. I'm not in the trench alongside you, I admit, but I'm here in the hospital and I see the effects of this war up close in all of its horror. It never gets easier but if you don't stay strong, how can you expect your men to follow your lead?' It landed on him like a blow. 'How about we make a pact, Captain Nash, that I won't give up if you won't?' The grey gaze glittered across him like quicksilver.

'All right,' he heard himself say, not sure if he'd been seduced or hypnotised, because he didn't want to make that pact. As she tapped the cot in which he lay as if to say, *Deal!*, he added: 'On one condition. Actually, two.' He couldn't let her get away with an admonishment without defending himself. Flirting was surely the only way.

'Really?' Grey amusement slid down to his lips and back up to meet his gaze head-on. He was impressed by her fearlessness, especially as lemon-lips Matron was hovering. 'And what are those?'

'If we both make it out alive, you'll let me take you to a dance.'

Her head tipped in the way he liked, and she smiled. He saw so much promise in it, it made him ache. 'I'm very good at stitching – as you'll see when you next look in a mirror – but I'm even better at dancing. Dare you take up that challenge, Captain?'

He found it hard to believe he was smiling, even harder to believe she was flirting back. It seemed primeval drive was never entirely obliterated. He nodded. 'I'll let you be the judge of that.'

'Then stay safe and I'll see you some time.' She scribbled something on a page on her clipboard. 'Here are some tips for helping you to look after that wound, because it's going to need re-dressing in a couple of days. I'll organise a sphagnum-moss one because that white bandage is a dreadful target and I'm looking forward to shaking a leg with you.' She laughed at his expression. 'Muddy that bandage up,' she advised as she handed him the scrap.

'That will happen in seconds out there.' Charlie glanced at the small torn-off piece of paper on which she'd scrawled. Her surname was Peterson and she was from Surrey. There was a phone number. Not a word about wound care, though; would Matron be fooled?

'Take care of yourself.' She shook his hand politely. 'You didn't tell me the second condition.'

He stood gingerly and let the tent swim around him before he nodded to say he was fine to move on his own. 'That you call me Charlie.' He winked.

'And me Ellie,' she matched.

Charlie raised a finger to his head in a sort of salute. 'I'll think of you when I shave and note your neat scar close up.'

Her gentle smile hurt so much more than his head. 'Stay alive, Charlie,' she whispered.

The memory of that whisper was only a couple of days old but it might as well have been years, given how Captain Charles Nash of the 8th Leicesters felt as the blood spattered on his face and he realised the man he had been talking with was dead.

Only a minute earlier Royce had offered him a cigarette.

'Not good for my breathing . . . or my shooting.' Charlie had grinned without amusement.

'You reckon you'll live long enough to worry about your lungs, sir?' Royce had observed with the typical mirthless humour of the trenches. The older man had taken two more long drags, and as he'd turned to flick the minuscule butt into the mud slime they stood in, he grinned. 'I'll count on your —'

Much of Royce's face was obliterated in that same heartbeat with the telltale whiz of a bullet.

Charlie caught him as he fell, more of the man's blood oozing onto his uniform. 'Oh, Royce, you stupid bugger,' Nash murmured, sickened by yet another close-range death. He ground his teeth, trying not to show it because that meant weakness. Even so, that German sniper across the way had to die. Word went down the line that Royce, the spotter, was dead. Charlie couldn't look away from the ruin of the face that had been grinning at him moments ago. He rubbed his own face, trying to offset the internal agony, and as he did, he shifted the sphagnum-moss field dressing that had been applied after a piece of shrapnel sheared open his head.

Even now, a few days on, he convinced himself he could taste the fragrance of violets that he recalled emanating from Nurse Ellie. Just for a heartbeat, the gagging smell of the latrines disappeared as he remembered her.

'You all right, Nash? Are you listening?' The major's vexation dragged him from his thoughts to the ugly present.

He snapped back to attention and let Ellie go. 'Yes, sir. Look, there's no point in keeping this position; their sniper knows where I am now,' Charlie said, trying to keep it matter-of-fact, averting his gaze, which had rested on Royce for too long. 'I'm going to get that bastard, sir, if just for Royce alone. Send me with the lads when the whistle blows, sir,' he asked for the umpteenth time. 'A captain moves and fights with his company.'

And for the umpteenth time plus one, his commanding officer shook his head. 'We can't lose you, Nash. You know that.'

'Sir —'

'This is not up for discussion.'

'Wait, sir. Please,' Charlie appealed, trying a new approach. 'I left my essential services role and joined up because I wanted to do my bit,' he said, fabricating around the truth of running away from his laboratory because he did not wish to make mass-killing gas for the Allies. Charlie had no desire to discuss the philosophy of war with his senior officer as the Germans cranked up for another morning's artillery fire.

'We all want to do our bit!' The major was becoming testy.

'By keeping me in this trench, sir, you are not letting me do what I came here to do.'

'Captain Nash, this is the last time you and I will have this conversation. You are doing the duty I demand of you by killing our enemy. You achieve more death in a few hours than we can in our pointless dashes towards them. I am not prepared to lose you, no matter how it rankles here,' he said, prodding Charlie's chest. 'I know you didn't plan on becoming a makeshift sniper. But firing a rifle with that deadeye shot of yours keeps a few of these lads alive,' he growled, pointing over Charlie's shoulder, 'just a little bit longer. And if you can keep doing that, some of them *might* just

43

make it out of this hellish place.' His tone told Charlie he would not tolerate further discussion. 'Now, what about a replacement for Royce?'

Firmly back in his place, Charlie had to look as though he was accepting. 'How about the new youngster, Hartley, sir? He doesn't wear glasses.' He was a poor choice, and the major's expression confirmed to Charlie that his superior knew this too. He pushed harder. 'He lied about his age; he's not seventeen for a few months. Doesn't need to go over the top, sir. Not yet, anyway – he's only just arrived. Looks like a startled hare.'

His senior officer nodded, resigned. 'You see, there is a heart beating in there, Nash; you just don't want to be reminded of it,' he said, this time prodding gently at Charlie's chest. 'I'll send him down.'

'Thank you, sir.'

Charlie selected a new part of the trench to work from.

The sniper who had been privately taunting him, while picking off members of his unit with ghastly regularity, had grown large in his mind as a monster. Suddenly, he wanted nothing more in the world than to kill him. Life was getting worse with the familiarity of war, not easier: wanting to kill someone was everything his pacifist soul deplored. The fighting sometimes began early; other days it could be quiet for hours, or it might only crank up at night. In between the carnage the soldiers on both sides filled their time coping with the filth and discomfort of daily life, spiced by the anticipation of death. Most, he realised, quietly accepted their end was near, but the concern was how it would arrive. Would it come quickly? Invisibly? With noisy warning? Painfully swift? Bloody and terrifying? Would the dying last for hours or just moments? The waiting and wondering kept them all on edge. In the meantime, their duty was to survive. Live through the anxiety that shredded their consciousness. Dodge the bullets and artillery fire, find some sleep in the impossible conditions, stay strong-willed on meagre rations, keep a sense of humour through what felt like the ending of humanity, shut out the grief for lost friends and fine, brave men. Kill, kill and keep killing more strangers you have no personal grudge against. Block the hunger, the chilblains, the trench foot, the rats, the excrement, the blood, the screams of the dying and the scared. Above all, don't lose your rifle and never give up, even as you feel your hold on sanity slipping. How did the others lean back against a filthy trench wall and smoke a cigarette? How did they find cheerful words to write letters or postcards with stubby pencils? He was amazed at the humour they dug deep to find; so often he would hear the soldiers laughing together, sometimes uproariously – as though they were sharing a huge joke at the pub, and not here contemplating their death at any moment. And most seemed to keep their consciences clear despite who they might be killing on the other side. Following orders. They were protecting Britain: their families, their friends, their country . . . everything it stood for. No doubt the Germans felt the same about their loved ones, their country, their Kaiser . . . their orders. It wasn't personal. Would it matter if the guns just stopped and the men emerged from both sides and shook hands, called it quits?

The Tigers Brigade, as the Leicesters were known, had arrived here in Polygon Wood in Flanders in late September. He'd volunteered a year into the battles, in time for the bright and murderous hell of the Somme. The number who died in that fray felt as impossible to contemplate as it was that he'd survived clambering over the top of a trench to run towards enemy machine-gun fire. Back in 1915 he couldn't have believed that the conditions or the attrition of men could get worse. Of course they had – much worse.

The 8th had been moved around so much now it no longer mattered which trench he found himself in. Ultimately, they all felt like the same tunnel of despair, and the landscape had begun to look like the same wilderness wherever they landed. Mud, a few tree stumps, grim skies overhead; below ground he was always at least ankle-deep in diseased, muddied water – and that's if the 8th were lucky. In 1916, the Battle of the Somme, in northern France; the Arras offensive on the Western Front during spring of this year and now here they were: another trench, another battleground in Ypres, and autumn was approaching. Not that Charlie could tell one season from another. All those delicious telltale signs he used to appreciate were no longer there. From the birds and creatures that heralded the seasons to the plants and the fragrances of the air . . . now it all felt the same. Dim, smoky, toxic-smelling, bleakly grey, with the sounds of pain and gunfire almost drowning out all others.

It was here in Ypres that Charlie discovered more about the gas that had sent him scuttling to join up. He learned that the Germans had helpfully marked their differences. The shells bearing a yellow cross contained mustard gas, which lingered and caused severe blistering, affecting the eyes in particular. There were those bearing a green cross, and Charlie's chemist's mind immediately knew this to be chlorine and phosgene – the mix that had enraged him sufficiently to volunteer, despite his pacifist leaning. He'd discovered a third since arriving . . . the one marked with a blue cross. This one had variations of diphenylchlorarsine that he understood had been designed to make the victim sneeze and cough, forcing him to pull off his gas mask and expose himself to the gas. He wondered if his old boss back in Lancashire had been involved in developing the filter that had been inserted into all their gas masks this summer to protect them from the gas in the blue-crossed shells. It was an idle thought that didn't help anyone, least of all Charlie himself.

The truth was that in this wasteland of trenches and shell holes, the mustard gas could saturate and dissolve itself in the pools of water. It was poison waiting to be drunk, washed in, boiled up for tea in the mess tin . . . Still lethal, in other words. He'd tried to explain this to his men, to make them take care, but were they listening when they were parched?

With a feeling of fresh disgust, Charlie began adjusting his Enfield.303 to take account of his new position. He didn't like to clean the outside of his rifle, believing that the grubbier it was, the less likely it would show up when the enemy scrutinised positions, although he was not entirely sure whether this was a just superstition. Internally, however, he kept it pristine.

A young man stumbled up, moving awkwardly, not yet used to trench conditions. His eyes were wide and worried.

'I'm H-Hartley, sir,' he stammered. 'Er, I'm to be your new spotter . . . sir.'

'Keep your head down, Hartley,' he ground out, roughly pulling the lad below the lip of the trench. 'Got a mirror?'

'I do, sir.'

'Good.' He pointed to the top of their trench. 'That's your ceiling. Never be tempted to peek over.' He turned and fixed the freckle-faced youth with a hard stare. 'You want to be alive tonight, yes?'

'Yes, sir.' The lad looked bewildered.

'Tell me about your girl.'

Hartley's face flushed beneath the smudges of mud. 'I wish I had one, sir.'

'Oh, you'll be fighting them off, I promise. You'll be a hero.' The youngster grinned crookedly but the smile died as a fresh eruption of artillery fire whizzed and exploded around them. Charlie could see the mirror shaking in his hand, the boy's breath coming faster. That had to stop if he was going to survive even today. 'Where are you from, Hartley?' They were waiting for the general signal that would send men clambering above them, but Charlie needed to distract his young companion, keep him talking.

'Burnley, sir.'

'I know Burnley. Whereabouts?'

'Queen's Road, s-sir,' Hartley stammered, back pressed hard against the trench wall.

Charlie could see it was taking all of his willpower not to simply shut his eyes and scream. He carried on conversationally. 'Ah, yes. Apparently that is the only road of its name in the country, making it unique. Did you know that?'

'No, sir. I don't think I understand, sir.'

Charlie kept checking his rifle sight, narrowing his world down ready for the moment his skills were needed. 'Well, there are probably lots of places called King's Road, or Princes Lane, or even Hartley Street . . . but there's only one Queen's Road in the whole of Britain – and it's where you live.'

'Heck!' Hartley said, scratching his head beneath his helmet and sounding impressed, and Charlie knew he had him. Now he had the lad's attention directed away from the fear, and perhaps the shame that even he himself felt that it was others going over the top. 'I must write to my mother about that, sir. She'll be right chuffed.'

'You should. Write tonight.'

Machine-gun fire escalated from the German line.

He straightened the boy's helmet and pointed at the mirror. 'Your world is in there. Don't listen to the guns, don't watch our men or get distracted. Just look in there. Hold it up . . . higher . . . bit higher. There. Now, take your time. I want you to help me search for their gunners but most particularly their sniper . . . there's only one of those at present in this section and I want him. Can you see anything interesting for me, Hartley?' he muttered.

'No, sir.'

'Go slow. I call him Adolph Topperwein in my mind,' Charlie admitted, ducking lower in the trench to finally look squarely at Hartley. He was such a baby-face, appearing younger than most at seventeen. How was Charlie going to keep this child alive?

'Why?'

'There's a man,' he began, fiddling again with his weapon, making a slight adjustment, 'who used to perform in travelling shows in America, and he would entertain audiences with his clever shooting. He could outline the silhouette of an Indian chief in bullets. That was his famous trick. He had the German name of Adolph Topperwein. So I think of him as our cunning shooter across the way; he's the best I've encountered. In these few days we've lost four men to his rifle. I don't plan on there being a fifth.'

'Let's get him, sir.' Hartley grinned.

'Sniping takes patience,' he began again, but shouting now, as around them the world had essentially exploded. 'No matter what happens, I must remain still, breathing evenly – slowing my breathing, actually – searching for the clear-sighted moment and the target.'

Satisfied, Charlie cast a glance around at the men of the company. The nervous tension was so thick it was now a presence around the soldiers, wrapping long arms around them and whispering that death beckoned. Most of those about to go over the top would not make it back, and almost certainly would not make it much further forward. Behind their position the bigger guns bucked and coughed fire as gunners slammed rounds into the breeches. No one could be heard above the ruckus now. It was as though one hundred orchestras had been given the signal to make as much of a discordant din as they could possibly achieve . . . as loud as they possibly could.

He imagined the conductor instructing, *As many cymbal clashes and hammering drums as you can . . . use your muscles, chaps!*

A shell exploded in their zigzag of trench and he felt his heart give to see Hartley cower, his face contorting with primal fear. The cries of men were a minuscule sound – a bare jangle of a triangle in the terrible symphony being waged – and still he could hear it.

It was as though only he was attuned to death, because those hit from that explosion had died without the soldiers a few feet away knowing. They were just gone, like Royce: here one moment, their heartbeats stilled the next. Someone needed to bear witness to their last breaths. And so that was him. The captain with good hearing, a deadeye shot, a heart he only knew was there because it kept pumping. He heard them and he wished them peace.

'Mirror, Hartley,' he yelled. 'Focus on that. And remember, we just have to survive today, the last of our four-day rotation, and then we can drop back into reserve. You can do that, can't you?'

'Yes, sir!'

'Good lad. Let's get to work.'

Machine guns bristled from the other side, their staccato noise a murderous chorus among the fire and explosions. Mud spat nearby and Charlie peered through the gloom and searched for his nemesis. As the second whistle blew over Polygon Wood, torrential rain began.

Men, terrified, nevertheless readied to haul themselves over the top of the trench while trying not to slip. Everyone's minds would be on the best way to run across the pocked battlefield, which was rapidly turning into craters that could suck a man down in moments. He felt a familiar chill spangle through his body, an animal instinct that meant every sense he possessed was now switched on, engaged and working as one. No more internal debate on whether to face the threat or flee. The mind had won; the body was resigned and obedient. *We fight*, his consciousness instructed every muscle. Instead of tensing as they wished to, they relaxed under its orders.

No wind today. Hopefully no chlorine gas, then, although it now arrived by shell and didn't need Nature's help. Even so, he pulled off the hateful mask. No special calculation for his shooting either. But so much noise that it was no longer possible to convey anything to poor Hartley. Charlie took a deep breath, aware of slowing his exhale, and then another. The final breath was even deeper, and as he emptied his lungs achingly slow, it felt like his breathing had stilled, and Charlie took one final, steadying blink, firmed his finger on the trigger, and saw the single giveaway glint of a machine gunner's weapon at the back of the opposing trench. Triumph trilled through Charlie as he narrowed his gaze still further and then depressed the trigger smoothly. The bullet left the barrel with an exhilarated sigh that at last it had a destination. It hurtled towards its victim, and in the heartbeat after the crack of its departure, Charlie watched a man's head snap back as the rifle bucked against his shoulder. He let the trigger return smoothly, and momentarily, silently, acknowledged a good shot. He took no pleasure in the result of his accuracy; he knew that if he paused to consider its repercussions on that man's family and those who loved him, his threads of composure might unravel. He moved on swiftly: it gave his men some time, but that gunner was not the prey he was hunting.

The third whistle screeched like a panicked bird and men clambered up and over the lip of the sandbagged trench. He was aware that several fell immediately, their bodies jerking and jumping as the bullets hit them. They toppled backwards or side-wards, like ragdolls. Not wanting to survey the greater carnage, he focused his gaze through the tiny sight of his rifle, then watched a man's head explode as flying artillery smashed into it. The body moved, headless, for a full revolution before collapsing like a half-emptied sack of flour. He closed his eyes on it and shifted his sights. *Look for Topperwein.*

Red and sulphurous yellow flashes began to burst in front of enemy lines and the machine-gun fire that had only just cranked up fell silent again. Charlie peered through his sight into what felt like eternal oblivion, but as he adapted his vision he could see his infantry stumbling about, up to their knees in mud, hauling themselves from one sucking footstep to the next, carrying eighty pounds of kit on their backs with their rifles readied to shoot. Everything around was as desolate as Charlie's state of mind. This had surely once been the prettiest of landscapes, surrounding a picturesque medieval city that was famous for its cloth. Now there were blackened tree stumps, the once verdant ripples of the land turned into a bog filled with the flotsam and jetsam of war: metal, timber, rubber and flesh.

He'd begun to believe that no matter the risks he took, there was no German bullet or shell with his name on it. No bomb would kill him. He wondered whether in this moment he should scramble over the top and just run at the enemy to test his theory. If he was right, then he would take as many of the Hun as he could before he was wounded. If he was wrong, well, anything, including death, was better than this. This was not life. This was not even existence. This was a caught animal, surviving a few more minutes by snarling at its trapper.

He hadn't realised he was moving until Hartley grabbed his sleeve. 'Sir?'

But Charlie wrenched clear and angled towards the makeshift ladder. 'Hartley, remember to write to your mum.' He used it to launch himself as others had minutes before. And then he was moving . . . more freely than he had in an age cooped up in the trench. If the marshy ground would only permit it, he could run. He was not weighted down by a pack; he had only his rifle. He would take as many of the enemy with him as he could. He didn't want recognition.

He ran into the back of a disoriented soldier, and as that man turned, Charlie could see half his face was gone. The soldier collapsed in his arms. Charlie laid him down, feeling the hot pain of fresh despair. Another mother's son, dying for what? A small piece of land? Let them have it, for pity's sake. Another soldier stumbled over him as he crouched.

'Keep moving!' the fellow yelled, eyes wide and terrified.

If he could see better through the chaos and smoke, he would take aim at Fritz; hell, he would duck and weave his way right up to that sniper and —

Charlie didn't hear the explosion; he only felt its effects. He didn't remember landing on his back. He had no idea how long he had lain there and whether he'd been unconscious or simply stunned. He felt first for his rifle. Nowhere close. Then he checked he was whole. He could feel sticky blood on his hands and he could move his feet, but was he pushing back towards the British trench or moving closer to the enemy line? He couldn't tell. Charlie checked that each digit of his hands moved on command. They did. So, perhaps not so badly injured. Winded, something broken – a rib perhaps because there was distant pain stabbing, and his mind felt gauzy, like it was suddenly filled with cotton wool and too dense for clear thought.

Another explosion: a piece of shrapnel missed him by inches, but he felt mud spatter him and harmless metal shards landing on his boots. There was no way to tell if the bomb was one from friend or foe. He could hear men crying nearby but couldn't see them. Charlie lay back, closed his eyes and this time felt himself drift.

Topperwein may not have had a target painted on his helmet but Charlie knew some things about him. The man liked to wear his helmet tipped arrogantly backwards . . . it made shooting easier, Charlie knew, but he preferred to think Topperwein was so certain of his invincibility that he invited the enemy to take a shot at his exposed forehead. He also knew that Topperwein had orange hair. Thick and aggressively cut so it stuck up, like carroty grass. He needed these insults to hold his hostility strong in his mind, for this man surely couldn't help the colour of his hair or the fact that he too was a deadeye Dick.

Charlie lay there feeling stronger as the hours passed. There was pain but he determined no fracture; bruising, no doubt, and ringing in his ears. *Be still*, he told himself, *and wait for evening to close over you.*

*Stay alive, Charlie*, he heard in Nurse Ellen's voice.

*I can't die*, he wanted to tell his men, especially the major, who would be convulsing with rage at his disobedience. *I've got to get Adolph*, he pleaded silently.

Charlie watched as the German side sent up its rocket. As it lit the immediate surrounds, he knew the enemy would be looking for any movement at all so they could pick off soldiers still alive in no-man's-land. He played dead, waiting for the light to burn out. Frustratingly, a second was sent up and, again watching through a slitted gaze, he didn't shift a muscle, knowing Topperwein would be scrutinising the fallen through his rifle's sight. He heard a bullet whizz and hit something soft and blunt nearby. He reckoned it must have landed in Godfrey and was pleased the poor sod had died hours ago, moaning gently, calling a woman's name until he fell silent. Despite the intimidation of the single bullet, shot by Topperwein, no doubt, Charlie still refused to twitch, trusting his invincibility.

The second shell lost its illumination and it seemed everyone relaxed on both sides. The Germans were done for the the day. But one more person would die this night and it would be at the end of his bullet, Charlie promised himself. He felt cooler air drift across his face, drying the mud he'd slathered over it as camouflage. Now he wanted to believe himself invisible as well. Even so, he knew Hartley would have reported him, and the major, cornered by Charlie's decision, might yet consider a decoy to help him. He certainly hoped so. Charlie bided his time, not concentrating on minutes passing but simply making his mind blank, flexing his fingers to prevent them from becoming too cold. He would give it a little longer just in case his side could help. He would use that time to get into shooting position. As slowly as a cat might creep up on an unwary bird, Charlie began to roll over in tiny movements. It felt like eternity until he found himself on his belly, up on his elbows, his rifle sitting comfortably in its familiar shoulder. *Bless you, Major*, he thought as he heard a song being whistled. It was their company's code. When this particular song erupted, it meant a decoy was about to take place. Over the whistling came a burst of laughter and then men's voices joining in with 'Happy Birthday to You' in one part of the trench. But he waited still . . . knew the major would have something in store. Someone lit a flare nearby to where a small group of men were singing.

Charlie smiled grimly. Even he had cast a glance at them, so he imagined it would have drawn Fritzy's attention and potentially Topperwein's. Holding his rifle as tenderly as he might a lover, he crawled away from the British trench. Slow and steady, working with tiny movements and with gaining confidence, he used his knees and the obliging mud to propel himself forwards as many inches as he dared.

Clouds covered the moon like Nurse Ellen's thin sphagnum-moss field dressing. He liked its sweet-smelling earthiness of Britain's peat bogs. In this pause, before he pulled the trigger, Charlie made a promise to himself as he lay there beneath the dull, ghostly moonlight that leaked around Belgium's autumn clouds. If he did outlive all that the war threw at him, he would commit his life's work to something that made lives brighter, easier. Trapped between two trenches in the land where no man ever wanted to walk, he made a solemn oath in the loneliness of his grim surrounds, which he shared only with corpses – some fresh, some ripe – that he would return to his chemistry background. Set up a distillery to make exquisite whisky or gin . . . or help to develop new medicines from nature's wealth of knowledge, like the humble moss stuck on his head.

Another deliberate burst of laughter: that was the cue.

He heard a cough from the German trench and that whip-cracked his focus. Charlie took a slow, shallow breath and turned his head in a motion as slow as the thickest of honey falling off a grooved honey dipper. It was as though he had all the time in the world; to Charlie it felt like the world was stilling anyway. Time no longer existed. There was just him and there was Topperwein; even if his enemy didn't know it, Charlie was coming for him. And there he was – ghostly in the thin moonlight. Whether it was the sniper's match or someone else's that flared briefly, a cigarette had been lit, a man had straightened and tonight he wore no helmet so his badly cut orange hair was on display. There was Topperwein, arrogant enough to believe no one would see him, even arching his back slightly to stretch. Yes, he likely was the smoker. Charlie could just see the glow brighten over the top of the trench position that he was staring at. It would be impossible for him to have such a clear view from a trench.

With excruciating slowness Charlie began, inch by careful inch, firmly tucking his rifle into place at his shoulder. It was primed and ready.

His legs felt numb from lying on the chilled mud but he was ready. 'Come on, Topperwein,' he whispered. 'Show yourself again.'

Raised voices came from his trench, pulling attention away from him. This was the only chance he'd get. Maybe Topperwein needed to stretch out his limbs for the coming day's carnage but Charlie could suddenly see his nemesis. A depression in the sandbags gave him a clean enough view of the redhead he loathed. Charlie held his breath, opened his eyes wider before narrowing his gaze once more into the rifle sight as he slowly pulled on the trigger, waiting for the buck of its explosion back into his shoulder.

'Farewell,' he breathed to the stranger. As the head of flame hair snapped back, Charlie didn't pause to wonder but immediately began scrambling backwards. He hoped with all of his heart that someone back in the trench was looking out for him because his numb legs felt as though they were working at one-third their normal speed and he dared not cry out for help for fear of showing his position. The other trench was still in shock; he could hear the yell go up.

'Grab me!' he risked calling out, shocked by his desire to live.

Strong hands gripped his boots and he felt himself being unceremoniously wrenched from behind and he slipped and slid into the trench like a huge fish being landed onto a boat. He flopped in a pile into the watery mud, still holding his rifle high and away from the slops, to wild congratulations from his fellow soldiers. He didn't know whether to laugh or cry. He was sure he was doing both.

Men were slapping his back.

'Keep your heads down, men!' It was the major coming through. 'Captain Nash! You're a bloody disobedient bastard but you're also a hero,' he whispered.

'Who pulled me back?' He glanced around. 'Was it Hartley? He was worried that —'

The major blinked. 'Hartley's dead, son. After you left, your part of the trench took a big one.'

Charlie stared at him weakly, all the excitement leaking from him. 'Are you sure?'

His major nodded. 'I'm sorry, Nash.'

*Sorry* didn't begin to touch it. The major squeezed his limp shoulder as Charlie stared sightlessly into the mud.

'We've got new orders.'

He noticed now that those still alive in his company had begun to move. The bombardment of this trench would soon be some other poor unit's problem.

Charlie frowned. 'To where, sir?'

'Some well-needed rest. The Leicesters are being sent east of Paris – the Marne region. It's gone a bit quiet down there as Fritz is all bunkered down in some forts and it's become a stalemate, as the French have got Reims held. We can get haircuts . . . maybe even drink some French plonk.'

'Reims and Épernay, that's champagne country, sir.'

'Well, you know more than I, Nash.'

'Why us?'

'Take a look around, will you? We've been smashed for weeks. I don't want to know the head count for the last days of this rotation, let alone provide the information already in my possession up the line so another wife, another mother gets that dreaded letter back home. But I have to. If someone offers this company an out from Flanders to a sleepy region in France, I will not say nay. Get your men organised.'

Charlie nodded, promising himself that when he got to this quiet area of France they were headed for, he would write to Mrs Hartley of Queen's Road in Burnley, to let her know her son died a hero.

# 4

REIMS

*April 1918*

Sophie, whom all bar herself considered to be a widow, stood in the great nave of the cathedral as the city burned once again. She recalled the deliberate attack on the sacred building at the start of war, in September 1914. While most had been scared, Sophie felt only fury, especially when the mayor of Reims sent out a missive for them to stay calm. The great city was to be an 'Open Town', he'd announced, which effectively meant letting the German army march through without resistance. It had galled her that while her husband was off fighting to keep France safe – to keep Paris French, no less – the Reims mayor was demanding they give the enemy a cheering squad on the way to the capital. She'd argued with him, saying that if Paris fell, they were lost, but he'd pleaded with her as a prominent citizen to help him keep everyone alive by not resisting.

She'd mourned to watch the cathedral aflame. Vast pillars of fuming black vapours had belched from it, as the scaffolding that had been hastily erected to protect the façade and the great rose window caught fire. Two forests had donated their trees for the roof, and she grieved for those forests, burning dry and bright. The lead lining had melted, leaving a few bare rafters and daylight beyond. Two kings of centuries past had gifted funds to provide the roof, which had now gone the way of its benefactors. As it melted and leaked away through the gutters and gargoyles, it created new destruction, including the Bishop's Palace. The kings – the two who'd had the vision to help build the cathedral, and those who had made the pilgrimage to the holy place since – had been anointed and crowned at the top of the nave, beneath the intense colours of the stained glass that shone its rainbow light upon them. A church had stood on these foundations for fifteen centuries, and yet it had taken a malicious act of a twentieth-century army to reduce one of the proudest of its churches to a shell. Sophie secretly believed the enemy had targeted the cathedral as a way of letting France know none of its pomp and royalty could help it now. It hit right at the heart of the proud history of France.

The fighting was strangely quietened today. Even so, from what she was hearing there was going to be a massive spring offensive in the region, which was terrifying simply in its threat. The reality would be one hundred times worse if the last few years were anything to judge by. She looked around at the once proud walls of their magnificent cathedral, hating the crunchy sound of ruins beneath her boots.

'I can't believe it's happening again.' The priest was standing nearby.

'It's deliberate, Father.'

'No, the Germans have denied that,' he countered – far too trusting, in her opinion.

She looked at him with the expression of an indulgent mother gazing at a child who was wondering about the little mouse who exchanged baby teeth under the pillow for gifts. 'They are using the spires of the cathedral as target practice to adjust their sights in order to lay waste to the town. They are lying to us and still we repair their men.'

'Don't lose faith in yourself or us, Madame Delancré.'

Since Jerome had disappeared, no one – not even Sophie – bothered to call her by her married name. They'd not been married long enough for the name to become habit, and everyone, even she, found it easier to use the name by which she'd always been known.

'Well, Father, for now we can no longer count on this space as a clearing site for the wounded, be they French, German, British or Australian.'

'There's always more room below,' he remarked.

'Yes, but the wounded need fresh air to heal. The tunnels are saving the lives of our people, but they are becoming ill from the atmosphere. It is unhealthy.' She sighed. 'We need to make room for more wounded, not keep a hospice going for those in recovery.'

'I know you are doing all you can, Sophie.' He was one of the few citizens who referred to her by her Christian name when he was of a mind. 'The women look to you, although yours are such young shoulders.'

She gave a sad smile and nodded. 'They're broad enough. I'm on my way down there now.'

'How long can you stay?'

Sophie gave a soft shrug. 'Today, at least . . . I must visit my vineyards around Reims. It is, after all, our most important time of birth among the vines.'

'There is little left, surely?' he remarked, sounding dismayed by her plan.

'Even so, I must protect those baby buds with as much tender-ness as I would a newborn in the tunnels.'

'But it's freezing.'

He was right, of course. 'And they could still die. This is the circle of life in the vineyards. But the vines look after us, Father, have done for centuries. It is our turn to look after them. You more than anyone should know that our attachment to our land is near religious in its intensity.' Her voice was light, not meant to sound accusatory. But the priest looked burdened when he sighed his understanding. Sophie continued. 'As the guns are quieter today, I might return to Épernay under cover of dusk. I'll check in on the school and the hospital first.'

'Stocks of disinfectant and dressings are low. Can you speak with your military contacts? Saint Just is around.' She cut him a frustrated glance. 'I know, I know, Sophie. I don't enjoy relying so much on the goodwill you have with important people, but —' he turned both palms towards her in appeal — 'we are trying to save the lives of their soldiers.'

She looked around to the clump of injured enemy men, clustered in an untidy heap around one of the cathedral's soaring columns. 'It's becoming more difficult to convince them when we increasingly look after Germany's soldiers too.'

'Under God's roof, all are equal.'

'I'm sure Gaston de Saint Just will understand that sentiment.' Again, she kept her tone deliberately wry, as the priest was one of the world's good men. 'Goodbye, Father. I'll speak with him when I next see him.'

She left him as he turned, hands on hips, to regard the desecrated holy space with a despair she could feel like a swirling entity. A rain shower had begun, and it felt like that spiritual entity was crying within the hallowed walls. She couldn't think any further on it. The war had taught her the keenest form of pragmatism; she couldn't fix the cathedral, but she could help with the physical and pastoral care of her people.

Sophie emerged onto the cobbles and watched a woman – one of the schoolteachers – leading a quartet of children, none older than five years. They held hands and moved like a dragnet. The youngsters looked up towards the clouds, excited to be above ground. They appeared understandably pale from living beneath the city for too long in its crayères, which had been built to house champagne, not people. The only boy in the gang grinned at her, and the moment of happiness that she sensed he was feeling touched Sophie's heart. She knew his name as Gilbert. The simplest of pleasures were all they had left; even she, with more money than most, had to find her joy in small events . . . like his smile.

She wished Jerome had given her a baby before he left to fight. A child to raise and protect would give her more reason to do what she did. There hadn't been time to become pregnant, and it was a constant ache.

'Bonjour, Madame Delancré,' the woman called. She urged her charges to follow suit.

'Good morning, madame,' they said in unison.

'Hello, children.' Sophie beamed at them. 'Are you well, Madame Rondeau?'

'We manage,' the schoolteacher replied, nodding. 'I thought as the guns are silent a brisk walk around the town would aid the children's breathing. They are struggling with their lungs.'

'Is there anything I can do?' She frowned.

'Stop the guns permanently?' the teacher offered before giving a rueful smile.

'Give me a gun, I'll stop them,' the boy said.

'Oh, Gilbert, hush now.'

Sophie crouched to be level with Gilbert. 'But we need you down in the tunnels. You have to be strong and protect all in your class.'

'Everyone is scared but I am not,' he asserted, and then dissolved into a series of wet coughs.

Sophie frowned, not trusting the sound of his ailment. 'I'll send some herbs. Gilbert would benefit from an inhalation,' she said to his schoolteacher.

'Thank you. I don't know how you do it, madame.'

'I'm a good negotiator.' Sophie grinned. 'Tonight, tell his mother she shall have the herbs. Where in the tunnels?'

The woman gave her directions and Sophie nodded. 'Goodbye, children. Listen to Madame Rondeau. Stay safe.'

They chorused a farewell and continued on, two skipping and laughing through their coughs, as though they'd never known a happier day. Their boots made slapping sounds on the smooth stones, which were turning shiny beneath the shower. Sophie was reminded of how resilient a child could be. She must learn from that, she told herself. The children were living in the moment; she could find some solace in that approach.

She cut away from the square to walk down one of the narrow connecting streets, whose destruction made them seem unrecognisable. On either side had once been homes, some above shops, but now she gingerly picked her way through smashed bricks and broken glass. Shutters hung forlornly from gaping windows clinging to the sides of structures that could be toppled with a strong wind. She risked a glance behind, forcing herself to confront the charred skeleton of the cathedral watching her leave. Its irreplaceable stained glass had been blown out, and from her vantage it now appeared to have a flat roof. It held itself like a black, ghostly testament to humanity at its worst, while inside and beneath it was humanity at its best, where nationality didn't matter, and life was precious.

Only the lampposts she passed in this street stood erect; they seemed to salute her – another survivor – as she passed on her way to the family's Reims mansion, beneath which the city now lived. It was another ten minutes of solid walking, much of it uphill, but relatively enjoyable given the relief of silent guns.

As Sophie approached the city house, she lowered her gaze to watch the progress of her scuffed boots; it was too upsetting to observe the pockmarks in the façade of the family's once proud home, which attested to more target practice by the Germans. Their attacks had collapsed one corner of the house that had stood to its majestic height on the edge of the city for a century. Now relentless artillery had broken one side of its elegant structure, and it looked to Sophie as though it was bending its knee to the Germans.

Gaston, the man she was charged to seek out, had smiled at her when she mentioned this on the morning the destruction had taken place.

'Sophie, don't ever forget that *you* are House Delancré, not this building. This building is mute, inanimate. You are the walking, talking, breathing version that carries its memories forward, who embodies your great-great-grandfather who built this house.'

'And then there's Épernay,' she murmured, taking a breath to calm herself.

'Yes, and then there's Épernay, another glorious mansion of the Delancré family . . . and let's not overlook the chateau in Sézanne.' Gaston placed his hands on her shoulders to force her to face him. He spoke tenderly. 'Your family owns much property and you could say any one of the many houses is Delancré, but —' he squeezed her shoulders — 'they are stone and mortar, bricks and timber. You are the flesh of Delancré . . . you are the living embodiment of its collective spirit and knowledge. You cannot be rebuilt like this house. So, let them break your property but not your fine spirit, Sophie.'

They were rousing words at the right time. Gaston could do this, had been doing this since they were children and the closest of friends.

It was he who had said to her: 'So, don't look at the house. Look at your feet, which keep you moving towards it and while you do so, think about something important and then go below. Confront it only when peace arrives. Then you can fix it. For now, all that matters is that you stay safe.'

She'd followed his advice ever since, and now as she descended the stairs into the crayères that tunnelled below the house, she reminded herself once again that this wasn't her childhood home, where she had also lived with Jerome and where the real memories lived. That was in Épernay, and in a safer position than the Reims dwelling.

Nevertheless, this city house was the face of the Delancré business and below it ran the city's cellars. More than one hundred of the limestone and chalk pits, which the Romans had carved out of the earth during their occupation of Gaul, had been purchased by the fourth-generation champenois Marcus Delancré, her great-great-grandfather. The crayères twisted, turned back on themselves and ran for several kilometres below the city. Hers were just a small part of the collective network that Reims had once proudly stood above, but over which it was now increasingly collapsing.

Sophie paused on the stairs to inhale. It was a ritual of hers. She breathed deeply twice: no matter her mood, her body responded identically each time. Sometimes the comforting smell of chalk and mustiness lasted longer, or like today, the pleasure was fleeting, but it was always reassuringly present.

She hadn't yet fully immersed herself in the cool that she knew awaited her sixty feet below on the floor of the crayères. For the moment she liked noting the first and most important sensation, which was the unique fragrance of the tunnels. At first it was like sniffing mushrooms . . . predictably earthy. She touched the walls, which felt moist and yet silken. The soft chalk was porous, wicking away rainfall and the damp that rose from below. Sophie put her fingertips to her nose to smell again; she had been doing this since childhood, loving the timeless flinty aroma of the chalk. She was smelling the Romans. She was smelling generations of her family. She was tasting the atmosphere that these tunnels could maintain, which led to the dry, crisp and, yes, even chalky flavour of the beverage that fizzed in the collective mind as the world's most desirable. The family crayères offered safety to her and others, and a womb in which the young wines could be nurtured.

She continued her descent, the smooth walls cast in a vague yellow from the lamplight and the rare and random electrification. Finally, on the ground, she did what she always did at this point, which was to look up towards the lip of the original pit. Daylight shone through its small circumference at street level in Reims, whereas down below, the tip of the funnel widened and led into a vast subterranean pit. As a child she had loved the idea of this secret domain running beneath the verdant countryside of her part of France.

She walked around a puddle from a recent rain shower before she headed deeper into the labyrinthine world that felt like her second home. The damp would bring more illness, she reminded herself, and stepped up her pace through the familiar winding tunnels. She'd been running along these narrow alleyways since she was old enough to run. Others needed arrows and posters to tell them where they were within the network, but Sophie had a mental picture of her precise location and could get just about anywhere, not just within her family's crayères, but within the maze beneath the city, if required. All the members of all the champagne households could do this. Champagne families raised their young to be independent within the cellars. And so she passed countless rows of bottles of Delancré champagne angled in their pupitres and tried not to think about the inevitable thieving that was surely going on.

Voices sounded in the distance. As Sophie turned into the dogleg of the tunnel, she knew it would get far busier from hereon, not just because of the hospital but following this opening would take her past living quarters, some separated by furniture, others more salubriously curtained off with heavy fabric. In these tiny nooks of the tunnels, once used to house pupitres, women now cooked, read or did their sewing by candlelight, rocked babies to sleep and wrote letters with stubs of pencils to send to their loved ones in the trenches.

Life – or at least a semblance of it – functioned like a busy beehive; everyone just got on with what had to be achieved, from council meetings to school lessons, from physical exercise classes to keep themselves limber, to laundry and an apothecary dispensing medicines. City hall had been moved underground, as had the headquarters of other essential services including the police and the fire brigade, into this upside-down world below the city.

Light was in short supply. It was the one elusive life giver that they all protected, whether candle or oil lamp, and yet everyone moved to the rhythms of daylight. Sophie had been astonished to discover that even the pet songbirds that now lived in the shadowy world of the crayères, lit only by glows and glimmers, nevertheless sang their songs without the help of the sun.

She passed an elderly woman who was busy knitting, her pet canary cheerfully singing as she worked with a soft smile – to all intents, a look of complete contentment. It reminded Sophie that even in the darkest corners the human spirit was strong enough to prevail.

Sophie wasn't looking forward to the meeting ahead but it was necessary. She made her way to the subterranean café, one of several, and lifted a hand to the man who had been shown down here to wait for her. Looking at him made her realise that another spring had rolled around. The war continued in its relentless bleakness. How had nearly four years passed since Jerome marched off to die? How had nearly three disappeared in the grief of his loss? These were the searching questions she tortured herself with only when she put her head down on a pillow. At other times, self-pity was banished, and thoughts of Jerome were pressed deep and inward. It was easier that way to put one foot in front of the other and help herself by helping others. Sometimes, though, helping others meant begging for assistance from people like the man seated before her.

'My, my, Sophie. It's been a while, hasn't it?' Louis Méa remarked. The small cane chair creaked a protest as he settled his weight into it.

She'd promised herself she would be accessible and even warm to Jerome's brother, especially as he'd made the time and taken the trouble to visit. No doubt it coincided with the opportunity to check the house and business at Avize but she shouldn't be churlish. He was family, after all, but more importantly, Louis was well connected . . . and that's what mattered to her at the moment. 'Louis, I'm sorry that we haven't —'

He stopped her with a tutting sound like tutor to student. 'No need, dear Sophie. We're together now, and I'm so very delighted that we can be. Your correspondence was timely.' He didn't explain why, so she stopped wondering as he continued. 'I'm thrilled to see you. You look as alluring as ever, my dear. Dare I say war suits you?' She didn't answer, giving him a wan smile instead. 'I'd rather see you in a gown, of course, but I'd be lying, my dear, if I didn't admit that this austere outfit makes you look powerful.'

'It's what I wear when I'm volunteering at the hospital,' she said, giving a once-over glance to her simple charcoal dress with a narrow skirt that brushed her ankles. She'd only removed her apron because it took so long to starch and iron, preferring to leave it hanging up in the nurses' area of the cellars. Alluring? Sombre, more like.

'Well, this is a novelty,' Louis remarked, moving on, casting a slow gaze around the hollow of this part of the cellars, which had become a popular underground café since the city of Reims had reinvented itself below ground. 'I had no idea you'd all become subterranean creatures,' he chortled, as if life had never been gayer.

'As you saw when you arrived, there is nothing left of Reims,' Sophie said, trying to anchor him with some pity but not letting any edge of disdain creep into her tone. 'We had no choice; we feel lucky to have these tunnels below our city.'

He nodded. 'Living in Paris, we certainly have our restrictions too . . .' She didn't think so, going by his girth, which had spread to make him rounder than she remembered. Meanwhile people down here in the champagne cellars beneath Reims had become ghostlike versions of their peacetime selves. Thin, pale, lacking vitality – it was all due to this underworld existence, where the sun and fresh air never reached them . . . not to mention existing just a breath away from the front, so nerves were often shredded. 'This is truly amazing, my dear,' he said, trying not to sound condescending, she was sure, but failing nonetheless.

'How have you been, Louis?' She injected bright interest into her query.

The few candles whose flames danced in the makeshift café dulled colour to create a crepuscular atmosphere that Sophie decided suited Louis. He liked to act flamboyant, but she suspected that was the theatre he hid behind; Sophie felt convinced that he preferred the cool of the shadows and that shadings of grey best described him, despite his ruby necktie, which perhaps unintentionally matched his lips.

He wet them now before he answered. 'Well enough, Sophie, thank you. I'm glad you extended this invitation. Actually, more than that, I'm genuinely touched. We share the same surname, we both grieve the same person, we are linked through the same interests. We have much in common, you and I.'

Sophie blinked. Louis was heading somewhere and wasting no time about it. She would follow his lead and not waste any more time with polite niceties. 'I did have a motive for making contact, I must admit,' she said.

'I'm sure,' he said, reaching to pat her hand. She watched his sausage-like fingers cover hers. They were soft and slightly clammy. She wondered if the signet ring with the family crest could ever come off that little finger. She doubted it: it appeared to sit in a valley of flesh, and she couldn't imagine it would ever slip over the mountain ahead of it. No persuasion of oil or soap was getting that off. She had to resist pulling away her hand and cut her gaze back to his narrow-set eyes – which were watching her intently, she now realised, glad she hadn't overreacted. He was testing her. 'I do wish us to be closer,' he continued, 'and I also want you to feel wholly encouraged to ask for my help at any time.'

Sophie answered with a smile that felt awkward. 'That's generous, Louis, thank you. Let's drink to family, then,' she offered, reaching for the bottle of champagne she had organised. It was her label, but she was happy to pay for it at the café and keep business ticking over. 'This is a vintage that I made at the start of the war, just as Jerome was leaving.'

They clinked glasses.

'Mmm, Sophie, my dear! Assaults my senses in every good way.'

She nodded, impressed by his remark. 'Shocking, isn't it, that our most memorable vintage of recent times was crafted in the most devastating of years. I recall weeping as we bottled and corked it.'

'Perhaps your sorrow, which I suspect was exquisite in its pain, is in here?' Louis suggested, taking her even more by surprise. She'd never got to know him well enough to understand that he might possess empathy for others. Sophie felt suddenly disappointed in herself for perhaps being impetuous – a quality her father had counselled against. Jerome had certainly tried many times to assure her that Louis had a good heart despite his pomposity. Her instincts had always told her Louis was greedy, though, and she'd trusted those rather than Jerome's generous and helplessly sentimental loyalty.

*He so wants to be loved*, Jerome had said repeatedly.

'. . . and in that way he is never gone. You can always uncork him, taste him . . . love him,' Louis was saying.

She blinked, arrested. She didn't expect such tenderness in Jerome's brother, but then she really did not know him well enough.

'That's a lovely way to view it, Louis, thank you,' Sophie replied. 'I feel like I've lived several lifetimes since I made this, and that time soon after we lost Jerome is such a blur . . . a dark cave of misery that had no light source, no way of finding my way back from that cave, or so it felt.'

'And still you did.' He smiled, letting the gesture curl and linger wide against cheeks that were more jowly than ever; the years were not being kind to Louis. 'And yet there's nothing dark or brooding about this,' he said, holding up the glass to admire the track of ascending bubbles in the low flickering light of the tunnel.

All the underground cafés were well patronised, and Sophie sold her champagne at subsidised prices to this particular bar. This was one of Sophie's ideas to help achieve a small sense of normality. Many a glass, over the past few years, of House Delancré's sparkling wine had been part of muted celebrations of sorts for birthdays, anniversaries, christenings and, yes, even weddings. She'd been amazed to see people gathered around tables adorned with fine linens, prized china . . . even a candelabra or two. The resilience of folk to take their lives underground into an upside-down existence hadn't failed to impress her. Even now, with nothing in particular to toast, sitting at a small table and sipping an aperitif or a flute of champagne could fool the participants – if just for a short while – that life was not all bleak.

'Tell me about this vintage. Jerome once said it was like listening to poetry when he heard you talk about champagne.'

Sophie was touched; he was trying to be charming, and she needed to recognise that and respond in kind. 'Well, now, I hear the rustle of silk skirts in the chorus of bubbles,' she began. 'Listen,' she urged.

He grinned and did as he was bid, putting the glass to one ear, which she noted looked too small against his large, marrow-shaped head. Thinning fairness on top was compensated with licks of hair around those small ears allowed to grow long. It was prejudicial to compare these half-brothers, as it seemed that in every way Jerome was handsome, Louis was not; that couldn't have been easy for the elder brother as they were growing up. Jerome was not perfect – a nose broken falling from a plum tree had lent a permanent kink to it; one eye was slightly narrower than the other, and he showed a dimple on only one cheek when he grinned, but she liked that these imperfections gave Jerome a rakish appearance. Her husband had been helplessly untidy, too. Clumsy, always dropping things or knocking into furniture, his hair rarely obeying a comb, his jaw always in need of a shave . . . even when he had shaved! She could recall now the scrape of his ever-threatening beard against her skin. She would give all the bottles in her cellar to feel that again.

His brother by contrast was pallid, smooth-faced, neat despite his roundness, deft and economical in his movements . . . and there was nothing open about Louis, nothing carefree, no abandon. His mind was quick and agile, though, whereas it used to make her laugh that Jerome was always slow to catch on, whether it was a simple jest or an undercurrent; he wasn't a sharp judge of character. He liked to trust and gave his trust freely. Jerome had admitted once that he left all the important decisions to Louis because he couldn't rely on his own prudence. 'Except for falling in love with you,' he'd said. 'That was my greatest moment of acumen.' She'd never fully understood that sentiment but there was no doubting that Jerome's brother was decisive, shrewd, driven. She had no idea of his role in Paris but knew it was important, part of the government, and no doubt, knowing Louis, he had his finger poised over any number of well-connected buttons he could push at any time. It was Jerome's honest, uncomplicated way, though, that had attracted her. She hadn't wanted complexity when it came to love.

'Where did you go?' Louis lifted a caterpillar eyebrow in query, although his next comment reminded her of his sharpness. 'You have to let his memory rest, Sophie.'

He was onto her. She sighed. 'I can't.'

'It's been three years since he died.'

'Not dead, Louis. Missing.'

He bowed his head at the correction. 'If he was genuinely still missing, though, do you not think we would have heard something by now?' He didn't make it sound accusatory; his tone was light, conversational. She looked down. 'If he was still alive, my dear, we would have been contacted by the various authorities, even if he can't reach us because he's injured or the like.'

'But what if he's lost?'

'Lost how? In his mind, you mean?' She nodded. He gave her a patient smile. 'Then even if he's languishing in a German prison, the wardens are obliged by international law to make known to the French Red Cross every prisoner they hold. You read the prison gazettes, no doubt?'

'Religiously.'

'So do I, my dear. His name has not appeared in any.'

There was a pause and she didn't know how to fill it. Louis obliged.

'To happier thoughts. Can I tell you what I hear in your glorious champagne?' She dredged up a smile. 'I hear a babble of women gossiping,' he admitted.

'Well, that would impress those who commentate on champagne. That's wonderful, Louis,' she replied, genuinely surprised. 'This is exactly what you should hear: excitement, teasing whispers and wicked chatter. Now tell me what you see.'

'I see these bubbles rising like shooting stars for position at the top.'

'They are busy forming what we call the cordon . . . crystalline and radiant. I wish you could view them with sunlight striking the glass.'

'One day we shall – when this wretched war is done,' he assured her, and there was something in that passive comment that felt proprietorial and sounded a distant alarm within her.

She moved him on. 'How would you describe the colour?'

'Almost silvery in this light,' he continued, sounding fully engaged.

'Louis, listening to you, I could be fooled that you are a champenois.'

He gave a shrug in an attempt at modesty. 'No . . . don't be fooled. I love to drink it, and like you, I enjoy talking about wine. I do remember your father impressing upon us to notice the grey-golden colour.'

She smiled, recalling the same, pleased that he remembered her beloved father so clearly. 'And he'd say these bubbles must explode into tiny motes of gold that collect in the cordon like a fragile necklace of diamonds to glitter elegantly.'

He smiled over the rim of his glass. 'Beautifully described. Sophie, I admit to having nothing but admiration for you. And that you can produce something as delicious as this despite all the trauma, is, as I say, incredible.'

'It's not just me. There are so many brave women, older men, even children who come out into those fields.'

'You take too much risk.'

'This is my way of defending France – its way of life, its flag. I have to do something. All you men at least have purpose,' she said, being deliberately generous given that Louis sat behind a desk most days in the relative safety of Paris.

'So, you walk out into fields under attack?' His tone was teasing. He was doing his best, but he had no experience of the fear they confronted each time they worked Jerome's vineyards.

'I know I defy our enemy every time I walk out into the vineyards. Every woman who walks with me, every child, every elderly man who would like to pick up arms and defend France but cannot knows that by working at our vines we show our attackers that we will not be broken. France will not break.'

'Your courage is exemplary, but few of your workers will survive if they continue to defy the Germans, and I'm especially frightened you won't either. It's about to get much worse.'

'Why do you say that?' She felt a current of shock trill through her. 'It's been so quiet. What do you know?'

He shook his head. 'I hear things, my dear, but I happen to know that some of the most battle-hardened troops have been transferred out of Flanders and are now down here in our Marne region, purportedly for rest.' She watched his moist lips balance on the edge of the champagne glass; it was like viewing a pair of slugs from beneath. He made a soft sound of delight as the slugs sipped their champagne. 'But you see, Sophie, the senior people I mix with don't trust the silent guns.' She frowned, tension curling in her gut like a piece of paper thrown into a fire. 'We all appreciate that this,' he said, pointing upwards towards the rubble of Reims, 'is the pathway our enemy needs, don't you think?' He formed it as a reasonable question and looked at her unblinking until she unhappily nodded. 'So, I'm being assured,' he said cryptically, tapping his beak-like nose, 'that the German army will not walk away from a direct route to Paris as long as this war is being fought.' The memory of the spritz of the champagne disappeared from her mind as his remark fully deflated her. 'Sophie, dearest, I know we've not been close but now is a time for me to take on my role as your only existing family. Let me protect you.'

She was still thinking about the German army boots stomping through Reims again, horror coiling and unwinding like a troubled serpent in her gut, so his final remark took a few moments to filter through. She shook her head. 'What do you mean? How?'

'By coming to Paris for a while.' He shrugged carelessly. 'Away from here, Sophie, these dark tunnels, the injured and the war that I am sure is soon to re-erupt.'

'You can't be serious, Louis?'

'But I am. I made a grave and binding promise to my brother that I would take care of you. I haven't wished to impose as I know what an independent spirit you possess, but it's about to get very dangerous for all of you here.'

*And what about everyone else?* she wanted to ask. 'You make it sound as if it hasn't been dangerous up to now,' Sophie offered up in an even tone instead. 'We live with danger daily.'

'I suspect what's coming is going to be far, far worse.' The snake in her belly coiled tighter. 'I cannot risk you being in its midst.' His tone had changed; gone was the conversational attitude. 'Look, I'm going to say it. I think we should marry.'

He couldn't have surprised her more if he'd reached over and punched her. She looked back at him in disbelief, only just managing to disguise her horror.

'Marriage?' she repeated, her voice tight.

'Sophie, my dear, I know this suggestion is somewhat of a shock, and you don't have to answer me this minute, but it is the right move for so many reasons. We can consolidate what our two families have before the Germans run rampant through the region. Never has this been more important than now. I can also fulfil my brother's demand that I protect the woman he loved.' *Loves,* she corrected in her private despair. 'Marriage gives you all the privileges I enjoy – and I enjoy plenty . . .' he said, having the graciousness to look down with at least a tiny sense of shame. 'My dear

Sophie, I can protect everything you care about.' *Take it, more like*, Sophie's inner voice railed. 'And we can start a family, keep our lineage strong. You're not getting younger. I'm certainly feeling my age,' he said, giving his midriff a shake, trying self-deprecation now, as though searching for a way through her stunned silence so she could appreciate how rational and sensible his offer was. Before she could speak, he held up a hand as if to ward off an explosion of objections. 'Don't answer fast, my dear. I don't for a moment flatter myself that you might marry me out of any affection. No, Sophie, I know you love my brother and that shall not change. But you see, it doesn't have to. Marriage between us would, we both know, have to be a strategic decision and it would be for all the right reasons. While you might think otherwise, I want you to understand that I loved my brother in my own way. He knew it too. Unlike you, though, I believe him dead and I think it would bring his soul peace if he knew you were being looked after in the right way by someone who bears his name, someone who does not dilute our shared family assets and someone, above all else, who can offer you absolute protection of the highest level. So, give it due consideration. Add to this that I would not expect you to change your life drastically, either; once we attain peace – and we shall – you can run a household in Épernay and indeed Reims. I can keep living in the apartment in Paris, visit Avize when I need to. We can lead separate and, I'm sure, content lives.'

She waited to be sure he was finished. He had managed to make something so far from her thoughts – so horrible – sound not just pragmatic but simple and indeed easy. It was shocking. Her slightly strangled tone clearly reflected it. 'Louis, I have to ask,' she said, pausing to clear her throat of its anguish, 'what is in this for you?'

'Other than the obvious, you mean?'

She blinked. 'What is the obvious?'

'A beautiful, intelligent, capable wife, of course. One who matches my intellect . . . even some of my interests, perhaps, but essentially someone I can introduce in my circles and feel proud.'

*A bauble*, she thought. *I'm to make you look good.* 'All right.' She nodded. 'Now tell me what it is that you gain apart from the obvious?'

His face creased into a thin smile that had no chance of reaching his eyes. She wasn't sure if Louis knew what that sort of smile looked like, or even felt like. 'I do want family, my dear, so . . .' He tried to look embarrassed, but his lips got in the way as he licked them and his expression changed to something more lascivious. It was unintentional, no doubt, but it was present. 'There is that important duty that would need to be considered in the scheme.' He gave a chuckle that sounded drier than the champagne she strived to make. Again, he faced his palm towards her to ward off an instant response. 'Think on it. No hurry . . . perhaps we can take some opportunities such as this one to get to know each other better. Start again, so to speak.' His expression shifted easily from cunning to bright. 'Now,' he said, his tone gushing, 'I don't for a moment think you invited me here for a social chitchat. I imagine I can offer you some sort of service? Perhaps you need to lean on my network of important contacts?' Louis shook his head and his chins mirrored the action. He was too shrewd for her. 'Please, don't in any way feel shame at this. It's how the wheel turns, my dear. You scratch my back and I will always scratch yours . . . and with pleasure.' He smiled at his cliché, which brought the ugliest of images to her mind. 'I'm at your service, Sophie, so let me help you. Turn to me first.'

Stunned, she managed to spit out the reason she had invited him, realising how many steps ahead of her he was.

'Supplies, Louis. The hospital is running too low on every-thing. We need —'

'Consider it done,' he said, waving his hand as if already bored by the request. 'Write down a list before I leave today. I'll have it on the next train down.'

'That easy?'

He gave a shrug so casual it took no effort. 'For you . . . yes. Providing we understand one another.'

Another chilling moment. The vision of Louis hoisting himself into her bed exploded in her mind, but it was as if he knew her greatest weakness. Not having a family was the pain that never lessened, and even a child from Louis was pragmatic, if not tempting. A true Méa. Maybe. She could love the child with purity even if she found the father hard to enjoy.

'Louis?' He looked back at her as if in innocent query. 'There is something else I need your help with.'

'Can I take a wild guess and ask if this is connected with finding Jerome?'

'You see right through me,' she flattered, hating herself for being so easy to read. 'Can you get me in front of someone more senior at the Red Cross?'

'To what end, my dear?' He didn't even sound surprised. His tone was measured, his voice even, as if preparing to explain something complex to an imbecile. 'The information doesn't change whether you're here beneath the ground in Reims or standing in front of someone's desk in Paris.'

'Please, Louis. Humour me.' She knew she looked desperate. 'I'll tell you what,' she said, deciding to use his tactics. 'Why don't we attend the opera together? A long time ago you said you'd enjoy that.'

His eyes, their colour indeterminate down here in the shadows but which she knew to be an unremarkable brown, suddenly glittered. 'The opera? Oh my, that is enticing. You are a terrible tease, Sophie. Is this quid pro quo, my dear?'

She couldn't imagine Jerome ever using a term like that against her. How different they were, and yet Louis seemed to believe he could make her content.

'I don't see it that way,' she said evenly. 'If I'm coming up to Paris to see someone from the Red Cross, I might as well take advantage of our beautiful capital . . . and enjoy something with you that I could with few others.'

The flattery worked, even though she suspected he was well aware of being manipulated. Sophie accepted that Louis chose to let it happen because it suited his needs. 'In that case I shall book tickets and send a telegram as soon as a meeting is set up for you.'

Louis raised his glass and she had no choice but to raise hers and let him clink his against it, as though they were sealing a deal. She prayed it wasn't for marriage. He looked genuinely chuffed. 'Let's continue my education on the 1914 vintage. We had reached taste, had we not?'

Sophie dredged up a smile, knowing through bitter experience that it was only wasted energy to dwell on all those aspects of life she had no control over. And she needed every ounce of her energy for those she could.

She put some lightness she wasn't feeling into her tone, and deliberately sat up straighter. 'Well, the flavours change from year to year and because we are sipping vintage, I can taste the barrels in which it developed its flavour.' He smiled, eyes looking lazily back at her as though lulled, and she was encouraged. 'I can sense floral notes – like white freesia – which scented the earth that the mother vine of these grapes smelled as she grew her fruit. And then it will change, reacting with the atmosphere, the damp of our tunnels and the flavours of the limestone giving us what we call a second nose . . . more complex, more mature, less bright on the tongue.'

'Go on,' he encouraged, as though simply enjoying the sound of her voice.

She distracted herself from her distaste of Louis by talking through the flavour of this exquisite offering from House Delancré. 'I always think of this vintage as being reared in blood. And when I feel it in my mouth, I believe I can experience the enthusiastic spirit of the twenty-two children who died while helping their mothers and grandparents to harvest the fields while their fathers were defending the country. This wine always tastes fresher, more ebullient than those that have come after it, and I believe those children live on in it with all their devil-may-care attitude and laughter. Their memories are here in the slightly sweet spritz and the fruitiness lingering on the palate and the smoothness, like their young skin.' She'd had no clue how moved she'd become. Her tears welled but didn't spill. 'Forgive me.' How she hated to look weak in front of him.

To her surprise he took no advantage from it. 'Then for the children of Reims who gave their lives for this vintage, I salute them, and I raise my glass to you for keeping their memory alive in this glass.' She nodded and sipped. At the inevitable sigh of pleasure as he swallowed, he continued. 'Do you regret not having children?'

That was unexpected. Her eyes flashed up at him, unsure whether to feel injured. Her gaze was met with genuine enquiry.

Sophie took a slow breath to ensure her voice was even when it came. 'I would love to be holding the hand of Jerome's child, knowing their father was still with us through this son or daughter. But, if I'm honest, I think all this fearlessness that people credit me with would never have shown itself if I were a mother.'

'You doubt yourself too much.'

'Because I might have had something to live for, do you mean?'

'No, because you'd make a fine mother with all that empathy roaring around in your blood. Even so, I've heard mothers say that having children makes one braver.' Did she hear a wistful note there? 'I often think of my mother and how she died before I had the chance to know her. My father always spoke to me with admiration of how courageous my mother was facing her death, telling him with her dying breaths that it had been worth it because she was leaving knowing she had a son. She named me too before she left us . . . called me her *little king*.' Through all this he had not shifted his gaze from her, did not seem awkward to speak of such tenderness and loss. 'I feel ready to be a father, to be important in someone's life.'

'I do regret that we never had a child.'

'Then together we must make it happen, Sophie . . . the Delancré and the Méa will not die out when we do. For that alone we have a responsibility.' He let that sit upon her while he drained his glass. 'On that thought, I must start making my way back to the surface after this most intriguing of visits. You'd better give me that list.' Appalled at how casually he spoke of wanting to make children with her, she pulled two folded pages from her pocket, trying not to tremble. 'Ah, of course you came well prepared.' He smiled, as though they had concluded a business negotiation. 'I shall look forward to our time in Paris together.'

# 5

Newly returned to Épernay from Reims and her meeting with Louis, Sophie stared at Étienne, the most reliable of her employees, now in his eighties, and she could see he shared her despair. The woman nearby began coughing; it was clear she was not recovered from whichever of the many ailments had struck, but still she had kept working.

'You've done your best, Yvette,' Sophie reassured her. 'Please go home and take care of your children.' The woman looked at her plaintively and nodded. Sophie needed her gone so she could never know how this news was shredding her mental state. She turned Yvette around by the shoulders and urged her out of the sheds. 'Rest,' she ordered. 'My housekeeper is in charge of the additional medicines I brought back from Reims. Call in at the house and take what you need.'

They watched the woman retreat and finally, in frigid silence, they turned back to stare at the few sacks of sugar remaining in the warehouse.

'How could she let this happen?'

Étienne sighed. 'She is doing a job out of respect and duty,

84

madame. This is her husband's role and Paul would never have let this occur. You know that. She doesn't.'

'I blame myself,' Sophie said, letting out a groan. 'I should have paid more attention.'

'Let us be honest, madame, and agree that whether she told you in winter or now can't make any difference to the situation.'

'I could have prepared, though, Étienne. I could have . . .' She didn't finish her thought. Life suddenly overwhelmed her in the moment and she fell silent.

'Madame, let us think on a solution and not fret on what is done.'

'No sugar, no champagne – the equation is simple,' she said, staring at the remaining sacks, which had travelled all the way from the Caribbean. 'The last time I checked, the Cuban sugar producers were doubling, tripling their production. It didn't occur to me it wasn't arriving.'

'I suspect they have increased production but getting their sugar out and across the seas in wartime is likely the problem.'

'What about Africa? We used to buy from there.'

He shook his head. 'Impossible at the present time.'

'When did you discover we were down to our last sacks?'

'Last week, madame.' She turned to him open-mouthed and he shrugged. 'I tried to solve it alone . . . My thoughts too leapt to the African supplier, but sugar is not available from anywhere.'

She knew Étienne would die for her family and changed her tone. 'None to be had?'

He shook his head. 'None to be bought, bribed for . . . even stolen. I think our sacks here are a few sacks more than anyone else possesses.'

She stared at them, helpless and impotent, feeling her throat closing. In her mind's eye she could see walls closing in on her . . . and Louis was outside those walls, beckoning.

'Is sugar beet out of the question? I mean, it's not my preferred —'

'The beet fields are now mud and trenches, madame. They don't exist any more in France or Belgium.'

She'd guessed as much and had just needed to hear it confirmed. They remained silent until she could bear it no longer. 'Right!' He looked at her, waiting for instruction. 'We use the last of it for bottling.'

He didn't need to say it, but he did anyway. 'And for the tirage, madame?'

Sugar was even more important for that process, but they both knew that unless they could add the sugar now to create the bubbles essential to champagne, there would be no product to bottle and sell. Worse, their wine would suffer, and potentially be lost.

'When tirage time comes, I'll have a plan.' She turned to him and, despite her rousing words, felt powerless. Without asking for permission, the short, old fellow who had worked in her family business since he was a child reached out and hugged her.

'I know you will, madame,' he soothed her as she leaned into his embrace, cried briefly for his blind faith, and then rallied herself as quickly as she'd felt overcome by despair. Sophie sniffed back her tears and let go. He had been around her all her life, and was old enough to be the grandfather she often treated him as, enjoying his wisdom.

It came now. 'You use the least sugar of the whole industry. If anyone can make a champagne with this little, you can.'

She nodded her gratitude. 'Except it's not enough, Étienne. We both know we need more, and I'll have to find it.' Her mind raced and her thoughts landed unhappily on her husband's brother, his touch still unpleasantly warm in her memory.

'What will you do?'

'I shall use my influence where it is best spent,' she said, and already began to think about that trip to Paris.

———

Was there ever a more beautiful time in this most beautiful of cities than spring? Sophie allowed herself a private smile of pleasure because she was standing in front of one of the most spectacular buildings of the city, one she had been visiting since childhood and which held only the happiest of memories for her. An evening at the opera at the Palais Garnier, where for a short time she could set aside her sorrows both old and new, to lose herself in the spectacle but especially the music.

Sadly, she had to share it with Louis Méa, but that was the price.

It was Rossini tonight. Easy to listen to, amusing and about love. If Jerome was ever going to listen to an opera, this was the one she'd suggest to him because it was fun, often loud like him, and built to a frenetic pace. No one in the audience, even if they arrived in a bad mood, could leave feeling that way, but then the opera house of Paris tended to shift one's disposition anyway. It allowed its patrons to enter a new and fantastical world of pure escape. Just walking into the bedazzling Palais Garnier, which dominated Haussmann's grand avenues of the 9th, could quicken her pulse as it was meant to, with its glittering opulence and bold design and decoration. Flamboyant throughout: a mosaic ceiling of Murano glass, mirrors everywhere reflecting the opulence and allowing the patrons to stare at themselves and their neighbours, rivals and betters indirectly. Every chamber seemed to outdo itself with outrageous grandeur, but she could argue all day about the functionality that led eager concert-goers to the horseshoe-shaped theatre – a feast of marble, stucco, velvet and gilt. But even all of that was a mere support act to the now infamous massive bronze and crystal chandelier that lit the auditorium with its three hundred and forty glittering lights. Its counterweight had fallen one night, killing a patron. The subsequent novel by journalist Gaston Leroux, which created such fascination when it was serialised as *Le Fantôme de l'Opéra*, featured the magnificent chandelier falling from its hoist into the audience. She loved to look at it and think of the disfigured man of the novel who menaced the famous opera house and favoured box five. She glanced to her left to where that box overlooked the stage, just above the grand box saved for royalty.

'Did you know that in days gone the men would sit in the stalls while their women sat in the boxes above, which could have red velvet curtains drawn across?' she said to Louis.

'I am happy that those rules no longer apply,' he admitted, her arm tucked tightly around his elbow, allowing his gaze to wander down from her neck and linger just a heartbeat longer than she found comfortable. 'You look exquisite tonight, Sophie.'

In a gown she hadn't worn for years, a favourite because Jerome had bought it for her, she felt strong, in control, and was able to field his compliment rather than feel cornered by it. 'Don't we all look rather splendid? Who would think we are fighting a war?'

There was a distinct lack of men in the audience but still enough to surprise her. In Reims and in Épernay, no man of working age was to be spotted unless he was injured or recovering from an injury. She wondered if Louis felt conspicuous but dismissed that thought quickly.

It had been so long since she'd attended the opera, she needed to hold her confidence and remain focused, especially as this expedition was not purely for pleasure. She intentionally recalled the moment when Jerome had given her the box containing the gown she was wearing this evening.

'It echoes the colour of my vineyards' soil at the start of summer,' he'd said, but she had always thought that fanciful. To her its colour was more a soft version of malachite that faded to rich cream in a straight column of drapery in the empire style. The dress was fringed with silk the colour of rich parchment and the bodice was beaded with the palest of pink pearls and pink chiffon rosebuds. It was a pretty ensemble with a modest train and elbow-length sleeves dangling prettily with silver beads. With her hair swept up, Sophie knew she was perfectly groomed for her evening but the misfortune was that she looked all the more delectable to Louis.

Sophie was pleased to find herself sharing a box with some of her parents' wealthiest friends, one of them the wife of a merchant she intended to press for help with her sugar crisis before she leaned on Louis, to add more to her side of the balance sheet. She smiled at her companion and told him she'd just seen a friend she hadn't spoken to in years.

The woman suddenly spotted her too and called out across the box. 'My dear Sophie!' she exclaimed, waving frantically. 'How long has it been?'

Sophie excused herself and moved towards her mother's friend.

'Years,' she admitted. 'Forgive my absence, Brigitte, I —'

'How could I not?' The woman chortled, sounding like a hen. 'The world's gone mad. And why would you ever want to leave beautiful Épernay?'

Sophie wanted to explain to Madame Charpentier that Épernay was in the line of fire and not nearly as safe as this uninformed and well-protected Parisian understood, but she needed access to the woman's husband so she bit back the response and instead smiled benignly.

'Sophie, darling . . . any news of that dashing husband of yours?'

'None, I'm afraid.'

'Well, they say no news is probably good news.'

'Do they? I hope so. I had to come to Paris, Brigitte, on House Delancré business, and in fact I wanted to ask —'

'Oh, my dear, no shoptalk. Let me introduce you to my new friend, Mademoiselle Guigon – she is engaged to be married to no less than . . .'

Sophie tuned out. She couldn't be less interested in whose ring Mademoiselle Guignon wore. She remained in the pair's company just long enough to give the new fiancée a few congratulatory words before removing herself to the back of the box to rethink her strategy. Louis looked to be engaged in conversation, so she had some time to herself.

Her neighbour, who seemed equally reluctant to mix with the gossipy crowd, gave her a sympathetic nod.

'And what are you trying to secure while you feel ridiculous in an evening gown while men are dying all over Europe?'

She stared into a roundish face with flattish features and a clear complexion. A soft cloud of gently coppered hair was caught up above her head. A cupid's bow of a mouth smiled back at her. Sophie blinked, measuring whether to take offence; she looked into the calm gaze of the round-faced woman, who looked uncomfortable in her opera finery, and realised her companion hadn't read her wrong.

'I admit to loving Rossini, but if I'm honest with you, *The Barber of Seville* is not why I'm here, my dear. I'm here to hunt donations.' She couldn't help the grin and shook her head gently. 'And what I need is sugar.'

Her companion frowned. 'Did I hear right?'

'I make champagne. We have no sugar left.'

'Ah, for your fermentation.'

Sophie's gaze widened. 'You understand winemaking?'

'Not like you. I'm a scientist, though. I understand the chemistry of what you do but with no knowledge of your amazing skill to turn grape juice into the magnificent drink we're all sipping tonight.'

'I'm Sophie Delancré. It's a pleasure and a relief to meet you.'

At this the older woman chuckled. 'Likewise, my dear. I am Marie Curie.'

Sophie's mouth opened in surprise. This woman had been awarded the Nobel Prize twice. 'I am honoured.'

'No need to be, but thank you. I should warn you, you're not the first person tonight to be angling to meet your friend's husband.'

Her heart felt as though it were drowning. 'Really?'

Madame Curie nodded. 'I'm afraid so. I think she's enjoying all the attention. He's not in Paris, I gather.' Sophie spirits deflated. 'Unlike you, though, I don't need him specifically. I just want a little of her money.'

'For research?'

The scientist shook her head. 'No, I'm building mobile X-ray machines that I can take to the front line. I need urgent funding to do that.'

The orchestra had finished warming up and the lights of the grand chandelier dipped several times.

'We must talk later,' Sophie suggested.

———

During intermission, Sophie moved away from the crowded hall of mirrors that echoed Versailles. Standing in a quiet corner, sharing a flute of champagne, she introduced Madame Curie to Louis, and they made some small talk before he began scanning the crowd.

'Forgive me, ladies. I know rather a lot of people here and they all want something. I must keep a sharp eye out for . . . um . . . incoming.' He turned away.

Sophie smiled at her companion. 'I understand from my reading that you discovered two new chemical elements and that you used radium to treat tumours. I am humbled by your research.'

'I'm delighted to meet someone so young who is familiar with my work. Thank you – it was hard-won. As a woman with a career you'll appreciate how hard it is to pursue a vocation beyond teaching or nursing. The higher education required for research was not available to girls in Poland. I could only achieve it in France, where I was lucky enough to study chemistry, mathematics and physics.'

'In French, though.'

'Yes.' Her elder gusted a brief laugh. 'I had to learn French very quickly so I could understand the lessons.'

Sophie shook her head in genuine awe. 'I was fortunate to know from a young age where my future lay. And my career was given to me along with my surname.'

Her companion gave that small smile that Sophie was beginning to understand was not easy to draw out. 'And yet you compete in a man's world very well, it would seem.'

'I have to. My husband went off to defend France and hasn't been seen since 1915.' She shrugged to show she did not want pity, but it struck her that none was forthcoming. Madame Curie was likely too wise to offer hollow platitudes.

Instead she fixed Sophie with a gimlet gaze. 'He would be proud of you for remaining strong in his absence.' She glanced at Louis's back.

Sophie sighed. 'He is well connected,' she whispered. 'Have to keep him on side.'

'Be careful,' Madame Curie warned, only for Sophie's hearing. Then speaking normally, she said, 'I haven't told many people this, but all the radium I have has been securely packed away in a lead-lined box and transported well away from Paris to be secretly stored.' At Sophie's look of surprise, she continued. 'I didn't want the Germans getting their hands on my radium, but I also couldn't sit idly by and watch this war from Paris. I felt I needed to help somewhere. Do you understand X-ray . . .? I don't mean that to sound condescending but most people do not.'

Sophie enjoyed her directness. 'I would appreciate learning what they can do.'

Madame Curie sipped her champagne as she began a brief explanation. 'X-rays are a type of electromagnetic radiation that can look through tissue to the skeleton. They can see injuries to bones and have also proven effective in hunting down foreign objects in the body, so it made sense that the machines would be valuable for finding bullets. Modern conical bullets twist to lacerate the flesh and cause bones to burst before they become lost some-where in the body.'

'I see,' Sophie said, her understanding dawning.

'And then there are the shell fragments buried so deep it's hard for the naked eye to detect them. When this ghastly war began, only city hospitals had the capacity to perform X-rays, but I could see we desperately needed them on the battlefields for urgent medical aid. And so I invented what everyone seems to call my "radiological car". Now, Irène – that's my daughter – and I can drive our van right up to the field hospital where army surgeons can make use of the equipment to guide their surgeries.'

'I'm in awe. How do you power this mobile machine?'

'We incorporated a dynamo.'

'Dynamo?' Sophie looked lost, prompting another soft smile.

'A generator,' she explained. 'The petroleum-powered car engine provides the electricity to drive our X-ray machine. Let me add, it was the Union of Women of France who gave me the money

I needed to produce the first car. That one was rolled out in your very region, in the Battle of Marne in 1914.'

Sophie was astounded by this news and also grateful enough to want to help. 'How many X-ray vans do you have now?'

'Mmm, I believe it's twenty – Irène will know exactly. We've trained women in the physics of electricity and X-rays, given them practical lessons in anatomy and also photographic processing, and then off to the front they were sent.'

'Incredible!' Sophie breathed. 'And how many of these marvellous volunteers do you have?'

'Again, Irène will know the true number but it has to be in the order of one hundred and fifty. The vehicles come in a variety of shapes and sizes and had to be adapted. All of them were donated by wealthy Parisian women, without whom none of this would be possible.'

'Marie, I will donate a vehicle.'

At this remark, Louis turned; he had clearly been listening to the conversation while pretending not to, and Sophie was relieved they'd been careful earlier.

'That's rather hasty,' he said, trying to smile through his warning to her.

'I didn't mean for you to feel obliged, Madame Delancré.'

Sophie glared his way. 'And I don't. I feel inspired. Let me arrange for you to receive a vehicle from the cars we have at Épernay, or better still, let me buy you a car from someone in Paris, if that's easier.'

'I'm astonished but immensely grateful.'

'I look at what you and Irène are doing, and I want to do more.'

'I can't imagine you not keeping busy?'

'Hardly,' Louis sneered. 'She's helped set up a subterranean hospital, she's still tending my brother's vineyards' – *my vineyards now, Louis* – 'and she's making champagne. She's a very busy person.'

'A hospital in the cellars? Now I feel awed. I can't get you sugar, but how else can I help you?'

Sophie didn't know she was going to ask until the words forced their way out. How could she miss this opportunity? She'd come for sugar but maybe she wouldn't return empty-handed. 'Will you visit Reims, Marie? We have so many desperately wounded men carried into our underground hospital directly from triage at the front line, and often we're digging around blindly for shrapnel and bullets.' Marie winced. 'Our surgeon is excellent, but I know he could work more magic if he knew what he was looking for. He could certainly save more lives.'

The scientist nodded. 'We shall come, Irène and I, I promise.'

'I don't know how to thank you.'

'You have – a car! I couldn't ask for more. Now, one more thing before we go back into the theatre and get lost in Rossini, and I don't wish to prod at a wound, but you said your husband disappeared. No word?'

She shook her head. 'Nothing. There are witnesses who say he fell.'

'Witnesses who attest to my dear brother being killed,' Louis interjected.

Sophie kept her patience. 'Not confirmed, though. His present status is missing.'

Marie considered this before pulling a face to suggest it was hardly conclusive. 'He is missing . . . just presumed dead, then?' Sophie nodded. 'He could have been taken prisoner.'

'We've left no stone unturned, Madame Curie,' Louis said over his shoulder, sounding peeved.

'No doubt you're in contact with the Red Cross?'

'Yes, since 1915 I've been badgering them. They're tired of me,

I'm sure. My brother-in-law has kindly set up a meeting for me at the Parisian headquarters tomorrow, so I hope I might be able to find out more then.'

'I don't want you getting your hopes up, Sophie,' Louis said, turning back to them. 'Please approach this meeting without anticipating too much.'

Marie took a different approach. 'Never tire of being a nuisance. Keep pestering – they're not infallible, and if you've never been to the front, I can assure you that mistakes could easily be made in the chaos of battle and rescuing the fallen and injured. Men might have lost their uniforms, or the items that connect them to who they are. I have seen the effects of shock. Some change personality. Anyway, my dear, I don't wish to frighten you but simply to ensure you don't give up hope.'

'We shan't,' Louis said, putting a protective arm around Sophie's shoulder. 'Shall we, my dear? Looks like the intermission is drawing to a close. It's been lovely talking,' he said to Madame Curie.

Sophie squeezed Marie's arm. 'Come to Reims . . . please. I will keep my promise regarding the car. Thank you for tonight.'

'Keep your hopes bright, Madame Delancré. Maybe he's hoping you'll find him.'

# 6

MARNE

*May 1918*

Captain Charlie Nash and his company found themselves marching through a sun-drenched landscape that, if not for their uniforms, rifles and all the other clutter of warfare, let him pretend that the world was at peace. After leaving their camp in Belgium, the 8th Battalion of the Leicestershire Regiment had begun their much-anticipated journey into France, towards the quieter sector near Reims. They'd marched and then boarded a train, not at all offended to be travelling in cattle trucks – the only available rolling stock in this part of France right now, they were informed – just relieved to be leaving behind the despair of Flanders. Grief from not having been able to keep Hartley alive until their rotation and retreat felt like a weight pressing on his chest, heavy as a grave-stone. But since arriving in France it had begun to ease.

He'd nodded as his major observed what a little spring sunshine and blue sky could do to improve the men's humour. 'Enjoying that warmth on your back, Captain Nash?'

'Appreciating it all over, sir. I think my uniform is feeling vaguely dry for the first time in months.'

The men around them had chuckled their agreement.

'How long, sir, to the next stop?'

'I don't really know, to be honest, but I think our boarding at Wizernes was the last for a while. Next stop is a place I cannot pronounce.' He spelled it out.

'Aougny, sir.'

'Yes, well, not all of us speak Frog like you, Nash. Anyway, it's on foot from there.'

'No one's complaining, sir,' Nash replied. 'It feels a treat to be able to move around so freely.'

The men were as good as Charlie's word, with not a murmur of discontent at having to march with their packs. They were treated so well by the French civilians in every village and town they marched through that Charlie began to wonder if his battalion would be able to get back into that lean, fighting frame of mind from Flanders. Not that he was particularly concerned, given the promise that the fighting in Marne was sporadic at most; he sensed they would simply be holding their positions as a deterrent. It presented a surprise opportunity for everyone's physical wounds to begin healing, their health to improve and hopefully for the mindset to turn optimistic once again. Minds were harder to get well, though.

In mid-May, as the Tigers passed through Jonchery, Charlie was astonished to see French soldiers forming a guard of honour to show their respect and gratitude to the Englishmen for helping to keep their people – and Paris – safe from German pillage. He penned a letter to Hartley's mother from Châlons le Vergeur when the 8th arrived at their new position, approximately ten kilometres from the front. He also finally got around to writing to his old boss at the laboratory in Lancashire. He had no one else to write to. No family, no good friend waiting on a missive . . . just a mentor he respected and still felt badly for leaving when he volunteered to join up.

*Truly, Prof, at Ypres, when we were rotated into huts, we'd sleep in dust on hard floorboards and wrap our puttees around our feet for extra warmth – not that there was much to be had. Here in France, we lie naked, mainly because of the southern warmth but also because of the fleas. I don't care about the itching because I can smell the living forest nearby, something Flanders couldn't offer. The trees have branches and thick, beautiful leaves . . . I can hear birdsong all day and I realise I haven't heard birds singing in more than a year. The grass is lush and long like a thick carpet, and although it's cold, the river is clean and we all jump in to bathe. The houses in the nearby town are deserted but they're whole. People closed their shutters and left. Everything appears intact and only the dead flowers in the window boxes give away that the place is unlived in. Mind you, if we walk a bit further to another town nearby, it's business as usual. I was sitting at a café, for heaven's sake, drinking pinard (that's French plonk) as if I had nothing more important on my mind than enjoying the sunshine! I do feel guilty for the poor sods left to fight in Belgium on those flat, grey plains with the explosions all night, like stab wounds in the land, and killing where they can.*

*The French soldiers smile at us wherever we go and the women blow kisses. Blimey, we are being made to feel like heroes. I will say the troops are building up in this region, which is a little unsettling as we thought we were being sent here for some much-needed R&R. I also note that the enemy positions have the high ground. They can watch everything we're doing. That said, I've counted six shells being fired in the ten days we've been here, and after the shelling we've endured, this is a paradise by comparison.*

*Enemy patrols are active but we're onto them. The orders down the line are to fire only when fired upon, although*

*I reckon we'll retaliate with vigour if it should intensify. No sign
of that yet and a lazy afternoon with some pinard beckons.
I'm not allowed to tell you where I am but suffice to say our
headquarters are on a hill, which is reassuring because it gives
us some sort of view of the canal in our immediate distance and
a lot of deserted trenches. The trenches here are clean enough
and not required but there are insufficient latrines should
they be. Again, my hope is that they are never called upon.
The canal I mentioned separates us from Fritz too, which is
doubly reassuring.*

    *Hoping this finds you well. It leaves me a little lighter
of heart than my last, and here's to sharing a beer with you
sometime in happier days.*

    *Yours, Nash.*

Charlie posted his letter to Professor Clunes that day. Over a small
flagon of wine, his back leaning against the warmed bricks of the
local café at Trigny, he considered his fortune at being here when so
many good men from his unit were dead.

'Follow orders, even if they're stupid, and then die,' Charlie
murmured into his cheap wine.

'Hey, soldier.' It was a woman's voice interrupting him. He
grinned, grateful to be distracted. '*Santé*,' she said, and he raised
his glass to her.

She walked over with a hip-rolling gait, encouraged by his
smile, and slipped into French. 'Do you understand my language?'

'I do,' he replied in French, and watched her eyes widen in
surprise.

'Ah, my handsome soldier is also clever,' she said, amused and
surprised at once.

'Only when I'm in the mood,' he quipped, still in French,
before draining his glass.

'You impress me, Englishman. Can I call you Tommy?'

'You may, but my name is Charlie,' he replied, pushing off the wall and immediately missing its soothing and silent warmth.

'Well, Charlie . . .' He rather liked how she pronounced his name with a *sh* sound. 'How about some French comfort?' she offered with a wink, her weight shifting to one of her wide hips as she paused, blocking the sun so he didn't have to squint to admire her attractive curves. 'Better than that vinegar you're drinking.'

He allowed a new and lazy smile to split across his expression; it had certainly been a long time since he'd felt the touch of a woman's skin.

'It is tempting,' he offered. 'But —' he pointed to his shoulder and the three stars on his epaulette — 'I am a captain, and I must take my men away from this lovely place so we can defend France and her beauties.' He nodded at her and she appeared to give a brief quiver of delight that he was speaking about her.

'Come with me, Captain Sharlie.'

'What's your name?' he asked. She opened her mouth to reply but he added, 'Your real name.'

Her gaze narrowed as she considered him. 'I go by the name of Coraline.' He waited. 'But my real name is Fayette.'

'That's pretty.'

'My mother's choice. She was pretty.'

'What does it mean?'

She shrugged. 'Little fairy. My friends call me Fay.'

He felt suddenly sad for her; something about that small disclosure and the fact that he knew she was telling him the truth. 'May I call you Fay?'

She nodded.

'Then I shall walk with you, but I don't have long.'

She gave him a smile of promise and led him to a tiny room over a shop which was bare of furniture save a small table, a cupboard, a bed and a small couch for two. There was a painting on the wall that looked primitive, as though conceived and executed by a child, and it hung crookedly. The room smelled of food whose aroma rose from beneath the boards; he could pick out garlic in particular.

'They're making garlic soup in the café,' she explained as he sniffed the air. 'Economical.'

It was not unpleasant and it made him hungry. When he remarked on this, she laughed.

'Hungry for what I have, perhaps?' she said flirtatiously.

'Can we just talk?' he asked, feeling ridiculous for asking.

She had been busy unbuttoning her blouse and paused now, staring at him as though he was feeble-minded. 'I think you mean that,' she said.

'I do.'

'What do you wish to talk about?'

'Tell me about your life growing up as a little fairy.'

He led her to the sofa and she obliged, first fetching a flagon of wine and some short, thick glasses before sitting beside him, placing the wine on the stool in front of them. The sofa's springs had long ago given up their bounce and wheezed with their weight.

'No, Sharlie. Tell me about *your* childhood. Tell me what that sadness in your gaze is about.'

He'd never told anyone before, but as Fay poured him a glass of cheap wine, he began to talk as freely as if they were the closest of friends.

'I don't know who my parents were. The orphanage was a dreadful place for any child to grow up. I went to a good school, though, by winning a scholarship, and my eyes were blackened regularly by the fists of a bully we called Nobby.' Charlie used gestures, balling his hands and punching, in case his French wasn't up to conveying the story. He gave a small gust of breath at the memory. 'He had everything – parents, a home, the best bicycle in the school, money in his pocket for sweets and penny dreadfuls.'

She frowned and he explained. 'Cheap, printed serial stories.'

'Ah, yes, I understand. Why did he hurt you?' She sipped her wine and he raised his glass to her.

'Because he could. He frightened everyone but he liked to pick on me because I was small and poor. One day I stumbled upon Nobby embracing another boy. He beat me until I was a coughing, bleeding mess – no doubt with a couple of broken ribs and bruised kidneys.' He pointed to where he'd been injured and she frowned deeply with concern. 'I told my schoolmasters that I'd fallen out of a tree while stealing apples from a nearby orchard. They tried several times to get the truth, but I stuck to my story. When Nobby searched me out by the school sheds, I remember putting up both hands in surrender.' Charlie made the gesture and saw only sympathy in Fay's face.

'I said to him: "If you beat me up again, I'll have to go to hospital and that will get the authorities involved." I needed to appeal to his smart mind. Nobby asked me why I hadn't spilled the shameful truth. And I just told him that I had no reason to share it. That it was probably hard enough without others knowing.'

He couldn't imagine why Fay was so intrigued, but she leaned in, entranced by the story.

'So what did this Nobby do?' she demanded, topping up his glass, her blouse half undone, exposing small but voluptuous breasts desperate to break out of a lacy brassiere. She crossed a lean leg over his thigh in an intimate but wholly unaffected gesture; she seemed genuinely interested in what happened next.

Charlie cleared his throat as his arousal tried to take control.

'Well, I was astonished to see Nobby reach out his hand. I was too frightened not to respond and I felt my hand being squeezed in a huge fist and shaken. He said he was going to trust me.'

'And?'

'I think I recall suggesting he ace his exams, go to university, be all the brilliance he could be and then enjoy the freedoms that so many of us never would.'

'And did he?' She leaned closer. He could feel the warmth of her leg through his uniform and the teasing beckon of her skin was intoxicating. Charlie felt drunk.

He swallowed his wine. 'I learned that Richard Hardwick – that's Nobby – had distinguished himself in war and died heroically on the Somme battlefield, trying to carry two injured soldiers to safety. It turned out that he had studied at Oxford – that's one of our top universities – and had become a man of letters. He was working on his debut literary novel when he became one of the first to join up.'

'You are proud of him, no?'

He nodded. 'I am.'

'I like this story, Sharlie. It is sad but it makes me feel uplifted. I am wondering why you chose this one to share?'

He shrugged. 'I suppose I'm just all too aware of how fragile life is. He could have given something to the world through his writing. We'll never know. He represents all the potential lost through this war.'

'I think you tell me this because Germany is Europe's bully and you don't like bullies.' Fay's legs were long and supple against him and he finally reached out his fingers to stroke the smooth skin. 'I think you need some loving, Captain.'

His faraway gaze returned to this woman who sold her body. 'Why do you do this, Fay?'

Charlie sensed her considering how to answer that: whether to smooth over it or lie. 'I have a child and a sick mother. My son's father is dead. I have no siblings, no other family. There is no work to be had in this town, but I have neighbours who help me with my child and who don't judge me, so I can't leave. This sort of work I do is plentiful. I can rely on it . . . I can pay rent, buy food, buy medicine for my mother, clothe my son and perhaps even look towards saving a little for his future. I am not ashamed. I am not unhappy. I don't live here,' she said, gesturing around the room. 'This is where I work. I can afford to rent this room from the café below. I would prefer not to earn my living this way, but it's my choice right now.'

'A pragmatic little fairy.' He smiled. 'A smart one, too.'

She nodded. 'The soldiers are grateful and generous but rarely as handsome as you, Captain Sharlie. It would be my pleasure to answer your need.' She glanced at his lap. 'And you have the most beautiful lips I've ever seen on a man. I do believe I would like to kiss them.'

'Next time, perhaps. I really must go.'

She smiled sadly with amused disappointment and watched him dig out some money.

Charlie didn't want to hand it to her, so he placed it on the table.

'That's too much,' she remarked.

'No, it's not. Not for how much I've enjoyed being with you, Fay.'

She sighed. 'Come visit again, Captain Sharlie,' she said.

He picked up his hat, sporting its growling tiger insignia, and settled it on his head. Charlie gave a half bow. 'To next time, lovely fairy,' he agreed, feeling bad for the lie, but he suspected Fay knew their paths would not cross again.

Still, he couldn't deny how restorative these last few days had been.

Invisible demons baited him as he took the stairs behind the café two at a time, leaping the final three to go and round up his men.

*How long will the good feeling, last, Charlie? Maybe tomorrow you die?*

*Maybe this is a glimpse of calm before the real ugliness begins?*

*Hey, Sharlie,* another taunted. *Maybe a bullet that has your name on it is being loaded now, and you'll never feel a woman's skin again.*

*Maybe, maybe, maybe,* he said over in his mind to shut them out.

# 7

*May 1918*

As a soldier in Trigny left the village with the memory of a generous woman and her smoky laugh still pleasing his thoughts, Sophie Delancré held the memory of a man with a loud laugh and smiling eyes in hers.

'Allow me,' Louis said, pushing open the door of the French Red Cross headquarters in Paris.

She wished he hadn't insisted on accompanying her but in truth she was excited to be another step closer to finding out Jerome's story. That's how it felt, even though Louis had impressed upon her for most of the journey here that it was a blind alley, and he cautioned her strongly not to let her hopes rise. Rise they did, though. Especially now, waiting for this man to invite them into his office. She looked around at the posters and the notices, and watched the crisply busy activity of people walking up and down the corridors and opening and shutting office doors. They were all pursuing the same end; knowledge of Jerome had to be somewhere in this building.

'Tell me again why you aren't fighting alongside your brother?'

'Because I was needed in Paris, my dear,' he said, dodging her question.

She refused to be avoided. 'But conscription. Surely? . . .'

He gave a shrug. 'Two reasons, dear Sophie. I am needed for government procurement,' he said, as though that explained most of what she needed to know, yet to Sophie, it was vague enough to sound like a rehearsed excuse.

'And the second?' she asked, determined to make him defend himself with a valid reason.

He covered his breast with one hand. 'Did Jerome never mention my weak heart?' She shook her head. 'I don't speak about it. From infancy, apparently, it was always a weakness. I couldn't do sport. Jerome was always the strong one.'

'Monsieur Déa? Madame Déa?'

He looked relieved to be interrupted. A woman arrived, and at their nods she smiled. 'Come with me, please?' She escorted them down the hallway and Sophie listened to the rhythmic click of the woman's heels on the parquet floors, hoping it would lead her to news. The woman paused finally at a door and knocked before opening it . . . they were expected, after all. As she announced them, a short, wiry man pulled off his glasses and leapt from behind the desk as if a thousand ants had just stung him.

'Louis, Louis, my old friend. How are you?'

Louis shook the man's hand warmly and told him he was perfectly well before formally introducing Sophie. 'Jean, this is Madame Méa-Delancré.'

'Yes, yes, madame, what a pleasure it is to meet Louis's sister-in-law.'

'I'm hopeful you can help me, monsieur,' she said, leaping right in, already past her tolerance for the inevitable small talk.

He gestured for them to be seated and withdrew back behind his desk, reached for his reading glasses and sat down, before leaping up again to ask if they would like some refreshments.

'No, monsieur,' she assured him and looked towards Louis,

who reluctantly declined with a shake of his head. 'I know you are busy, so if we could . . . ' She sat forward on the edge of her chair.

'Yes, of course,' he said, returning to his seat and carefully wrapping the arms of his thin wire glasses around each ear. The wait as he did this felt taut. 'Now, Jerome Méa,' he said, sounding triumphant as he opened a file. 'Yes, yes. Acquitted himself most heroically on the battlefield, madame. You and brother Louis here can feel justly proud.'

'We do,' Louis assured him, sliding Sophie a reassuring nod.

Jean returned to the file. 'He went missing in . . .'

'April 1915,' Sophie answered for him.

'Yes, yes, I see that. We have two witnesses who —'

The tension was too tight in her chest. She snapped free of it by interjecting, 'But you see their accounts differ, monsieur. One says the man was broad, dark-haired and tall, and that he fell after being shot. The other, sir, describes him similarly, although fails to mention that he's broad.' She gave a nervous smile; she knew she was speaking too fast and that this man did not like to be hurried. 'And that he fell from the gas attack.'

'Er, yes, this is what I read here,' he replied, and she detected that he was indeed miffed to be jostled along.

'Surely that strikes you as odd, monsieur? They are differing accounts.'

She didn't have to look at Louis to know he was exchanging a look with his friend that was asking him to indulge her. She wanted to scream at both of them.

Jean frowned and took his time reading through both witness accounts once again. Louis cleared his throat and Sophie got through the protracted pause by wringing her hands and counting backwards in the little Russian she had. 'Not so strikingly different, though, madame, if you'll pardon me,' he said, finally looking up.

'The description is of a lieutenant from your husband's unit falling from being shot following a gas attack.'

She knew it in her heart but had nevertheless felt it worth trying to make the distinction, even though it was weak. 'I understand but neither witness mentions anywhere that this man actually died.' She could hear that her voice had gone higher. She sounded as desperate as she felt.

Jean sat back. His gaze flicked to Louis, then back to her, embarrassed. 'Er, madame, pardon me, but it is tacit in these military witness accounts; they are being given for the very reason of us trying to find out who has died on the battlefield.'

'Tacit,' she repeated. 'But not proven.'

He looked again at Louis, more nervous now. 'Your husband's name has not appeared on any lists that we have, madame. Since your brother-in-law contacted me, I have taken the trouble to make my own enquiries after your husband. I have repeatedly received the same information that there is no record of a Jerome Méa in any prison, in any hospital, or surviving anywhere close to the region where he fell. I know you have pressed upon us, madame, and we are keen to ensure we follow every avenue of possibility . . . and we have.' Helplessly, and in case she hadn't been able to grasp this previously, he began to hold up his fingers and repeat what they already knew. 'He is not a prisoner, he is not injured, he is not being held in a field hospital or a town or village facility anywhere that we can find. He is certainly lost – and by this, I mean we have not recovered a body . . . pardon me, madame,' he said, and she realised her eyes were tearing up. 'The French courts will make a final recommendation at the right time, madame, but for the purposes of your query, we are taking our information from the military regarding your husband being missing, as being lost for good.'

She heard Louis shift to reach for a handkerchief, but she dug in her handbag for her own and shook her head when he offered.

'He is one of tens of thousands of brave French men who litter Belgium's battlefields. Given the time that has passed, I suspect he has not been found because Ypres has become his grave. We may yet find those men who were buried over time but for now we term them as "missing, presumed dead", madame. But if I am to be candid with you, that is our way of saying your husband is likely dead and we may never recover his body.'

It was a long speech and now his eyes, made large behind his spectacles, darted between Sophie and Louis. The silence made him more nervous, it seemed, so he filled it. 'I have tried everything, I promise you.' He sounded earnest, almost pleading.

She hated that she was openly weeping now. It felt so weak to be crying in front of men, especially as this was exactly what Louis had anticipated. He was making soothing sounds, apologising to Jean and thanking him profusely for his generous efforts.

'Come along, my dear. I think we both need a stiff cognac and to gather ourselves.'

Louis made all the appropriate polite noises to Jean before he led Sophie out of the Red Cross building and onto the damp streets of Paris. His arm around her felt less about protection and more about ownership; she'd come here hoping to be a step closer to finding Jerome, but all she had achieved was taking a step further into the debt of Louis. In a blur of fresh despair, Sophie lost track of their progress; she remained quiet in the taxi that rolled them around this most beautiful city, past Madeleine, and down towards Place de la Concorde at the bottom end of the Champs-Élysées. The vehicle rounded the corner, to where the much admired neoclassical façade of the Hôtel de Crillon overlooked the wide square. The hotel had opened nearly a decade earlier to high acclaim, and her family's champagne had been served at its grand opening; her parents had attended, little knowing they'd be dead the next year.

Louis had been talking throughout the journey. It was a soft babble, probably designed to soothe. Only now she heard what he was saying.

'. . . and the Count of Crillon bought this palatial house at the end of the eighteenth century, and his descendants lived here until just past the turn of this one.'

Sophie nodded. She knew she had to engage with Louis, be better company; she still needed him. She also needed to rein in her emotions and put them away again or she'd be good for no one. There was still a champagne house to run. She reminded herself that she may be no better off but she was certainly no worse off than she had been this morning. It was a setback, yes, but they still had no body. And Jerome would not be dead for her until they proved it. As she'd been retreating to this position in her mind, Louis had assisted her from the taxi, linked her arm around his elbow and led her through the grand entrance and into the famed restaurant Les Ambassadeurs.

'Come on, my darling,' Louis cooed. 'I've always thought life looks better on a full belly.'

*Darling.* He'd taken his intentions up a notch, she thought absently as the maître d' glided up and exchanged a hushed, brief conversation with Louis before bowing and saying, 'Of course, Monsieur Déa, please follow me.'

They were led across marble floors to a round table laden with heavy linen and crystal. Above her the frescoed ceiling joined marble walls while chandeliers hung low and twinkled seductively. She permitted Louis to consult the menu and discuss it with the waiter, remarking that she would only manage a single course, which seemed to disappoint him, but she did agree to cognac. Over the honeyed fumes of her Rémy Martin, she absent-mindedly picked out flavours, from the florals of honeysuckle and iris through to the stickiness of candied fruit, and she could swear there was a hazelnut quality to this marc. But she didn't mention any of this; she sipped and let the alcohol's effects work their calming magic.

'Oh, that's good, isn't it?' Louis said, licking his lips clean of the syrupy liquor.

'Thank you. It's delicious.'

'Let it soothe you, Sophie . . . I'll talk and order while you gather your thoughts.'

It was kind of him. He chose the sole meunière and she approved for its clean simplicity. He let her sit quietly and allow the cognac to inhabit her until their meal arrived, which was surprisingly fast. Once the food was set before them, he began to talk.

'Do you know,' he began conversationally, as if testing the waters at the edge of her tolerance, 'that Marie Antoinette took piano lessons here?'

She didn't know that. 'Really?' If she wasn't so concerned that he was trying to manipulate her, Louis would be interesting, intelligent company.

'Oh, yes. And as you know from your Revolution history, right outside there,' he said, flicking a sausage finger towards the satin-draped window nearby, 'she lost her head. Guillotined right outside the very place she had enjoyed living briefly.'

'There you are, I've learned something,' she admitted, trying to smile, reassure him.

'How's your fish?'

'It is delectable, though how food like this is found for Parisians while —'

'Now, now, dear Sophie. Just enjoy,' he admonished her lightly. They ate in a companionable silence for a few more forkfuls before he made a soft sound as though only now recalling something. 'Oh, that's right, forgive me. I did overhear you mention something to the Curie woman last night.'

'Remind me,' she replied absently.

'About sugar?' He sounded innocent enough in his enquiry.

'Yes. I desperately need some.'

He fixed her with a smiling gaze, and she felt like a mouse pinned down by a hungry cat. 'How desperately?'

Sophie blinked, unsure of how to answer that. She shrugged, swallowed a final delicious morsel, and shook her head. These actions bought her a few seconds of time. 'Er, well, I suppose we are down to the last couple of sacks.'

'And that's a death knell, is it?'

She sighed and it sounded halfway between a laugh and despair. 'Yes, you could put it like that.'

'How would *you* put it, Sophie?' He leaned in, chewing, and she could see some of the buttery lemon sauce slick on his lips. He dabbed at them with a napkin.

'I would put it that if I cannot source sugar in the next couple of months, I will not be putting out a vintage this year. It will be the first time in the history of our house. But it feels more dramatic than that.'

'Dramatic?' He frowned.

'This is the fruit from the special vineyard of chardonnay that is in jeopardy.'

'Ah, the wedding vineyard,' he said. 'Jerome's experiment.'

'Which has worked. I want to make an all-chardonnay champagne to honour him.'

His expression rearranged itself; on anyone else Sophie was sure it would appear conspiratorially friendly, but on Louis it came across as pure cunning. 'What if I said I could get some?'

'I would call you a liar.' She laughed teasingly, although she realised there was little mirth in the sound, and Louis clearly did not appreciate the accusation. His even expression hadn't changed but the narrow-set eyes had darkened and something in the way he put his fish knife and fork down told her she had trespassed. She tried to make amends. 'I mean, if all the other champenois are strug-gling to find sugar with all their powerful friends, I cannot imagine where you might locate it. These are all men like you, Louis, with connections.'

His cheeks permitted his smile to stretch, although it generated no warmth. 'They are not like me, dear Sophie. You say you are desperate, but I sense you're not at the very end of your tolerance?' He formed a question by raising his eyebrows.

'I have a little time.'

'Then I suggest we have something sweet to finish.'

'You go ahead, Louis. I'm feeling delicate today.' She wasn't lying. The visit to the Red Cross had left her feeling faintly ill.

He nodded and signalled to the waiter, who glided over. 'Some madeleines and some sabayon to dip them in, I think.'

'Very good, monsieur.'

She found a smile as the waiter moved away. 'Jerome loves sabayon.'

'Entrenched in us both from childhood. Our mother used to make it regularly. In spring she would serve it with a buttery almond cake that our father enjoyed. He'd pick the almonds for her. In summer she would spoon it chilled over slightly crushed berries that we picked for her, and in winter she would serve it straight from the stove, warm and silken, with those long, thin biscuits to dip in the frothy custard. Oh, what are they called?'

'*Langues de chat*?' she offered.

'Yes! I used to tell Jerome when he was little and gullible that they were real cats' tongues.'

She joined his amusement. 'Dear Jerome. He always believes the best of people. I can imagine he'd trust you when you told him that.'

'He did! Poor fellow. He must have believed my mother was out gathering the tongues from cats and baking them for our pleasure.'

This made them share a genuinely indulgent moment of laughter.

'It's very uplifting to hear you sound . . . well, I was going to say happy but I know it's not that. Even so, it's a pleasure to hear your enjoyment.'

She shrugged. 'I search for any moment connected with happier times,' she admitted, 'even if it isn't from my own childhood.'

'You said you have a little time.' Sophie frowned in confusion until she realised he was referring them back to their previous conversation.

'You mean before the sugar situation is beyond just desperate?'

He chortled at her understatement. 'I do. And when you feel you are at that point, do ask me and perhaps I can prove that I never offer something I cannot provide.'

'All right,' she said, hoping she sounded contrite. 'Perhaps you could find out some costs and —'

He made a tutting sound of vexation as he finished his sole. 'You let me worry about that. I know someone who knows someone, and everyone owes each other favours. I can get you sugar.' He nodded as though that was final. He pushed his plate forward and raised his gaze to meet hers, fixing it so she dared not look away. 'I will not want money from you, Sophie.'

'I see.'

'Do you?'

They regarded each other.

He dipped into his pocket and produced a ring box. She sucked in a breath, wanting to let it back out as a scream and run full pelt from the room. She did nothing but stare in horrified and helpless fascination as he flicked it open. Inside sat a gold ring with a central sapphire. It looked like twilight beneath the glitter of the chandeliers, and its two equally large diamond sentinels kept guard, winking and twinkling at her in invitation, while smaller diamonds clustered between them like minions. 'My mother's. I can think of no one else's hand but yours that I would prefer to wear it.'

She couldn't speak even if she wanted to; her throat had surely closed, her mouth was certainly shut fast.

Louis continued. 'Last time we met I said there was no rush and I did not wish to pressure you. Nothing has changed, but Sophie, while I will not press you into marriage right now, I would like you to wear my ring.'

'Louis, I am married!'

He denied her remark with a swift shake of his head. 'Married to a man considered dead. You are a widow in most people's estimation.'

She had to break her tongue free from a dry palate. 'Why?' she murmured. 'I mean, why now?'

'It's the intent it will offer to me.'

'You want people to see it, you mean?'

He shrugged. 'I suppose. But between us it would mean that our relationship is not all one-sided. I must have something in exchange for my trouble.'

Sophie removed the napkin from her lap and folded it slowly before laying it on the table. 'Well, Louis, this has been an enlightening visit to Paris,' she said carefully. 'You've been generous and I'm grateful. However, I think it's important you understand that while you've accepted all that you've heard about Jerome, I haven't.'

*You need his help*, she kept reminding herself privately. *Don't offend any further.*

She watched his façade wrinkle slightly at her words, but he righted his expression quickly. 'What more do you want, Sophie?' he said, deliberately sounding weary.

'I want proof.'

'A body?' He sounded as though he wanted to laugh in her face. He didn't. His expression turned scornful. 'That's impossible. You heard the man.'

'I need more than I have now because all I have is vague remarks from traumatised men, and your friend at the Red Cross is keen to accept whatever hearsay there is.'

Louis looked back at her as if she was simple. 'You have a military record that attests to no Jerome Méa still walking around in any shape or form.'

'That the people who compile these records know of,' she impressed upon him, her voice turning angry, and she took little pleasure in watching him twitch with suppressed frustration and possibly carefully concealed anger of his own. She did admire his control. 'Louis, I've seen men come into the hospital who don't even know their names any more.'

'So what?' She frowned at his careless attitude. 'We know who they are,' he continued. 'They have a uniform, a number, identification!'

*Don't let him cast your objections aside*, her inner voice demanded. *Push!* 'Jerome might have lost his,' she appealed to him.

'What, all of it? That's just too easy. You're reaching, Sophie. You want him to be alive, I understand it, so you're constructing any excuse you can to ignore what is so clear to everyone else. And you are hurting yourself by holding on to this hope.'

'Please help me, Louis,' she said, hoping feminine appeal might work better than objection.

'I thought I had,' he said, his face unable to fully hide his disgust.

'Help me to find emphatic proof.'

'And then what?' Now he sounded sulky.

She must tread carefully now, she realised. 'And if it's as you believe, then we'll talk about us.' She couldn't believe she'd said it but now it was out and between them. 'I won't wear any ring of yours, not yet. Find me Jerome . . . proof of his death. Find me sugar.' She shrugged. 'Then we'll talk about us.'

Sophie knew she could look past the fact that he held no physical appeal to her, but if she was being entirely truthful, she would admit that Louis and she had enough common interests and intellect that on considered observation they would make quite an evenly matched couple. Unfortunately, life was rarely considered; she did not want to be married off simply for convenience. Her mind tried to wrap around the notion of having a child with Louis. It couldn't – she shied away helplessly with revulsion – but the sugar? The sugar was like a beautiful lure to a hungry fish. Without sugar she would let her family name down . . . more importantly, she would fail Jerome. Honouring him and staying true to her father's name and his brand's history felt like the only aspect of life that was keeping blood flowing through her body. Hope felt lost in this war and she no longer cared about her life, which was essentially empty – no husband, no children, no family . . . she was living off the pure emotion that rose from hope and a relentless sense of duty. The emotion of not being able to turn Jerome's wedding vineyard – his prized grapes, such a rare and special gift just for her – into champagne had no comparison. Not even agreeing to marry Louis felt worse than not making this wine, not having the sugar to do so. Could he sense her desperation? If he did, he didn't care. He had his agenda and he was happy for his potential bride to have hers. She tried not to shudder.

He watched her carefully before nodding, mindful not to speak and burst whichever bubble had just formed around them. Sophie felt the bile wanting to rise. Was she really bribing him with the promise of herself? What had she become?

She had become strong, she assured herself. It took strength to make these decisions.

*Whatever it takes*, she told herself.

'Quid pro quo, Louis.' She smiled and had to swallow back the desire to return all that sole meunière to the plate.

———————

Louis Méa had kept his expression even as he kissed his sister-in-law farewell and waved her off on the train that would return her to Épernay. Now, though, as he paced distractedly around the parquet floors of his Parisian apartment, which stood halfway between Opéra and Pigalle in the 9th arrondissement, he let all his rage come to the fore. But as was his way, he showed no tantrum; instead he let it seep out. He stepped by a magnificent credenza of inlaid wood and marble adorned by a decorative oval mirror, and moved past a Boldini painting of a nude stretched out on a sofa, to the tall window that overlooked the square, around which so much illicit pleasure could be found.

This was the neighbourhood where France's other revolution had occurred, for any and every manner of sexual predilection could be catered for here, and of course the people flocked, especially at night. He partook freely of its offerings, just a brief walk from those most splendid and conservative avenues radiating out from Opéra. If only Sophie would think of herself as a widow, it would make life far easier for both of them. He couldn't tell her of his financial stresses. In fact, if he could get her to agree to an engagement, then he was sure his debtors would see him through a different lens. The Delancré holdings were vast – all that property, and the champagne house itself was profitable . . . even through this wretched war. He smirked; how ironic it was, then, that Sophie needed sugar to make her champagne and that he had invested so much of his private wealth into building new sugar mills in Cuba. His money, in part, had helped to fund three new mills in 1914 alone but he couldn't convert his investment to cash because the sugar couldn't be shipped. Even so, he could get some, enough to back her into a corner. He considered his finances. A hefty chunk of his wealth was tied up in passenger shipping and much of it had sunk with the RMS *Lusitania* during the spring of 1915 – around the time they had received the news of Jerome.

'Stay dead, Jerome,' he muttered.

It wasn't that he didn't love his stepbrother – he did, but Jerome had stolen Sophie Delancré from under his nose four years ago and he wasn't going to allow Jerome's ever-present ghost to steal a second opportunity for Louis to have Sophie as his wife and get his hands on her wealth. She needed proof. He had turned this over in his mind repeatedly, recalling the bargain. She would wear his ring if he would help her to prove Jerome was no longer alive.

'That's the goal, then,' he said to the shifting humanity in the streets below him: mainly women, but plenty of military men and senior male government workers. He should be behind his desk, but he was too distracted today, too edgy, and that needed to change if he was to think clearly.

He saw a flash of red and followed it, the wearer of that coat. Marie. A whore who would soothe his edginess for a couple of francs and some wine. He licked his lips. Yes, Marie would help clear his thoughts on how to keep Jerome dead.

# 8

REIMS

*May 26, 1918*

There was excitement in Reims and Sophie was feeling it as much as the doctors, the nurses and the other hospital volunteers. The arrival of their special visitors from Paris had caused the surge in spirits.

Dr Langevin was the most excited of all. 'Head of the physics laboratory at the Sorbonne,' he said. 'A woman!' he added, as though it were blasphemous. Sophie knew the doctor did not mean to sound the way he did. She understood he was deeply impressed by this scientist. 'She took over from her husband as Professor of General Physics in the Faculty of Sciences after he died – the first woman ever.' Sophie wanted to laugh at how aghast he sounded.

'Be careful, Dr Langevin, there may be a woman president one day.'

He shook his head and she wasn't sure whether this gesture was one of alarm or admiration. It didn't matter. What she did know about Madame Marie Curie was what mattered right in this moment, which was that the famous scientist had kept her promise and brought her mobile X-ray machine to Reims. That she had responded to Sophie's invitation so promptly was a blessing they all celebrated. Now they knew exactly where the bullet was located in the young French soldier recently brought in, and Langevin was preparing to operate on him; they could see precisely where the bone was broken in the leg of one of the Algerians, which meant it had been set properly, maybe even allowing him to go back to his unit within a couple of months. Most of the townsfolk had come to the surface and gathered to cheer the arrival of the famous scientist, and Sophie was able to offer a brief welcome of her own to Madame Curie and her daughter, Irène.

'Hello again, Marie.' The two women had hugged with genuine affection. 'Thank you both for coming – and I hope you got your new car,' she whispered as she embraced her elder over the mayor's formal welcome.

'Arrived last week,' the woman replied, smiling beatifically. 'Thank you.'

Now they were sitting underground after the two visitors had spent a full day with patients in the hospital.

'We have a concert tomorrow night, if you can make it?'

'Underground?'

Sophie grinned and shrugged.

'Well, well, Madame Delancré, you are full of surprises and innovation. You should get a medal!'

'It's nearing ten-thirty. What am I thinking, keeping you up so late, sipping champagne?'

'Do you see me complaining?'

They both laughed. 'I should let you go to your accommodations. I'm sorry I can't host you at my house. I do believe it's too dangerous and I'd rather have you both far from the range of the guns.'

'We understand and are grateful for your consideration, Sophie. Please don't apologise. But the guns are so quiet . . . I think your concert tomorrow evening will go uninterrupted.'

Sophie nodded in agreement and yet it never paid to take the silence for granted; nearly four years of war had taught her that much.

———————

It had been a mild spring evening that stayed light for hours, but night was finally closing in and the chill of darkness was stealing across them. Charlie's company had been moved up to the front line to relieve their regiment's 6th Battalion and they were settled in now.

The landscape he could see was hilly and still lush from the thaw of winter, with none of the bleakness of Flanders. He wondered if Belgium would ever recover from the devastation of war. Here the forest was intact and there were woods at the top of one of the higher rises, but that's where the German position was strongest; the enemy had an overarching view of whatever the Allies chose to do. He couldn't imagine that even the most optimistic general could view their situation as one to win from. So Charlie began to accept that he, and all these men bunkered down in trenches, were simply more fodder – for the time being a deterrent rather than any sort of genuine threat to the Germans. For now, he was absently grateful that their enemy had seemingly lost interest in reaching Paris via Reims. All was quiet and the real fighting was in Belgium . . . the other route into France. It had been so calm since they arrived in the region – and while Charlie had no reason to think that would change, he nevertheless possessed a sense of disquiet. He assured himself this was just his duty kicking in; it was his job as captain to be alert and in a position to think through all the possibilities for his men should fighting break out. He was likely being over-analytical, given the lack of fighting for weeks. Even so, he considered the Aisne Canal and how it could help and yet hinder them. It felt like a protective ring to their backs, but that same protection could become a burden should they need to retreat.

Retreat, however, was not on anyone else's mind, as far as he could tell. The mood was genuinely jovial as the weather was so warm, even with a threat of storm. He'd heard some rolls of low thunder a couple of days ago, which at first everyone had naturally presumed was a resumption of shelling, but no, it had been a grumbling overhead that amounted to little more than a single flash in the far distance and then all was quiet again. The change of scenery had achieved a dramatic change in the men, reflected in their laughter, and the undisturbed evenings meant his company helplessly relaxed. They began to play cards, tell stories, reminisce about life in England, sweethearts they intended to marry at the first chance, and the yearning for the taste of an English pint. It was small, domestic, healthy talk of men looking towards a future again. Charlie didn't share their optimism because the silence to him felt ominous . . . prophetic, even, similar to what could be experienced before a natural disaster. He wasn't sure what he even meant with that thought.

'Want to pick one, Captain Nash?' One of the blokes shuffling cards interrupted his thoughts. A cigarette hung lazily from the corner of his mouth. He had been performing tricks to amuse the fellows around him.

'You carry on, Green. I'm not as gullible as the other lads here.'

Guffaws and sounds of mock offence erupted and even Charlie smiled in response to his quip.

'What's on your mind, sir?' one of the older men wondered, sidling up.

He regarded Davies, a man he liked and respected for his calming influence on the others. Davies offered him a sip of something from a hipflask.

Nash frowned. 'What's this?'

'Cognac,' Davies said with glee. 'Delicious stuff, Captain . . . I bought it a few days ago over in Trigny. Never tasted it before.'

He sipped out of politeness. It was rich and syrupy with fumes that zoomed into his nose and to the back of his throat. 'That's strong.'

'Good, though.' Davies winked. 'Just a little nip each night before I turn in.'

'Not too sleepy, I hope,' Nash warned, but there was no real accusation in his tone.

They stared into the darkness in shared silence.

Finally, Davies murmured again. 'You look worried, sir. What's on your mind?'

He didn't mean to spill precisely what he was thinking, but out it came. 'I was remembering geography lessons at school.'

'Oh, yes?'

He gave a small gust of a laugh. 'The lesson that most of us found fascinating in an otherwise boring subject was connected with the continental drift.'

'You're losing me, sir,' Davies admitted.

'How our great land masses are in motion.'

'I see, sir,' Davies said, sounding as though he regretted walking over and even more deeply regretted asking the question. He clearly had no idea what his captain was banging on about.

Charlie picked up on the man's lack of interest, but it didn't stop him talking. He'd begun now and it felt easier than the silence. He gestured the action with his hands without even looking at his companion. 'Land masses shift, crash into each other, break away . . . this all happens over millennia, of course, but there are some fascinating observations of mountain ranges, for instance, on different continents being capable of a perfect fit . . . like a jigsaw.' He knitted his fingers.

'That so, sir?'

He was aware of Davies looking around for escape. He should let him go.

'Enough of my schoolboy reminiscences, Davies. Carry on – I think our card sharp has another trick underway.'

'Right you are, sir.' Davies sounded relieved, touched his temple in a sort of salute. 'Sleep well, sir.'

'Thanks, Davies . . . and for the cognac.' The man grinned and turned away, moving further into the trench where the fun was.

Nash couldn't let go of his thoughts of continental drift, and the fact he'd learned that earthquakes at the seabed could create tsunamis.

Charlie looked around, noting that most of the men had turned in, except the sentries, of course . . . and him. They dozed where they'd been seated, leaning against each other, while some had created enough space to lie down. He turned his back to them, watching the forest on the high ground. His mind returned to tsunamis and the curiosity of a sudden tense silence beforehand.

*An oddly tense silence.* That's how it felt now. He wished Davies were still alongside him so he could make his point.

'It's too quiet,' he murmured beneath his breath. It was, to Charlie, the archetypal pregnant pause, as though this silence fore-shadowed something significant about to occur. He let his thoughts run free. *The birds already know the wave is coming, because even the night birds and nocturnal creatures have gone eerily silent.*

Charlie checked the time. It was one minute to 1 a.m.

---

She should have been asleep hours ago, having hugged Marie farewell, but she was restless and Sophie had long ago taught herself to be productive if sleep didn't come easily – it became a time for letter-writing, making a list of errands or accounting . . . that last one always helped her to achieve sleep. These days she was normally bone-weary and sleep couldn't come fast enough but there was the occasion, like now, when it eluded her. And yet nothing in particular felt like it was hankering for her attention. If anything, this had been one of the war's better days – no fighting, no bloodshed, no queue of fresh injured needing immediate attention or beds they couldn't find. It had been a day of smiles and inspiration, so why did she feel agitated?

Was she feeling guilty that she hadn't offered to host the Curies in the city mansion? She tested this question and came back with a clear conscience. No, it was too dangerous to have them sleep here. Granted, there was no shelling, not even the sporadic gunfire that occurred from time to time. *But why take the chance with important people who are making a difference in this war?* she had reasoned. She'd kept the invitation trapped in her throat and felt content that her decision was wise when she embraced the two women and bid them a quiet sleep in a house far from any immediate threat.

Sophie hugged a dressing gown around herself. It wasn't especially cold, but it felt comforting as she walked over to the window that overlooked the furthest edge of Reims and stared out across to her vineyards. All was as well as it could be. No flashes, no explosions, no bullets whizzing. Allied soldiers and German soldiers were all safe this evening, she thought.

Everything was still.

The quietest time of the day.

No haunting hoot of owls. No scurrying squirrels in her front garden. That was odd.

Too quiet?

Sophie checked the time on her wristwatch, which she could just see with the aid of the watery moonlight seeping in.

It was 1 a.m. and already tomorrow.

———

Gaston de Saint Just shook off his melancholy thoughts with the reminder that all was quiet and there had been almost no fighting for many weeks. He'd seen more than his fair share of the ugliness – been gassed, been wounded, watched too many of those he liked die. Now he and his Algerian Tirailleurs might just see out this war with no further losses if they remained here in the Marne region. They'd been busy cleaning and repairing trenches in the quiet time and everything seemed so orderly around his regiment's narrow tunnels that he'd given his men the night to themselves to relax.

He'd remained on watch because his mind was filled with gratitude for his cousin bringing the mobile X-ray machines to Reims. Now many of his wounded men could get much faster, better care and have a chance at achieving a full recovery. And if that wasn't enough, Sophie's latest venture was a rare event to look forward to. She had come home not only with the promise of Madame Curie but she'd also managed to persuade a number of musicians to visit and give a recital. He had no idea how she'd pulled that off, but in truth he didn't think Sophie could fail at anything towards which she really bent her will. He hoped he might make it back into the city to spend tomorrow evening with her.

He checked his new trench watch, sent by his sister with a sweet note that it had been made in Switzerland by only the best watchmaker. He was glad she was safe in neutral territory, away from the troubles; wished Sophie had taken up her cousin's invitation to move to Zurich. But that had always been an empty hope; still, the two women, good friends, wrote often. A luminous hand told him it was exactly one in the morning and he should probably consider getting some sleep if he was going to —

Gaston never did finish his thought because the world around Reims began to explode.

---

No one had stayed in their beds, but Sophie – not only alert but up when the bombardment began – was one of the first to be dressed in work clothes and out in the street, clutching a shawl around her shoulders more out of fear than cold. People began to gather around her house on the furthest reach of the city to see the night sky lit with its deadly orange of war. They had an appallingly good view from her house.

'It begins again,' the mayor said, arriving with a look of dread, still fastening his belt around his trousers, his shirt tails escaping.

'I'm afraid so,' she said, already glancing away from him. How incredible that only moments ago she'd been marvelling at the silence and its safety. That had changed in a heartbeat. She couldn't bear to watch the fresh anxiety pinching at the faces of people she knew well. She could sense the collective worry about whether the tunnels could cope with more casualties, whether they'd have enough supplies and food should they be cut off. Some, like her, were thinking of family, friends and homes in Épernay and other surrounding towns and villages. And she suspected, like her, no one wanted to so much as allow the question into their minds regarding what might happen should the Germans breach the front line that protected Reims. That's where Gaston was.

This was the landscape he and his men protected. He was out there now, perhaps fighting for his life. She didn't know enough about battlelines and trench lines or even front lines. These words were thrown around and everyone used them, but few understood the network, least of all her. She hoped all the generals did because her best friend was on one of those lines, giving orders, no doubt leading his men heroically to keep Reims safe. She couldn't lose him. Not after Jerome.

She watched a shell explode in the direction of her vineyard, feeling all the more wretched for being unable to do anything to help Gaston. She could stand and observe the spectacle of the battle unfolding before her or she could head into the vineyard and do what little she could to protect it.

Action won through.

# 9

His worst fears were confirmed. Charlie felt, as much as heard, the first explosion soon after the luminous radium hand of his wrist-watch confirmed that it was one hour past midnight. He started because he hadn't heard that sound in many weeks. The men around him stirred too, groggy from real sleep, but they soon heard their captain's voice yelling at them.

'This is real, lads! Not thunder. The Germans have begun shelling.'

It felt like chaos breaking out, but the men were well drilled and while the activity was sudden and untidy, they were upright, rifles ready, if not wholly awake.

'Gas masks!' was being howled by several people, as more than just Charlie noted the sinister cloud of gas mixing with the night's mist and beginning to drift their way.

'Yellow cross!' Charlie yelled, his voice muffled through his mask. *Chlorine.* 'Yellow cross!' He bellowed as loudly as his throat would allow, even though he suspected there would likely be other gasses.

In less than half an hour Charlie was informed that all

communication with the various battalions had been cut.

'I'll let the line know, sir,' his runner said, but he didn't wait for Charlie to reply; the lad was already out of Charlie's trench and moving towards more officers in other trenches.

The bombardment began to intensify over the following hours and Charlie's men were trapped, not just by their lack of knowledge or orders, but due to the low light and the gassing, as much as the devastating news from the French regiment to their right that the Germans had crossed the canal. An hour or so later, Charlie was informed by their brigade, the 110th, that no runner was getting through – but worse, the enemy had breached their sector and had crossed the canal in the region they were protecting.

'What now, sir?' Charlie asked his superior, not wishing to state the obvious that their flanks were bare. 'It's a maze of trenches that we can't man.' He squinted into the murk. 'I reckon Fritz is taking up positions we haven't secured and now can't. Shall we call the retreat?'

The major and Charlie had a good understanding; certain matters didn't need to be openly aired, but the man giving the orders looked deeply distracted, as though he hadn't heard the question. 'We've had a pigeon that the Germans have taken Chasseurs, advancing in large numbers over open ground straight at us now.'

Charlie kept his expression even and thus hid his fears for what this latest news meant for the Tigers.

'They're bombing their way through,' the major said, his tone sounding hopeless.

'If they cross the main road, we're doomed, sir.' It was out before he could censor himself, nor did he care any more. They had to move.

The major didn't notice his bleak tone. 'I think our actual front line is only being held by our snipers now.'

Charlie nodded, appreciating that the sentries usually withdrew through the night to at least four hundred yards back. He waited but there were no orders forthcoming.

'We have to sit tight, Captain Nash. I have not been given further instructions. Stay watchful.'

'Right, sir,' Charlie replied by rote, but he didn't agree. He tried again. 'Er, sir.'

'Yes?' The man sounded tetchy.

'I think we should fall back, Major. If they're running right at us and our flanks are exposed, it won't be long before we're encircled.'

'Retreat?' The major sounded aghast.

'Fall back to a stronger position, sir,' he reasserted. 'We need to use the bridges across the canal before the Germans have them. A lot of the men under my command are new recruits. They're paralysed with fear and have no experience to draw on, so let's give the men who've already been to hell and back a fighting chance, sir, to help those new lads. The boys from Ypres know how to advance or stand their ground. None are cowards, sir. But we need a bit of space between us and Fritz in order to get organised.'

'We don't know how long we've got,' his superior said, sounding unsure and as though he could be persuaded.

'Well, you have no orders to the contrary, sir. So let's fall back before we're overrun and maybe we can get ourselves relinked with the 64th so we're in a position to defend.'

He could see by the unknitting of the major's brows and the relaxing of his expression that the suggestion made sense to him. 'We can't see anything, anyway!' the major growled through his gas mask, disgusted.

'They could be on top of us in minutes, sir,' he agreed.

'Right, Captain, your men are to fall back. If you encounter a runner, let him know and pass it on. Let everyone know we're moving closer to the N44 but not as far as the canal.'

'Yes, sir. Good luck, sir.'

As he saluted the likeable major, Charlie would never know whether the man had smiled, replied, or even survived the massive explosion near their trench that had them all dodging or ducking. Urgent orders were then being yelled and passed down the trench.

None came directly from the major.

Charlie took control and urged his men back; they found themselves in a trench in what he presumed was the local area known as Le Godat. It was also the last time he would see his company as a collective again despite moving with them, hauling himself from the trench and leading them so they could drop back towards the main road that led into Reims. Every soldier began to look the same even as they became rapidly fewer in number.

What occurred over the ensuing hours felt like being on the Somme and Flanders at once. It seemed impossible and yet here he was, running around in it. Charlie had never heard battle like it, and he'd been in some of the worst. It was as though the world itself were fracturing, and no one had control any longer. Soldiers were being catapulted into the air, limbs flying in various directions; others were simply obliterated by the force of a blast. Shells maimed, destroyed, murdered. The smoke, the flames, the vile gas and the tunnel vision of the mask he wore meant Charlie's world was reduced to a small window.

The explosions had raged for a couple of hours in his estimation, but Charlie noted the shift in sound that told him machine guns and rifles were taking over from larger field guns and artillery.

'They're advancing!' and as he yelled to whichever men were left standing around him, the forward outposts of his company came running back, hurtling through the communication trenches and falling back to their second line of defence, where Charlie had brought the survivors.

Their fearful expressions told him all he needed to know, and the retreat was called. He had to get what was left of the men he commanded back to the road at least. He checked the radium hands again, squinting to see: it was nearing 0400 hours and Charlie came to the gut-twisting realisation that no runners had likely got through, which meant no reinforcements were close. They were now likely surrounded, and this would certainly be their last stand.

He would go down firing.

'Shoot for all you're worth, lads.'

The order prompted a tirade of bullets and yelling but it seemed useless: even he suspected he was firing at shadows in the mist. He was trying to decide whether they should save their ammunition or just continue the rally and risk firing at ghosts until they became ghosts themselves.

At some point in the confusion he had dragged himself onto open ground but now he felt trapped by what he couldn't see; there were no more Tigers, nothing ahead but a wall of smoke, sudden flashes of fire that made him veer left or right, and that was when he might bump into another man. They'd tried linking arms to stay together – it was Davies, he realised only from the muffled voice – but they'd been separated when his companion fell.

Charlie bent down. He couldn't risk pulling off his mask, but he could see enough to know that Davies had drunk his last nip of cognac on this earth. Disgusted, enraged and filled with despair, he gulped back a sob and left the dead man behind with all the other dead Tigers hidden in the morning mist. Why Davies and not him? Why couldn't he just die?

The noise meant no one could hear or keep track of the others. He ran on alone, unaware of what might be a few feet in front of him. Disorientation quickly set in. Pausing with Davies meant he'd lost his direction. A fresh terror was hearing the German language being hurled all around him. The enemy was overrunning them. Grief collided with confusion like the atoms he liked to study in the abstract. There was nothing abstract about this morning, though.

He was living it. Living the hell that had erupted. He thought he knew war, thought he'd survived the very worst it could throw at men. He was wrong. Charlie stopped running suddenly; he wasn't sure why. Perhaps he wanted to take a measure of man's potential to destroy. His surroundings had turned a filthy, murky grey-green. No more bright summer grass like velvet, no more ancient trees in full leaf; man's weaponry, his cleverness at science and engineering, was reducing nature. And Charlie knew he was part of that ugly machine . . . he was one of the clever men of science.

He heard the word *Flammenwerfer* yelled nearby and realised at the blast of fire that the German soldiers were now using flame-throwers. Grenades began to explode among the carnage. He fell backwards into a trench and only just stopped an enemy soldier with a bayonet to the gut. The man's mouth opened but only blood oozed from it as his eyes bulged and then his weight collapsed onto Charlie.

He didn't know how long he lay in the mud with a German bleeding on top of him, but he felt feet stomping over both of them, heavy German boots treading on the back of his enemy. As he found his wits again, he understood that the German soldiers were flowing towards the canal.

Surely now he must either surrender so he could preserve the remaining precious Allied souls under his command, or make a run for the canal and try to beat the Germans to it so they could protect it. He shouted for his sergeant with the thin hope of forming a breakout party to make a stand at the canal, but he knew it was hopeless. Who could hear in this din? And through the slowly clearing mist he could see only his own dead in the trench, looking to all intents like discarded litter.

A hand grabbed his shoulder. There was a face he recognised and then another.

'There you are, sir. This is bloody hopeless,' the man said, in one of the finest understatements that Charlie was sure he would ever hear. 'You're wounded, sir.'

Charlie shook his head as if the observation was meaningless.

'I've got Harper with me, sir.' Their voices sounded distorted coming from behind gas masks, and they were barely able to see one another.

'Good boys. Harper?'

'Sir?'

'Somehow you've got to get a message to Battalion HQ. We are falling back all the way to the canal and we'll make our stand there.' He pointed. 'I think it's that way.'

Harper nodded and started to run. He'd hardly made four steps before he was felled. Charlie froze in shock, feeling responsible and useless at the death of yet another man in his care. He found his voice again, and despite the gas mark's muffle it still sounded like controlled rage. 'Let's go,' he said to his remaining companion. 'The canal is our only hope.'

Frightening himself and his fellow soldier, he lifted off his gas mask. Perhaps there had been sufficient time for the gas to disperse. He felt no characteristic sting, and used the brief moment to smell the air and use his primeval sense to locate the stagnant canal. Dragging on his mask again, he led the way in silence, moving counterintuitively to where he had originally thought the N44 would be and thus the waterway. After half running, half staggering for several minutes, Charlie felt sure they should have reached it, but he realised they must have been running at the wrong angle, perhaps even towards the Germans. Charlie looked to his side but the soldier – he couldn't remember his name – was no longer there. He looked around wildly in the filthy smoke and mist but could see nothing. He felt a new stinging pressure at his shoulder. Not pain but a fresh sense of alarm. Had he been hit? No time to consider it – sadly not dead yet, which gave him no choice but to keep moving. *Change tack, Charlie*, he urged himself. He turned in another direction, feeling a fresh surge of hopelessness and helplessness at once. There was no fear, although he was absently glad to acknowledge that he would most likely die in the next few moments. *Come on, Death*, he railed inwardly, *I'm ready for you*.

He caught glimpses of staggering soldiers – a suggestion of men, nothing whole – and then they were gone. He couldn't tell whether they were his men or the enemy. It no longer mattered. Maybe that's what they'd become: ghosts moving on to other worlds.

Perhaps he was already dead? He might already be a wraith.

An enormous explosion told him otherwise.

When Charlie regained consciousness, he had no idea how long he'd been oblivious. He blinked at his watch, struggling to make out the enamel dial, clogged with mud and useless in the hideous grey light of a strange morning that made him think of the Underworld. He kept blinking, trying to regain his wits, and gradually, like a creature emerging from hibernation, he began to feel as though he was returning from a deep sleep. How long had he been trying to retreat before he was brought down? Maybe ten minutes, perhaps fifteen? It could have been thirty for all he knew. Nothing had changed, though: the bombardment was still underway with massive, reverberating force, although the explosions were not as many. Lots of gunfire around him. He had no idea whose rifles were shooting and in which direction. He knew he wasn't thinking clearly; his mind felt woolly. Had something happened to him? Was he hurt? He was sure he'd seen blood on himself – was it his? He couldn't stop now to check.

*Keep moving, Charlie.* 'Stay alive, Charlie,' he heard in Nurse Ellen's voice. 'You promised dancing.' He mustn't let her down.

Charlie found a fresh well of strength and redoubled his efforts to move. He'd never felt more alone than in this moment, even though his life had been one of relentless loneliness.

Now, though, as this horrendous battle raged all around him, he'd lost all that he thought he possessed: his will, his sense of self, his fellow soldiers – his whole company, it appeared – his country. Charlie was sure his desire to live had long ago been dismissed but now he sensed he was surrendering something far more important. He was giving up his faith in himself and indeed humanity. His spirit wanted to let go and drift away from all the ugliness. And still his animal drive meant he fought that urge. Even now, amid this despair, he was surprised to discover a tiny part hidden deep reminding him that if he had counted on anything in his lifetime so far, it was his instincts and personal trust. Surely this was life's ultimate test, to live through this carnage?

Another shell exploded nearby, knocking him off his feet. He felt earth, grass, and something wet hit his face. There was a curious pressure on his arm, but he felt no pain. Perhaps he was pinned down? Charlie considered this as one might peruse a menu in a café, deciding whether to have eggs poached or fried. Nevertheless, he forced himself to shift position and concluded he was free of any burden, except that whispering desire to let go and take the easy path from this hell. But the stronger voice that lived within spoke now, demanding he strive until the last breath was squeezed from him, until the last drop of blood from his final heartbeat was pumped out of him. *Don't capitulate to a bully*, it demanded.

Charlie chose. Wholly disoriented now, his rifle lost, he moved, hoping to find someone, anyone, from the 110th Brigade. They could run together, perhaps grabbing more of their regiment as they travelled. His gas mask was gone, knocked off when he fell, or maybe he'd pulled it off in his confusion. Yet it was a blessing: somehow he was sure he could smell water. He did his best to angle towards the Aisne Canal. At least then he'd have something to follow.

# 10

All communications were lost at the moment of the surprise German attack: precisely 0100 hours, or so the radium hand told him. Gaston looked at his field watch out of habit and imagined that men all over the region, enemy and ally, were doing the same. The sound of the guns awakening across the valley, having been so quiet that he was sure most soldiers believed they might remain silent evermore, came like a dark omen.

Was this the end for Reims? For Paris?

For Épernay? *No!* For Épernay, then, and the cousin he loved and the family to which he belonged and the place he was born, he would strive harder than he ever had. And he did: organising his troops and inspiring them to find the courage to be braver than they ever had before, to stop their enemy from changing the lives of the people they loved. It was easier to relate it to their homes in northern Africa and how the Germans would run rampant through their lands if they beat the French, if they were allowed to get one mile closer to Paris than they were now.

The Tirailleurs could hardly be expected to pity Parisians but he could certainly persuade them to think about important cities that their own people depended upon.

When he realised the British were retreating, his regiment's exposure came into stark focus. Their position could be overrun; it could be a slaughter. Counterattack. It was the brave option but in Gaston's reckoning it was the only option, or they might as well all just sit down and wait for a rain of bullets and the inevitable murderous spree that was coming.

As his watch ticked past three in the morning, he ordered the attack. The far side of the canal had been lost. If the Germans crossed, Reims would be lost, and that meant Paris was lost. Already he'd got word through a courageous messenger that some of the trenches on their side of the canal were being overrun.

'We take them right back!' Fighting words, but the casualties would be significant. Nevertheless, he gave the order.

Gaston called a runner, demanding the youngest in the regiment, and in the moments it took for the man to arrive he scribbled a note. 'Here,' he said to the youth, who was no more than seventeen. 'To Reims. Find this woman,' he said, pointing to her name on the paper. Grubby hands took the note and Gaston felt a moment of sadness to see mud already staining the white of his fine stationery. It summed up his life at present. 'Into her hands only! Do you understand?' He spoke in Arabic to be sure.

'Yes, sir. Madame Della . . .' He struggled.

'Madame Sophie Delancré,' Gaston said. 'Delancré. Say it for me.'

The youngster repeated it.

'Say it all the way to Reims so you don't forget. Now run!'

---

The shelling had been going for almost an hour now. Night's mantle at least disguised the war that was now at Sophie's door again, showing itself as bright explosions and bullet tracings. The darkness on the other side of midnight was misted and acrid – the smell of heavy shelling, cordite, or perhaps more accurately picric acid that she knew the British called Lyddite and the French Melinite. She blinked at even pondering this; it didn't matter who called it what, it smelled appallingly bad especially combined with chlorine gas and the pungent odour of gore from the men and animals it had been designed to kill. Sophie loathed the familiar, nasty bouquet travelling on the wind. The cordite brought with it a sweet taste that surely had no place in war.

Sophie needed to be busy so she didn't dwell. Besides, the vines needed warming, and she had always intended to work in the vineyard over these cooler nights. Others might consider she was losing her perspective, but no one – perhaps only other champagne makers – understood that to not take care of the precious grape buds was akin to not taking care of one's babies. And so she would light torches this cold evening and she would warm the buds that would bring life and fruit . . . and a good harvest if she protected them.

A handful of people had drifted up to help, to keep earning despite their fear. She nodded her thanks as she emerged from her Reims house. Trailing her were four of the helpers, one of them a teenage girl and another a young boy. Although guilt-ridden that children were part of this dangerous work gang, she had still accepted their offers of help because it was impossible for her to refuse. The teenager, Antoinette, was desperate to escape the tunnels and her mother had begged Sophie to let her help; the boy – an orphan who had lost his father in the first months of the war and his mother to a recent bout of influenza – had taken to shadowing Sophie when she visited the vineyards.

'Henri, will you carry this for me?' she said, keen to let him believe he had an important job. 'This is the can of fuel that will light our torches.'

'May I light the torches, madame?'

'We can do it together.'

'Will the flames keep the grape buds safe, madame?'

'Oh, I hope so, Henri,' she admitted, recalling that it was around this time last year that Gaston had come into the vineyards with her to perform the same task. 'I'm glad you know what we have to do.'

'My grandfather taught me. But he died and now my father is dead, so I will learn from you, madame. I want to be a champenois one day.'

'Well, that's a fine aim to have.'

'May I work for you, Madame Delancré, when I am bigger?'

She grinned in the lowering light. 'We are already working together. I don't see why we won't still be working together when you are taller than me.'

He flashed her a smile. 'I will make you proud.'

'How old are you, Henri?'

'I am nine, madame, but my mother said although I am small, I am the smartest nine-year-old she knows.' He blinked and corrected himself. 'Knew.'

Sophie squeezed his shoulder, unsure of what she could possibly say to ease his grief. Adults were easier to comfort; children didn't respond with the resignation or the understanding that they were not the first or the last to be bereaved. The grief of a child was total. It wasn't less or more than an adult's, Sophie believed; it just felt absolute because a child lived in the moment. Except Henri – here he was talking about being grown-up and working in her vineyards, learning her skills in making wine; she loved him a little for that. Maybe he could be the son she didn't have . . . she had a responsibility to teach the young. He had aspirations; he had a dream he wanted to follow and that was more reassuring than anything she'd encountered in the past few years.

She would employ Henri. She would help him to learn the craft of the champenois. She would invest in a child's life and help him to achieve the dream his grandfather had set in motion when he began teaching his grandson about protecting the precious buds that showed in April and needed protecting if the May nights remained cool.

'We know what to do, Madame Delancré,' a senior man assured her. 'Would you like me to organise the work? I am told you have spent most of the day at the hospital. Me? I have had my long afternoon nap and my energy is high.'

She smiled at him. 'Jean-Claude, you are always so gallant.'

'My mother insisted,' he said, lifting a cap that seemed as old as he was.

She watched him begin to organise the folk who'd come to start working the rows and turned back to her young shadow.

'The chardonnay grapes tend to bud early, Henri, which makes them more likely to suffer the bite of a cold night. It's not frosty but I don't wish to risk them. The chardonnay is too important.'

'So we tend to them first.'

'Yes, we will do our utmost to protect them.' She handed him some matches she'd kept in her pocket. 'Be careful with those. Do not strike one until Jean-Claude gives permission. First take the fuel and help douse the rags on the torches.' The lad hurried off obediently, catching up with the older man who pointed towards the far end of the field, where the others were beginning.

'I'll catch up, Jean-Claude; let me inspect the plants. I can see better here,' she called, gesturing with her lantern at the vines near the entrance.

'Madame, if you'll forgive me, by lighting these torches we are giving the Germans a target.'

'Yes, but I don't believe they're interested in us right now, Jean-Claude. The fighting is in the distance, making the way clear to

Reims. If they win over there, our city is open to them anyway, but it will not come to that. I am not scared.'

'Then neither am I, madame.' The man hobbled away.

She smiled sadly. Despite the booming noise of shells in the distance, it felt better to be in her vineyard than below ground in the hospital. 'At least I know what to do here,' she murmured to herself, bending down to inspect the closest vine, holding the lantern close. Sophie became lost to her buds over the next few minutes and was so focused on how much protection might be required for the vines in this particular field that she did not notice the escalation of artillery fire around her.

It was only when she straightened and looked back up the field that Sophie became aware that the sky around her was lit up. The bombs were close . . . far too near. Their flames were turning the atmosphere a murky, unpleasantly yellow version of night. She looked for the nine or so people who'd come into the vineyard with her to call them back. This had become too dangerous; they would have to abandon their plans for tonight, regroup tomorrow, perhaps, depending on the horrible guns. The buds did need help, but they could wait another day.

She squinted into the shadows. 'Jean-Claude?' she called loudly.

They were already moving swiftly back towards her. No doubt the old man in his wisdom had deemed it suicidal for them to continue working, although she could shake her head at the reck-lessness of previous years when she would have done anything to save her vines, standing in the midst of the artillery fire, defying it to wound or kill her. Perhaps she'd found wisdom, or she'd seen too much blood on too many dying to put a plant ahead of a life.

And then came the sound they all dreaded. To Sophie it was like a steam train hurtling out of control, threatening to jump its tracks, with madmen at the helm feeding it more and more fuel to make as much steam and noise as possible.

She knew this sound from her nightmares. Everyone did.

Sophie scanned the hurrying people, now running, convinced all were accounted for as she urged them on to safety. They'd never make the city, but if they could get to the entrance of the vineyard, Sophie was sure they too would be out of range. This was not the sound of the huge field guns; her hearing had become so accustomed to the orchestra of war that she could determine that the shell surely arriving in their direction had been launched from a smaller mobile field weapon.

'Why?' she yelled into the night, helplessly raging at the Germans. There was no need for them to direct their explosives at innocents, or at vineyards, or at a city they'd already levelled.

The sound strained through the air towards them at speed. She waited for the shell to land or burst, but the ghostly roar of its power continued to herald its imminent arrival.

'Run!' she screamed impotently at those who were already running, her shrieks joining the ghostly wail of the artillery fire that wanted to devour her vineyard and everything it contained.

In her terror, she saw that the lit torches in the vineyard illuminated a yellowish burst of smoke that experience told her meant the shell had reached its apex and would now begin its descent. It was almost directly above the group. Then it announced itself, hitting the ground behind them, smashing vines, exploding to release murderous shrapnel that flew low and at tremendous velocity to cut through branches, leaves and limbs.

Sophie was knocked sideways and landed painfully on her hip. Scanning the field for her companions, she dragged herself back upright. The guns sounded muffled as though someone had stuffed wool in her ears. She felt dizzy when she stood. Nausea threatened too. Her first concussion, she thought absently as she searched desperately to see the first of the gang emerge from smoke. It was Antoinette, and she was dragging two of the women from her household with her. Others staggered towards Sophie, and although she wanted to move quickly to them, her feet felt inordinately heavy, as if the vineyard was trying to suck and hold her boots within its mud. She knew those were her outstretched arms but only because they were clothed in her garments. She could feel nothing, hear so little, and the disorientation from the smell and the smoke, the worry about gas, the sight of bloodied faces made the scene feel like a piece of theatre she was watching and not participating in.

As the women reached her, they fell into each other's arms. The sensation snapped her senses so time catapulted back to normality. Mewls of despair arose but there was no time for tears.

'The others?'

'They fell,' the girl said, gesturing helplessly over her shoulder.

Sophie ran despite the dizziness, finding it hard to focus on the count in her head. Were there three or four missing? Four, she was sure.

'Jean-Claude!' she called, but it came out more like a scream.

She heard a groan and ran in its direction, where she found the elderly man prone. Sophie knelt at his side. 'Are you wounded?'

'I can't tell,' he admitted, his voice raspy. 'I thought I was dead until I heard your voice.'

Sophie helped him to sit up. She fumbled in her pocket for the other box of matches, lit one and used its brief illumination to cast a swift glance over the man. He appeared whole: no blood, no bones sticking out at odd angles.

'Pain?'

He shrugged again. They heard other voices: it was the remaining man, helping his wife, who was bleeding. The man was hard of hearing, she recalled. He was a superb vineyard worker, one of Sophie's favourites, and she swallowed with relief to see him.

'Alain,' she said in a voice that spoke only of regret, wondering if he heard her.

'Chantal is hit,' he bleated. There was a significant wound in the woman's shoulder, but Sophie had seen enough in the hospital to know this would not kill her; the danger was sepsis.

'We'll get her to the hospital immediately,' she assured him, all but dragging Jean-Claude to his feet.

She called to Antoinette. She came, the other women flanking her, coughing, still bending this way and that to check they were only bruised. The blood on their skin and clothes made no sense. They seemed whole and not injured seriously enough to account for it.

'Henri!' she suddenly screamed, and this time she really did run.

As bullets and artillery fire traced arcs and intermittently lit the sky, she found what remained of Henri in what at first appeared to be a ragged pile of clothes. He had been lifted off his feet by the blast, which explained the odd angle of both knees, collapsed in on themselves. He looked like a ventriloquist's dummy waiting to be animated by its owner. It was only when she lit a match that she could see the blood still bubbling at his lips. His head was angled to one side and his eyes were downward-cast.

'Henri,' she whispered, tears spilling down her cheeks, her conscience burdened, the heart she'd tried so hard to heal breaking again, this time for a child.

'I just wanted to light the first torch,' he struggled to get out. The words were mashed but she understood.

'I know,' she replied, stroking his cheek. He would be dead in moments; there was no point in trying to move him to lie down. His middle was opened up by a row of shrapnel balls that had all but cut him in half. Sophie suspected he would be feeling little pain.

She sat down next to him and put her arm around his narrow shoulders. He gratefully leaned into her.

'I will dirty your fine clothes, madame.'

'I don't care.'

'I was never a fast runner,' he ground out, resigned.

'Perhaps, but you're a good vineyard man. I would be proud to have you in any of my fields.'

'Thank you, madame. That would make my parents proud.'

She wept harder but silently, hoping he couldn't feel her shaking frame or the tears dripping onto his head.

'I wish I had a mother to hold my hand, madame.'

'I will hold your hand, Henri,' she said, quickly taking his cold fingers and wrapping them up in hers.

'Can you kiss me farewell too, madame? I am a little scared of dying.'

She bent and kissed his damp hair, which smelled of cordite. 'Adieu, my proud little champenois.'

'Adieu,' he whispered, and she felt the tension leave his slim frame and his body leaned lifeless against her.

Sophie believed that in the next moment she had made a silent plea to the heavens to forgive this carnage. Instead, fully unaware in her despair, she had turned her face to the heavens and issued a guttural cry of anguish that made the tendons of her neck strain and her throat turn raw. The noise of despair, however, was lost to the roar of the guns and a different form of desperation as the German army made a last massive push to claim Marne and open the way to Paris.

The explosions all around her attested that no vineyard, no innocents, no conscience mattered any more . . . only winning.

———

As he lurched through the mud, which was at least crusty in parts at this time of the year, Charlie's vision was compromised by smoke, dust and especially his state of mind. He was not scared – he knew that much; he welcomed the killing explosion or the flying piece of shrapnel. But while both legs still moved and his mind remained active, albeit blurred, he was obliged to keep moving. It was his duty to do so. He had no helmet, but he now had a rifle, which he didn't remember picking up from a fallen soldier who would not miss it. He already missed his own.

As he tried to piece together the jigsaw of this day so far, from images and vague recollections of being in and out of consciousness, he felt the land disappear. Charlie was sure it was another mortar shell exploding, but when he felt the shock of water it took him a moment or two to understand that he had slipped down the canal's muddied bank and into the filth and freeze of the Aisne. Though unpleasant, the sensations brought him some clarity and a tiny prick of elation that he knew where he was. His mind felt as though it was clearing; he could hear voices in the near distance, all speaking German. He had to presume he was surrounded by the enemy now and the canal was his only chance of survival, slim though it may be. Debris bumped around him – mostly floating timber that he presumed to be the remains of boats. He wished he knew where on the canal he was. It was no use staggering around in the shallow water and hoping not to be noticed; the best cover, he reasoned, was hugging the bank, and so he paddled towards it, only now noticing that his left hand was not working; it looked mauled. He couldn't remember how it had happened, and that was likely, he decided, because he couldn't feel it just now.

The Germans were definitely closer, almost at the canal's edge, and the water – only as high as his knees – was not deep enough for him to disappear beneath. The canal after years of warfare was now almost dry, littered with muck and the occasional rotting barge hulk. They would surely spot him if they looked into the river. His rifle was wet, he had no mask, and his only other weapon was his bayonet, which so far had enjoyed its most use opening cans and killing rats in the trenches. Charlie turned and then glanced back to where he saw what remained of one of those abandoned barges once used for floating goods down the canal. It was smashed up in parts but still upright, if leaning badly in the shallows. He needed to make a decision, and without trying to think through his options he quickly launched back into the water and half paddled, half lurched to its blind side. Around the hull he spotted a small enemy group emerging from the murk of the battlefield. Far too close for comfort.

Again, without trying to second-guess himself, Charlie moved as far away from the group as possible, behind the cover of the barge, and with difficulty, hauled himself slowly onto its flat, shallow deck. Crawling inch by inch he located the manhole and lowered himself into the small hold.

As he took a silent, shallow breath he turned to find himself face to face with a soldier. He was German.

# 11

Sophie was uncharacteristically teary as morning arrived but she forgave herself for it. The death of young Henri had affected her deeply; his loss seemed to represent this war in the most poignant way. Innocence, hope, patriotism – it all felt useless. Henri had possessed all of those and none had saved him from the enemy's death blow, which others now believed had been a stray mortar, not aimed at the vineyard. There had been no other explosions in the field, but that single blast had taken with it all her faith. Why Henri? Why then? Why would a stray mortar find him when he was trying to help save her vines? Why did Jerome have to disappear? *Why?* was the worst question to ask during this war because there was never an answer.

She was back underground, tending to those in the hospital. She'd tried to distract herself by making a fresh inventory of stock with some of the other nurses, working out what would need to be rationed. Most of the seriously wounded would be taken to the battalion doctor, who was located near Gaston's post. There they would be tagged and assessed. Those chosen to be sent back to the city would go by divisional ambulance to the underground hospital in the hope that they could be further cared for, or at least kept as comfortable as possible until they passed away.

Gaston had scribbled a note, sent with his runner, to her personally to ensure she understood that the number of casualties would be large and the wounds horrific. The youth who had brought it was wide-eyed and exhausted. Apparently, he was emotional, not because of the battle, but because he couldn't remember how to say her name. He had no French, but a passer-by had helped him and recognised the name on the note.

'Are you all right, madame?'

'Yes, I shall be fine,' she told one of the senior volunteer nurses. 'Where's that Algerian?'

'Eating breakfast, I'm told. Eating our tunnels out of food, apparently. He's only seventeen.' It was said kindly and both women found sad, silent smiles that were gone in a blink.

'Don't send him back too fast. I can't have another lad on my conscience.'

The woman nodded sympathetically. Everyone had lost dear ones.

'Henri was a very sweet, if a little serious, child. I think if he could hear you now, then what you say, even with his tender years, would make him proud.'

She shook her head. 'He should not have been in that vineyard with me; he insisted but I should have said no.'

The nurse said no more but gestured towards some fresh bandages. 'May I, madame?'

'Of course. But —'

'I know. I shall be sparing . . . and selective.'

Sophie swallowed, hating herself for being forced to choose between lives. 'Have we heard from the Curies?'

'Yes. They wish to stay a little longer after the shock of the bombings.'

She sighed. 'They know we'll be getting so many desperate casualties.'

The woman nodded and reached for a pen to record the dressings she was removing from the storeroom. 'Perhaps Madame Curie could telephone Paris for us?'

'I'll ask. If anyone can get us more equipment, she can.'

Moving through the tunnels, Sophie made a point of stopping at various points along the way. She visited the two small schoolrooms; as she passed by she lifted a hand to the woman behind the counter of the café she regularly frequented, and then called by a couple of the older people whose men had been favourite workers of hers. It struck Sophie as incredible that people could still be so cheerful in these circumstances. Of course, they had not just held a brave child in their arms as he died, and nor would she make them suffer the knowledge that she had, but even so, she took some inspiration from their resilience and lack of complaint.

'You need some fresh air,' she advised old Madame Dellaport.

'I have no desire to breathe in the cordite,' the old girl grumbled but without any real rancour. 'I prefer the damp chalk of our beloved cellars, madame.'

'I think I do too.' Sophie smiled, squeezing her elder's arm. She risked it. 'Any news from Jean-Paul?'

The woman's eyes lit up and she drew a letter from her apron pocket. 'Yes. He is managing to stay alive. This is dated from nine days ago. I hold on to hope, Madame Delancré.'

'As you should,' she urged her. 'I'm glad his letter got through so fast.'

'I told him in my last one about your concert.'

Sophie waved a dismissive hand as though it were the last thing on her mind.

'Oh, please tell me we shall still go ahead. We are all counting down the hours. The musicians are already here, are they not?'

'They are, but I was thinking of cancelling out of —'

'Oh, no, madame! Please! It will cheer us all.'

She frowned. 'Let me ask the others who are involved. So long as it's not disrespectful.'

'To whom?' The woman shrugged. 'The dead don't care. The living will have their spirits lifted to hear music.'

'I hadn't thought of it that way.'

'Well, do!' her elder admonished her. 'I've washed out my dress,' she added.

Sophie left. She'd better find the mayor and ask his opinion on the concert. Perhaps bright music was precisely the sort of defiance that was required. And the orchestra had already arrived. She would dedicate the concert to Henri and she would not sleep . . . not until every last wounded soldier had been cared for.

---

Charlie rolled over swiftly and instinctively covered the German's mouth with his hand. The soldier's eyes bulged behind their lids and Charlie noted the pain in them. He glanced across the man's body and could see, even in this dull light, that the German was bleeding. He put a finger to his lips and stared at the man, who nodded with understanding. Gradually, testing him first, he eased the pressure of his hand on his enemy's mouth. All the man did was sigh softly as he was released.

'My name is Charlie,' he murmured in German, once again glad of his grammar education and his ability with languages.

The man's eyes widened. 'Willi,' he responded softly. 'I have no English,' he admitted.

'Let me see to your leg,' Charlie offered, continuing in German.

The man didn't have the strength to be impressed. 'Why?'

'Because I'm tired of killing.'

'Me too.'

Charlie frowned. 'How old are you?'

'I shall be forty tomorrow.'

Charlie nodded sadly. The man looked older to him. 'Not much of a birthday.'

'This will be my fourth in this war if I survive until then.'

'Why wouldn't you?'

'Because we both know you have to kill me.'

'I'm not going to kill you. I told you —'

'You *must*. I would kill you.'

'I doubt that, Willi. We know each other now.' He couldn't believe he actually winked. 'That would be rude.'

Charlie found an old rag nearby and used his teeth to rip it in half to make a tourniquet. Together they tied it above Willi's knee and Charlie covered the man's mouth when he sensed the injured German might cry out. Again, Willi nodded, and when released he breathed out the pain.

'The tourniquet will slow it, but won't stop it. You need help,' Charlie said.

'Shall I call for it?' Willi whispered, finding a grin. They could both hear German voices nearby.

Charlie returned the amusement, amazed that he could. 'I'd rather you didn't. Are you hurt anywhere else?'

Willi nodded and pulled back his jacket where another hole had been blown in his side, also bleeding wetly. 'I'm not for this world any more, you see, Charlie.'

'Try harder so I'm not wasting my time while your friends look for me.'

'Are they?'

He shook his head. 'No. But I'm the last one left, I think. Everyone's disappeared or dead.'

'I wish we could all just stop.'

'Every soldier feels the same way, I'm sure.'

'I have a daughter I've never seen.'

Charlie ignored his own wound and got busy trying to staunch the bleeding of his new friend. 'You have to help me, Willi, because my hand is suddenly useless.' He began to suspect his efforts were hopeless but he banished the thought and worked on anyway. 'Tell me about her.'

'We called her Agnes, after my grandmother.'

'Agnes,' he repeated with a smile. 'Well, you think of your little girl and stay alive for her.' Willi winced as Charlie bound him as best he could.

'Why aren't you married? You're a good-looking man.'

Charlie gave a mirthless murmur of a laugh. 'I've enjoyed women. Never met "the one".'

'You haven't looked hard enough.'

'Probably not.' He'd not admitted such a thought to himself, let alone out loud to a stranger. Somehow with Willi it didn't matter being so frank.

'If you survive, you must find her.'

'I promise.' He grinned.

'What now, Charlie? The voices are getting closer.'

He was right. The men sounded as though they were right next to the barge. He listened closely to their conversation and worked out that one was wondering aloud whether they should check inside.

'Still feeling like you must call them?'

Willi shook his head. 'But go, or you will be shot. They are not in the mood to take prisoners and I'm sure they'll feel obliged to look in here.'

He nodded, bent down and kissed both of Willi's cheeks. 'Stay alive, my friend. I'll look you up after the war. My name is Charles Nash.'

'Wilhelm Becker from Bavaria. My town is Freising, a pretty place not far from Munich . . . best beer in the world. It's called

Weihenstephaner. Can you remember that?' Charlie dutifully repeated it. 'Good. We shall drink together in peacetime.'

They clasped hands. It seemed so ridiculous that he felt closer to Willi, his enemy, in this moment than any other person, living or dead, from his life. 'Think of Agnes,' he reiterated. 'Give me two minutes to get away and then call to your fellow soldiers. They'll get help for you.'

'I'll distract them for you too,' Willi grinned and winced again. His breathing was laboured. 'Charlie?'

He looked back.

Willi pointed over his left shoulder. 'There's a hole back there. If they're on the bank, they won't be able to see you. Head in that direction down the canal —' he pointed — 'towards Courtine Basse. The French snatched it back earlier. There's a culvert . . . use that.'

Charlie didn't understand all the words – his schoolboy German wasn't that sophisticated – but he grasped enough and nodded his thanks before gingerly standing up. He let go of Willi's hand and moved towards escape.

---

Gaston had watched as gas and explosives raged through the dark hours, and when dawn began its creep across the sky, the German infantry began its move. He had looked on with increasing horror as the Germans made rapid progress towards the canal, destroying the British lines as they roared through.

By midday the British had fallen back, lines broken, men dying, whole units lost. As Gaston picked up his field glasses yet again, one of his men arrived, breathless.

'What now?' he asked in Arabic. The terse tone was unavoidable today.

'The sous-officier sent me to fetch you, sir. We have pulled a strange man from the water.'

'What strange man?'

The soldier pointed to his temple. 'He has lost his mind, sir.' He shrugged. 'Dressed in an English uniform, we think, but not speaking English . . . or French.'

'British uniform? You realise that's impossible?'

'Come, sir, please.'

They'd got it wrong, Gaston was convinced, because the Germans had cut off the English; he would have had to break past their lines to reach this position, but he followed his soldier to where a man, who was indeed wearing a British uniform, was babbling in German. Fluent in the language, Gaston could tell this man was using very basic words that suggested he had only a bare knowledge of it; he was not the enemy. He was, however, wounded, and was slumped on the ground between Gaston's men, who had encircled him and were watching him warily.

'Who are you?' he said in French, shaking the man's shoulder.

'Err . . .' He shook his head.

'Regiment?'

The familiar command seemed to snap him into focus somewhat. 'Tigers. Everyone's dead,' he said. The wounded man fell forward and Gaston caught him, sighing at the blood that spilled all over his mustard-green sleeve.

He called for the salts. One of his Tirailleurs ran off. Gaston held on to the wounded soldier, who leaned his head against him. He thought the man said 'thank you', but he couldn't be sure. His runner returned with a small blue bottle. He waved the salts beneath the man's nostrils and waited for the inevitable kickback of the fellow's head. It came soon enough.

'Try again. What's your name, soldier?'

The wounded fellow remained silent but frowned as though trying to remember. 'Charlie, I think.'

Gaston ran out of patience. 'Any ambulances?' he snapped,

exasperated, but this time in Arabic to the men gathered around. They shook heads.

'Another couple of hours, sir, perhaps,' one replied.

'I want a tourniquet onto that arm above the elbow, and then this man is to be taken to the toubib. Get him gone. He's the battalion hospital's problem now.'

# 12

*9 p.m.*

Sophie glanced across the largest of the caves and saw Gaston.

All day it had seemed as though a balloon was inflating within her chest, pressing against her ribs and crowding her organs. She hadn't realised how tightly she was holding her body: everything clenching instinctively, with despair over Henri and worry for her cousin. And now to see his crooked smile over the heads of the audience, it felt as though the balloon had been punctured. All the air rushed out of it, returning her insides to their rightful positions and forcing her to inwardly slump and bend her head as her anxiety was released. Sophie heard sighs of pleasure and soft claps of congratulations from other guests, who too were relieved to see the commandant safely back in the city. His Algerian troops were popular simply due to the collective appreciation that people from far away had come to France's aid. But that these men were led by one of their own – not just French, but a man of Reims – well, Gaston could always raise a cheer . . . from women especially, she thought.

She could hear him apologising to people as he manoeuvred his way past their seats to where she stood, her back against the

162

cool limestone wall, its familiar chalky smell giving her a sense of security she clung to. The German offensive was not yet twenty-four hours old, but this day had felt like a lifetime. The ignorance of what was happening above them, the shaking of the earth, the unrelenting sounds of weaponry. She couldn't remember a fiercer day and she dared not dwell on the casualties that had begun to flow in as Gaston had predicted. She'd had to welcome the musicians into war instead of the quiet she'd promised.

All that aside, the fact that Gaston was here, alive, grinning at her, was a balm.

'Sophie? Are you unwell?' He leaned an arm against the wall, searching her face, and she felt the space between them close – it was nearly an embrace. It was so welcome.

She looked up, teary with relief, seeing him as though he stood on the other side of a rain-pelted window. 'No . . . no, I shall be fine. It's been . . .' She couldn't find the words to describe the loss of Henri, especially to a man who was having to see people he cared for die all too often. No, Henri was her ghost and his memory was hers alone to live with and grieve for . . . like Jerome's. 'I'm just glad you're here.'

Gaston pecked each cheek gently as people began to glance their way. 'I told you, I won't die if you promise to stay safe.'

'I thought I'd lost you.'

'And still you held the recital,' he jested.

'Gaston, don't. I couldn't —'

'I know,' he whispered, making her look straight at him again. 'I know, Sophie. And I'm proud you have.'

'Then don't make light of it. Of course, you've missed the first half. Vivaldi. After intermission it's all Mozart.'

'I hate to tell you I was busy,' he began, still in an ironic tone.

She sighed. 'You don't have to explain anything. This is relief talking.'

People moved to congratulate Gaston and speak with him about the battle above them. Sophie let him talk to the eager cave-dwellers, not really paying attention, focusing instead on the musicians who were returning for second-half tuning up . . . easier than thinking about a little boy. She listened to the tuneless, haphazard sounds that seemed to echo how she felt in her mind at present. There was no song. There was noise but no rhythm . . . just anxiety.

'It's been the bloodiest, most brutal fighting I've experienced in nearly four years,' she heard Gaston admit to the mayor.

'The Curies are not here for this splendid evening because they felt they could be more help at the hospital, given the casualties. For the rest of us, we feel helpless, and Madame Delancré insisted we press ahead.'

'She was right to, Mayor.'

There was more small talk and then the few musicians began to clear their throats, taking their formal positions as the pianist arrived. Sophie shook her head to think that they'd managed to set up a piano in the cellars. It sounded glorious, too.

It was only now that she saw the telltale stains on his uniform. 'Oh, Gaston, you're hurt,' she said, anxiously looking for a wound.

He shook his head. 'None of it is mine,' he whispered. 'I'm sorry I didn't have a chance to do much more than use a flannel and brush my hair. I was eager to see you, to let you know I was alive, because I figured not knowing might ruin your evening.' She glared at his grin. 'All right, I'll stop. Most of this,' he said, looking at a large stain on his sleeve, 'belongs to a curious fellow we dragged out of the canal.'

'Curious? How?'

'Because we don't know how he came to be where he was. Anyway, he's injured, not saying much, and from an English company, but he has excellent French.'

The orchestra stopped its tuning notes and the mayor arrived on the makeshift stage. He apologised for interrupting proceedings and began to explain what Gaston had told him about the battle that had raged; no one minded because the fighting was in everyone's thoughts.

'Ladies and gentleman. I know we were all using the recital as a distraction for those of us who couldn't offer assistance on the battlefield, and . . .'

She couldn't bear it any longer. 'Gaston, can we leave?'

She didn't wait for an answer, threading a path around the back of the cave, making gentle apologies that she was feeling light-headed. Gaston obediently followed until they were in a dark, lonely part of the crayères.

At his worried glance she shrugged. 'I'm fine.' The thinnest of watery light stole its way to where they stood as their eyes adjusted to the dim tunnel. 'Tell me what happened.' And for the first time since Gaston had shouldered his senior responsibilities when this war began, she watched the bravado leak out of him. He leaned back against the wall, steadying himself with the hand that emerged from the blood-soaked sleeve. She couldn't stop staring at the drenched uniform, wondering at the man's life that had leaked onto Gaston and which woman's or child's life – or both – had irrevocably changed because of it.

'I've never experienced anything like it, Sophie, and I pray I never do again. It was carnage. It was as though the land outside Reims had become a special hell on earth. The devil was among us, killing gleefully and at random. I'm sure as many Germans lost their lives as our side. On the ridges, no one could see for the explosions; I'm sure most of the men were lost because they ran the wrong way, and who could blame them?' He shook his head. 'It began with German bombardment —' and Sophie nodded, remembering it, and determined not to speak of Henri or her vineyard — 'but they soon realised we'd set up a line of false trenches manned by only a few.'

'A deception?'

'Yes, our commander-in-chief put the strategy in place to buy time while the Germans emptied their artillery and their gas into the forward battle zone of cleared trenches. By the time it dawned on them and they reached our real front lines, we met them with ferocity. Our enemy suffered heavy casualties and this helped us to set up for a major counterattack.'

'So what happens now?'

'The Germans haven't surrendered. They're fighting on but they're making only minor gains. I am anticipating a call from my superiors to confirm what we all suspect.'

'Which is?'

'That we thought we were clever. Meanwhile, their whole offensive was a blind.'

She frowned.

'A bluff to distract our armies,' he explained.

Sophie looked back at him, horrified that any general would fling men like chopped wood into a fire in order to trick their enemy. 'Distract us from where?'

'Flanders,' he answered, sounding weary. 'We think the Germans have now decided the only effective way to Paris is via Belgium, and so they threw a big effort down here to distract us, because they knew we believed they wanted the easiest access to Paris. But they're retreating now, back to trenches between the Aisne and Vesle rivers.'

'*Bon sang!*' Sophie covered her mouth in despair, words about Henri, killed through trickery, dying on her tongue. She sucked in a breath and finished her thought. 'How many are now dead for the sake of a ruse?'

'Thousands . . . on both sides. One lucky Englishman, though.' He pointed to the blood on his sleeve.

'So the real war is elsewhere.'

He nodded. 'The Germans are massing now for a final push out of Belgium.'

She groaned. 'It doesn't feel pretend.'

'No, and I can assure you that it doesn't look make-believe either. I've recently sent another two dozen to the underground hospital, the Englishman among them.' Sophie gave Gaston a fresh look of frustration. 'What am I to do? They need care. Useless on the field, a burden to their company. Just do what you can to patch them up and send them out again. Some, of course, won't make it through tonight, others we may just have to send home.'

'Why can't you send this English fellow to his own field hospital?'

He gave a soft snort of bafflement. 'Sophie, to be truthful, I don't even know how he got as far into our territory as he did. He was with a regiment called the Leicesters, who were to our left. They've been obliterated from what I can tell. It is a miracle that he got through. Actually, he swam – or I should say half paddled, half waded – through waters considered enemy territory. He used the canal but don't ask me how, because at some stage he would have needed to get out and run alongside Germans. No wonder he was muttering in that language. I realise now it was his only defence – his clever use of German and the misty weather helped him.' He shook his head as if in awe.

'What do you want us to do?'

He shrugged. 'Our medical facility at the front line is little more than a parcel force. *Wrap, label, post,*' he quoted, with a shrug. 'I sent him to the battalion doctor at our field hospital, and I presume he was tagged.'

She nodded. 'Probably red.'

'I would have thought blue for surgery, but who am I to say? We couldn't send him back to the British.' He gave a helpless shrug.

'The line was so badly crushed, no one knows where anyone else is . . . as it is, I've had to have some strings pulled just to be here but I have to go; I need to be with my men a few kilometres from here.'

'I know. I asked a lot of you to be here.'

'I'm sorry I can't stay for the second half of the concert. Every man is needed at his post.'

'Don't apologise. I'd rather be useful too – I'll go over and see this English soldier. Maybe my language skills can be of help.' They wearily hugged farewell. 'Please stay safe, Gaston,' she whispered as he pulled away. He cut her a jaunty smile and disappeared into the dimly lit corridor, while she headed in the opposite direction.

They'd all made the effort for the orchestral recital but now she imagined appearing foolish as she hurried through the corridors having to lift her skirt; although she wore no jewellery but her wedding ring, she was certainly in an outfit that caught attention. Normally she kept her clothes dark and plain, for mourning and modesty. This crimson she was dressed in, though appropriate for the concert, felt far too loud all of a sudden.

Unlike Gaston's uniform, it would have masked the blood though, and she now went in search of the man who had bled it.

---

He would not talk. It had been two days since his arrival. The Curies had left, the musicians with them, and he had been among those X-rayed, with damaged bones in that mangled arm. Men had died around him with regularity in the hospital, but he had not shifted from his position on the bed, staring at the ceiling. The nursing team had tried to get him to speak. Even Gaston had tried again but the English soldier – their only British wounded – may not have been aware that all around him men had called out, taken final breaths, groaned in their morphine-induced sleep, while he made no sound.

'He never closes his eyes,' a volunteer admitted. 'It's unsettling.'

'Maybe he does not dare, with all that he's seen,' Sophie said sympathetically.

'Why is he any different to our boys?' the woman asked, instantly offended.

'He's not. He's hurt, that's all, Jeanette. And he's in shock, clearly. We have to be patient with him.'

Gaston squeezed her shoulder. 'I'll make enquiries about getting him across to his own people, but I'm not holding out much hope at the minute.'

They said farewell. For the rest of the day and night Sophie kept a watch over the unknown soldier. He was an enigma simply because he was English and had dodged the German army. Just like her concert, this man's survival was a defiance against the odds, and she couldn't help but hold a private admiration for him.

It was deep into the night when the French Red Cross sister, who was in charge of the hospital for the next twenty hours, came to her side with a mug of coffee. 'Madame Delancré, you are in danger of putting the rest of us to shame with your dedication.'

Sophie smiled. 'I wish you'd all call me Sophie.'

The woman, only slightly older than her, grinned. 'Nursing is a bit like the army, madame. It needs structure. It's not that we're not friendly, but the hierarchy gives confidence. You are intrigued by this Englishman, no?'

She shrugged. 'I would love to know what he's thinking. He's in there. Perhaps he's frightened, surrounded by people speaking a strange language.'

The sister shook her head. 'Tenderness can never be mistaken. He could not believe he is among anyone but those who care.'

Sophie nodded. 'I think I am intrigued by his story. I hope we'll learn it.'

'I gather his arm will need to be amputated in the next few hours.'

Sophie raised her hand to her mask with alarm. 'Oh no!'

'You're not surprised, surely? Sepsis waits for no one. Best it's removed and then he gets on with healing.'

'I've been trying to imagine what he did before he came to the war. What if he was a musician like those marvellous players we've just enjoyed? What if he is an artist and paints with his left hand? What if —?'

'What if he lives? That's all that should matter to us,' the senior nurse admonished her gently. 'That's our role: to comfort, to care, to ensure survival. The rest is up to him.'

'How does one treat this shock from the shells if he doesn't speak?'

The senior nurse sighed. 'There's no right way. We're still learning about how the war affects the mental state of soldiers, but I'm assured there are sanatoriums to take the men returning who are no longer sound of mind. Many are intact, not showing physical injuries, but here —' she tapped her temple — 'they are like an open, bleeding wound.'

Sophie frowned. 'Sanatoriums?'

'Fresh air, simple good food, quiet days, walks, visits from other soldiers rather than family, they say, because only other soldiers know what they've seen, what they've experienced. The routine is about anything peaceful and safe that prompts a return to their normal mindset . . . not that life is ever going to be normal for any of us again.'

'What if I took him back to Épernay with me?'

'Madame Delancré, why would you suggest such a thing?'

'Because all of those elements you mention can be provided there.' Sophie lifted one shoulder in a defensive gesture. 'Maybe we can start the healing process so that when he can be repatriated, he is more attuned to the present.'

'But what about his hand?'

'What else can be done for him after that dramatic surgery except changing dressings and making sure he's comfortable? I do that here anyway. I know how to take care of him, and we have a full-time doctor and two nurses. We're registered now as a hospital.'

The woman's gaze softened. 'I didn't know that. How many patients are at your home there?'

Sophie frowned. 'Oh, I think there are about twenty men now.'

'Twenty!' she repeated. 'That's impressive.' Sophie shrugged. 'I see no reason for you not to take him if you wish to. We need every bed we can get.'

'That's my thinking. He's able to move and he will be easy to care for, and you may want this bed for another soldier with serious wounds needing nursing care around the clock.'

'Oh, I think our Englishman will be getting that, all right. He's handsome enough.' She winked.

# 13

It was the early hours and so long since she'd slept that Sophie couldn't remember the last time she'd lain in a bed. She should return to Épernay, where soft pillows beckoned and there was plenty of work in and around the vineyards that needed to be attended to. And yet she felt somehow closer to Jerome here in Reims – probably because it was under constant threat from the guns that had killed him. It also felt nearer to Gaston, whom she worried about daily. And now an English soldier for whom she suddenly felt responsible.

Sophie was alone on the ward and had done the rounds as she'd been instructed. It was nearing three, perhaps the loneliest hour of the night, when even nocturnal creatures were silent. Everyone was asleep. It was uncharacteristically quiet with no groans or soft snores from the patients. Even the soldier who never closed his eyes was properly asleep now, but that had been forced upon him by the anaesthetic.

She walked over to his cot and stared at his heavily bandaged arm. Miraculously, his hand had been saved. How useful it might end up being was still to be seen, but he appeared whole and that meant saving his dignity and perhaps even his life down the track. The surgeon was always under enormous pressure to save lives, to get to the next patient, to just patch up and move on. And she had chosen to create a fuss over this man? Why?

She would never speak it aloud but the first trill about saving his limb had sounded when she began to clean him hours after the concert. He'd arrived filthy with blood, some his, but there was too much of it to be all his own. She tried not to imagine what he'd experienced two nights ago when she was cradling a dying child: this captain had dodged bullets, artillery fire, mortars, bayonets and who knew what else.

He was hurriedly wiped over for surgery. Langevin said his quick thank you for her assistance, given with a look that glanced off her and back to the mangled hand. 'Immediate amputation surgery, please, Matron.'

She looked desperately in the direction of Matron, who turned away. It wasn't cruel . . . she was simply being realistic. Sophie understood, but that didn't mean she would give in without a fight.

'Dr Langevin, please, the Curies are still here,' she interrupted as he began speaking to Matron.

'And?' He was clearly in a hurry.

'Could we not do an X-ray?'

'We could, but it would be a waste of time, Madame Delancré. I know you like to save every poor unfortunate this sort of surgery.'

'But —'

'Madame, we have walked this path before, no? Remember the young man from Marseille?'

'I do. His leg couldn't be saved, you were right,' she said, deciding to flatter him. He nodded. 'But I don't regret us being sure.'

'This man's hand is a mess.'

'Please, Jules,' she said, deliberately breaking protocol. They had become good friends over the course of the war, and he'd enjoyed plenty of her champagne . . . at no cost. She was going to lean on that friendship now and leverage her generosity. 'Please, let's try. I know your expertise has always been with the small bones; wield your magic now if it can save his hand.'

He looked exasperated, but Jules was one of the people who really did appreciate how hard she worked for everyone in and around Reims. And it was no hollow compliment: the man was a wizard when it came to repairing bones. Plus, he owed her. He shrugged. 'What's a little more blood loss to this poor fellow?'

'Thank you.'

She held on to hope and it was rewarded. The British soldier returned from surgery with a small welcoming party around him.

'We've tried, Sophie,' Langevin said wearily. 'I did my best, and while I am not holding out hope for its use, he has a hand at least.'

'Keeping him looking whole can make a difference. Thank you, Doctor.' She stood and kissed his cheek, whispering, 'Thank you, Jules.'

But now the man deserved to be cleaned properly. She felt a duty to bathe the soldiers as best she could, so they felt free of the battlefield. As she tended to him, she kept up a constant gentle chatter. It was in French so she wasn't sure how much he understood. It didn't matter; Sophie knew that words spoken in kindness sound the same in any language.

His uniform was gone to be washed and patched; he was now dressed in a nightshirt.

She wondered about his life before the war. Was that hand essential for his work? He was of an age, she guessed, to still have young children if he was a family man, and he would not be able to pick up those youngsters easily without the use of that hand. He might never play a sport again. He would certainly never pick up a rifle again, so his war was over, thank the stars, but his life was now on a different path . . . unless that hand could heal itself.

But then this was how Sophie's thoughts always flowed with each new injured soldier, and she comforted herself that his life had shifted its direction since the day he joined this wretched war. Maybe it was his luck to be injured so badly he could leave it? Others, after all, were leaving their lives behind on the battlefield.

And still Sophie couldn't help herself. The English soldier, presently lost to the morphine, was a novelty. She studied him, enjoyed watching him. He was slim and hard-bodied – they all were in the trenches, but she guessed he'd never been strapping – and his reasonable height had probably distracted from his trim frame. While she had helped the orderly to remove the uniform from the limp soldier and get him into a nightshirt, she noted he was muscled but rangy. His features in repose gave nothing away. Even forced into relaxation by the drug, he gave the impression of a man who held his thoughts close. The set of his square jaw looked like it preferred the clamped position of someone refusing to speak. There was no fresh blood blooming at his face as she cleaned it to reveal a straight nose and plump yet well-defined lips, the bottom one almost cherubic. *Kissable.*

Sophie's breath caught in her throat as that thought passed through her mind. What was wrong with her? Clean him up and move on to the next man. There were bruises all over his slim body and there had been collective mutterings about broken ribs, but mercifully no one had seen any obvious signs of internal bleeding.

The mild warm and soapy water had begun to reveal the man beneath the filth of the trenches and the battlefield. She put a towel beneath his head and began to soak off the blood and mud matted in his hair, and around a couple of small wounds that had scabbed over on their own. She observed an old head wound that had been stitched . . . extremely neatly, she noticed. The hair was still trying to grow over it, though, and his hair wasn't entirely sure what colour it was, being neither dark but certainly not fair, sitting somewhere in between. From a distance it appeared earth-brown but this close up she could see thin glints of a dark gold, as if someone had dripped amber toffee through it. That brighter colour began to peep through as she dabbed away the soap with a damp towel. He could use a shave, but she wouldn't attempt that now. His heavy brows gave him a serious expression and that lovely mouth was still pinched as he dreamed; she wondered what horror roamed through his sleeping thoughts to make him frown like this.

Because he had not shared a word on the ward, no one knew what his voice sounded like; it had not occurred to her before now that the tone of someone's voice was important. A voice was vital, now that she pondered it. Jerome had possessed a rich voice; he liked to use it to sing and to make people laugh, letting it boom out around a large room. It drew people to him. Gaston's voice was attractive for the opposite reason: it was intimate, cultured and seductive. He used it softly to woo, and she was sure just as softly to intimidate and to make people pay more attention to him. She helplessly thought of Louis; his had an affected sound, as though he'd rehearsed it. There was a vaguely effeminate way he lingered on certain syllables. 'How do you sound, Captain, I wonder?' she murmured as she tended to him.

And if she allowed herself a moment of honesty, she would have to admit that the cast of his face was attractive in a way that men as much as women could appreciate. He had the looks of someone that film producers would chase. The camera would love him, she thought. There were worry lines embedded in his expression that didn't leave, even though to all intents his body was relaxed. She liked them; she dismissed the nightmares of war and instead convinced herself it was endearing, that even in sleep he was fretting . . . perhaps thinking about his wife, his family, the men he was responsible for. Gaston had told her he was a captain, having recognised the insignia on his uniform, and that he belonged to a regiment from northern England, but that was meaningless to her. She had only visited London, so to know any difference between north or south, east or west was impossible for her. It was such a small island, how could there be much difference anyway? she wondered, smoothing back the twist of hair that had fallen across his forehead. He needed a proper bath, that was certain. Despite her ministrations, his hair beneath her fingers was greasy, still clumped with mud and heaven knew what else.

Instinctively, believing affection was what was needed, she held his unbandaged hand. It's not as though she had any other work to do this night. A new shift would be coming on in an hour, so why not try to send some silent comfort to a stranger who was lost, hurt, trying to find his way back to consciousness and a new life when the British army transferred him home. The Red Cross would soon get busy making enquiries on his behalf. Everyone had drifted away. She and he were alone in a corner of one of the tunnels attached to the hospital.

He was emerging from the morphine. Eyes gently fluttering their wakefulness but refusing to show awareness. It was a false awakening and wouldn't last, she was sure. She kept murmuring.

'Well, as you're not in a talkative mood, I shall do the talking. What shall we discuss? How about I tell you about my private passion. I don't tell anyone about this because few here understand. But I don't mind sharing my secret of how much I love opera.'

His eyes flickered open fully. Sophie held her breath as he turned his head; he was moving of his own volition for the first time since he'd arrived. She didn't want to burst whatever bubble she'd managed to put them in, so she continued. 'Why do I love opera? Because it mirrors my love of champagne.'

His eyes found focus and his gaze rested lightly on her; it seemed to swim almost immediately. He was struggling to concentrate – normal.

'Hello,' she said, in English now. It was rusty but she was thrilled to use the education her parents had insisted upon. 'Don't be scared. You're in Reims, in the champagne cellars.' She couldn't be sure he was taking the information in. His expression had a vacancy about it, probably due to the morphine.

'I always wanted to visit Reims.' He said this in English. Relieved to hear him speak at all, she thanked her stars that her father had insisted on her learning this language for business.

'Visit Reims? Why?'

'I like cathedrals.' He had moved into French effortlessly.

She chose not to tell him about the ruins of the cathedral above them.

'And I do like champagne,' he added.

At this she smiled. 'I am Sophie.'

'Sophie,' he tried to repeat but half of her name got lost in his throat. He was drifting in and out of his drugged sleep.

'Sophie Delancré.'

'Like the champagne,' he mumbled, back in English. 'I heard men talking Arabic. I might have begun speaking in very poor German because I thought they could be Turkish. The kind French commandant set me straight.'

'His name is Gaston de Saint Just. We all admire him,' she said. 'If you remember Gaston, you will surely remember your name?'

'Captain Charles Nash of the Leicesters.' It was slurred but there. His mouth lifted at the corner in an attempt at a smile but failed. 'Everyone calls me Charlie.'

'Sharlie,' she repeated. 'Why are you amused?' she enquired at the lift of his eyebrows.

'You sound like Fay when you say my name . . .' His voice trailed off as he slipped away from her again into his dreams.

Fay. She must be his wife or sweetheart. At least she'd drawn some words from him. Everyone would be relieved to know he could speak and make sense, even sedated, and that offered some hope for his recovery. Plus, she'd heard his voice. It wasn't particularly deep or light. It didn't have a musical quality like Jerome's or the alluring quality of Gaston's, but she heard something potentially idealistic in it. She liked that and its mellow pitch.

# 14

Charlie hadn't been struck dumb from shock, he didn't believe, but he couldn't think of a single word he needed to say. The horror of what he'd lived through had to be somehow worked through in his mind, and no one could be more surprised than he that he'd survived. Some kindly Arabic unit had fished him from the water when he was doing his best to drown in the shallows. Now even kinder French nurses attended to him, checked his dressings, spoke gently to him. Someone especially beautiful had just washed his face and spoken of opera. So much kindness after so much terror.

His left arm was in a large bandage so he couldn't tell anything of his injury, or even if he still had an intact arm; a new fear erupted that he might now be an amputee. It would be tricky to explain to a team of people working tirelessly to keep him safe that he really would rather die. There was nothing and no one waiting for him back home; this war had taken everything that mattered and now it may have taken a part of him that meant any sort of life would now be seriously compromised. He didn't want that life. He didn't want sympathetic glances for the war veteran, now an invalid. Who knew how long the war would continue, but he knew as he emerged from his fretful sleep that he would be sent back to England to see out the war. Pensioned off. Useless. He'd be one of those men who walked around with a shirtsleeve pinned up or a jacket draped on the shoulder with the sleeve empty. He knew this was heinous self-pity but he indulged in it all the same, because if life had looked bleak on the battlefield, at least it had felt like honest endeavour. Going back to England as a failed soldier, and a pathetically injured one at that, seemed a lot worse.

It was the presence of the opera lover, the woman whose name sounded like champagne, that brought him back. He was sure he was in a dark trench walking around looking for his hand, which had been sheared off by a flying mortar. He followed the sound of that voice, as airy as the bubbles in the champagne she spoke of. It had an alluring huskiness that resulted in a softly spoken way and he followed it gladly, out of the trench and back into consciousness and the underground hospital.

He sensed she was making an effort to use his native language. 'Hello, Charlie. We are making all the right enquiries to get you back to your people.' She shook her head. 'But I cannot say when that might happen. The fighting is ongoing.'

He could hear the dull thud of guns, now that she mentioned it.

'Charlie, they need this bed. There are more wounded coming in each day.'

He nodded and tried to clear this throat. His voice came out as a croak. 'I'll leave.'

'You have nowhere to go just now until we can find someone to claim you.' He loved her gritty voice. It sounded as though her breath carried it over fine grains of sand before it was allowed to sound. She smiled. 'I have a better idea. Until you heal, would you agree to come back to Épernay with me?'

He looked back at her quizzically, shrugging and opening his palm. It felt as though he were opening both his hands but on checking it was only his right. He hated that he could still feel his numb limb, but it wouldn't work for him. 'With you? Why?'

He enjoyed her smile when it came, more restorative than the shot of the cognac he now recalled sharing with Davies just before the world blew up.

'Because I think you will heal faster in Épernay and you have nowhere else to go until we can get you repatriated to the British. We will have to leave immediately.'

It didn't require much pondering. Charlie nodded. 'Is it safe? I mean, for you?'

She grinned. 'Safer than here. Besides, my vineyards need me.'

So, she *was* connected with the champagne house. 'Then let's go,' he said.

She laughed and explained her plan to the senior nurse who had hovered into view.

'But you surely have no room in your formal house, Madame Delancré?'

'Always room for one more,' she said gently.

'How will you get him there? There are no ambulances,' the nurse reminded her.

'He is sitting up in bed,' Sophie observed, her voice even. 'So he can surely sit up in a cart, can't you, Captain?'

She didn't sound in the slightest defensive. Charlie nodded. 'Of course. Another soldier needs this bed.'

The senior nurse sniffed. 'Whatever you say, madame.'

Sophie glanced at Charlie, her gaze sparkling with triumph. He wanted to wink to congratulate her, but nothing seemed to work very well for him right now.

Sophie Delancré's arrival in his life was like something bright and shiny in an otherwise dull, metal-grey world; it gave him a curious sense of hope that was trilling deep inside. He suddenly felt like a champagne bottle, its potential effervescence within.

Could he find joy again after what had felt like the Somme repeating itself? Now, looking at that conspiratorial grin from the woman of Épernay, even returning to Britain for a new life as a disabled soldier suddenly felt possible. His emotions were all over the place.

'We need to get you dressed, Captain Nash,' the nurse was saying to him. 'We can see to it, madame.'

'Let me know when the captain is ready to be collected.'

'As you wish,' the nurse replied, even more lemon-lipped, Charlie decided. Clearly Sophie had some sway around here; not just a wealthy volunteer doing her bit, then. She became more intriguing.

It took them half an hour to ready him before a lad was sent running to find Madame Delancré. She re-emerged looking like a new doll, out of the overall-type uniform she wore around the ward and now outfitted in a grey pinstriped frock that, though utilitarian, could not hide her trim waist or long neck. Its three-quarter sleeves and V-neck revealed skin that struck Charlie as being the colour of light honey. He imagined her in her vineyards. A straw bonnet, modestly trimmed with a single pale ribbon, would hide the dark blonde hair scooped up beneath it.

*You're a picture*, he thought, glad his voice couldn't betray that notion to the women gathered there.

'He's all yours,' one of the younger nurses said, and then blushed furiously after a frowning glare from her superior. 'Forgive me, Madame Delancré,' she said, all but curtseying. 'I meant —'

'Suzette, I know what you meant, and yes, Captain Nash is now my responsibility. I will continue the relevant enquiries for his repatriation to the British. Thank you, everyone.'

'Suzette and young Paul will aid you to the surface, madame.'

The pair immediately offered themselves for him to lean against. It was awkward, with his second arm flung almost uselessly around Suzette. What help a sling would be. He would suggest it.

He wanted to tell them he could probably walk for himself, but the truth was he did feel light-headed, having been prone for a couple of days, and he suspected he would never make it to the surface. It was amazing enough that this underground hospital existed. He continued with the awkward gait as he shuffled between his two aides, highly aware of the presence that followed them.

They loaded him into a wagon and Sophie climbed up alongside him. He tried to convey his horror and sadness at seeing the great city of Reims levelled.

'I know, Charlie,' she assured him. 'Even we don't have words.' She changed the subject. 'I would normally transport you more comfortably in a car, but I've given my Reims car over as an ambulance.'

He waved his good hand as though this was of no importance.

'Comfy enough?'

He could feel the length of her thigh next to his; the novelty made him dizzy. 'I feel like I'm off for a picnic.'

'Drive on,' she said with a chuckle to the man in front.

Vineyards sprawled along the bumpy ride to Épernay, and he enjoyed that soft scratch in her voice as she kept up a steady flow of conversation about the champagne makers of the region.

He turned his gaze back to her. 'So you are a Delancré of the champagne house?'

She nodded. 'The current generation.' It looked to him as though a sorrow ripped through her. 'The last one, I fear. It ends with me. How about you – anyone at home?'

'No parents or siblings. Perhaps that's easier, though.'

'Why do you say that?'

He thought about it. 'There's so much more fear when you have something meaningful to lose. I know from experience that on the battlefield nothing matters any more – money, possessions, career. It all fades, and all that remains in the front of one's mind is who is missing you. And I have watched men crumple when they talk about the family they are fighting to stay alive for. It's no longer about king and country – that's there, yes, but every day is the battle to survive to the next day so you can write home, let them know you're still alive. It's easier being alone, I imagine. Are you married?'

'The army says I'm widowed.' His brow furrowed in readiness to apologise but he felt her hand on his arm. 'I lost my husband, Jerome, within months of the war's beginning.' She sighed. 'Like all these women you see, I am learning to live alone.'

'Don't. You're too young to contemplate life alone.'

'I could say the same for you, Captain Nash.'

He nodded. 'Then let's make a private pact: we won't say forever.'

She smiled, and its warmth upon him felt like the memory of a hot bath, and sinking into its depths.

———————

Charlie couldn't remember a happier time in his life than this bumpy ride in a horse-drawn cart.

'These belong to Pol-Roger,' Sophie remarked in English, suddenly puncturing the quiet, waving a hand. She had long fingers and nails trimmed blunt but shining a healthy pink. 'Maurice Pol-Roger was our mayor at the start of the war. You know, Charlie, when all the authorities we counted on began to withdraw, it was our mayor who kept us going from his own pocket. He was like a mint, committing his funds to the bills being written for the town of Épernay. We bestowed the honour of chevalier in gratitude, and later he was made an officier de la Légion d'honneur.' She sighed. 'Collectively, we have lost a lot of our vines. The vineyards are a network of trenches now, and some terrible fighting has taken place between the vines in the Marne Valley. Merchants will be weeping at the destruction, but what can we do? The situation in Épernay is much easier; we feel insecure because of the air raids and there has been some damage, but it doesn't stop our work and there isn't the relentless artillery fire that Reims has contended with.'

'Have other champagne houses moved from Reims to Épernay?'

'Yes, many have set up their operations in Épernay, but there are problems with supply – getting glass bottles is hard enough that we are having to salvage and reuse, which we would normally never do.'

'Why is that?'

'Ah, well, the pressure in the glass is enormous so traditionally we would not take the chance in case the structure has been weakened, but these days no bottles get broken if we can help it. Our women have still been producing hundreds of thousands of bottles of champagne through the war.'

Charlie gave a look of surprise.

'Yes, never underestimate what women can achieve. I'm proud of us for keeping up that sort of production through these years.'

'What about transport?'

'That is always a problem. Champagne, though passionately desired in Paris, London, Moscow, New York and beyond, cannot be made a priority. We suffer dangerous routes with limited opportunity . . .' Sophie shrugged. 'The Nancy–Paris line that serves the Marne Valley is regularly bombed from the air, so we have to choose our moments. Exports are harder with a shortage of vessels to cross the Channel. The German soldiers pilfer at every chance; I might even claim that if we ever prevail, our champagne has played its part in keeping the enemy well soused and unable to shoot straight.' She grinned. 'But I'm assured we have enough in storage for ten thousand different battles of Marne. I will gladly keep them drunk if it keeps us safe. What did you do before the war, Charlie?'

'I was a chemist,' he replied.

Her eyes widened with surprise. 'But how wonderful! In what area of chemistry?'

'I worked in a laboratory. Essential Services. I defied my boss, and the government . . . ran away to war because I was frightened.' He was admitting this for the first time, but it felt like a burden being lifted to tell someone, even this beautiful stranger. *What is it about French women*, he wondered, *that makes a normally private man open up his soul?*

'You were frightened so you ran away to war?' She was understandably bewildered. 'Men are very confusing creatures. My husband joined up the evening we were married and left soon after.' She shook her head sadly. 'It was both the happiest and saddest day of my life. How could he do that to me?'

'Duty . . . patriotism . . . and, above all, because he loved you.'

'So he left me?'

Charlie could tell this was a question that had obviously been burning for a long time. It rode on tremendous pain . . . He could see it in her plaintive expression and those eyes that made him want to hug a tree. She was the colour of nature, this woman. Beautiful dark blonde hair, a glance he didn't dare meet for too long for fear of being found out, but he knew they were a green of sorts . . . but an earthy green. 'He left you, Madame Delancré, to save you.' He watched her take a slow breath; he hadn't meant to cut so deep but there it was: the open wound of longing and despair, of love lost and even rage that she'd been denied what was hers. 'I would fight . . . I would give my life twice over if it was you at home to keep safe.'

'Oh, Charlie,' she groaned, furtively dabbing at her eyes, frightened perhaps of the driver seeing her tears.

'I'm sorry . . .'

'Don't be. I'm ashamed of myself now for being so angry at him . . .' She sniffed. 'Years of pent-up fury that he chose war and it chose him as one of its early victims.'

'It doesn't choose; it doesn't have intellect or the capacity to select. It destroys all in its path. And the most terrifying aspect is that we can stop it tomorrow; we could have stopped it the day after it began. We are the ones with intellect, and we choose not to stop it. Blame the generals, not the courageous men like Jerome.'

She kissed her fingers and laid them on his hand in thanks: for wisdom, for enlightenment, for tenderness at the right moment, he couldn't say, but the gesture sparked a rolling charge through him as if a hundred-gun salute were being unleashed. 'Tell me what you were frightened of, Charlie?' she said, smiling through her drying tears as she composed herself.

'It was 1915 and we'd begun hearing about the Germans using poison gas to attack on a large scale. It was singularly the most horrific moment of my life when I realised that our government had instructed our laboratory to help with the design and manufacture of something more painful, more lethal, in retaliation. In a matter of hours, I'd gone from being an eager lead research chemist working on a new chlorine process to potentially a mass murderer.'

This time she took his hand. 'Jerome was lost during that first gas attack at Ypres. You could have saved yourself by staying in that privileged position, but I think you're a hero for refusing to be part of that.'

He didn't know what to say, but he did wish for her never to let go of his hand. Sadly, she did, clearing her throat, brightening her tone and gesturing to the landscape around them. 'Well, as you can see, we have now left enemy territory and —' she gave a soft sigh — 'we are entering beautiful Épernay.'

He followed her gaze towards gently rolling hills and the fields beneath them quilted in various shades of green, some bright, some darker, one patch almost luminous beneath the summer sun. There was no smoke, and although he could smell the cordite lingering in the air, the landscape was a patchwork of untidy rows of vines in full leaf. The sense of unruliness gave him a flutter of pleasure. He held her gaze momentarily with a smile, before sliding it away as the driver began urging the horse to slow. It didn't need a lot of encouragement, placidly bringing its trot to a walk as they rounded several corners and moved slightly uphill. Charlie could see a row of splendidly tall mansions dotted about on some high ground. Below them was a stream, and around them the village life of women, children and elder men moved at an unhurried pace. Across the water he could see houses and enclaves that no doubt adjoined other villages.

To Charlie it felt like he'd entered a picture-book world, far from the madness. There was an overwhelming moment when he felt he might cry, but no, he wrestled that urge back down. What would his men think to see him blubbing? Cool-headed, ruthless Captain Nash weeping? None would believe it . . . but then none was likely left alive to think it, he realised.

They continued in silence, swooping around a village, and he felt a slight incline as the horse brought them onto a wider boule-vard flanked by many grand houses. 'This is la rue du Commerce. Many of the well-known champagne families have, over centuries, built their private homes here.'

Charlie gave a slow whistle.

She smiled, appreciating his awe. 'You can see for yourself they are not uniform, the idea being that each building is somehow a reflection of that family's brand and its product.' She chuckled. 'Many say it is perhaps the most expensive street in the world.' He frowned, thinking about many streets in London and those he'd heard of in New York. 'Not because of the houses themselves, Charlie,' she said, guessing where his thoughts had roamed. 'But because of what you cannot see lying beneath these homes, which began construction more than two centuries ago.'

'Crayères . . . I've heard about them.'

'Exactly. Endless tunnels of magnificent champagne are stored beneath us. This street was actually once called le Faubourg de la Folie . . . er, how you say, the Mad Place, or the Crazy Place.'

He grinned.

'By the end of the eighteenth century, this avenue was the address of choice for all the pioneering producers, but the region itself has become a place of beautiful chateaux not just for champenois; indeed, some very wealthy members of the clergy have always appreciated the fine drop of our region and set up vast country homes. Moët et Chandon – perhaps you know this champagne?'

He nodded.

'Napoleon and his empress, Josephine, were among many important guests who visited the Hôtel Moët & Chandon at Épernay. I could go on, but I fear you'll get tired of my voice and my passion for my birthplace.' She grinned, continuing: 'Ever since the arrival of the railway, of course, and the increased export of champagne all over the world, I think our architectural taste on the avenue has been leaning towards the grandiose, if not monumental, but I'm glad to say not here.' She sat forward and Charlie felt the wagon slow to a stop. 'Welcome to my home, Charlie. This is House Delancré.'

Charlie looked through spiked iron railings to a tall, typically French-looking country manor of greyish stone. A steeply pitched, hipped roof of charcoal slate, which looked like a tall hat, sloped directly to the walls of the two-storey building. Within the hat sat dormers with gabled windows. The second storey was as distinctively tall as the first, giving the manor its height but also its aristocratic symmetry. And yet this fairytale castle that Sophie called home was modest in comparison to the palatial dwellings they had passed by, and it struck him that if he'd had to choose one of the many structures for her, it would have been this one. If these houses were supposed to reflect their owners and their champagnes, then he believed the understated sophistication of this building was a mirror of the Sophie Delancré he was beginning to understand.

Charlie soon found himself sharing a light-filled bedroom on the second floor of the mansion house. The three other recovering soldiers in the dormitory were all French and none spoke English. Sophie had explained his situation and how he came to be here in their midst.

'Commandant de Saint Just was standing there as they fished him out of the canal,' she said. 'Now, he speaks very good French but don't tax him with your questions, Philippe. I know how inquisitive you are.' She grinned at a young man with a bandage slanting across his head and his arm in a sling. 'Just let Charlie be quiet for a while.' She let her gaze return to Charlie and rest there. 'Be well, Charlie. Our doctor will want to inspect your arm.'

He felt her departure like a loss and it was nearly a week before he saw her again.

# 15

Sophie hungrily scanned the *Gazette des Ardennes*. She couldn't help but rush over the pages, hoping for Jerome's name to leap out from the list of prisoners the Germans habitually published. It wasn't a generous act, she'd discovered. The enemy took pleasure in letting their opponents know just how many of their civilians and soldiers they now held in captivity and put to work for their war effort. Sophie suspected that Jerome, if he had been captured, would not be worked to death like a regular soldier, and she hoped his status as a lieutenant gave him protection from that exploitation. As her gaze roamed the lines of names, she knew she didn't have enough room in her heart in that moment to think about all those who weren't officers and didn't have that veneer of protection. Only one name mattered but she couldn't find it; she likely never would but still she had convinced herself not to give up this habit.

The first pass was cursory, so maybe she'd missed his name – that's how she comforted herself as she moved on to a more studied examination of each line. This time slower, focused. It took close to an hour, sitting upstairs in her mother's chair; the same light that was nourishing his vineyards was trying to shine its brightness onto his name as Sophie sat near the window and turned the pages of the newspaper. A familiar disappointment snagged in her thoughts and she uncharacteristically flung the gazette down to hold her head in her hands until the despair passed . . . it always did.

She had contacted Jean at the Red Cross twice already since their meeting, hearing the impatience growing in his tone, not caring at being the cause of his vexation. She understood. There were probably tens of thousands unaccounted for; every family wanted to know whatever the Red Cross knew. Pointedly assured, most recently by Jean's assistant, that according to their records, and the military's advice, Jerome Méa had not been rescued, taken prisoner or registered as dead, Sophie took pleasure in saying: 'Still missing, then?'

'Presumed dead, Madame Delancré,' the woman murmured, having the grace to sound abashed.

'Please keep me informed,' she had said into the telephone, even though it was a redundant request.

Sophie let out a sighing breath and forced herself to stand, shake out her tense shoulders, and move on to another task. She knew the time was fast approaching to let Jerome go, let him live on in her memory . . . through his vines and the champagne with which she would honour him. Mentally, she shrugged, reminding herself it was no one's life but hers, and until there was a reason to let go, she wouldn't. She looked over at the parcel that had arrived from Paris this morning. She knew what it contained, having organised for its purchase and delivery on the day she'd left Reims with Charlie. She'd delayed seeking him out; he was surely wondering why, given it had been her idea to bring him to Épernay. Even so, she had plenty of soldiers recuperating here and there was no need for her to feel driven to seek out one in particular. He wasn't special.

*Well done. Keep lying to yourself, Sophie*, a small voice cautioned her. *That will protect you.* She stood, making a sound of disgust, and was glad to hear someone urgently calling for her.

A week of quiet days had passed and during this time he attempted to answer the frequent questions of curious Philippe. The others were older; they understood more keenly and observed Sophie's warning. They nodded greetings, shared the wine that was sent up and made the odd remark about the food, and he noted they paid attention to his conversations with Philippe. All the other soldiers recovering in the house, he'd gathered, wore a French uniform. Charlie presumed they were as intrigued as Philippe but chose not to show it. There really was so little to know but he was different – he was English, that was the distinction.

Suddenly hearing Sophie's voice in the garden drew him to the window to see people gathered in the sprawling back garden. They looked excited; there was weeping, hugs, and Sophie was in the midst of them, but it was as though she sensed him watching and she happened to look up. Her broadening smile warmed him and he actually lifted his hand in greeting. He barely knew her yet he'd missed her presence keenly these last few days, especially as she'd broken him out of the underground hospital and given him the impression that they were co-conspirators.

He could hear intermittent clapping and cheering throughout the house and now he joined his roommates on the landing to peer over the stairwell in the hope of learning what the excitement might be. Sophie arrived moments later, her expression so impossibly bright it could only be news of the best sort.

'Gentlemen – we've just learned the city of Reims is saved!' she said, arriving on their floor. It was a message she was delivering to all the rooms of her makeshift hospital. Charlie wished he could clap like the others; instead he banged his fist on the banister in time to their applause. 'The line is stabilised,' she continued. 'Commandant de Saint Just sent me word that the Americans have held the line around Château-Thierry and counterattacked at Belleau Wood.

It was the bloodiest of battles, I gather, but they're not just holding; together with our allies we are pushing the enemy back.'

More cheers. Charlie joined in. His companions began moving downstairs to join their comrades in celebration and he followed; it meant he could greet Sophie Delancré as well as join in the happy atmosphere.

'There's a glass for each of you being served in the gardens. Get some fresh air and enjoy this news,' she said, laughing, before turning towards him. 'Hello, Captain Nash?'

'Charlie, remember?' he insisted. He looked at her expectantly.

She nodded, corrected. 'How are you feeling, Charlie?'

He found a lopsided smile. 'Pinching myself that I'm here and not in some filthy trench.'

Sophie nodded. 'I wonder, could I trouble you to come with me, please? I have something for you.'

'For me?'

'It's . . . er . . . private,' she said, giving him a small, awkward grin.

Charlie was intrigued. He followed her onto the landing and then up a short flight of stairs to the top level of the house.

'These rooms I normally reserve for visiting dignitaries. We have none at the moment.' He frowned as he watched her undo a trap door with the aid of a long-handled hook before she pulled down a ladder. 'And this is where I stay.' She laughed at his expression. 'Can you make it, do you think?'

Stung by the presumption of his helplessness but privately delighted by the mystery at hand, he gestured towards the ladder. 'Don't worry about me – lead on.' It was harder than he'd imagined, and he was breathing heavily and feeling slightly clammy by the time he'd hauled himself through the opening and accepted her help to clamber up and emerge into the attic.

Inside her attic space he smiled. In here was Sophie Delancré's private world away from everyone who needed her. He wondered why she would permit him into this haven. Was he not a reminder of all she needed to escape?

She obviously could see his bewilderment and explained. 'I've brought you here, Charlie, because what I have I didn't want to give to you in front of the others because . . .' She hesitated. 'Well, it doesn't matter why. Perhaps you'll indulge me in a little white lie that Commandant de Saint Just sent it for you in honour of your impossible feat breaking through German lines . . . and his thanks to the British who fought so courageously in our region.' She seemed apprehensive.

'Of course,' he replied, watching dust motes dance around her like attendants in the soft light of the attic. Charlie wanted to tell her how beautiful she looked today with that glow of optimism suffusing her cheeks, and strands of dark blonde hair escaping her neat chignon. Those escapees were backlit, turning them into golden outlined threads wafting about her. It gave her a girlish appearance and he felt sure he could glimpse the child who had learned from her father about his world of champagne. 'I'll gladly lie for you, madame.'

'Sophie, remember?' she insisted, mimicking him from earlier, and smiled.

'Have you heard the saying *a sight for sore eyes*?'

She shook her head.

'It goes back a couple of centuries – means your presence can make everything feel safe.' He knew that his translation skimmed the true meaning, but it conveyed just enough.

'I make you feel safe, Charlie?'

'You do. I can't imagine anywhere else I'd rather be right now than here in the attic of a beautiful house where champagne is made by an extraordinary woman.'

She gave a low laugh. 'It's nice of you to say so, but surely you'd rather be home?'

'I don't have one.'

'I mean England. No woman pining for you?'

He shook his head, smiling at her probing.

'Whatever have you been doing with yourself? I would have thought women would be trying to catch your attention.'

'Maybe they do,' he admitted, trying not to sound in any way arrogant, realising they were flirting. 'I'm just not very good at noticing.'

'Well, pay attention, Charlie! Handsome, single men shouldn't go to waste.'

He laughed properly.

'I like to think any soldier who finds himself here under my roof can find his smile again. It's lovely to hear you laugh.' The pause between them was awkward only because he felt the connection locking into place, bonding them to each other. He knew she felt it too, which is why she turned away suddenly, busying herself tidying up papers that didn't need to be tidied. 'I hope Épernay will help you to recuperate. You deserve it after all your heroics.'

He shrugged. 'All I was trying to do was retreat, find the Allied line.'

'You were very brave. We all think so.'

A soft silence laid itself around them. He moved to the window and she joined him. 'You're looking at my favourite place in the world.' She pointed out the small villages, picked out the river running behind her property, drew his attention towards the railway station and Paris. And then directed him to where the chardonnay grew. 'My husband planted a special vineyard for our wedding just over that hill,' she explained.

'He's a romantic.'

'Aren't you?'

He blinked and knew she had seen the self-conscious gesture, but the question was too revealing.

'I hope we all are, given the way of the world right now.'

He looked back at her but found her direct gaze too intense and sighed, embarrassed. 'Thank you for inviting me here. I feel privileged.'

'Thank you for talking about my husband as though he's alive. No one else does.' Sophie turned and reached for a box. 'Charlie, it occurs to me now, in this awkward moment, that I may offend you with this.'

He gave a soft frown.

'I want it to be a gift, but I fear you may take insult.' She looked up at him helplessly and he saw now only the little girl of her past, unsure and fretful. Yet she had nothing to fear from him; if anything, her composure and courage intimidated him. All he wanted to do in this moment was reach for her and kiss her. It was such an outlandish, rogue thought that he had to clear his throat.

'Nothing you do or say could offend me.' Standing so close to Sophie, Charlie noticed how the diffuse light glanced off her skin in a way that said it wanted to touch her, gently but swiftly so she didn't notice the intrusion. He blinked in private annoyance at all this schoolboyish desire.

'That's kind of you, Charlie,' she said, and the warmth in her smile brightened him like an awakening. It was a beacon worth following, out of the darkness of his many years of war towards this place of safety. Actually, no, it was her – Sophie was the sanctuary.

Perhaps she sensed his struggle, which was likely why she hurried to open the box and redirect his attention. Inside, sitting on a bed of navy velvet, was a hand brace. It was fashioned out of polished metal and leather. He stared at it for a long time, well past any period that could be considered polite, but she held his tense silence with one of her own.

Charlie felt as though he disappeared in this interval, as if he were released from the confines of his flesh, his spirit free to roam, and it took him on a journey over the course of his war. He glimpsed battles he recognised, even trenches he could pinpoint exactly on a map. He knew the landscape of Arras and the bone-freezing winter of Ypres. He saw men he recalled, now dead, and he watched himself being dragged back into the trench, bloody-faced and unconscious after his fateful shot that murdered the killer Topperwein. And now it lifted him free of the fighting to enjoy mild days in eastern France and the gratitude of the people in those towns and villages. He could taste the wines of the region and the warmth against his back from a sun-drenched stone wall outside a café where a wide-hipped woman propositioned him . . . But then he could taste blood, smell it too. He watched himself killing and others dying around him. He was running, he was falling, he was drowning in a few feet of water. He met a German; made a pact of mercy together. He heard Arabic, he knew pain, he listened to a good man, a French officer. He knew kindness, felt tenderness, smelled bandages and disinfectant . . . and then he saw Sophie. She now represented the light he had been running towards these last three years; she didn't know it, nor had he a day or so ago, but here with Sophie he felt like he wanted to embrace life for the first time in nearly four years. He felt at home here, too . . . home was such an elusive notion for him. He'd never felt he had one, until now. Home was an emotion. Home was a feeling – it was security, a place where he smiled, felt affection and returned it . . . Home was where Sophie Delancré lived and laughed.

He had at last found all that he could want . . . and yet he could have none of it. She belonged to another.

'I don't know how to thank you. It's beautiful,' he murmured in a scratchy voice.

'Now you can heal faster.' She put the box aside, and clearly without any thought towards propriety, she pulled him towards her and hugged him as close as any lover might. It was instinctive, her affection spontaneous. 'I am so happy you like it and will let it help you.'

He held on . . . held on for dear life, because without this moment, this hug, this woman, it felt as though there was no life for him. Long, slim arms encircled his neck and he dared to lift his good arm and hold her. He could feel her small waist and the ribs that suggested she ate too little and worked too hard. How could he have ever wanted to die when this meeting was around the corner? To hug Sophie Delancré . . . nothing compared to it. *Nothing.* The softness of her breasts against his thin shirtfront was a sensation worth fighting to live for – and one to wake up desire that had been so lacking for too many years. And still he clung to her, with one good arm, as she whispered fresh congratulations.

Finally, she pulled away and he turned, clearing his throat, and Sophie made a sudden fuss of fiddling with the leather arm in the box. She spoke to cover her sudden awareness of the physical embarrassment she had caused him. 'Forgive me, that was inappropriate of me.'

'Don't apologise. I think every soldier should be hugged daily.'

He heard her soft chuckle. 'I saw this aid just before the war began in a shop in Paris that sold curios. I was attracted to it because of the workmanship, and the owner told me its story. It was made for a wealthy officer from the war in the Crimea who had lost his hand to cannon fire. There is another whole box of magnificently crafted tools that he could attach to this brace, although you don't need them. I was in luck when I sent the telegram – not only did he still have it in his shop, but the owner was kind enough to send it immediately to Épernay on a train with some returning officers from our army. I'll show you the tools in a minute because the shop owner couldn't bear for all the parts to be separated, even though he understood that I only needed the brace. I think it might fit you very well, Charlie.'

He looked at the dangling leather laces, feeling a fleeting moment of sadness that this was what he'd been reduced to, but then he saw her eager expression and grasped that it was time to accept his lot.

He nodded with another smile. 'The kindness behind this is a little overwhelming.'

'The British army is helping to save France . . . your company has been obliterated, I gather, to save Reims and Épernay from being overrun again. This gift barely touches my gratitude to you and your fellow soldiers.'

He didn't know what to say to that. She was right, though, when he thought of all the British lives lost in just this region of France alone.

'May I try it on you?' she offered.

'Of course.'

'We'll have to be gentle so soon after surgery.'

He grinned. 'My hand is numb anyway.'

She led him to a small chair. 'Please have a seat.' He did as he was asked, embarrassed to crunch over a newspaper cast aside on the floor, as she made herself comfy sitting on the window ledge.

'Put your arm here, Charlie,' she said, gesturing to her lap.

'I'm afraid that would —'

'You should not worry about my sensibilities. I am not embarrassed if you are not?' She waited.

He gave a lopsided shrug and then grinned. He placed his arm onto her lap, still bandaged. Charlie felt a momentary relief that his hand lacked its normal ability to sense touch, certain if it weren't he would be unable to resist allowing the sensitive nerves of his fingers to send all sorts of messages back to his hungry mind: the warmth of her body through her skirt and the curve of her thighs. He dared not ponder anything more or another awakening would embarrass them both.

He tried conversation to quell all the new feelings charging around. 'Er . . . you read the gazettes?' he said, glancing towards the publication.

She nodded. 'The German jails take delight in publishing lists of their prisoners, which is re-published faithfully in our gazettes. I search for Jerome in every edition.'

'I should read them too. Look for any news of members of my company.' He wondered if she would ever become resigned to not finding her husband. He shifted his attention back to where Sophie was gently easing the glove over his bandaged arm. He watched her long, slim fingers at work. 'I have noticed that your hands are sun-tanned.' It was something to say in a discomfiting moment.

She nodded, didn't seem perturbed. 'Before I was married, I was pale because I was in my cellars so much. These days I spend as much time in his fields as I can.'

'Tell me about the vineyards.'

Sophie began to thread the laces through the metal eyes that drew the two flaps of the glove together, encasing his arm in metal so polished he could see himself reflected. He could already feel that it was giving his arm more strength.

A smile danced across her face and he sensed this was a subject she never tired of talking about. 'Well, over March and April as the winter is beginning to thaw, the vineyards are waking up too and beginning to show signs of new life. It used to be my husband's job but now it's my responsibility in this period to shape the canes of our vines in a way that controls both the quality and quantity of grapes they are capable of producing. We call this *les travaux en verts*.'

'The green work,' he translated. 'Sounds odd in English, doesn't it?'

She considered it, smiling. 'I would like to learn this language even better, because I would like to sell my champagne more easily into England.'

'Tell me more.'

She gave a knowing sigh and moved back into French. 'The most important task was taking place just before the recent battle. It's a debudding procedure.' At his puzzlement of unfamiliar French terms, she tried to reword it. 'Er, we take of some of the new growth to prevent the goodness from the soil being devoured.' He smiled his understanding. 'And precious water. This is hard work, done by hand with deep concentration, as a decision has to be made on each bud.'

'Exacting work.'

'Yes, and tiring.' Satisfied that the brace was sitting neatly on his hand, she began gently tightening the laces.

'What happens next?'

'*Relevage*. The branches of the vines will have begun to grow by the beginning of June and they'll grow in all directions. It is time to raise them off the ground, and in my husband's vineyards we use two wires for the branches to wrap around, which allows air to circulate. This creates space for people to move through the rows freely to work and keep track of maturity. We might do this several times to keep the vineyard orderly and give the grapes their best chance to thrive.'

'*Relevage*,' he repeated, as if committing it to memory.

Sophie was tying a neat knot now at the top of his brace and had to hold his arm in place using her thighs. He could tell she was being careful, and he tried not to add any extra pressure, but he suspected they were both acutely aware of how intimate this moment had just become.

'And then?' he asked, desperate for something to puncture the quiet.

'And then through these next weeks, something called *palissage* will occur. Because of the anarchic way the vines choose to grow . . .' She saw him struggle to understand again. 'Er, let me see,' she said, straightening the small, neat bow at the top of the brace, 'let me think of another word . . .' She tapped her lips with a finger, and he wanted to kiss those lips so much he had to look down at his newly braced arm instead. 'Wild!' she said suddenly. 'Do you understand my meaning?'

'I do.'

'So, in this period we are separating those branches to get as much sunshine and fresh air to all the buds but in a way that they're shaded by leaves that are not twisted against each other. It's all about improving that ordered architecture, and when we do all this labour, we can get the very best result from that year's growth. It's very hard work for the small hands of the women and children and the weaker hands of the few older men who help me. But we do it because Épernay must survive – the champagne must keep flowing.'

He knew the fitting of the brace was complete and he would be expected to remove his arm from her lap, but he didn't want this private moment to end. Besides, he liked listening to her and hearing the wistful tone in her voice when she spoke about the vines. 'So, you can leave them through the summer to grow?'

'Well, there is another stage during their growth called *rognage*.'

'*Rognage*,' he repeated.

She grinned. 'It's a trim . . . like a haircut – something you need, Charlie.'

'Do I?'

'I shall organise it for you.' She touched the hair around his ears to demonstrate its unruliness but all it did was send a fresh thrill through him. 'I think this newly braced arm is going to work. Maybe not the hand yet but this will give rigidity.' She raised her gaze to his. Eyes the colour of the grass right before meadow turned to forest were now shining with delight. He wanted to run around that forest, lie down in that meadow. 'I suggest you do not wear it for too many hours. Your hand is too weak still. Maybe try keeping it on for a few hours at night to keep the muscles strong, straight. At other times a sling might help. Even so, this does look very handsome.'

He barely heard her words; instead he watched the way her mouth moved with economy, always a smile ready to broaden across it. It was obvious she was excited for him, but he dared not wonder aloud about why she was so thrilled, given that the addition simply amounted to a more elegantly clad piece of useless flesh.

'How fortunate that the owner of the curio shop happened to have a left-handed one of these things,' he remarked, his voice gritty, finally lifting his hand to turn it so they could admire the fit.

'Coincidental, I agree, but your good fortune, no? I hope it doesn't feel, um —' she moved her head from side to side, searching for the right word — 'sinister?'

'No, not at all. I'm grateful.'

'Does it feel uncomfortable?'

'Surprisingly comfortable,' he acknowledged. 'I think it could be tightened, but for now I think it's fine. I mean, it's rather splendid with its polished buckles, and the craftsmanship is exacting, very beautiful, but my hand is still unable to do anything.'

'But it might! Give yourself time, Charlie. I accept, as I presume you must, that your hand may not function again as it did, but if we can strengthen it, the body is an amazing structure – it can heal, rebuild itself in so many ways. Remember, the bones had to be straightened, repaired, and tendons had to be reconnected. There's healing to be done. For now, you have to be patient and we are going to do lots of exercises to keep you strong so you can heal.'

'Such as?'

'Such as turning bottles in my cellars for dexterity.' She grinned. 'There are thousands, as I've warned you.'

He liked the idea of working with the champagne. 'I'd be so glad to. What else?'

'Hmm, well, you can learn how to lift the vines – that work is always plentiful at this time, so you can get some strength back into your whole body . . . use your good arm.'

'Anything else?'

'Well, tasting, of course.' She saw him look at her lips, lingering a heartbeat too long, and then turn away quickly. 'Er, so we might test this hand regularly in lifting a champagne glass for tastings.' She grinned and knew he saw it was defensive. 'If we can make champagne this year, that is.'

'Show me the rest,' he said, gesturing towards the other box. She placed his braced arm back in his own lap and stood up. His arm felt more complete for the tightness of the brace. He could swear he felt the nerves jangling in his useless hand, fingers like ghostly extensions, yet all the same aching to touch her again.

She returned with the second box. 'Ready?' Sophie flipped open the lid to reveal seven implements, each exquisitely crafted in the same polished steel, finely rendered to lock into the end of the brace and offer useful assistance: everything from a knife, a fork and a spoon to a tool for holding a pad. 'Look, there's even a small hammer,' she pointed. 'I'm not sure why you'd need it but it's there.' She sounded nervous again.

'Blimey,' Charlie said and gave a soft whistle.

'The hook is a bit fearful, I'll admit,' she continued, touching it.

'Useful, though.'

'Do you think so?'

'Of course.' He lifted the glinting hook from its place in the box, studied the end momentarily and then nodded. 'Do you see this?' He pointed to a glimmering, beautifully fashioned half-sphere with elegant carving. She nodded, looking intrigued. 'Well, that would fit onto the end of the brace – presumably the poor man who owned this originally had lost his hand entirely.'

'I believe so, yes.'

'The hook and all these other helpful implements would then twist into place on that mount.' He knew he'd used the word *mountain* instead of the correct word, which made her twitch a smile, but she understood and encouraged him to keep using his French with an eager nod. 'It's like a bayonet on a rifle,' he said, demonstrating how easily the two ends fitted. 'You see?'

Charlie shifted to stand and turned the newly mounted hook in his working hand, so it glinted in the sunshine that was slanting into the room. 'He must have felt like a . . .' He didn't know the word for *pirate* – had never had cause to use it. He said 'sailor' in the end, but it lost the point of the humour. He tried again but found himself in English. 'Buccaneer?' She shook her head, perplexed.

Charlie took a step away from the chair and mimicked brandishing a cutlass. He covered one eye in another attempt at a pirate cliché. 'You know, sailors who steal from other ships . . . er, er, oh yes, how about *corsaire?*'

'Ah!' She looked gleeful.

Charlie swished his make-believe blade with his hook.

She laughed at his swashbuckling. 'You look very handsome brandishing your hook, Charlie. I wonder what it was used for?'

'Oh, I can think of several uses.'

'Such as?' She was still smiling from the levity of the scene, perhaps relieved that he liked his new hand, and in that moment Charlie felt like his old self, the one who had been charming, amusing, good company for women. And so it was with shock at his own recklessness that he responded not only audaciously but with so much risk that even a regular gambler might have rejected the odds.

But Charlie continued because he had always taken risks. Perhaps it was the orphan in him, who knew that unless he did, the world would push him down because no one else was looking out for him. He didn't dare count the risks he'd taken in the fray of battle, any one of them able to blot out his life in a heartbeat. And yet what he did now took all of his courage – he had never felt more vulnerable as he tipped his gaze back to Sophie.

'Such as this,' he said, daring to snare the gleaming hook into her belt, and pulled her towards him. 'In order to do this,' he said; the hitch in his voice was all about desire.

Astonishingly, Sophie Delancré did not resist.

*Is this really happening?* was Charlie's final thought as he tentatively closed the gap between them. Their lips touched, both of them hesitant initially. The kiss was soft, not fleeting, but he didn't want to risk lingering. He pulled back slightly, looking with longing, searching for permission, but it was Sophie now who led the way, those slim arms of hers looping around his neck and not only giving him sanction, but showing that she would be their guide into this unknown territory.

'I've imagined kissing your lovely lips since the first hour I was alone with you,' she admitted softly, sounding aghast at herself. 'I feel so guilty . . . ashamed of myself.'

Charlie smiled, filled with happy disbelief. 'Why didn't you?'

'Matron wouldn't approve.'

They both let out embarrassed chuckles.

'Sophie . . . it's been three years, hasn't it? No word? No sighting? No information?'

'Nothing.'

'Dare I say that this is more like potential for life beyond war – and I wouldn't flatter myself that it's with me, but that you can glimpse a new way ahead . . . that you don't have to be lonely, or a widow. And enjoying others is not a betrayal.'

He couldn't tell if she was convinced but it was Sophie who encouraged him, pulled him close again, as if she could no longer resist her own desires. He let go, gave himself over to her, and couldn't imagine a happier place to land than into her kiss.

# 16

It wasn't planned. But deep in her heart Sophie knew she needed to confront the truth that she'd felt a strong attraction to Captain Nash the day Gaston had sent his curious river find to Reims in an ambulance.

And now here she was with the same soldier, his healthy arm wrapped around her waist, his injured hand saved by a talented surgeon and her determination to keep him whole. Then there were those lips, which had been so inviting on her first proper look at him. They had borne out their promise, not that she would have believed a fortnight ago she'd test that potential. They were pillowy soft against hers and his kiss was tender, not searching, as she had imagined the kiss of a man starved of affection. He was holding back, allowing her to decide how far this episode went and at what speed.

He turned his head and his lashes brushed the top of her cheek. Curiously, that feathery touch felt more intimate than any other romantic experience of her life. It seemed to sum him up: so gentle, so light, it was as though he might disappear.

The very thought of kissing a man other than Jerome had felt abhorrent, especially with Louis now firmly making his push for marriage. The idea of him touching her intimately enough to make a child was so revolting, she had to put the image out of her mind. And yet look at her, carelessly giving her affection to a stranger. But until a few moments ago no man except Jerome had made her catch her breath – and in that moment, as Charlie risked making that daring move, she felt clarity arrive. It warned her that unless she opened herself to others, she would never kiss again. Charlie was right: it was not a betrayal. Jerome used to say that mouths were for kissing, not arguing, whenever they disagreed. Of all people, she knew he would be disappointed if she gave up the potential for love and laughter simply in his honour; in a way her loyalty to a dead man dishonoured his gregarious, life-loving personality.

Charlie withdrew again and rested his forehead against hers.

'Sophie, as mad as this sounds, this scares me more than war,' he whispered in French.

'What are you scared of?' She didn't mention that she felt the same.

'Losing this,' he replied, touching the left side of his breast. 'I've never had anything much to lose before.'

Sophie didn't mean to let a smile drift into her expression. 'You've never loved a girl, Charlie?'

He shrugged, earnest as ever. 'Only from afar.'

'She never knew?'

'All the boys loved her.'

'How old were you?'

She was expecting him to have been in his late teens, a gorgeous youth too shy to approach the girl of his dreams. 'Six.'

'Six!' She exploded into laughter.

'You shouldn't laugh. It was a serious love.'

'No adult?'

'Not if you don't count the crush on our school nurse, Miss Peabody.'

'I won't. But I cannot believe you've not had a meaningful relationship.'

'Plenty of dating, some that lasted long enough to be considered a relationship. None were women I felt strongly enough about that I could see myself spending my life loving them. I think I loved my work too much . . . until I didn't and then I was off to war.'

*Why him? Why this Englishman?* She could imagine Gaston saying it; she could certainly imagine Louis almost spitting on the ground at her feet if he learned of this. *You've been so strong, so committed to Jerome in his absence for years. Why now?* It was Charlie who answered that question pounding in her thoughts.

'You've saved my life in every way,' he admitted.

And that was it. She was someone's hero.

'That's dramatic,' she answered, although she was excited by his remark. It felt like a new life beckoning.

'I thought I wanted to die so many times and that's because I had nothing to live for. You've made me want to live again.'

There it was. Charlie's words summed up her feelings.

She kissed him again to show him how much his words meant, and that she felt the same. She pulled at his unruly hair and hugged him as close as two bodies could be. And then she broke the kiss abruptly as shame threatened to overwhelm her. Guilt wagged a finger at her from behind the English soldier.

'I must get back, Charlie. People are waiting in the cellars. Come on, I'll give you some work to do.'

The *Gazette des Ardennes* rustled again beneath their feet as they reluctantly pulled away from each other.

They emerged from the attic room, looking like guilty children.

'I want to stay up there forever,' Charlie whispered in French, just as one of the young hospital aides came running upstairs.

Sophie let go of Charlie's fingers as if stung.

'Slow down, Marie,' Sophie urged the aide. 'Has something happened?'

The youngster's gaze locked onto Sophie with relief. She sounded breathless, as though she'd run up the pathway to the house as well as the various flights of stairs. 'Commandant de Saint Just is here, madame. He can only stay a short while. He asked me to find you quickly.'

'Thank you, I'll come right away,' she replied brightly. 'I think Captain Nash needs his arm bound in a sling by day, and in this brace by night. Can you organise that for me?'

'Yes, madame. Shall I cut up another sheet?'

'We're out of slings and bandages already?'

The girl nodded. Sophie sighed and unravelled the scarf she wore habitually.

She handed it towards Marie. 'Use this.'

'Oh, madame, if you please, I —' Marie began.

'I have others,' she said, dismissing the concern with a wave of her hand. 'Besides, it will make a perfectly soft sling.' She cast a glance backwards at him. 'I'm glad that brace works for you, Captain,' she said over her shoulder. 'Come to the cellars later. Always work for you there.'

And with that she was gliding down the stairs, disappearing from his view.

# Part Two

# 17

The new young guard looked at the prisoner in surprise. 'How come you speak good German, Bouchon? Convenient to have you as a translator, of course.'

The man who had become known as Jacques Bouchon shrugged. 'I must have learned it.'

'You use our slang well, so you have obviously spoken it since you were young.'

'Perhaps my family lived on the border. I have no memories of my past.'

'Nothing at all?'

'Oh, yes,' he admitted, in a slightly grudging tone. 'I get flashes. Voices in my dreams. I sometimes have snaps of scenes in my mind like single photographs, but they leave as fast as they arrive.' He shook his head. 'I can't hang on to them.'

'Like what?'

'There's a woman.'

Rolf's eyes widened with intrigue. He laughed suggestively.

'I never see her face, but she has dark golden hair to here,' Jacques said, tapping a finger just below his shoulder. 'It's thick and it shines glimpses of fire when the sun catches it . . . and I hear her voice. It's slightly raspy.'

'What does she say?'

'I can't hear the words, but she beckons to me. I see other people now and then but they're all strangers in my mind.'

'You're lucky that other French soldier recognised you as an officer or you'd have been sent to a much tougher prison.'

Jacques nodded. 'I wish he'd lived and I could have asked more, but he was vague even in his recognition of me. He knew me as an officer and said he thought I was Jacques but he had no surname; it was hard enough to get that much from him. I'm grateful but I don't trust it.'

'Why?'

'I don't feel like a Breton.'

His companion laughed.

'And if I am, why am I not speaking the language of Brittany?'

'How should I know? I'm German! You've probably forgotten it. The shock they talk about in the trenches took it away.'

'But left me with French, German, English? Pfft!' he said dismissively.

Being able to translate had made him popular with everyone, especially the German guards, who between them had very little English. There were no other French prisoners left here.

'I was in Belgium,' Jacques explained, taking a drag on the final centimetre of his cigarette.

'Gassed?'

'You can tell?' he asked the guard, expelling smoke into the air.

'Your cough,' Rolf admitted. 'I recognise it from others. It was far worse in the prison I worked at before. That cough of yours is not from the tobacco. It is distinctive. What did gassing feel like?'

'What a callous question.' Jacques shook his head with a soft smirk. 'I wouldn't even wish it on my enemies. Curiously, it's something I do remember. It burned my throat and I felt like I would suffocate and die there in the mud, gasping for breath.' He gave another shrug. 'I was one of the lucky ones to survive but I was told the best I could hope for was damaged lungs for life and being susceptible to respiratory problems. It may still kill me.'

The man looked curious rather than moved. He drew deeply on his own cigarette and changed the subject. 'Why are you with the English, not with your own men? If you are French?'

Jacques sighed, looked away from the freckled face of his jailer and took a final drag before stamping out the butt. Rolf was one of the kinder ones: he was new, and Jacques suspected he would rather be out drinking beer and hunting for female company than standing in a makeshift prison.

'I only know what I've been told,' he said. 'Everything else remains lost to me.'

'Tell me what you've been told, then. I have nothing important to be doing and I'm about to run out of cigarettes.'

Jacques hugged his arms around himself. It probably couldn't hurt to strengthen his relationship with any of the guards. He couldn't know when he'd need to lean on the thin friendship, or more likely when his fellow inmates might ask him to find out information. Indeed, one of the guards might spill a nugget of news that could bring them fresh optimism.

'Apparently, I was caught in the gassing at Ypres three years ago, and while I survived it, I walked around in a fog and became separated from my regiment but also from the men I was in charge of – I was found alone when I was taken prisoner by your boys. As I understand it, I was half-naked, with no identification left on me. I was lost.' He tapped his temple. 'In here. I couldn't make a single thought stick; I had no idea who I was. I simply followed others on the long march out of Flanders and into Germany. Someone, perhaps one of my men, seemed to know

I was a lieutenant, but I couldn't tell you who that was because by the time I arrived here there were only a few French soldiers with me. I don't know if they died from their injuries or whether I was carved away from them because I spoke English.' Jacques sighed and could tell that Rolf was still helplessly engrossed. 'We slept in all sorts of places – I'm sure you know this?' He was trying to avoid having to say more.

'Go on. I like listening. Stops me feeling hungry,' the young guard admitted, beaming one of his smiles. There was little enough food here for the guards, let alone the inmates. Everyone was lean, hungry on meagre rations and desperate for news from the front, especially about when this war was going to end.

'Well, I do remember us linking up with other captives, plenty of civilians and soldiers mixed together. We slept rough . . . barns, sheds, open fields, and at some point through the coldest weeks I caught a fever so maybe I was muttering in English, I don't know; I was put with the English soldiers. From what I can gather, by the time we arrived here there might have been one other Frenchman left, who was from my division but not from my unit – I mentioned him earlier. Your German need for records wanted a name to be given to me. It was clear I wasn't English, only that I spoke the language. Even though I had only a ragged shirt and had somehow acquired a blanket to wrap around myself, I was wearing the blue trousers of the French army.' Jacques touched the scar on his head where no hair would grow back. He wished he could remember receiving this wound and the others that had changed him forever. 'The British officers called me Corky.'

'Corky,' Rolf repeated, confounded.

Jacques pulled out the cork he habitually carried and was grateful not to have lost. 'Because of this,' he said.

'What is that? A champagne cork?'

'One day maybe I'll remember. But I keep it close. It was in my pocket. As no one could put a name to me, the prison orderly wrote the word *cork*, translating to French as "*bouchon*". I must have nodded or simply accepted it, but either way it was never corrected. I truly cannot remember when I acquired the name Jacques, but it was likely on the long march to Germany.'

Rolf whistled. 'So you still don't know who you are, in truth?' The guard sounded full of wonder. 'Maybe the woman in your dream gave you that cork. Perhaps before the war you had been with her . . . celebrating . . . you know . . .?'

Jacques watched Rolf's face flush pink at the innuendo. 'Maybe.' He winked, hoping to end the painful conversation, and won a conspiratorial laugh from the friendly guard.

They heard a shout and both turned at the sound. Another guard was beckoning angrily at Rolf.

'I must go,' he sighed. 'I'll see you around, Jacques.'

Jacques dissolved into a fit of coughing. *Damn that gas*, he thought, wondering yet again whether his ailment would slip into the dreaded tuberculosis that killed so many with weakened lungs. Finally finding his breath, he raised a hand to Rolf. 'I'm not going anywhere,' he quipped, making the younger man grin. 'What's the rush up there, anyway?'

'We're preparing for some visitors,' Rolf said.

'Berlin coming here?' he said in a wry tone.

'No, no, nothing like that. A team of doctors from the neutral zone.'

Jacques frowned. 'What for?'

'I don't know. I am not told these things, but I shall get my backside kicked if I don't go and help tidy up the space for them.' He waved farewell, flicking his cigarette butt away.

*Doctors from the neutral zone*, Jacques thought. *Well, that might be something to take to the English officers over tonight's gruel and bread.*

It was two days later he was hunted out. Jacques looked up, frowning as the guard yelled his name.

'Here,' he called, standing, hoping he wasn't in trouble.

'You've been summoned.' It wasn't one of the friendly guards.

'Why?'

'Don't ask questions.'

Jacques looked back at the men he shared quarters with. A couple gave jeering but affectionate whistles.

'Give 'em hell, Jack,' Captain William Jones said, still finding it easier to anglicise the French pronunciation. They joked all the time that they'd made him an honorary Englishman.

'Ask them if we can get some more wood – it's bloody freezing in here,' another senior officer, Major Hugh Blackman suggested.

He grinned, offering sarcastically: 'I'll ask for some fresh stocks of tea too, shall I?'

'Yes, please, old chap. Make sure it's Vickery's Darjeeling – second flush, mind. Best bloody tea on earth.'

Everyone laughed as he saluted.

'And I'll have a tin of caviar, thanks,' Captain Jones said.

He followed the loud click of the German guard's boots on the grey flagstones. They travelled from one end of the castle to the other, where the administration and the enemy were housed. He had never seen this part of the castle, and the further they went, the plusher it became. There were tapestries and other soft furnishings, and the sinister *clack* of the guard's boots was intermittently deadened by thick rugs. Armchairs were grouped around carved stone fireplaces, and in the distance he could hear music. It was a new world echoing the old one.

Finally, he was escorted through double doors into a vast room where three men with sombre expressions sat behind a large table with paperwork strewn on it. Behind them to their left sat a stenographer with thick-rimmed glasses; she was the only person who greeted Jacques with any hint of a smile.

The man in the middle spoke first. 'Thank you. You may leave him with us.'

The guard glanced at Jacques, his lip slightly raised in a sneer, and departed.

As Jacques regarded the panel of strangers he helplessly dissolved into a fit of coughing. He couldn't focus on their awkward silence for his cough was wet and all-consuming. To his surprise and gratitude a tumbler of water appeared and there was a gentle hand on his back. The tone was friendly too. 'Here, drink and find your calm.' It was one of the men, and close up he could see only sympathy in the fellow's gaze. The man spoke in English but with a European accent he couldn't guess at.

'Thank you,' he struggled to get out, and continued coughing, unable to drink for at least another half-minute.

They waited patiently until his struggle subsided.

'Forgive me,' he said, clearing his throat a few times. He drained his glass and awkwardly shook the hand of the man who had assisted him, and remained silent but nodded again as the European in civilian clothes returned to his seat. Jacques cradled the empty tumbler in his lap and regarded the trio once again.

'May we conduct this meeting in French?'

He nodded.

'Thank you. Mr Bouchon, may we call you Jacques?'

'You can. It is the only name I have.' It sounded sarcastic, which he hadn't intended. 'I mean, you've probably been told I have lost my memory? It is the name I go by – one given to me.'

The lead man nodded. 'Yes, we do understand. Let us introduce ourselves. I am Dr Anders Keller.' Keller spoke the names of the others; Jacques paid little attention to them but graciously accepted their nods and brief smiles. It was only now, as Keller gestured towards the fireplace, that Jacques noticed a man, not in uniform, with a pencil-thin moustache and a neat razor-like parting in his oiled hair. 'Dr Kurtz is German, but he is here simply to ensure we make wise choices.'

*Choices?* He waited, baffled.

Keller continued in his kind tone. 'We are one of ten delegations from neutral countries who have the responsibility of selecting imprisoned soldiers in Germany to be transported to Swiss internment camps.'

Jacques gave a low scoff but turned it into a sniff and then an embarrassed cough when he realised no one in the room was jesting. 'H-how has this come about?' he stammered, unsure of how else to react.

'Switzerland, in conjunction with the Red Cross, is working hard for humanitarian reasons to help those imprisoned in German jails to be sent to several camps in Switzerland to improve their health.'

Jacques wanted to pinch himself. Was this a joke? He hadn't realised he'd spoken this thought aloud.

'This is not a joke, Lieutenant Bouchon, but I can understand your bafflement.'

'After years in prison, you can imagine how odd this is.' He began to cough again, struggling momentarily to regain some ease of breathing.

'We realise it is surprising for prisoners. We are committed to this aid, and I hasten to add,' he said, glancing at the German in the room, 'you will not be a free man but you will be free to come and go within the confines of the town or city to which you are sent.'

The man peered at him over rimless spectacles, and the message conveyed in that look told Jacques that the term 'prisoner' would be considered loosely in Switzerland. Was this really happening? He needed to focus on what the man was saying.

'. . . and it is our understanding that you suffered a poison gas attack in 1915.'

He nodded. 'At Ypres, yes. That was where I was taken captive.'

'And you have no memory from before then?'

'I remember the green mist. It invades my dreams to this day, but of the hour – even the moments before I first saw that killing mist – I have nothing. The memory of that mist brings on a sort of panic and I find it hard to breathe, my pulse races and I feel like my heart is going to explode.' He looked back at the man help-lessly. 'I have tried, sir. I've spent the last two years of captivity feeling like my brain is bleeding, I've pushed it so hard to recall. I have small, er, how shall I say . . . images – vignettes, even – that unfold now and then. There is a woman and there are other people whom I don't know, should know, but are strangers still. I don't know if I'm a lieutenant. All I know is that I am French, rather than specifically Breton, and was fighting in Ypres by 1915.' He stopped talking, realising he had been speaking too fast, sounding perhaps a little aggressive through his frustration. Jacques scanned the panel of doctors with appeal in his expression.

'The cough you display is a result of the chlorine gas we see in your file.'

'I am not a doctor,' he admitted with a shrug. 'But I feel sure I had strong lungs before the war.'

'May we examine you, Lieutenant Bouchon?'

'Am I being chosen to go to Switzerland?'

'Quite possibly,' replied Keller amiably, and the other Swiss doctors smiled as they stood. 'Perhaps you would remove your shirt for us. Do you need help?'

Jacques looked down at his arm, which had been poorly amputated at the elbow. 'No, I've learned how to manage, but thank you.'

'You are tall – you must have been strong,' Keller observed as he ran through his prodding and listening checks.

'I suppose so, sir.'

'I notice your handshake is extremely firm – more powerful than most.'

Jacques looked back at him queryingly.

'Makes me think you worked with your hands, perhaps? Something repetitive that strengthened the grip.'

He shrugged.

'Keep it in mind when those flashes of memory hit.'

The German joined in, speaking in clipped French. 'It is intriguing that you are French, but you are with the English officers.'

Jacques looked towards Kurtz. 'It is, but I suspect all known details are noted in the files. It changes nothing, for all of my company as I understand it are dead, mostly from the effects of the gassing.'

'And yet you survived.'

'I survived. I don't know how or why.'

The German gave him a slit-eyed nod and seemed satisfied.

The doctors gave him a thorough examination, listening to his lungs, tapping his back, checking his blood pressure and nodding and whispering to each other in Swiss French, which he mostly understood.

'Thank you, Lieutenant. You may dress. And you shall hear news soon.'

'How soon, Dr Keller?' he risked as he pulled on his shirt and dexterously buttoned it with one hand as he'd taught himself.

'By week's end,' the man assured him. He turned to the stenographer. 'Thank you, Lena.'

Lena tinkled a bell and within a moment the unfriendly guard returned to escort Jacques back to his dormitory.

'Thank you for the opportunity,' he said, not entirely sure which day of the week it happened to be or in how many days the week would end.

After some cooler days, the weather had 'fined up', as his fellow prisoners termed it. They were taking advantage of it: one of the inmates was a doctor who urged them to get the sun on their backs whenever they could, especially those like Jacques with respiratory problems.

He had just finished a meagre midday meal of rough bread with jam in the courtyard. Everyone shared their parcels from home. He was one of only two officers who received no packages from relatives.

As usual he declined anything extra because he couldn't reciprocate.

'Come on, Corky, you know we don't care,' Captain William Jones remarked. Jacques didn't mind the nickname. Most seemed to have one. Jones was known as Ducky but Jacques never understood why; something to do with the English sport of cricket, he'd gathered, but it still made no sense.

'Even so, I feel, how you say, awkward,' he said to Ducky, whose blackberry jam it was.

'Well, don't. I want you to taste my village in this jam. I used to pick blackberries from these same bushes when I was a little tacker and used to go fishing at the local stream. We never caught much more than tiddlers.'

Jacques didn't bother asking what a tiddler was.

'I hope I see that village again.'

'You will, Captain,' Jacques assured him.

'You might see it before me if you get out of here. Switzerland, eh? Taking that with you?' He nodded at the cork that Jacques had been absent-mindedly turning over in his hand.

'Given this is all I have that connects me to my past, I would weep to lose it.'

'That's dramatic, old chap. You might have just drunk some

old plonk during rotation. It could be meaningless.' His companion stared at it. 'What does that say?' He squinted.

'*Ancre*,' Jacques said. 'Means anchor.'

'Who names a bloody champagne Anchor? You're nowhere near the sea in Champagne country.'

As the captain said it, something snagged in his thoughts, tried to reach out to him and he to it, but at that moment two guards stomped up; one was Rolf.

The other guard addressed Jacques. 'Lieutenant Bouchon? You must come with us.'

'What's happening, then?' Ducky asked, standing.

'We need a French translator. We've got two new prisoners and can't make sense of them,' one said to Jacques.

Jacques nodded, told the captain what was happening and left with the guards, amused that they'd sent a pair, both armed. Where would any of them run to in Germany, anyway? He'd asked his fellow prisoners that question and it was a major who'd replied that, for the British, it was every soldier's duty to try to escape.

'Old Fritzy knows that,' Major Blackman had explained. 'So they're careful.'

'Where are the new captives from?' Jacques asked the guards as they entered the building.

'No idea. One's an Arab. Moroccan, perhaps. The other is short and hairy, so from the south, we think.'

They showed him into an office where two men sat with their heads hung.

'Ask them for information. We need names, ranks, division.'

The Arab looked up first. He wore a greenish mustard-coloured uniform. Jacques spoke to him, unable to fathom the fizzing sensation at the back of his mind that this man seemed to prompt. He couldn't know him. He was a native of Algeria, and

Jacques explained this to the fellow's jailers, giving the name and rank they demanded.

'. . . and they're called Tirailleurs. He's from Constantine, to the east of the capital, Algiers.'

The man recording the information looked at the other fellow, who was yet to raise his head.

'Capitaine?' Jacques prompted. The man looked up and focused the far-off gaze of his rheumy eyes. Jacques introduced himself. 'We just need to mark your arrival down, sir, so we can enter your name into the lists. Your family . . . other soldiers will be looking for you.'

'I am Jerome,' the man said.

Jacques felt the fizz in his mind boil and spill. He didn't hear the man speak his surname but soon felt Rolf shaking his arm.

'Bouchon!'

He blinked several times in confusion. His breathing was shallow and a coughing fit erupted. Mercifully it was short, but it had distracted everyone. He staggered slightly and Rolf caught him.

'What is wrong with you, Bouchon?' he growled in German.

'My name isn't Bouchon. It isn't Jacques, either.'

Rolf looked at him, perplexed, and cut a glance to the other Germans.

'We're aware of that,' snapped Otto, another guard, taking a step forward.

'Yes,' he wheezed. 'Except I've remembered who I am.' He looked into Rolf's young face with wonder. 'I'm Jerome.'

'Yes, I said Jerome,' the new prisoner insisted.

Rolf looked between them and then back at the man whose arm he held. 'Your full name?'

He pulled out the cork from his pocket with helpless excitement. 'It's not *ancre*. It's Delancré! Most of the name has been rubbed off.'

'Jerome Delancré?' Rolf asked.

And Jerome shook his head. 'No. But I know why I carry this cork now, and the house that made the champagne it once belonged to. My name is Jerome Méa,' he said triumphantly, his voice breaking as he spoke his name for the first time in three years. He swung around to the man recording the prisoners' details. 'You need to change my details. Now – it needs to be done now! They will be looking for me.'

'Calm down, calm down,' Rolf urged, whispering, 'I'll sort it out. Get this man's details.'

With his mind scattering, and still holding his triumph in his throat, Jerome Méa gained all of the information that was required from the new inmates. As he was being escorted back to the prisoners' courtyard, he grabbed Rolf's arm.

'You have to help me, Rolf.'

'Be quiet!' Otto warned.

'Oh, come on, Otto. He's going to Switzerland, anyway.'

Rolf won a glare from his elder.

'I'm definitely going?'

Rolf nodded. 'Tomorrow.'

'All the more reason. I have to get a letter out, Rolf. Please.'

'I'll see what I can do,' Rolf said, glaring straight back at Otto. 'Don't worry, he'll speak kindly of us to those doctors. Maybe we'll get a cushy transfer.'

---

It was Ducky Jones who filled out the special form letter for him that prisoners could submit; Jerome was shaking too much, and a one-handed man with a tremble was going to take far too long, especially one who'd lost his writing hand. Clutching the envelope that sealed his fate, held his very life in its note, he sought Rolf, beckoning to him later that day and pressing two-dozen cigarettes through the fence. The officers had each donated to Jerome Méa's cause, which had created a ripple of optimism among the men, not just one of their own escaping to Switzerland but one of their favourites breaking through the fog that had held him in its sinister clutches for years. This was something to celebrate and they were even planning a shared feast tonight, all chucking in whatever food they could gather up from biscuit tins and jars.

He had to get this letter away before he left Germany and was taken further from his home in Épernay . . . his wife . . . oh, his beautiful, darling, suffering wife. Had she given up on him? Could he blame her? He was still shaking with excitement when Rolf ambled up.

'For me?' Rolf said, eyeing the cigarettes.

'Sell them if you want. I just need you to take this letter and have it sent through the Red Cross to Paris.'

Rolf sighed. 'Otto said it could take an eternity, the way this war is going. Letters take many months – you know that.'

'It's already been an eternity, Rolf.'

'We're very behind in prisoner documentation. You have to understand this. I checked. It's not just us. It's all the prisons, I'm told. You will be gone from here before we can even get it away.'

'Will you submit it for me?'

'Yes. But you're being transferred as Jacques Bouchon. It is too late to change any of the paperwork. They'll be moving you in a few hours.'

'You said tomorrow.'

He shook his head. 'I don't make the rules, Bouchon.'

'It's Méa,' he corrected Rolf firmly.

'Well, that may be but it's Lieutenant Jacques Bouchon who is getting on the transport to Switzerland.'

# 18

ÉPERNAY

*June 1918*

It was several days after the kiss and Charlie hadn't seen Sophie since. He could smell her distinctive perfume drifting up from the scarf wrapped around his arm. He wished he could still feel the warmth of her skin on it, and worried that all the rigid control he'd imposed upon himself over the years was being rapidly dismantled. It had taken endless days of war to turn him into a ruthless, seemingly cold-hearted murderer who apparently couldn't die. It had taken just one kiss from a woman he admired and desired to make him feel vulnerable and, he now realised with shock, feel a genuine fear of death because it would rob him of Sophie.

Charlie hated to feel weak, but he would sell himself twice over if it meant he belonged to Sophie. He shook his head in private surprise that this was the same Charlie Nash from the trenches at Ypres. He should feel ashamed, perhaps. Instead, he leaned his cheek momentarily on the scarf at his shoulder and inhaled; in a blink it felt as though she were walking beside him. The fragrance had a sweet spiciness to it that spoke to him of burnt orange and sandalwood. It reminded him of how much he'd wanted to study perfume-making during his university days, but the notion had been ridiculed by his tutors and he'd conformed to the image of the man in the white coat rather than go where his heart was leading him.

He mourned that weakness of youth. Inhaling the luscious scent, he understood that it was as much a signature for a woman as if she'd written her name in ink. She might have left a room minutes before and yet, from her distinctive perfume, could still be identified as having stepped into it. He knew he could catch a drift of this perfume anywhere and he would instantly think of Sophie Delancré, even though he didn't know its name or what its bottle looked like. Charlie felt sure he could pick it from one hundred perfumes.

He liked seeing the scarf's paisley pattern tied around his arm . . . his neck. That felt romantic: from her neck to his. She had been right: his numb arm had a new weightlessness now that meant it didn't hang as heavily from his wounded shoulder. As his shoulder healed with this support, it would be able to lift and carry his arm more easily.

As he'd been urged, he walked around the property, wearing a woman's scarf and feeling only vaguely ridiculous. The truth was he had never felt happier, unless he considered glimpsing paradise in Sophie's arms. He'd been with enough women to know that she was someone to fall for. When he considered all the lovely women in whose company he'd enjoyed affection, he couldn't compare a single one to Sophie. What was it about her? There had been other, more traditionally beautiful girls with straighter, more elegant noses, perfectly arched eyebrows, creamier complexions. The small scar on Sophie's brow gave her a permanent look of gentle amusement; he must learn what had caused that injury. One of her eyes was ever so slightly darker than the other but that could only be noticed if one was as close to her as he had been as they kissed. *How many have got that close?* he wondered in a flash of jealousy.

He flicked the thought away and let his mind shift to her hands; most women took pride in theirs. Hers were long-fingered, made strong from years of hard work; the skin of her hands was distressed with tiny wounds and the odd bruise, which she wore without embarrassment, perhaps even with a sense of pride. And while most of the people she worked with in Reims were milky from their subterranean lives, Sophie's skin was slightly burnished and she didn't seem to care. And that's where Sophie's magic lay, he realised: she did not possess the vanity that might make her arrogant or precious. Here was a woman wealthy in her own right, and although she carried herself confidently, it was not with superiority but with a sense of belief in herself. There had been other confident women in his life but again he couldn't raise one to mind who came close to Sophie in terms of her commanding presence; gazes, including his, followed her, and fortitude did not compromise her femininity. If anything, that quiet strength enhanced her, shone through that woody-green gaze. Her beauty lived within her smile – when she had turned it on him, he experienced for the first time the sensation of his heart skipping a beat. He'd always sneered at such sentiment but no, his whole body had felt itself pause when she greeted him with a smile that seemed to warm all of her features . . . but just for him. He knew he was being mawkish, but this was a new emotion for him, and it felt enlivening.

Her husband's presence threatened to invade his thoughts, but Charlie pushed him away. Not yet. He would confront that issue soon but not now. He did wonder how she might be rationalising the same question. But she had kissed him willingly. She'd stepped over that line of her own desire.

Charlie passed sheds like insect hives, full of industry. Women in one shed were cleaning barrels; the smell of damp oak was prevalent. He strolled in to watch and saw them sluicing water around the big barrels that would soon hold the liquor from this year's harvest. In another they were washing bottles, elbow-deep in thin suds, chatting above the clank of heavy glass. There was an eager atmosphere around the property; the women believed that the end of this torturous war was nearing. He watched a cartload of sacks being delivered and his acute sense of smell told him this was yeast, while another shed held what he realised was cane sugar – there didn't seem to be much left, but what would he know?

Two little girls skipped towards him. They were of similar age; one was without front teeth, giving her a delightful lisp.

'Are you a soldier?' she asked.

'I am. I'm not French, though.'

'But I understand you,' she said in a singsong voice. Her friend, or perhaps it was her sister, giggled.

'Because French is such a beautiful language to speak,' he replied. 'What is your name?'

'I am Clemence,' answered the lisper.

He looked to her friend with enquiry.

She pointed to herself. 'My name is Marcelle.'

'Would you like to see all the bottles?' Clemence offered.

'I would,' he said, unsure of what they meant.

Without hesitation, Clemence took his hand, Marcelle linked arms with her and they led him down some stone steps.

'Mummy works here,' Marcelle said, 'but I don't like it.'

'Why not?' he asked, enchanted by the youngsters.

'Oh, that's because she's scared of the dark. I'm not,' Clemence informed him. 'I'm like Madame Delancré.'

'Are you?'

'Yes,' she assured him. 'She's not scared of anything.' Her lisp made her brave words sound all the more courageous.

A musty smell, not dissimilar to mushrooms, captured him. He felt the warmth of the day disappear as he arrived at the bottom of the steps and stood, mouth slightly open with awe. Women, like worker ants, stood behind tall timber shelves that held seemingly endless rows of bottles at an angle. The women were twisting the bottles and he could tell it was with precision but they were fast and focused.

'Maman!' Clemence yelped and both girls ran to her mother, disturbing her at her work.

Charlie noticed she was softly vexed but found a smile and smoothed their cheeks, whispering a gentle admonishment. They pointed to him and she turned. He quickly strode up to her.

'Forgive me. Madame Delancré suggested I explore the property – I am one of her wounded,' he said, lifting his damaged arm to demonstrate.

'I can see.' She smiled. 'I recognise Madame's scarf too.'

'We needed an urgent sling,' he admitted and grinned. 'Are these your daughters?'

'Clemence is and Marcelle might as well be. They are insepar-able.' The girls skipped away, their attention caught by something else. 'Her mother died recently, her father killed in 1915, so she's part of our family now.' She shrugged. He didn't pursue it. Everyone helped everyone around here.

'I didn't mean to interrupt your work. What is the name of this procedure of you turning the bottles, changing their angle? It is marvellous to watch.'

'We have many words for it. Boring is one.' She laughed, and he smiled.

'We call this *remuage*,' said a familiar voice. 'Hello, Adeline.'

'Madame.' The woman half curtsied.

He turned to see Sophie arriving. 'Remuage,' he repeated.

'In English they call this riddling. Someone as skilled as Adeline here can turn many thousands of bottles each day. Her husband held the record of twenty thousand in one day.'

He stared at Sophie and back at Adeline. 'That's extraordinary.'

'It is. We'll leave you to your work, Adeline. Would you care for a tour?' she asked Charlie.

'If you have time.'

'I do.'

After their intimacy he loathed their aching politeness but with others around he had no intention of compromising Sophie's standing.

'Do you understand the making of champagne, Charlie?'

He wanted to ask her about the kiss. Had he imagined it? He could be forgiven for thinking he had. Charlie cleared his throat, allowing Sophie to decide when to raise what had occurred in the attic room. 'Treat me as a beginner,' he said.

'Well, the riddling process is designed to move the sediment in the bottles, left behind from the fermentation process, down to the neck so we can rid the wine of what is essentially waste matter. Remember, this wine has been maturing first in barrels, then in bottles.'

'All right,' he said, encouraging her to go on, loving the passion in her voice.

'Now, riddling looks easy enough, doesn't it, that even a one-handed man could perform this?'

He grinned, liking her gentle barb. 'It does.'

'Aha,' she said, eyes sparkling with amusement, 'but the riddler has secrets, knowing just how far to turn each bottle – today left, tomorrow it might be turned right – all the time adjusting the angle so minutely that a novice can't spot that change. And while this action happens, what we call the must is eased towards the bottles' necks until we can be rid of it.'

'How many turns per bottle?'

'Thirty, perhaps.'

He whistled at how impressive that was.

'I learned this at my grandfather's knee. I used to turn the lower bottles until I grew tall enough to turn an entire pupitre.' She cut him a glance. 'Adeline was teasing, by the way. She has worked for Delancré since before the war. And she's even better than her husband was. She has more empathy for the young wine and its needs.'

'That sounds maternal,' he remarked as she led him deeper into the tunnels, past more workers, some of them children, which made him smile.

'Well, it's true,' she replied. 'I care for my wine as lovingly as a mother would her child. I have to. Look at all these people it must support.'

'How far do these cellars go?'

'They twist and turn for a while yet – not as extensive as Reims, of course, but they run the length and breadth of the property. Don't worry, Charlie, I have run around these caves since I was old enough to stand up. I could navigate them without a lantern and blindfolded. Come, I want to show you something.'

She led him into a very quiet part of the cellar network where horizontal bottles now sat at peace. It was silent, the only light coming from a lantern she picked up on their way.

'It feels monastic here,' he said.

Again she smiled. 'We are certainly all praying for a good year. Yes, these bottles are now resting. I have high hopes for this vintage.' She glanced his way and put the lantern down. 'Vintage is made only from the three important grapes that make up champagne. These are pinot noir, chardonnay and meunier.' She counted them off, lifting a finger for each as she did so; he understood she was impressing upon him the importance of those grapes. 'And all from the same year.'

'So, this is your best stuff?'

She frowned and he watched her run her fingertips over the seals in a gesture of affection. 'That could be a misconception. Younger champagne is full of its effervescence and fruit. It is delicious when made with care and the blend achieved with precision.

Vintage is enjoyed less for its spritz than for its complexity. The flavours exert themselves over time and if you can get it right, it can make exceptional drinking. But it takes a lot of time, a lot of storage, with potential problems —'

'War, for example.' He smiled sadly.

Sophie nodded. 'Yes, war and —'

She was not permitted to finish her thought. Charlie had pulled her towards him and swallowed her words with a kiss, but not one that lingered.

'I couldn't resist that,' he finally said, touching his forehead against hers. 'I've missed you.'

'Charlie . . .' she began.

He heard her hesitancy and felt instantly dismayed that he'd read her wrong or taken advantage of her kindness. 'Were you just being kind before?'

'I'm really not *that* kind. I don't make a habit of kissing every wounded soldier who crosses my path.'

'Have I overstepped?'

'Your face would be stinging if you had,' she replied with a soft smile he couldn't read. 'I think I'm the one who should be apologising.' He frowned, unsure – he didn't want to let go of her, but it no longer felt right to hold on to her in such a proprietorial manner. 'I took advantage of you.'

'Why do you say that?'

She gave a shrug. 'I think I'm feeling . . .' He watched her choose the right word carefully, her features falling into soft resignation as she found it. 'Vulnerable.' She touched his cheek. 'And you're the first man in a long time who has caught my attention in a way to make me forget myself. I never thought it possible . . . I mean, the thought of being with anyone but Jerome is . . .' She smiled. 'You're easy to fall for, Charlie.'

'But your defences are up now?'

She nodded with an even warmer smile. 'I have regained my wits,' she admitted. 'Reminded myself that my husband is missing, and only presumed dead. I am the one to blame. I should not have allowed my feelings to spill as they did.'

He fixed her with a harder gaze than he intended. 'So you admit to feeling something for me?'

She nodded, looking ashamed. 'And I feel guilty for it. I've suffered for days berating myself over being weak.'

'Or simply attracted as well as lonely, looking for affection?'

'All of those.' She sighed.

'Nice to know,' he said, hating how flippant he sounded.

'Charlie. Please understand that I can't,' she said, firm but with an appeal in her voice. 'Until I can be sure about Jerome's fate. I must remain faithful to the man I love, the man I married. It was a moment of madness and selfish desire.'

He lowered his head. 'Do you believe in your heart he's alive?'

'I'm frightened if he's not.'

'Frightened how? You've been years without him already, I —'

'It's his brother,' she blurted.

He narrowed his eyes. What an odd admission. 'What about his brother?'

She let out a low sigh, looked away and finally eased out of his encircling hands. 'Louis seems to believe he has a claim on me.'

'Pardon?' He was astonished by her remark. 'Why?'

She shrugged her slim shoulders, looking distressed. 'Louis feels a right because he saw me first.' She told him the story of that first meeting. 'But it was Jerome I fell in love with . . . almost the instant that he walked into the room. Cliché, no?'

He gave a sad shrug. 'Oh, I don't know, I think I felt the same about you, chattering away about opera and stroking my skin as you washed it.' He watched her blush and found her all the more desirable for it. 'And you mean this Louis hasn't forgiven you for falling for his brother?'

'No, it's not that, actually. I think if that were the case, I could almost feel a sympathy for him. Unrequited love is the worst sort of love, isn't it?'

'I suppose so.'

'Charlie . . .' she said, fixing him with a stare. 'It doesn't take much imagination to think on the women whose hearts you have broken, simply by your elusive manner.' She smiled. 'It's part of your charm but it would frustrate any woman in your life.'

He nodded, as if admitting the truth of this.

'No. Louis feels entitled.'

'Has this become a serious problem?'

'He is making his intentions clear to me. He believes with Jerome missing, certainly dead in his opinion, not only that he should but that it is right he step into Jerome's shoes. He utterly believes it is the correct action to take and this is all apparently linked up with the promise he gave his brother to take care of me.'

'Not marry you, though, surely!'

She lifted a shoulder in confusion. 'In his view, it is the next step. He's doing me a good deed and remaining true to his brother. While all it does is horrify me, it all makes neat and loyal sense in his mind.'

Charlie's expression darkened. 'And keeping assets tight, no doubt.'

She nodded, looking at him with certainty. 'No doubt,' she repeated. 'Louis is no farmer. He will not tend to vines – nor, I imagine, will he shoulder any workload of mine. No, Louis will reap the benefits of House Delancré and, under the guise of reasserting the family name of Méa, bring balance to our lives.' She shuddered and Charlie shook his head, not quite understanding what she meant. 'He wants to have children. He has insisted that it is part of the deal. He has thought it all through, it seems, and I am permitted to lead a wholly separate life – living apart in Épernay while he lives in Paris.'

'But you must bear him a child?' His voice was tight with disgust.

'Children,' she countered and cut him an anguished gaze. 'He's the antithesis of Jerome. I find it loathsome that he would press this upon me.'

'Bloody hell, Sophie. You don't have to succumb to that pressure. He doesn't wield any power. I look around me. You're a wealthy woman in your own right and bearer of the family name . . . is that not correct?'

She nodded, touching the dust on some aged bottles in the nearest pupitre.

'I don't understand,' he said, opening up his palm. 'Why does Louis have any say over your life?'

'Because he's helping me with the Red Cross. He's connected to all the right people that I can't reach.'

'Wait,' Charlie said, shaking his head. 'That's counterproductive. Why would he help you to find his brother if by what you're saying he wants his brother to remain missing, presumed dead?'

'I agree,' she said, making a face as if to say, *It's complicated.* 'We have an understanding. If he leaves no stone unturned and there's still no word of Jerome, then I must agree to wear his ring. Except it's not going to happen, Charlie. You see, he – like everyone else – believes Jerome is dead and so he's more than confident in reaching this bargain with me. Meanwhile, I will use all his contacts to prove him wrong.'

'And if you're wrong?'

'I will never marry Louis. I will never consent to what he wants.'

'But you will lead him on?'

She swallowed, horrified. 'I need his help. And it's not just to help me find more information about Jerome. He has contacts that might supply me with sugar.'

'Sugar?' He made the leap. 'I saw a few sacks in the sheds.'

'And that's all we have. It's not enough for this year's wine-making. And of all years I must make a champagne from the wedding vineyard's first harvest. Staying on good terms with Louis means I can get sugar.'

Charlie shook his head with exasperation. 'On good terms? It's bloody outrageous how he's cornering you into this!' he hurled helplessly at the walls. It echoed back at them. 'You deserve better than that.'

She smiled sadly, apparently unshocked by his curse. 'The cellars hear everything, store it all in their ancient memory. Thank you for summarising exactly how I feel.'

'Sophie, come on. You do not have to agree to this lunacy. What a creep he is.'

'I don't want Louis anywhere around me, but I need the assistance only he can provide, and he has this way of making everything he's proposing seem so reasonable.'

'An oily, creepy blackmailer, then.' Charlie paced and she let him do so in silence, her expression half amused, half sad. 'Tell me this – Louis aside, let's imagine you had never met Jerome. Could you love me?'

Charlie watched her weigh up whether to tell a fib just to make him feel better, but sensed it was only the truth she chose. 'If my situation were different, then I would be lying to you if I didn't admit that I already feel something dangerously close to love. When I married, I couldn't imagine myself ever having even the spark of interest for another man. Until a short time ago I believed myself wholly and utterly devoted to Jerome, or no man.'

'And now?'

'And now I'm appalled by how easily you moved beneath my defences; I wasn't ready for you, Charlie. I really didn't see this happening for me, and I'm unnerved. Yes, of course I could love you . . . and maybe what terrifies me most is that I might perhaps already be falling in love with you, so I have to be strong now. I have to stop this before it creates despair for you, for me and for Jerome if he is found.'

'Then tell the brother about me,' he replied. 'Throw him off the scent.'

'I can't risk that he will stop helping me to find Jerome,' she said evenly.

'Sophie, you lost him in 1915 and haven't heard anything in connection with him since, am I right?'

She nodded.

'This is brutal to say but knowing those battlefields of sucking mud, it's unlikely he will ever be found. I've fought there. Jerome is likely already buried there.'

'I know.'

'Do you, though? It's just a massive graveyard.'

'And still I hold out hope.'

'And still you kissed me,' he countered.

'I told you, it was a moment of —'

'No, Sophie, it wasn't. I was there. I don't believe you do anything you don't want to, including being blackmailed by Louis.' Surprise at his accusation flared in her gaze. 'You're allowing him to do this because it suits you for now to use him, but you should be careful with this man – he doesn't sound like someone who can be easily manipulated.' She nodded, more gravely this time, letting him know she agreed. 'And your kiss was not the kiss of a friend . . . or idle error. It was the kiss of a lover; it was deliberate, it had intensity, and you said more to me in that one kiss than dozens of women have said to me in a much longer time together.'

'Dozens?' she repeated.

He blinked with frustration, stepped closer and pulled her to him. 'Sophie, I've never wanted any woman like I want you. They've come and gone through my life like lovely fireworks that burn brightly and briefly. But you're like a scorch. You're the first to leave her mark. Now I'll fight for you, but you have to want it.'

He let go of her arm, could see she thought he was going to kiss her again after all that passion blazing in his voice, but he needed her to feel it again too. The news of the brother, yet another obstacle, felt like a dark blow.

Sophie looked back at him, clearly torn. At least her uncertain expression told him she was being honest with him and not just controlled.

'I do want it. I want you, Charlie, but I have to be sure about Jerome. I need proof. I'm pushing Louis to get me proof. If anyone can, he can.'

Charlie nodded unhappily. 'And what if he proves me right? Beware, Sophie, you may find yourself trapped by Louis's demands because you owe him.'

'Let me be clear. I have no intention of being his wife.'

'Leading him on is dangerous!' he said, frustratedly running his hand through his hair, which had flopped forward.

'I have no choice!' she said, flinging her arms wide. 'I'm trying to establish whether my husband is dead . . . so I can . . .'

'So that you can what?' he demanded. 'Tell me, Sophie.'

'Be with you, Charlie!' She walked away, looking angry with herself, with him, with the world. 'Until now I have searched for him because I had to know – I refused to take their vague label of "missing" as adequate – but now, suddenly, I have a new reason to know the truth.' She appeared anguished to admit this.

Charlie's fury dissipated as rapidly as a fire being doused with water.

Sophie sighed. 'Telephone connections have been repaired . . . I spoke to one of the senior army people I know in Reims.'

'Yes?' He wasn't sure he wanted to know what she had learned.

'The French can't reach anyone from your Brigade at the moment, he said. He asked me if, for the time being, you could remain here another few weeks.'

That surprised him. She could have easily off-loaded him. 'What did you say?'

'I told you him you were a dreadful nuisance. Always needing to be kissed and hugged.'

He turned on his heel to look at her and sighed out his relief when she laughed; he was helplessly compelled to join in. The sound bounced around the limestone walls and filled his heart with its echo. Laughter was the only tonic for the way they were both feeling. He needed to be genuinely heroic now and let her off the hook that he could see she was wriggling on. 'I know, needy soldiers are such a drudge.' He grinned for her. 'Sophie, I'm sorry.'

She met his gaze firmly. 'Don't be. You're right. I was there. I encouraged, I participated . . . I enjoyed it too and it meant something. However, while I am coming to terms with the notion that Jerome is dead, I'm not ready to fully let go and that's not fair to you, so I would rather not have us fall in love.'

'Too late for me, I'm afraid.' He could see how hard this was for her. 'Louis is more dangerous than you think.'

'I am *not* scared of Louis.'

'So, you wish me to stay?' He waited. 'You have to say it, Sophie, or I walk away today.'

'Yes, I'd like you to stay, because I'm weak and selfish.' She gave him a sad smile. 'You are welcome to remain here, especially as you are not yet healed enough to travel easily or return to any unit.'

'The British army will want to repatriate me to England.'

'Well, they have to find you first. Can we be friends without being lovers?'

'We can be close friends,' he said softly, as if making a promise, 'but Sophie . . .'

'I know, Charlie. Just give me some time.' She touched his face with gentle intimacy. He sighed, frustrated. 'Come on, walk the vineyards with me.'

He wanted to stay in the chalky cocoon of the tunnels forever: Sophie in his arms, the champagne praying for deliverance into a perfect vintage while the war raged above them. He was no longer desperate to die for his country, he was not prepared to kill another soul for his flag, and he never wanted to put on a laboratory coat again. He followed, helplessly feeling the loss of her touch as she bent to pick up the lantern and lead him back into the sunlight.

# 19

The vineyard she wanted to inspect was down past the back of the property. She and Charlie had to cross a stream that Sophie worried might bring back memories of his escape from the battlefield, although there was no sign that he'd been recalling trauma, and if he had, then he'd banished those thoughts quickly. She led him through villages so tiny that they were past them within minutes.

'Can you make it up the hill?' she asked, aware that he was breathing slightly harder than she was. She suspected there was pain in his body, given all of his injuries.

'That's what we call a hillock,' he said in English. 'That's no hill. I'll be fine.'

She went along with his bravado but took it slow, deliberately talking him through the ascent, which was causing him to huff and puff. She covered his heavy breathing with her words. 'Most of our chardonnay is grown just outside Chouilly at Côte des Blancs, which is on the other side,' she said, flinging her arm in the direction of the back of the house. She pointed as they crested the small hill. 'And Hautvillers, down there, is for pinot noir.'

He looked in the direction of her hand and saw rows of bright green leaves. The vines were in full roar, looking healthy and basking in the summer heat, developing quickly the size of their fruit and the sugars it contained. She turned to him and felt a curious hitch in her breath at his almost boyish expression of wonder. All that she'd sensed he held so tightly coiled within now seemed to Sophie to be unfurling of its own accord. She could feel its effect on Charlie as years of war and despair were sidelined momentarily as he gazed upon something that she too considered one of the most beautiful sights: a healthy vineyard.

'These grapes, Charlie, are vital to good champagne,' she said.

'You can't make champagne without them, I'm presuming?' he asked.

'How can I put this? Pinot noir is like your spine, Charlie. Without it you'd be confined to the ground; you wouldn't be able to stand up strongly.' She gestured again. 'It's the same for champagne. Without the backbone that this grape gives the wine, it would be weak, lack strength in its . . .' She rubbed her fingertips together, searching for the word.

'Body,' he said, understanding.

Her expression brightened, eyes widening. 'Ah, that's it. It would have no body. This is the most obvious of the three grapes in terms of what it brings to the wine. It doesn't, how you say . . . er, beat about?'

He grinned.

'It doesn't wait to evolve, it is what it is on your tongue, in your nose, around your mouth. Lively but not round . . . nothing to mellow with this one.'

'I see, but I'm guessing now that it's a game of balance because you mentioned chardonnay.'

'Yes . . . my favourite, in fact.' She hesitated as if she wanted to say more but continued quickly on to her new thought. 'Of course, then there's meunier . . . resistant to cold weather, brings a sort of vivacious quality, attacks fast, with a delicious fruitiness and flexibility to the flavour, if I can say that. It is supple and can round off the champagne in one's mouth in a way that pinot noir does not.'

'I love hearing you speak of your wine. I could sit down and listen to you talk about it all day,' he said, staring hard at her, his gaze not wavering. She felt it look inside her, searching for what she knew he needed. Could she give it to him? Was she going to capitulate to the enigmatic English captain? 'Don't stop,' he urged, perhaps sensing her arrival at a crossroads. 'Tell me about your chardonnay, your favourite.'

'Ah,' she said, sighing, happy to be distracted. 'Shall we?' She gestured for them to continue to the wedding vineyard. 'Chardonnay is considered king around these parts. We bow to His Majesty, and yet,' she said, waving a finger, 'for all the power we invest in him, it is he who yields the delicacy in our wine. It is chardonnay that brings all the, how you say, charisma. This vineyard was Jerome's wedding gift to me.'

He gave her the widest smile. 'Go on.'

'It is chardonnay who adds all the grace, the characteristic notes of flowers and citrus . . . even minerals.' She was lost to it now. 'Without chardonnay there is insufficient complexity, no difference from one champagne to another. Where it grows, this grape brings with it the flavours of that region. Slow in development – and because of this aspect it is the grape that can carry the wine through its years, because it is slow to age.'

They began to walk up a row.

'Sounds like your hero.' He smiled.

She nodded. 'My heroine, if I'm honest,' she admitted. 'Everyone around here thinks of him as king . . . emperor. But privately, she's my queen.' She grinned. 'I will tell you more about her sometime. You would make a good champenois, Charlie. You grasp that the grapes have personality, that it is a balancing act of

making all those characteristics shine at their best and not aggra-
vate each other. The strength of the pinot must be smoothed out by
meuniere, while the mellow nature of meuniere is enhanced by the
complexities that chardonnay layers in.'

He smiled. 'So . . . when the cork is lifted and the champagne
has the stage, they have to perform together – no matter their
differences – and in harmony for the greater applause,' he summa-
rised with a flourish.

She stared at him and wondered if he could see how much
delight his remark had provoked. 'It's a great pity the world cannot
behave like a good champagne. Harmony, peace, pleasure – every
grape giving its utmost, its very best to the champagne experience.'

'I don't know a great deal about wine. In England we drink
a lot of beer . . . and, to a lesser extent, spirits. Only the wealthy
drink wine.'

'But this is not wine, Charlie. This is champagne . . . a holy
trinity of grapes.'

'Sounds blasphemous,' he said, arching an eyebrow.

'No, not at all. I think what they can do together is a gift from
the Divine. I am a mere mortal doing —'

'Heaven's work,' he finished as they arrived beneath a tall oak
tree. 'Blimey, he's a giant.'

'It's always been here. It provides shade for the workers;
I climbed to its reaches as a child and I think my father did the
same, as his father did before him.'

'And your children will too,' Charlie assured her.

She gave a sad smile. 'Perhaps.'

Sophie found it hard to look at Charlie and not want to lean
forward and kiss those lips she found impossible not to enjoy
watching. Making her decision felt right, felt responsible, but
despite how correct it was, it made it no easier to resist this man.
Their meeting felt predestined; there was absolutely no reason why

a chemist from Liverpool should be falling in love with a champagne maker of Épernay and yet they had kissed and the inevitable tumble into something wonderful had begun. It had happened without any conscious or deliberate intention. There was no warning, which was why her mind was hurting. She'd thought herself a fortress against all romantic feeling, not just because she loved Jerome but because it hurt so much to lose him. That she could even touch and enjoy the kiss of another had come as such a shock that she was sure her decision was half as much shame as it was her love and loyalty to Jerome. She was relieved Charlie had accepted her position but she knew in her heart that she really should have sent him away because his patience would wane . . . and soon. She'd had the chance during that conversation with her army contact. He'd offered to get Charlie on his way to where a lot of the British were gathering; he didn't sound eager to take Charlie but the offer was there. She should have taken it. Her responsible side admonished her. *You cannot have it all ways, enjoying him at a respectable distance while still actually keeping him close.* Her selfish side won. *He needs to get stronger and then I'll let him return to England.*

Later, strolling back down to the roadway, their fingers entwined once and then let go. It seemed Charlie was wise enough to sense all her concerns and had no intention of compromising her standing in the community.

They had just about reached the top of the hill, which would once more give them a view back to the house across the small villages. Charlie was telling her a tall tale about the day he'd been called upon to help ease an extremely large lady out of a narrow stationery cupboard at school. He was exaggerating in his storytelling, of course, because he could see how amused she was, and it was obvious that he was going to exploit that laughter. She didn't mind at all – loving how entertaining he could be and how she hadn't thought he could possess such fun if she recalled the man who had woken up in the underground hospital.

'. . . and being only this tall, by now my face was wedged between Mrs Slocombe's left buttock and —'

'Ah, there you are, dear Sophie.' They stopped in their tracks, amusement trailing away like a wraith, as Louis Méa crested the hill. 'They told me I'd probably find you here. I thought that was your laugh. It's wonderful to hear.' His smiling gaze flicked between them, but Sophie, who knew this man much too well, could see the expression was pasted on for their benefit. 'And you are?' He directed this at Charlie.

'Louis, what a surprise.' She knew her voice was tight with guilt and he was too perceptive. She needed to be smarter in this moment than he took her for. 'Er, I'd like you to meet one of the brave Allied soldiers who is recuperating at my Épernay sanitorium.' Louis fixed Charlie with a gaze that, if she wasn't mistaken, was vaguely adversarial. 'This is Captain Charles Nash of the Leicesters. Captain Nash, this is my brother-in-law, Monsieur Louis Méa.'

'Ah,' Charlie said, cutting her a glance. 'The very man we were talking about just moments ago. Forgive me, I can't shake easily.' He gestured to the sling.

'Talking about me?'

'Yes, Madame Delancré was explaining that you are as committed to finding your brother as she is.'

'Indeed. That's a pretty scarf,' Louis noted.

'I'm tired of hospital bandages, sir,' Charlie said. 'I've decided to be more colourful in my recuperation.'

'How very flamboyant,' Louis said as Sophie sighed in private relief that he didn't recognise it. 'Your French is excellent, sir. I must congratulate you on being so bright of personality, with flushed cheeks and so much laughter that I could hear it from the other side of the hill.' He blinked with perplexed enquiry. 'Madame Delancré has this effect on all. They should bottle up her spirit as some sort of magical potion that brings every wounded soldier back to good health.'

'Louis.' She stepped up and kissed him on both plump cheeks. He would recognise the soft warning in her tone, even if Charlie wasn't familiar with it. 'This is the man that my cousin Gaston saved.'

'I owe him my life,' Charlie said.

Louis shrugged. 'I have heard about you, Captain, from the Commandant. From what I can tell, you saved yourself. It was a remarkable tale of your heroism.' All of this was said with a rip of sarcasm tearing through the otherwise sweetly veiled words. 'Gaston de Saint Just assured me that his men simply hauled you out of the water, but you'd navigated through enemy lines on your own while badly wounded. Quite the hero.' He gave Charlie the benefit of his podgy smile and Sophie felt a pit open in her stomach because she alone could tell that Louis had already decided that Charlie was a new obstacle. 'And all the girls love a hero, Captain Nash. Even Madame here has no defence.'

She felt Charlie demur. 'I don't know about that. I can't remember any of it.'

'Why were you looking for me, Louis?' Sophie enquired, her voice deliberately light but as pointed as an arrow. She hoped he could feel the poke of it. 'You didn't say you were coming.'

'Er, I can find my way back, Madame Delancré,' Charlie offered. 'Thank you for showing me the vineyard, and I'd like to help . . . whatever use you can find for a one-armed soldier, I'll do it.'

'Thank you. I'll think on your offer.'

Charlie gave a formal nod of thanks. He turned again to Méa. 'Goodbye, monsieur. I hope there is good news of your brother to come.'

Charlie departed down the hill towards the house and Sophie looked back at Louis.

'What on earth drags you up here, Louis?'

'You can't take your eyes off the captain.'

She cut him a look of disdain. 'No, Louis, I can't take my eyes off my vineyards right now . . . not if I want to have a harvest this year. Captain Nash accompanied me. I think the walk, the companionship, will help him to recuperate.'

'It would help any of us, Sophie.'

'And because of that notion you would begrudge him the time?'

He shook his head, embarrassed. 'No, but be careful.'

'Of what?'

'Of shaming your good name.'

She swung on him. 'Are you accusing me of something?'

'Not at all. I am simply cautioning you.'

'Meaning?'

Louis sighed. 'Do they all get turns wearing your scarf? Are they all at some time singled out for special attention, including the personally guided tour . . . or is the English captain somehow above all the other injured you care for?'

She had thought the scarf had slipped his notice as hers and she was reminded once again of his acuity. 'The scarf was merely convenient a week ago in the hospital. And yes, I find him to be good company.'

'A dog is good company. That man's in love with you.'

'Don't be ridiculous.' She stomped past him, hating that she might be so transparent to him.

'Am I being ridiculous? I'm simply protecting my —'

'Your what, Louis? I hope you weren't going to say "assets".'

He smiled unpleasantly. 'I was going to say I was simply protecting my brother's wife.'

She breathed out her anger. 'Your fears are unfounded.'

'Good, because I have some news.'

Sophie stopped walking and glared at him. 'What news?'

'From the Red Cross. It's why I'm here. They've found something.'

253

# 20

From a distance Épernay did not look touched by almost four years of hard warring that had been fought on its doorstep. The miracle was that Reims, for all its destruction – where no street had been left intact, its magnificent cathedral a broken giant, stooped and smashed – had held. The city had not capitulated throughout what felt to Charlie like the sounding of the seven trumpets, which had fascinated him at school, studying the Book of Revelations during religious instruction. The city's implacability and its ruin made Épernay appear like a scene from a holiday postcard. While eastern France exploded, burned, fell over, Épernay looked like a beautiful girl enjoying her first adult summer.

Charlie's romantic musings were arrested by the sight of soldiers marching along the road, reminding him that this region was not altogether untouched; it only appeared that way to the casual observer. Their combined heavy footfall and dark expressions spoke of the death they'd witnessed and the companions they'd lost. This region too had given up its sons to the bloodbath; from the women working the fields and those around Sophie's cellars and outbuildings, the war had taken husbands, sons, lovers as it had taken from every other woman around France and indeed beyond. They might also lift a cautionary finger and remind him that for all its delicious beauty, this region had lived under four years of constant fear of being overrun. Other areas of France had not spotted a German uniform – but that might be a churlish thought, given their men had still marched to war. He waited, holding back at the bottom of the hill to let the weary pass. Only a couple looked at him, their gazes cutting his way and then sliding off slowly. He couldn't tell if their looks were levelled with disgust or envy . . . perhaps both. He knew any one of those soldiers would swap with him in a heartbeat and he guessed that to them he must look quite the sight: half-dressed in his English soldier's uniform, the collar undone, and a silken paisley scarf holding his arm as a sling. Were they scorning him for not marching back into the fray, or wishing him luck for escaping the next battle? He raised a hand to acknowledge them but not one returned the gesture.

He arrived back at the house to find Gaston de Saint Just waiting in the vestibule. 'Commandant,' he said, nodding as Gaston stood, despicably smart, golden hair glinting along with his smile.

'You're looking brighter, Captain Nash.' Gaston gave him the full breadth of his smile. He was taller and broader than Charlie. He wore his uniform with pride, and he deserved to feel that pride, Charlie presumed, for this man was surely a heroic figure in the region.

'Thank you, sir.' They might be distinct armies, but military rank prevailed no matter which country one hailed from. Charlie knew to respect his superior. 'What news of the Brigade, sir?'

Gaston's glad expression dissolved to graveness.

'What is left of your Brigade is to the south of Épernay; they are mostly in the town of Étréchy. I have taken the liberty of informing them that you are here and recuperating from your wounds. It is not such a great distance if you wish to make contact – as I'm sure you do. I can assist with that.'

'That's kind, thank you. What about the Leicesters . . . is there any information about them specifically, sir?'

At this, Gaston's expression shifted to one of deeper sorrow. 'Your Tigers took a terrible beating, Captain. I'm sure you don't need me to tell you that, because you were there in the worst of it. It was nothing short of a slaughter.'

'How many?' Charlie asked, and the grit of despair crunched in his voice.

'All,' Gaston replied, clearly deciding not to step around the question. 'There is no easy way to give this news. Your battalion, as I understand it, is down to cadre strength.'

*Cadre.* Only its administrative people and perhaps some wounded. Charlie felt broken by the news, so much worse than he had imagined. He had to steady himself with his good hand gripping the banister.

'I'm sorry to be the messenger of this news.' Gaston waited, and when Charlie said no more, he continued. 'As I understand it from my enquiries, the regiment has been formally transferred to the 25th Division.'

'Any stragglers at all, sir?'

'Again, only as I understand it, Captain, any remaining soldiers, of whom there might have been just a handful left standing, were transferred to the 6th and 7th Battalions.'

'This means the Leicester Tigers no longer exist.' Charlie shook his head, and his companion remained silent out of respect. He let out a low breath before he looked back to Gaston. 'Thank you for finding all of that out, sir.'

Gaston nodded. 'I am full of regret for your men, Captain, but they were courageous to the end. I am sure the Tigers will re-emerge.'

Sophie and Louis arrived at this moment. Charlie thought she looked pinched and pale, but he was sure his own complexion was waxy to match. He watched her find a smile for Gaston, allowed him to greet her formally with kisses to each cheek. She glanced sideways at Charlie; he sensed a message in it, as Gaston greeted Louis with surprise.

'Yes, I made a trip down from Paris, as yesterday I received some news of Jerome.'

Charlie blinked, cut a glance back at Sophie, but she wasn't looking at anyone.

'News?' Gaston repeated, reaching for Sophie's arm.

She nodded. 'The French military believe they've found his tunic,' she admitted. 'No one's quite sure. It's filtering down from the army through all the various departments into the Red Cross, so we wait.'

'I am certain it is his,' Louis said.

Charlie could not measure an iota of sadness in his tone; if anything, he was matter-of-fact.

'I've waited this long,' Sophie said, sighing. 'I'll remain patient.' She dredged up a wan smile. 'Anyway, how come you're here without warning, Gaston?'

'I brought news for the captain,' he said, looking slightly awkward.

'A big news day,' Louis remarked. 'I hope there's something hot and decent to drink in the parlour. Good day, Captain Nash.' He nodded at him and turned to the commandant. 'Gaston, always a pleasure. Come, my dear,' he said to Sophie, making sure Charlie saw the squeeze he gave her elbow. 'Let's leave the soldiers to their soldiering, shall we?'

'What news?' she asked, looking between them, ignoring Louis. He sighed and remained at her side.

'About the captain's regiment,' Gaston replied. 'I thought he might be eager to be done with France.'

'Actually, I'm not ready to leave France, sir,' Charlie admitted.

The commandant gave a confused smile this time. 'You've done your bit, Captain. No one should ask any more of you. And let's be practical now, you cannot be of any further use to your country, or indeed France, in your state.'

'I wasn't referring to being useful to my country. I wasn't even referring to the war. In this regard I do remain useless, sir.'

'Then you should go, Captain,' Louis said, deciding to re-enter the conversation.

Charlie turned and directed his next remark solely at Louis. He hadn't realised he was going to step so purposefully in front of Sophie, like a chivalrous knight, but he had no intention of letting the domineering, almost effeminate Louis step into his brother's boots. In the few heartbeats that had passed, he made the decision that he would prefer Jerome to return and scoop her up into his embrace than allow the coercive, underhanded Louis to have his way. It seemed he'd left one war to step into another. 'I am not, however, useless to Madame.'

And there it flashed. It wasn't hatred; it wasn't even jealousy. Far more complex, Charlie grasped: this was a man used to getting what he wanted, and he felt threatened by Charlie's presence. Charlie was an outsider, upsetting the order of life. He could see all of this in the barely detectable sneer that the Frenchman was nonetheless unable to disguise.

'What do you mean?' Gaston asked, frowning, looking towards Sophie for guidance but Charlie replied.

'I believe I can be of service to Madame Delancré, sir.' He glanced her way and she looked down, hiding a sly smile. 'I can —'

'Madame Delancré has no need of a crippled English soldier in her life, Captain Nash, if you'll forgive my insensitivity,' Louis interjected.

'I can,' Charlie said evenly.

'Pardon me?'

'Forgive your insensitivity.'

Louis bristled as Gaston straightened to his full height, seeming to have taken a measure of the undercurrent. 'Captain, I shall leave this decision to you although I would be glad to take you to where the British have gathered in the region.'

The more senior man's perception of what was right for Charlie's next move was wholly correct. It could be considered desertion if he didn't acquiesce and join his own brigade, regiment . . . whatever it was that was gathering south of Épernay. Even if he did want to help Sophie, army protocol came first.

'Oh, I might help out, Gaston,' Louis said in his most condescending tone. 'I will more than happily take the good captain all the way to Étréchy, spare you the trouble and him having to change transport. I have my car.'

Gaston glanced at Sophie, and then slid a look Charlie's way, as though taking a measure, before removing a map from his pocket and unfolding it on a nearby table. Louis took keen interest, poring over the map. 'This is where you'd be going,' Gaston gestured. Charlie glanced at where Épernay was and where the commandant's clean fingernail pointed. 'Just south here.'

'This all seems rather fast,' Sophie remarked, looking between the men. 'The captain is really not healed sufficiently.'

Charlie addressed the commandant. 'Did they say what was going to happen with me?'

Gaston shrugged. 'No, but I suspect you'll be going home to England.'

'Tea at four with . . . what do you call those things?' Louis searched for the right words. Charlie frowned, feigning interest. 'Ah yes, with cream and scones.'

'Scones,' Charlie corrected him, explaining that the word rhymed with *shone* not *tone*. Louis blinked with irritation, which absently pleased Charlie, given the Frenchman had aimed to insult him. He continued, still directing his attention at the commandant. 'It's really not that far away from here, is it? I can easily get to this place, Étréchy?'

Gaston blew out a breath as if to say the distance was neither here nor there and his remark purely academic. 'Not too far, no.'

'Then I suggest the captain remains here to fully recuperate; even I can get him to Étréchy within an hour or so,' Sophie remarked.

'It's really not a problem,' Louis said offhandedly. 'I will take him. Go pack, Captain Nash,' he urged.

She blinked with annoyance. 'Charlie, wait, please. Gaston, while I realise you've got infinitely more influence, I've already been assured that no one can get in touch with the British at Étréchy until the lines of communication are properly reopened.'

Charlie looked at the commandant. 'Forgive me, sir, I presumed you had spoken directly with the British army and received word back about me?'

'Actually, no,' Gaston qualified. 'I sent the message that we have you.' He shrugged. 'I'm trying to help out.' He looked between Sophie and Charlie as though he was sorry that he took so long to catch on to their reluctance.

'So they do not actually know you're bringing me, sir?'

The commandant shook his golden head. 'They may do if they've paid attention to that message but in the scheme of their problems, you are not a priority, no.'

'Captain,' Louis interjected, frowning. 'I imagine you would want to return to your regiment as soon as possible. We can all see that the commandant is simply expediting normal procedure.' The insinuation of malingering was there.

Charlie refused the bait. 'But my regiment doesn't exist, Monsieur Méa, and I suspect I could be more of a problem just turning up.'

Sophie gave a sigh of exasperation. 'Gaston, I doubt very much that the captain in his present state is considered valuable. More of a burden, wouldn't you say?' She glanced at Charlie. 'I mean no offence.'

He shook his head to let her know that he had not taken any.

'What do you mean, Sophie?' Louis asked, as though his opinion mattered in this discussion.

She kept her voice light. 'I mean that Captain Nash was brought here to recuperate. It's obvious he cannot be returned to active duty and that he will likely be repatriated to England.'

'So?' Louis exaggerated how perplexed he felt by her words. 'Isn't that what we're going to achieve?'

'No, I doubt that. The English may not find it very helpful for a civilian to deliver to them someone who is obviously just another problem to be dealt with. Captain Nash is not a problem here. In fact, I find him rather helpful.' Gaston suppressed a smile but she continued, ignoring the bristling Louis. 'He must remain until he's fit to travel, when that arm is slightly stronger, and then – even through my network – I can ensure through his line of command that he is reunited with the British army. I'm guessing, Gaston, they really don't want the injured at Étréchy if they're taking stock and reorganising regiments?' She didn't wait for his answer, Charlie noted. 'I could be wrong, of course, but it strikes me they would far prefer us to deliver someone such as the captain directly to the docks where he can be directly transported home across the Channel. You agree, surely?'

Charlie wanted to murmur *bravo* but held his tongue and waited, trying not to look overly interested in the decision.

'Yes, I think you could put it that way . . .' Gaston agreed carefully.

'I don't know how else to put it,' she said in such a friendly way that Charlie wanted to clap.

Instead he spoke to stop himself appearing smug. 'That probably is wiser than going via Étréchy.' He nodded, as if this were a decision they were making together. 'And I'm not helpless. I'm sure I can get a message to my division along those lines.'

He glanced at Louis and could swear he was holding the sly gaze of a crocodile: patient, sinister, ancient.

Sophie smiled briskly. 'And what is happening with your regiment, Gaston?' It was said as if the matter were settled. All of Sophie's side of the conversation had been spoken in a gentle but straightforward way. She was quite the diplomat, Charlie decided, and yet had a spine of steel. *That's what war does to the survivors,* he thought.

'Our boys are being moved out,' Gaston replied.

'Then I hope you'll stay for dinner before you leave with them?'

He nodded in pleased agreement.

'Louis, let me see you to your car. I imagine you are keen to find out more on that other business we discussed regarding Jerome.'

Her brother-in-law's gaze turned narrow. 'Very well – if the help is not needed here, I shall be on my way,' he said, lifting a shoulder in a casual shrug that Charlie felt was anything but. 'Doesn't the captain tie up one of your precious beds?'

For one alarming moment Charlie wondered – hoped – Sophie would say: *No, because he will be sharing mine.* Instead she beamed a smile at her brother-in-law. 'No, he's moving down to the sheds today. You didn't give me a chance to explain. Our guest, whom you may not realise is a chemist, has some clever ideas on how to improve this year's vintage, haven't you, Captain Nash?'

Charlie swallowed, tried not to bluster in surprise at the fib, and kept his features schooled as he smiled back. 'Well,' he began and then smiled, as if embarrassed to admit to his *clever ideas,* 'I'm pleased by your faith in me, Madame.'

Méa turned to him. He didn't look convinced. 'And you can assist with champagne?'

'Er, yes, I was going to brief Madame Delancré on those ideas this week. They're just some early thoughts that arose as she was showing me around today. I think I can help House Delancré with its production, if I dare be so bold?' Where was he getting this from? Even Sophie looked impressed, and she'd set the lie in motion. He was sure she wanted to laugh. He thought he might too if this continued.

'I see. And this is because you're a chemist when you're not a captain of the British army?'

'That's right. We chemists have our uses.'

'Beyond designing poison gas, you mean?'

Gaston raised his eyebrows at the barb, and Sophie gave a sound of disgust. 'Really, Louis, is that necessary, given what happened to your own brother?'

'It's because of people like this and that German Haber fellow that killing gas exists.'

'Captain Nash joined the army to escape being coerced into researching poison gas,' she said, sounding astonished at Louis's attack.

'Well, you seem to know a lot about his life and work, my dear, but I fail to see how an English soldier who used to work in a laboratory – and has probably never tasted champagne – can know that much about yours. It's highly specialised.'

She'd fought for him, so now Charlie would fight for her against this bully. 'I won't bore you with my ideas, Monsieur, but one is how to assist the fermentation process in its balance.' He had not thought about this with any sincerity but now that he'd aired the notion, he realised maybe innovations had been quietly developing in the back of his mind. Ideas rarely announced themselves loudly; they gathered momentum like a steam train gradually hits its full power. He was going to mention this metaphor but thought better of it. Instead, he added: 'I really don't know how to thank you for all your help, Commandant, not the least of which was saving my life, but I will take all the necessary steps – and responsibility – to get myself back to my own army, sir. As Madame suggests, they likely will insist, for expedience, that I travel straight to the coast from here, rather than going via Étréchy. I will remember you to our general for your men's generosity and bravery, Commandant de Saint Just.' He saluted.

'You're welcome, Captain.' He responded with a salute of his own.

'With your permission, I think I'll start moving my gear into the sheds, Madame Delancré.'

'The others will show you where,' she said, deliberately casually. 'Gaston, would you care to refresh yourself?'

He nodded, smiled and fell in alongside Nash. Before they peeled off in different directions they heard Sophie say: 'I'll walk you out, Louis.'

---

Outside, following him down the steps to where a car and driver awaited him, Sophie knew she needed to appease Louis.

He punctured her thoughts by suddenly swivelling around. 'Did you deliberately wish to humiliate me back there?'

'Heavens, no,' she said, feigning innocence and astonishment. 'I thought you were kind to offer to drive the captain to Étréchy.'

'You didn't sound it, my dear. Truth is, you sounded rather subversive.'

'Louis, the plan made no sense. Besides, he really does have some cunning ideas that can help my operation.'

'The Americans have entered the war, Sophie. You won't have him long.'

'I doubt the Germans see it that way.'

'They will. Their push for Paris has sputtered to a halt, especially because of what has happened here recently.'

'Well, when the guns finally stop, I'll believe the war is over.'

He blinked, irritated by what he presumably considered her indifference. 'We had a bargain.'

'I would call it a loose understanding,' she said, 'but nothing is proven.' Sophie knew she was walking a tightrope.

'You asked for something that proves he's gone. I think this comes as close as we possibly can. I had wished to shield you from this information but let me give it all to you, Sophie, so you're in no doubt about what my brother succumbed to. I was told this by the man from the Red Cross – a doctor. The gas attacks the respiratory system. It is our understanding that many of the soldiers attacked by the gas claw at their throats, and some pull off their clothes in an effort to breathe.' He gave a small cough. 'Forgive me for that vivid description. But this is likely why there is only his tunic.'

She refused to be baited, knowing he was being deliberately cruel. 'And where is Jerome, do you think?' she asked evenly.

'I cannot say accurately but the collective opinion is that Jerome is buried in the mud of Ypres along with thousands of his compatriots.'

Even though this echoed Charlie's counsel, Sophie refused to crumple, astonishing herself with her composure. 'So we shall never fully know?'

He cleared this throat. 'In terms of his remains? No, not unless we start digging up kilometres of mud and are ready for the tens of thousands buried with him.'

'I need more, Louis.' She tried to sound apologetic.

'Be careful, Sophie.'

'With what?'

'You know very well. He's dangerous ground for you.'

'Louis, you're not making sense,' she said, smiling and leading him to his waiting subordinate, who saluted at his approach.

'And you're being deliberately obtuse.'

'Am I?'

He held her with his gaze. 'I can see what is occurring.'

'Then I am blind, because I cannot.'

He took a step closer, waving away his driver. 'He's in love with you. That man has no place in your life, no place here . . . no place in the hearts of the people of Épernay. If you allow this to go further, you will break their hearts.'

'That's rather boorish of you, Louis. I think the folk of Épernay are grateful to all the Allies.'

He squeezed her arm. 'Don't insult me.'

She shook off his hand, careful not to display rancour, even though her following words cut with a keen edge. 'And don't lecture me or presume upon me. I will run my life as I choose and as *my* conscience and instincts alone will guide me. And please do not forget I live alone as a widow and answer to no man.'

'And don't you forget our agreement. As we speak, both the French army and the Red Cross are finding out more about the uniform. I feel confident I shall have the proof you demand that my brother is dead, although it will be up to the courts to confirm that. I might add, I can get you the sugar you need. It's ready and waiting for transport to Épernay.'

It landed precisely as he'd intended: like a blade cutting into her flesh to where it could inflict the most damage. 'Enjoy the summer and the harvest without threat. But if you decide you do want to make champagne, you know how to reach me. But it's going to cost you and you know what my price is. Farewell, Sophie.' He kissed her hand rather than her cheeks. She wiped the back of her hand as soon as he turned away.

Louis clambered into the car and he didn't look back as it turned the corner and left the avenue.

It was summertime but Sophie had never felt colder.

# 21

SWITZERLAND

*June 1918*

Taking a train bound for the border was the most exhilarating experience since Sophie had said yes to marrying him. What a different lifetime that was. Memories were returning to Jerome like the Paris flood that had brought her into his life. Each recollection, no matter how small, was a gift. He could remember his vineyards – down to the very detail of how the soil smelled in any season. He could taste his grapes, pick out the flavours of the terroir in their juices. He could remember the summer sky over Avize, but most of all the sight of that summer sun throwing glints of gold off the hair of the most beautiful woman in his world, and what her skin tasted like when he kissed it as they made love. Sophie Delancré. He could hear her voice once again in his mind; he recalled her touch, her lips. He could bring together a perfect image of her face, which had eluded him throughout his incarceration.

What had been happening to Sophie while his mind was imprisoned by amnesia? If the poison gas was going to take his life soon – if he was to succumb to the lung scarring that others had – he needed to see her once more, kiss her once more, lie with her one final time. He had to hold her close and explain that he never meant her to be hurt by this cruel absence. He wanted her to know that although he'd gone off to war to fight for her, he'd been fighting his way back to her ever since . . . she just didn't know it. Jerome pulled the window down to breathe out his fury at being lost for so long, walking around as someone else. He had pleaded with everyone in authority at the prison before departing for Switzerland, but his pleas had fallen on deaf ears; no one cared that he was not the man stated on the paperwork.

'Prove it!' one of the most senior prison administrators had scoffed. He'd tapped a file. 'You yourself said you were Jacques Bouchon. Be careful you are not court-martialled for lying if you are this Jerome Méa.' He sneered at him. 'You can do what you want when you're in Switzerland, but you leave here as Jacques Bouchon, which is how you arrived. All the paperwork is done.'

'My wife, my family have no —'

'Please – stop trying to make me care. I don't. Take him away,' he said, already moving from behind his desk to pour himself a cool drink from the jug on the sideboard. 'And get me a better fan!' he snapped at his aide, pointing at one that wheezed from the corner of his room, Jerome already forgotten.

'Make your request to your humanitarian jailers,' one of the guards jeered as he was led off to the van, still helplessly arguing for someone to telephone Paris.

So now here he was, standing in the train's corridor, where another soldier was smoking. They'd exchanged the briefest of salutations and then fallen quiet; he suspected the man was equally disbelieving to be on this train. He doubted his companion was on the tuberculosis list – more like shellshock, given the way he paced, the restless movement of his gaze, and the way he seemed to startle at any noise. Jerome wasn't interested in making a new friend or explaining his war, so he turned away and allowed the warm summer air to force his eyes closed and rush through his hair, as he absorbed the notion that he was free in spirit, if not officially. He'd been briefed that the Swiss military would be taking charge of him but to be assured that he was still considered a prisoner of Germany.

'On paper only,' the gentleman recording his details had said, winking.

The man was not in any position of authority, Jerome gauged, so he didn't waste his breath claiming his real identity. The problem was proving it – he knew that now – so he'd need to think on that before he reached Lausanne and people who might be able to help. How on earth to prove he was a man who had gone missing in April 1915? He had no identification papers as Jerome Méa. He didn't even have his uniform tunic to confirm his status, his division . . . he had only his returning memory to convince someone in authority that he was not this fellow whose name he had been labelled with for years through misadventure.

'So I won't be sent back?'

The man had smiled kindly. 'Certainly not. That is the last you'll see of Germany, Lieutenant Bouchon.'

Which was the single reason that Jerome was privately smiling with a mixture of relief and a genuine sense of freedom.

'You've done your country proud, Lieutenant. Switzerland is glad to grant you her safety.'

He was blessed. He reassured himself that from Switzerland he would get help to contact Sophie. So many lost years. She would be frantic; knowing his Sophie, she would have tried everything within her power to find news of him. But she would have drawn blanks everywhere because Jerome Méa had disappeared somewhere between Ypres and Munich: lost in his mind, lost to his army, lost to France.

And now a new enemy invaded his thoughts, just as he was savouring the notion of starting life again: had his beautiful wife beaten him to it? In her ignorance had she accepted his loss, put away her grief and accepted a new suitor? She might already be remarried; it had been more than three years and no doubt all the authorities had impressed upon her that Jerome Méa was dead. Even if she hadn't taken the step of remarriage, had she discovered a new love? It hurt him like a fresh wound to think it but he couldn't blame her if she had. Instead, he would pray that no one had discovered her. Louis wouldn't let it happen, he reassured himself – his brother would not have given up hope of Jerome being found even if there was no confirmation of death. He would keep Sophie's hopes alive too.

Feeling better for this reassurance, Jerome opened his eyes and gazed upon the scenery. What he noticed most was how green it was. Such lushness had been missing in his life for so long he'd forgotten how uplifting a wildflower meadow with drifts of happy blooms could be. Such a simple sight. He'd taken it for granted all of his life. Now it was as if he'd been granted a glimpse of heaven.

The steam train had left Konstanz in southern Germany, a city that had grown up around its lake, close to the Swiss border. He'd lost count of how many hours he'd been on trains since he began his journey from the castle in Heidelberg; they'd changed at various stations, none whose names he recalled, but always connecting with longer trains carrying fortunate prisoners like him. He knew he'd been following the Rhine River Valley south. At one point he could swear he heard in the far distance the familiar sounds of trench warfare, bullets and bombs, but that too had disappeared – as had Germany, to his gratitude. When the train stopped at Montreux it was greeted by a horde of smiling Swiss and a band of musicians. Cheering people lined the tracks as the train moved on to an alpine village where many were offloaded. He and his fellow soldiers were astonished by the rousing welcome. He hoped the crowds would forgive their slack looks of shock.

When the steam train finally hauled into Lausanne, women

threw flowers on the tracks and scattered them on the platform in welcome. A choir of children sang and the men, standing back, had casually assembled a guard of honour to applaud and guide the prisoners as they made their way off the train. One kind soul gave Jerome a patch to cover his left eye, which stared into the distance, milky and blind. Miraculously, a French tunic was given to him and the sleeve on the side of his missing arm, from the elbow down, was pinned neatly back, as another kind Swiss helped him to shrug into it. His limp was pronounced but not troublesome and he politely declined the use of a crutch.

Jerome paused on the platform, feeling to all intents as a returning hero, and yet these were not his compatriots. There were thousands of them; their joyful noise felt solid, as though he could be lifted up on it and carried triumphant through the streets. Some of his fellow soldiers were openly weeping; other had expressions of awe. One fellow stumbled against him as if swooning.

'We've left 'ell and found 'eaven,' the man exclaimed as Jerome struggled to steady him, nearly losing his own footing.

Jerome could only nod, too choked up to speak.

Guided by more smiling Swiss, who were obviously part of the official humanitarian team, and escorted by military personnel, the soldiers headed for a new life in Lausanne were finally ticked off and transported to their separate accommodations. Jerome found himself staying in a swish hotel not far from Lake Geneva. His room was tiny, up in the gods of the building. It was his, no one sharing with him, which was the final surprise. It had been so long since he'd had space to himself that he had forgotten what it was like to have privacy.

'I'm sorry, Lieutenant,' his escort said in flawless French. 'There are no notes that tell us of your injured leg, or we would have made better arrangements for your accommodation. I will certainly make sure a walking stick is made available.'

He looked at the man who had helped him make it this far with an expression of surprise. 'Thank you for the stick but please, no apology. I don't think you can imagine what this feels like. And I am fine – I expect the stairs are good for me. I can't thank you all enough for this generosity.'

'We are glad to help in any way we can.'

'But you have food shortages too, surely?'

The man nodded. 'Even so, it is the only way we can make a contribution. We were shocked four years ago when neutral Belgium was invaded and we have been offering humanitarian aid since 1916. I wish we could have received you sooner.'

Jerome wanted to shake his head at the graciousness of this man, who was obviously emblematic of his people. A coughing fit caught both of them unawares and the man watched with sympathy as Jerome doubled up and struggled through the attack, gasping for air as the spasm wracked his body. He wheezed to stillness and gave a wan but apologetic smile. 'And all of this is truly for me? I have to admit, I'm not used to having my own space.'

The man shrugged kindly. 'There is no tourism in Switzerland, Lieutenant. No one takes holidays here any more – the hotels in the Alps are only too happy to fill their rooms with internees. And this hotel has been used to having German and British travellers in particular, so you can imagine it is more than glad to have people staying again.' He cleared his throat. 'Er, a few formalities to get through, Lieutenant. Um, you understand that while you are a guest here, you are also considered by the Germans to be their prisoner and so we have agreed to keep a certain level of discipline.'

Jerome nodded. This room alone felt like freedom. 'I have no problem with that. What about moving around the town?'

'Roam freely, Lieutenant Bouchon, but do not go beyond its outskirts. You understand our relationship is based on trust, and while we do not need to be made aware of your every movement, we are relying on the internees to observe the rules so that we can continue to offer internment to the sick and injured prisoners without complaint or interference from Germany.'

'I have no intention of breaking any rules.'

'Thank you, Lieutenant. If you would read and sign that understanding right here,' he said, pointing to a dotted line on a form, and Jerome saw his alter ego's name.

'I have something important to ask.'

'Yes? How can I help?'

He pointed. 'It's just that . . . I am not this man.'

His companion looked bewildered. 'I don't understand.'

'I know. It is complicated. But I am not Lieutenant Jacques Bouchon.'

The man blinked. 'But you've been answering to that name?'

'I have. As I say, it's complicated.'

The man snapped his file closed. 'Oh, this is most unusual and troubling. Who are you, sir?'

'I am Lieutenant Jerome Méa.' He reeled off his company and division but knew the man was no longer paying attention. 'Perhaps we need to take this to someone in command?'

'Yes, yes . . . we most certainly do. Oh dear, this is perplexing. This, I suspect, will take some time, Lieutenant. I have no idea of the protocol. How has this come about?' Before Jerome could answer he held up a warding hand. 'Actually, it is best you don't explain to me for I will surely confuse others, and it is right that they should hear it from you. Can you leave this with me for now?'

'Of course. I'm sorry, I didn't mean to upset —'

'No, please. It's just that we can usually count on German record-taking and we pride ourselves on keeping strict, accurate files.'

'This is no one's fault. It is a misunderstanding that dates back several years. I will explain it all when you can find the right person for me to speak to.' Implicit in his words was the recommendation that neither of them allow a chain of different people to carry this story forward, as information had a way of being changed with each telling. 'I am patient, sir,' Jerome assured. 'And I am very grateful for everyone's help and patience with me.'

'I was going to mention that we can try to contact family for all our internees, but in this case it would not be prudent for me to be contacting family members of a surname that does not match your records. I'm afraid we would not permit telephone calls either, not that the telephone exchanges are particularly reliable in France right now. But I hope you understand our predicament?'

'I've waited this long, what's a few more days?' Jerome offered as graciously as he could manage. He didn't want to let on how his heart felt like it was trying to break free of the cage it had been in. He needed to reach Sophie.

His companion still looked mortified. 'My apologies.'

'Please, don't apologise. You've all been so kind . . . none of us are used to soft living, soft voices, soft care.'

'You are welcome. I'll leave you settle in. Sir, for now we will have to refer to you as Lieutenant, er, Bouchon, until we receive formal confirmation.'

Jerome felt like crying but he gave a crooked smile. 'I do understand.'

'Thank you, sir. The evening meal is served from six, breakfast from six in the morning.' He tried a smile and looked relieved that he could. 'You'll get used to the routine. There is a small folder on your bed with all the details relating to your confinement and the rules we must adhere to.' Jerome nodded. 'I'll let you rest, sir. There is always someone at reception should you need anything.'

'I don't know how to show my thanks.'

The man smiled. 'No need. You will likely begin doctors'

appointments and treatment the day after tomorrow. We are giving everyone more than twenty-four hours just to settle in.'

His escort departed, closing the door with a gentle click. No more clanging doors or studded boots of jailers. Dinner served at six? He wondered if there was a formal suit awaiting him in the tiny wardrobe. He would laugh if the situation weren't so moving. He wished all the men he'd become close to at the prison could share in his good fortune. It seemed unfair that one had to be desperately ill or injured to win this reprieve, but he couldn't be more grateful. Maybe his last few months of life would be pleasant enough and allow his mind to fill with memories of Sophie and the life stolen from them both.

'So come on then, Death,' he murmured. 'You've let me glimpse heaven. Don't find me before I can find Sophie again.'

# 22

Charlie was back in his sling, using the brace at night to keep his arm and wrist in the right position for healing. It had been weeks since the confrontation with Louis Méa and Sophie had been absent for all of it; the news of the discovery of her husband's uniform was surely the cause. He had become resigned to their separation, giving her time to sort out her thoughts and loyalties.

Being without close contact, without watching her moving, hearing the voice he loved and catching a glimpse of the smile that could undo him, had given him valuable thinking time. That he loved Sophie was not in question. It was whether she had fallen entirely in love with him . . . and could ever love him enough to let go of Jerome. Jerome was like a wraith that threaded his way around them and now he was back, larger than life even, with the finding of that tunic. Charlie's instincts told him that Sophie was no closer to finding Jerome than she had been before the tunic was found, but he suspected that Jerome's ghost was now less invisible, more solid. He felt a keen sympathy for her – it must seem like that ghost had watched them kiss, watched every glance between them, each time their fingers had curled and uncurled around each other's hands. Jerome was there: in her thoughts, in her heart . . . in her bed, which is where he wanted to be. He wanted Jerome to be dead as much as Louis clearly did but he would accept Jerome alive and her happiness if it meant getting rid of the odious Louis from her life.

Already after three weeks of hard work in the vineyards, doing the best he could with the one arm that obeyed his commands, he was feeling stronger and indeed brighter about rejoining the army and following whatever protocol it required of him. To all intents the war was over but the Germans weren't fully convinced, and until they were, Europe remained locked in battle and constant vigilance.

When not working he used the quiet time to get to know the property better, walking the vineyards and chatting to the workers who didn't seem suspicious of his questions. He'd peeped into all the sheds and tiptoed through the tunnels, beginning to gently test his strength by clasping a lemon. He didn't have the strength to squeeze it yet but just being able to cup it in his palm meant that all the right bits were working. He enjoyed helping the women with the riddling – something he'd learned how to do quickly one-handed – and teaching his two little friends how to play jacks with pebbles. And then there had been that morning of excitement when Clemence picked up the stones and placed them in his hand and he felt the tips of her fingers against his skin. For a man who believed his hand to be dead to sensation, it had the effect of someone emerging from the shade of a forest into warm direct sunlight.

He had closed his eyes momentarily to savour it, to be sure he wasn't imagining it. It was fleeting, replaced now with a vague tingling in his palm. His fingers still felt numb but there was defi-nitely a strange stirring as though nerves were beginning to reawaken. Could it be happening?

There was hope, suddenly.

There was a future . . . as a whole man. It was a start. Something to build on. A life to believe in.

He left his small friends playing their new game and wandered down into the tunnels to be alone with these thoughts of an actual future, albeit without Sophie, but a future nonetheless. He wanted to think about what his next move might be. Down here in the cellars it felt like a different world to the trenches they had been forced to live in on the front line and yet it was still cave-dwelling. Down here in the darkness it felt like a womb, where life was safe and it never changed.

He strolled past a lit cavern where men were pouring water over barrels and moved closer to watch, his expression inquisitive. The men were used to seeing him around the property; many had begun to raise their hands in a wave to him. He enjoyed the pleasure of doing the same, as though acknowledging friends.

One removed the cigarette hanging from the corner of his lip. 'A precaution, Captain,' he answered the unasked question, then shrugged as if to say, *Who is to say if it might work?*

'Against what?'

'Madame is a savant in her sensitivity to temperature change. She feels it is slightly warmer than we want.'

'Fermentation is going faster than you prefer?'

'Than Madame prefers,' Étienne qualified with a grin from an unshaven, deeply lined face. Charlie figured the older man *preferred* just as much as Madame. He surely had many years of experience. 'We want the fermentation to go slow and steady so the champagne can develop its flavours. I fear we didn't put these barrels deep enough.'

Charlie nodded, pleased to learn yet another new fact about the making of champagne. He had begun to believe it was nothing to do with chemistry, although chemistry was its foundation. No, this was an art like any other; just like painting, storytelling, writing poetry, it required emotion. Chemistry removed all emotion.

'Have you always worked here?' he asked.

'I worked with Madame's father. As a four-year-old I used to run messages for her grandfather.' The older man nodded, reminiscing. 'My father worked for House Delancré.'

Charlie gave a low whistle. 'The history of people alone in this firm is incredible.'

Étienne chuckled. 'Just us old-timers now. All our sons are fighting or . . .'

Charlie watched him struggle. He stepped closer. 'I'm sorry.'

'Both sons dead. No one to continue the family name in this business. One died before he could marry, the other before he could make his wife pregnant. They were both Delancré men too.'

'Any other grandchildren?' he dared to ask.

The man nodded. 'My daughter has given me two. My granddaughter is a joy. I hope this war ends before it can claim my grandson to its armies. He too is Étienne.'

Charlie gave him a crooked smile. 'Ask your daughter to let him keep your family name as part of his.'

The older man stared at him, his large, gnarled hands clutching the edge of the oak barrel, and considered this. He looked away and stroked the curve of the wood, darkened over years of use. 'I am in here,' he murmured. 'There's a part of all of us in this wine. A little bit of each of our souls flavours the new year's champagne.'

Charlie loved what the old man was saying; it spoke to his heart about everything he had begun to think was important in life. Suddenly material needs were irrelevant; he'd lived four years without anything more precious than a weapon with which to kill others. He didn't want one ever again in his possession, but it had taught him how few elements of his earlier life mattered any more. Promotion, status, reputation, earning capacity, the dream of owning a car, buying some bricks and mortar he could call his own: it all seemed worthless in the face of what he'd experienced. None of it could have helped him on the battlefield. War, certainly in the trenches, made all men equal – reduced each one to a finger on a trigger.

Emotion mattered, though, in the trenches. It was what drove them, kept them strong. Love mattered too: for each other, for those back home, for the country they defended.

But this . . . this spiritual connection that Étienne spoke of and he suspected Sophie shared – that too was something worth fighting for it. It spoke of the way of life of a region and its people, of ancestry over generations, of the future; it attested to achievement in striving to be better than previous years – not for payment or status but simply for satisfaction. In these barrels lived all of Sophie's workers down the decades, as the barrels never fully gave up their past . . . always holding back a little to be absorbed by and scent the next vintage.

Charlie wanted to leave the old fellow with some of the optimism he was feeling. 'Your sons are alive in these cellars – within these barrels and within the wine they hold.'

Étienne smiled with pleasure. 'Madame retained her family name. Her husband never seemed to mind that she did.'

That hadn't occurred to Charlie until now. 'A modern woman.'

Jerome tapped his large nose. 'A modern man. I gather he encouraged this. He wanted her to be proud of her family name, to keep it going. And if only they'd had a son, the boy, well . . .' He sighed.

Charlie nodded. 'She is young. There is time.'

'Yes, yes, she is young enough, Captain, but they were the most popular couple of the whole region. Everyone loved this pair. They were well matched in every way, from here,' he said, pointing to his face to suggest they were a handsome couple, 'to here,' he added, now pointing to his temple. 'Madame Delancré is as wise as she is beautiful; she is the perfect mix of her parents, bless their souls. And she finally found the right man, who respected her intelligence, encouraged her use of it. It is very hard on all of us that he is no longer with us.' The old man gave a shake of his head. 'That is a barrel that would be very hard to fill.'

Charlie felt guilt gnawing at him. Who was he to try to muscle in on what sounded like the perfect relationship? The perfect man had already found Sophie. Charlie forgave himself for falling in love with her – what man could resist? – but these simple words from old Étienne were telling as much as they were illuminating: he really did need to step back and not put her in an awkward position. Maybe he should leave immediately. Facing her again would only make it hard for both of them.

'Will young Étienne work here?'

'He already does. He runs errands.' At this the old man laughed as if he'd made a joke about history repeating itself. 'Drink with me to my grandson.'

He could hardly refuse. 'All right, what are we drinking? Bit early for champagne?'

'It is never too early for champagne,' his elder cautioned him. 'No, have a taste of this.' He gestured to an upturned barrel and a couple of stools. Charlie watched him pull out a squat, dark, unlabelled bottle from a bucket of chilled water.

'What is this?' he asked as the fellow released the cork and poured two nips into tiny, grubby glasses. The liquid appeared light gold and syrupy.

'Taste,' the man urged him.

Charlie took a sip and was surprised at the powerful jolt of alcohol together with a rich sweetness. 'Blimey! What is this?'

Étienne shrugged in that French way and then roared his laughing pleasure. 'We call it ratafia. Madame's is the best of the region.'

Charlie repeated the word. 'But what is it?'

Étienne chuckled. 'A mule's kick.'

'It is,' Charlie agreed. 'Powerful stuff. How is it achieved?'

'The marc.' Étienne could see he didn't understand. 'So, this is the liquor left over from making our wine.'

'Before or after fermentation?' Charlie asked, taking another sip, impressed by its cool, deliciously sweet flavour that he imagined would be as good an aperitif as a wine served with dessert or cheese.

The man shrugged. 'Usually it is the liquor that comes when the grapes are pressed and from the skins, seeds and stalks before fermentation, although fermentation begins once the juice is released.'

'It's incredible.'

'Hers especially; she takes pride in it. Madame Delancré ensures a fine taste. However, every family around here makes ratafia, monsieur. We all have bottles of it at home for guests, and to add to other things. Some women add it to their sweet cakes; others use it to be flavour for other flavours.'

'Like what?' Charlie was intrigued.

Étienne didn't seem to mind teaching Charlie. 'I know some houses sell theirs to makers of aperitifs that have lemon or cherry, perhaps apricot, even aniseed . . . You know grappa?'

Charlie shook his head.

'Italian. Every country in Europe would have a version of it, monsieur.'

'Ratafia,' Charlie said again, liking the sound of the word. 'It's so sweet!'

'You like?'

'I like,' he confirmed, and drained his glass to prove it. Charlie stood. 'Good day to you, Étienne, and thank you.'

'Come again. There's any amount of it after each crush.' Charlie's new friend grinned and waved a hand in farewell.

Charlie ambled off into the tunnel, taking a piece of chalk to make a small mark if he happened to make a wrong turn; he had none of Sophie's childhood navigation skills among the cellars and didn't trust his sense of direction. Here, hugged by the dark and seeing only with the lowest of lamplight, he could sense an idea beginning to form in his mind that was all chemist now.

---

It had been easier for Sophie to remain in Reims with the pretence of overseeing preparations for harvest, which would be early this year. It was a helpful excuse; returning home to Épernay would bring an avalanche of the memories she'd clung to, which she'd not had to put away but soon would, given the impotence of her persistent enquiries. But having found the courage to go, she'd slipped back home yesterday under the cover of night.

Louis would be arriving soon from Paris, ready to gloat with news that the discovery of the uniform and papers had officially made Jerome one of the unconfirmed dead – no longer considered missing. A simple rearrangement of words was about to change her life. Now it was time to pack up Jerome's clothes once and for all – give them to others who could use them. For his three decades on earth Jerome had not acquired much that was entirely his. He owned plenty as a brother. With Louis he had inherited the sprawling family mansion at Avize, the vineyards and their equipment, as well as all their parents' belongings. Even so, and in spite of his personal wealth, Jerome had not spent much on himself at all. He was not acquisitive; in the time she'd known him she'd never heard him want for anything but her. He wore no adornments, had no desire to own a car – *Why, when the nag does such a faithful job?* He didn't appreciate new furniture, new shoes, new clothes. Jerome preferred everything old and lived-in.

'I like being comfortable. I like the familiarity of clothes that have shared my life,' he had said to her when she darned his vineyard trousers for the umpteenth time.

Her husband desired little.

'Only you. You are all I desire in life. Your happiness. Your health. Your love. Whatever makes you happy gladdens me.'

So there was little in either of her houses to speak of the month that they had shared there as man and wife. His compass, perhaps, which he had pressed into her hands on his last night as they'd laid together and wept.

'Keep this, knowing I hold it here,' he said, touching his breast over his heart. 'You are my true north. I'll find my way back to you.'

Sophie leaned against the wall and looked out the window of her attic room towards Avize, where Jerome was born, and her tears flowed. No one shared them but no one needed to. These were hers to indulge as she came to terms with the news, and worse, the realisation that Louis might get his way and Charlie would only be a lovely memory she took out from time to time to enjoy. They hadn't got in so deep that Charlie couldn't surface and survive. In a different life, a different situation, she knew they would have been lovers, a strong couple – made a good marriage. War had brought them together and now it needed them to part. She knew her decision was the right one, and now with Jerome's status official, she no closer to finding any sugar and the war still dragging on half-heartedly, she needed to make a decision about this year's champagne.

She punished herself one last time, recalling her final discussion with Jean from the Red Cross on the telephone.

'Are you convinced, monsieur, that my husband could not be wandering around lost, so injured he can barely remember his own name?'

'I do doubt this,' Jean had replied, sounding emphatic. 'And I understand your pain, madame, and why you hope against hope. You are not alone in your sorrow at not having your loved one's body returned or even knowing precisely where he fell.' When Sophie didn't say anything – she couldn't, she was biting her knuckle to prevent herself sobbing, imagining Jerome clutching at his throat and gasping his final breaths before the sucking mud swallowed him – Jean hurried on with formalities. 'Following the discovery of his tunic and his papers we are adjusting his status accordingly. The Red Cross now officially regards him as permanently lost.'

A nice way to say *There's no more hope. Consider your husband dead . . . and move on with your life, as millions of other women have had to.* He said none of that, of course. Instead he remained polite and sympathetic.

'You have my deepest condolences, Madame Delancré,' he added, as gently as he dared.

So now all she had to look forward to – if she was going to stay true to Jerome and keep his vineyards going, making champagne in their name, hoping to keep that name alive through a son, even – was marriage to Louis. At the thought a shudder erupted through her and reminded her that she was out of excuses, out of time and out of sugar.

# 23

*August 1918*

It had been a fortnight since that phone call. Most of that time she'd plunged herself into work at the hospital, barely sleeping for more than a couple of hours a night, preferring to be moving, busy, confronting other people's problems rather than her own. Jerome tended to visit when she was alone, trying to sleep, frustrated that she wasn't more exhausted. He was telling her to forget about him. Make a new life. She was young and wealthy, she had years to look forward to, so much love to give another . . . especially to children.

And yet, two days ago, when she'd returned to Épernay to essentially pack up his memory, he had seemed larger in her unsettled sleep and was conveying the opposite.

*Look for me. Don't let me die.*

She forced herself to wake. Checking the clock, she noticed she'd been asleep for less than two hours, all of it restless and invaded by Jerome, she was sure. This would not do. She was functioning, but it was as though she were a wind-up doll. Time to take control, as she had when she'd first lost Jerome to this war. Well, the war was won. The Germans were retreating. They'd achieved nothing but nightmares, pain, fear, death and destruction across Europe, including Germany.

Maybe this was the time for new beginnings . . . for all of them, and for her especially. She had slipped back into Épernay unannounced, looking for Charlie but also hoping not to see him, and hiding out in her attic, taking no food and worrying her household as she brought herself to fully face her pain and reach a truce with it. Finally, after two days, she had bathed, dressed, agreed to take a small breakfast of a sweet roll and jam, smiling thanks and hugging those around her, assuring them that she was feeling strong.

'My husband was presumed dead just over a fortnight ago and I am resigned to it now. And nothing has changed with this news,' she admitted to the small row of concerned people who stood in the parlour. 'It simply reinforces what we have all had to accept.'

'We're all very sorry that it has reopened the wound, madame,' said the housekeeper.

Sophie smiled at her loyal staff. All had lost someone important. 'We all share each other's grief. Thank you for your kindness.' Sophie didn't want to ask about Charlie, even though the question was searching for a way out of her pressed lips. Instead she chased it away and found a sad smile. 'Now it's time for me to return to the cellars. Always plenty of work there.'

Later that morning, she checked in with the kitchen team to show she was fully focused on being head of the house and overseeing its smooth running again.

'Captain Charlie has been looking for you, madame,' the cook mentioned as she turned to stir a pot on the stove. She had dutifully sent up food for the last couple of days and Sophie now had to swallow her guilt for refusing it.

'Oh?'

'Most days he asks about you,' she added, still stirring.

Sophie knew she wasn't fooling her wise cook. Marie had been in the family for two decades, had known her since she was a girl, annoying the kitchen staff by trying to sneak a pastry before they'd cooled.

It smelled like a rich vegetable soup was being cooked up for their large midday meal. Freshly baked bread from the flour Sophie had brought back with her scented the air. She blinked. 'Well, that's kind of him. I'm sure I'll meet up with him.'

'He mentioned that he works in the cellars each day with Adeline,' Marie said over her shoulder, sounding casual but her gaze said otherwise. Sophie knew Marie had a soft spot for Charlie and would not be a critic should Sophie pursue a romantic relationship with the English captain.

'I see. Well, thank you. I shall make sure to look for him.'

She departed the house via its back entrance and headed down the pathway that framed the back garden towards the cellars. There was no sound of guns, no smell of cordite. *This is how life used to be*, she thought with a sense of wonder breaking through her sorrow as she began her descent into the labyrinth below.

'What do I do now?' she asked aloud, knowing the cellars listened; they'd been listening to her thoughts since she was a child wandering around them and singing rhymes or reciting her times tables. They'd listened to her when she was upset over what had felt like insurmountable problems at six and seven, but were in fact trivialities. They had heard her despair at losing Jerome and had held her close, reassured her, and helped to get her through these last few years. Although they never replied, the cellars gave her the space and, more importantly, the right frame of mind to think through her problems. And here she was, still walking these corridors, inhaling their mineral bouquet while listening for their soothing, silent advice.

Charlie heard the gritty sound of footsteps but didn't turn immediately; he imagined it was one of the other workers going about their business in this world underneath Épernay in which they spent so much of their lives.

Sophie found him holding a lantern above his shoulder so he could light the cavernous space in this part of the Delancré cellars.

'This section always struck me as having the quality of a chapel,' she admitted, breaking the silence. It was the voice he'd been longing to hear but now that he did, a fresh surge of sadness began to tear at his resilience; he hoped he'd find the right words and stay true to his decision.

'How are you, Charlie?' she asked, as he turned.

He removed his hand from the sling and surprised her by being able to open and close his fist. His fingers still felt stiff and no doubt appeared that way, but his hand was obeying most of his invisible commands, it seemed. 'The exercises are helping,' he remarked.

She found a smile. 'That's good news, Charlie. I'm happy to hear it.' She looked hollow, her complexion wan.

'Sophie, have you been ill?'

'I've been sad, Charlie. No sadder than anyone else living through this war but learning to handle the grief that is all mine.'

He frowned. 'Were you in Reims?' It sounded accusatory. He couldn't help that.

'Yes.' She glanced down, looking to him as though she did feel shame for her absence, but he watched her raise her chin, perhaps reminding herself that she did not have to answer to anyone for her actions, and certainly not to him.

He simply nodded. Charlie had been told on countless occasions by a good number of people that he could be infuriating in his silence. He waited for her to speak.

'It's nice to see you,' she said.

He heard the hesitancy. 'It's nice to see *you*,' he remarked pointedly, and they both regarded each other in an awkward pause. *Do it, Charlie*, he told himself. *She's suffered enough and so have you.* 'Listen, Sophie,' he began more gently. 'I waited for you because I didn't want to leave without saying goodbye properly.'

She couldn't hide her shock from him. 'You're leaving?'

'Gaston was right that I should be finding my people.'

'The war is all but over. The Battle of Amiens made sure of it —'

'I know, Sophie. But I have to say I feel awkward now. Every minute that I linger I am trespassing in another man's footsteps.'

'Charlie . . .'

'Let me finish,' he said softly. 'Everything I hear about Jerome reiterates that you and he were meant to be. You were right to stop our affections going any further. I agree that what occurred in your attic could be viewed as a mistake, a misunderstanding, an error of judgement.'

She impaled him with a gaze that told him he'd offended her. 'It was none of those.'

He opened his palms, pleased that his wounded hand obeyed. 'Nonetheless, we can pretend because it will make it easier on my heart if you can go along with the notion that it was a reckless moment in which we forgot ourselves.'

She nodded reluctantly.

'I love you, Sophie, but I'm going to leave because each moment with you makes it harder. I should be honest and thank you for this enforced separation. It gave me time to think straight, get my thoughts organised for what feels like the first time in years . . . and my good sense has prevailed. I can only admire your decision, heartbreaking though it is for me, to hold out hope of finding Jerome and stay true to him. No soldier could ask for more from the woman he left behind, and maybe it's that very notion that is keeping Jerome going in some hellhole somewhere, whether real or in his mind. And one day when he walks back into your life, we can silently thank each other for honouring him in this way.' He nodded encouragingly, needing her to agree, needing her to accept it.

'Charlie, Jerome is not coming home.'

He watched her eyes glisten with tears that had not been there a moment ago. 'Now why do you say that?'

'Because it's been confirmed.'

He blinked, taking time to make sense of what she was saying. 'Dead?'

She flinched at the word. 'His uniform and now his identification papers have been found, badly bloodstained. No doubt because of what happened between us, and so that I didn't feel disloyal to Jerome after all these years, I put more pressure on the Red Cross for information, and here it is . . .' Sophie pulled a crumpled piece of paper from her pocket. Her voice was unsteady. 'I, er, wrote it down so I wouldn't start to think I'd imagined it.'

Charlie stared at her with pain in his gaze, his face crestfallen. The news might be hers but it profoundly affected him. His decision hadn't changed – she was in no state to love another, but it made it so much harder to leave her. 'What were you told?'

She sniffed, wiped at her cheeks, but the tears still ran; she cleared her throat so she could speak. Her voice trembled slightly as she told him about where the items had been found, which was in the region where the poison gas had been unleashed, and their significance in terms of corroborating witness accounts. 'Apparently, some were able to run as far as two miles – including Jerome, helping others as usual – before the gas overwhelmed them. Many corpses from his unit were found there.' She sniffed again. 'I don't feel like reading any more.'

'They have his body?'

She shook her head. 'But they did find his bloodied uniform and papers. I've been counselled not to hold out any further hope.'

'You said he was helping others. The blood could be someone else's,' he tried.

She nodded. 'Yes, that was my counter too. But the authorities firmly believe him buried with so many others in the mud of Flanders. They are changing his status to "permanently lost", another way of saying "killed in action". And there will be no further investigation into Jerome.' She seemed to tremble but her voice was steady. 'They seem to have run out of patience with me . . . even Louis has refused to make another enquiry.'

He did take a step towards her now and she allowed him to wrap his arms around her as she sobbed.

He heard her voice muffled against his chest. Forbidding himself to read anything more into this moment of affection, he let her speak on. 'On an intellectual level, I knew he had to be gone . . . After more than three years, I would have heard if he were alive, or in a hospital, or prison. But you know, my heart just wouldn't let go.'

He didn't comment but simply held her tightly.

'So please don't go just yet, Charlie. Just a few days. I could use your friendship right now.'

He pulled away, knowing his expression showed how torn he was. 'I'll stay until harvest is complete.'

'Thank you for waiting a little longer.'

He blew out a tightly held breath; he desperately wanted to comfort her with affection, with a kiss, but knew it was a complication she might not welcome. 'Come on. Shall we walk? I know you love your cellars, but breathe some of the fresh air of your vineyards.'

Charlie felt trapped in a stalemate as they walked. The affection they had once felt – which he still felt – had been put on an imaginary shelf for the good of them both. It would be hard for him to explain it to anyone else, but he knew Sophie understood how they were able to do this. Certainly for him, the desire had not waned. All she had to do was perhaps look at him in her soft way and he would deliver up his heart, his life, all over again. He suspected this sensible armistice of theirs wouldn't, perhaps couldn't, last and he was glad there was a deadline on it. Just a week or so more.

They were seated in the nearby vineyard of chardonnay, its grapes gone, crushed, now fermenting in barrels until the following spring, when they would be woken up to the winemaker's magic that would turn the wine into champagne. Meanwhile Sophie's workers were busy in other fields gathering the fruit from vines that were more patient.

They were sharing a bottle of champagne from 1915; both knew it would be their last private time together, so Sophie had decided to open a bottle to mark their farewell.

'What do you taste?' Charlie asked, keen to break the spell of misery and forbidden love.

'Grief,' she said, and he didn't think she was being flippant.

'Nineteen-fifteen was a horrible year in both our lives.'

She nodded. 'Champagne is best drunk at a party or when one is in a good mood. It loves happiness. It should taste like falling in love. It should make its drinker feel light-headed quickly but in a good way, as though intoxicated by life in the moment of the joyous sparkle of its first sip.'

'Like a first kiss?' He was disgusted that he'd let the remark slip out.

Sophie smiled, fielding it as though it hadn't felt like a barb. 'Like dozens of kisses with someone you can't resist being with.' She returned to the champagne quickly. 'This is not our best. I swear I can taste gunpowder in it.'

He changed topics. 'How is Gaston?'

'I haven't heard from him.'

'I have no doubt he is stretched thinly at present. He'll be back in your life soon. What about Louis?'

'Angry and ignoring me for now. That too will change, I'm sure. I'm going to miss you, Charlie.'

He shook his head, refused to be drawn into it. 'Tell me about the wine from this vineyard. It can be my final tutorial with you.'

Sophie's gaze rested on him for longer than was comfortable, and it was Charlie who demurred. She spoke into the silence. 'I told you, she's a goddess with several personalities depending on where she grows. She's too important to be kept waiting, which is why we harvest her first.'

'Go on.' He plucked a grape and casually crunched it to release its juices and his eyes widened.

'Sweet, isn't it?'

'Yes,' he said, his tone filled with wonder. 'Surprisingly so.'

'Most people think the grapes we eat at our tables are sweeter, but this is a fallacy. And did you note how thick the skin is?'

He nodded.

'Full of flavour, which is why we cultivate grapes specifically to become wine.'

He spat out the pips. 'How many grapes do you need for a glass of champagne?'

She laughed; it was a delicious sound, he decided. 'It doesn't follow that way,' she said, shaking her head at him.

'Approximately,' he encouraged her.

Sophie shrugged her thin shoulders. 'Perhaps a typical cluster . . . there, like that one we've missed picking.'

'And so, this goddess . . .?'

'Well, as you can tell, she is sweet when she is ripe.'

He nodded.

'She is also capricious.'

'In what way?'

'She teases. She can be delicate at times – a terrible flirt.' She grinned. 'But she can take on flavours that can astound, depending on terroir . . . er, do you understand this term?'

He frowned. 'The soil?'

'Yes, the landscape. Where she grows. What is growing around here?' She emphasised this by pointing to the earth, a dark red as though it had absorbed the blood of the fallen. 'What is flavouring *this* soil?' she insisted. 'Chardonnay can be neutral and simply absorb, then throw back flavours from terroir as significant as those erupting from the skills of the champagne maker and what he or she adds or balances those flavours with. She can be austere – lots of minerality. I want to say she tastes like the swipe of a steel sword.'

He gusted a laugh. 'The picture in my mind is brilliant when you describe it like that.'

'Or she can be fruity, like crunching into a fresh apple. Best of all, with one hundred per cent chardonnay you are almost certainly going to achieve a very dry, crisp, citrussy experience. Imagine rubbing the skin of lemon – that's what you get.'

'She has no characteristics of her own?'

'Ah, no. That would be wrong to presume. I said she *can* be neutral. She isn't always. Sometimes she's bold, and will deliberately confuse us with something jammy like apricot, or astound us with a spicy anise, even ginger.'

He laughed. 'How can that be?'

'You should be seriously impressed with this grape,' Sophie said, playfully wagging a finger. 'She is a chameleon.'

'I can tell you are impressed.'

'I love her . . . She encourages me to step away from all that has gone before, to snub tradition – to ignore the people like my father, my grandfather, his father, and so many through the decades.

She wants me to disregard all the expertise we have in Épernay and have followed through the passage of time . . .'

'And do what?'

'Be a rebel, as Jerome always hoped I would be with my wine. She wants me to make my own champagne entirely from her grapes. She doesn't believe we need the others. It's why he grew me that whole vineyard of chardonnay as a wedding gift.'

The chemist in him was aroused, his interest piqued by someone daring to step away from the known and trusted. 'What would happen if you did?'

She smiled thoughtfully. 'I would be relying on the capricious nature of this grape for a vintage. It could mean an entire wasted crop: a year of work for everyone involved . . . all the toil, effort, ingredients and —'

'Why haven't you tried it?'

'I think I prefer to dream it. I'm scared of the reality.'

'All right, explain to me then why is this important to you, other than the obvious reasons of flavour you've described?'

'Well, the beauty for me is that it needs less sugar and that means less interference. She and I would have a relationship based entirely on trust. She would trust me to pick her at the right time, crush her gently, extract her juices quickly, knowing in my heart,' she said, placing a hand across her chest, 'that she knows what to do next. And then I would hand over all the trust to her to do just that – to ferment as she inherently knows how. You tasted her sweet ripeness. I feel she could do it alone, but if she needed me – and I would be with her all the way – I could always help by balancing. You see, we would be like a perfect pair of acrobats, balancing each other and flying through the air on trust.'

He whistled his praise. 'You must do this.'

'Until the start of war, I suppose I was mindful of Jerome's fields, his hard work, our very limited chardonnay.'

'No, you've just said this is what he encouraged . . . what he wanted for you to achieve.'

'He was a generous man, but his grapes were like his children. He would never see them abused or taken for granted . . . or used on a whim.'

'Come on, Sophie . . . surely?'

'Chardonnay is precious. We couldn't spare them for my hobby . . . for an experiment.'

'Promise me you will create this champagne one day.'

She pushed him affectionately. 'I promise.'

He felt such an urge to kiss her but instead he walked away, determined not to go where he'd sworn he never would again.

He wanted to entwine hands like the tangled vines around them, growing not in neat rows but haphazardly. The scientist in him wanted order: straight rows, neatly tied-up vines. Perhaps. Generations of knowledge meant doing it this way and he should not interfere. He resisted taking her hand. 'Tell me about this year's wine needing to be made.'

'Well, now, my private dream aside, let me say the three traditional grapes are all queens in their own right. I have elevated chardonnay – my favourite – to goddess status but all should be acknowledged as their majesties.'

He chuckled. 'And I'm guessing each with their own special gift to bring to the final dazzling wine.'

'Exactly,' she encouraged him, eyes sparkling like the champagne she made. 'When the balance is perfect you taste the perfection of three different queens, combining to form one whole glass of majesty.'

'I want to learn. Describe them for me.'

'You know chardonnay intimately now – you have tasted her, you have a feeling about her. Let me test you. If we discount winter, because winter is when the landscape slumbers and my vineyard will relax into his waiting arms to sleep . . . Ah, yes,' she said quickly, noticing him about to interrupt. 'I see the landscape as a "he". He embraces the three majesties. He looks after them. He is their knight . . . their lover . . . their protector.'

Sophie, his love for her, her voice, her stories . . . they were winning his internal war to return to life and sunlight, no longer those dark thoughts from the trenches. Could she possibly know how much he needed her or how hard it was going to be to leave her in a week or so?

He let her speak on over his sad thoughts. 'So, with winter left aside, we have three seasons. If you were to attribute one season to chardonnay, which would it be?' She had a hungry look on her face as she posed her question, clearly desperate for him to choose the right one. 'This is not, how you say, a trick question . . . but what do you feel?' Sophie put a hand on the left side of his chest. 'This is how I make champagne: with emotion, with my heart.'

Charlie took a slow breath. He wanted to get this right for her. Chardonnay. The grape, he recalled, had exploded with sweetness, but the sweetness wasn't so overpowering that he couldn't taste the other element Sophie had mentioned: that crispy apple, and its citrussy element.

'Think about the colour you tasted, Charlie,' she urged. She handed him a grape. 'Taste again.'

He crunched the grape and the first colour that leapt into his mind was green; he explored it, knowing she'd insist, and decided it was a muted green, like a new apple still filling out into its fecund shape. But then he tasted the sun, not rich and bright, but like the early warmth of morning – yellow mingling with the silvery, steely sensation of the moon's memory. This was not summer or autumn. 'Spring,' he said, and wanted to hold his breath. *Please let me be right*, he cast out, feeling as though this was the most important test of his inner self that had ever been presented to him.

She squealed pleasure. 'Charlie, my Charlie. Yes! She is spring.'

'Now you describe the woman she is,' he demanded. 'Good grief, that was exhausting,' he admitted quickly, blowing out an exaggerated breath. 'I was terrified to get it wrong.'

'There is no wrong . . . it's like art. It's what *you* feel and see and experience when you taste. But I'm glad you share the same vision as I.' She looked radiant in her pleasure. 'The woman who lurks in this juice is chic. You know this word?'

He nodded.

'She is an accomplished woman . . . she is as good at tennis as she is well-read. So she's sporty but also loves art, the classics, and yet she is avant-garde in her manner. She can breeze into a party and entertain everyone and then she is gone.'

'Where?'

'To the next party, of course!' Sophie said, as though appalled he couldn't guess. 'She has an ethereal quality to her. You can watch her but don't touch – she is unreachable; there for you but not entirely. Does that make sense?'

'It does, actually.' *You are chardonnay, Sophie*, he thought, watching her become passionate and abandoned because they were talking about champagne – not war, not love lost, not misery, but pure joy.

'Next we have pinot noir. Here is a grape that brings to the champagne her directness. She is spontaneous and can be fun, but she can have a sharp edge – don't take this woman for granted. She is mature . . . she is a mother and therefore she is strong.'

'Her colour?'

'This queen is all shades of red, from the brightest scarlet to the darkest maroon. Always warm, and so with that comes the potential for her unpredictable temper that needs calming.'

'Her season?'

'What do you think?' Sophie asked.

'Well, for the fieriest of our majesties, I would have to say summer.'

'You would be right.' She smiled. 'Summer storms.'

'Damn, but I love talking with you, Sophie. I could sit here against this plum tree for the rest of my life, and if all I could have were your voice and stories about your grapes, it would be enough.'

She turned to stroke his stubbly cheek. 'How many women's hearts have you won with that sort of talk?'

He demurred. 'I think most women consider me a scoundrel.'

'"Scoundrel"?' I don't know this word.'

'Well, they think of me as someone who isn't around for the long term.'

'But they fall in love with you all the same.'

'I didn't say that.'

'Charlie, you don't have to. Every nurse in Reims wanted to care for you. You are a handsome man, but you hurt inside. You hurt before the war . . . I think the war gave you the right excuse to unleash your pain.'

He looked at her, not knowing what to say. She saw all of him; Sophie was not just the first woman but the first person who seemed to understand him. No wonder his shattered mind had repaired itself and returned from that void for her. She was a reason for any man to return.

'We have one woman of champagne left,' he said, lost for how to respond to her insight.

'We do. We have meunier. Now, she's our friendly, loving woman – the grandmother. She's got fancy jewels in her possession, earned over time. However, she doesn't always wear them with a lot of taste.'

Charlie gave a bright laugh. 'She needs chardonnay and pinot noir to know which jewels to show off.'

'Exactly! This woman owns the ochres, beiges and browns so she gives us a lovely backdrop for the brighter colours. She is our autumn. Mellow but not without strength, and perfectly capable of being lively as much as she is welcoming. She brings roundness, softness where needed.'

'And so traditionally the champagne makers only use these three grapes?'

'They worship them. They must balance them, though.'

'And you, you rebel, you want to break free of all that tradition to the three queens.'

'And pay homage to only one . . . yes.'

'You will.'

'I fear her.'

'You are already making champagne that people revere. You know what to do, how to do it . . . you feel it here.' He banged his chest over his heart.

'And still I haven't tested my theory.'

'Because that takes risk. And you have spent your life being reliable, I'm guessing. Everyone here relies on you and trusts you. But why not take the chance of being wrong? Letting them down, letting yourself down? Dare to fail, Sophie . . . and I suspect in that gamble you may just win.'

She looked helplessly buoyed by his rousing words, stood up and offered a hand to haul him up. 'I will think on this, Charlie. I'm closer now than I've ever been to taking that risk, especially now that Jerome is gone. Maybe next year in peacetime when my chardonnay feels no fear from bombs or fire or frightened vineyard workers.' She sighed. 'Charlie, I know this is us saying goodbye. We've just not said the word "farewell". Instead may I hug you without . . .?'

He nodded and sighed into their embrace. They held each other without changing the pressure, without trying to communicate anything more than all that had already been spoken. The embrace said everything anyway.

He risked kissing her head, hard and briefly, hoping the misty gaze he was looking through would clear before she noticed. He cleared his throat. 'I'll write.'

'I hope you do.'

They regarded each other awkwardly. She had no one, he had no one, and now the loathsome brother stood between them. He wished he could find the courage to suggest she wait – hold Louis off and he would come back in a year to see how she might be feeling, but he didn't. The line had been drawn; only Sophie could cross it and change their future.

'And I'm hoping that the champagne you make this year . . . from last year's crush —' he pulled a face that suggested he hoped he was getting that right; he was, because she gave him an appreciative nod — 'is one of triumph. For France, for Épernay, for House Delancré. I will search it out in England.' There was a pause that didn't feel right and she looked crestfallen. 'What's wrong?'

'I can't make champagne this year.'

Charlie stepped back further with a look of puzzlement as he regarded her. 'Why ever not?'

She gave a small shrug of hopelessness. 'We have no sugar left. We've used the last of it for the first fermentation of this year's crush. We have nothing for the disgorgement, topping up, balancing to make this year's champagne.'

'But you don't add more sugar, do you?'

'I add as little as possible, it's true. So little sometimes as to be negligent, but I must have it available to balance the liquor if I need to. Going ahead knowing I have none really would be wasteful and unforgivable.'

He let out a disappointed sigh. 'Can you buy from others?'

She walked away. 'No one has any. I had the most plenti-ful stocks at the start of the war because I do use less than most; I prefer cane and pay the much higher price for it. But we cannot get any more at present – not from Africa or the Caribbean. Beet is local, but . . .' She sighed, looking dejected.

'Where does the sugar beet grow?' he pressed, determined there had to be something they could do.

'In places that are now nothing but battlefields . . . besides, there is none to be had for none has been planted, and what is left is being used to feed people, livestock. We have to wait until the land can recover and the crops can be replanted.'

There was more, he could tell. 'Or there is Louis.'

'He has access to sugar somewhere. He either knows where to get it, or he has actually accumulated sugar, knowing it would likely become a desirable commodity as war pressed on.'

'No, Sophie, no!'

'You know it's a choice I have to make.'

'Then wait!'

'For what? Years for sugar beet to grow successfully again? Or for commerce to recover and ships to get through with cane from overseas? Years in which my vineyards will grow, their fruit left to wither?'

'So be it.'

She blinked at him with annoyance 'You have no idea what you're asking.'

'I'm asking you to be wise. To be good to yourself. Forget me in all of this! But Louis? He will destroy you.'

'He will leave me alone. We could live separate lives, as he suggests.'

'Sophie, you are not thinking clearly. You're being emotional. Do you really think this is what Jerome would want?'

She couldn't answer him, or chose not to.

'I am going to think on this.' He didn't mean to make it sound like a threat. 'And I am going to find a solution that does not involve marrying your brother-in-law for sugar, or for security, or for the sake of your dead husband's vines.'

He sounded angry and just a little disgusted. He couldn't blame her for the edged comment that followed.

'So, you are going to magic up sugar for me, are you, Charlie? Perhaps you can magic up my dead husband as well! This is the only way I'm going to be able to make the wine in honour of Jerome, or be able to use the juice from the first-ever grapes to flourish from that vineyard. Sentimentally, emotionally and professionally, being able to make champagne from those grapes this year means everything to me. You make it sound like I want to have Louis at my side.'

'And you make it sound like you've discovered the easy solution.'

She slapped him. Hard. Strength gained from years in the vineyard powered it. His head whipped to the side and Charlie lost his balance but regained it fast. He knew that if he looked in a mirror right now he would be able to see the print of a woman's hand on his face. It wouldn't be the first time – or perhaps the last, because he had a way of infuriating women – but he doubted a similar mark would ever be left again by someone he loved as much as Sophie. And he hated that she was squandering herself for a ghost. He looked back at her, wounded, sad and angry.

'Oh, Charlie . . . I . . .' She put her fighting hands to her mouth and her eyes filled with tears.

'Don't apologise. I deserved that. But you don't deserve Louis. So before I leave, Sophie – and I am leaving you,' he said, a flinty edge to his voice, 'I'm going to put my chemist's brain to work for you. If this is the champagne that heralds the end of the war and means more to you than the rest of your life, then it must be made.

But you certainly do not need Louis's ring on your finger to make that happen.'

'Then work some magic for me before you leave, Charlie,' she said, her voice small, apologetic even, but also accusatory. He'd hurt her with his words as much as she'd hurt him with the blow.

Charlie left her standing in the vineyard of the chardonnay she loved so much, and as he turned his back on her, he already believed he knew the solution – but he had to act before Louis could load any more pressure onto those narrow shoulders.

# 24

It had been weeks of regular visits from the doctor, long walks around the lake and a summer to be remembered as much for its warmth and clear skies as for its sense of freedom. Internees were encouraged to join in sport as best they could and Jerome, in spite of his damaged leg and no use of one eye, was not backward in participating in everything from easy hikes to canoeing. His lungs felt to be improving, which was a surprise, and he put it down to having a nourishing diet again.

He had admitted to his doctor that he was looking forward to trying tobogganing, which the Swiss clinical team felt was fine for the soldiers who had suffered from poison gas but not necessarily those who had lost limbs. He could read that last bit in their troubled gazes.

'Let's hope you don't have to do a winter in Switzerland, Lieutenant,' his nurse said as she was changing the dressing on his eye. 'You've got the doctors worried that you'll take up an inappropriate sport.' They shared a conspiratorial smile. 'I must find you a more elegant eye patch.'

'Why?'

'So you can attend the events and look very handsome.' There was a flirtatious note in her tone that unnerved him.

He gave a soft snort. 'There's a dinner and a concert tonight, isn't there?' he said, to distract her and move into safer conversation.

'Will you be going, Lieutenant?' She grinned. She was a pretty little creature, ten years his junior and new on the team that looked after him. It wasn't hard to understand that she'd taken a shine to him . . . and he was careful not to encourage her. He wanted to counsel her some time when it was appropriate that she needed to be careful around the younger soldiers – especially any French ones – with her open and friendly countenance. Most hadn't been touched by a woman or even seen one in an age. And here, where they enjoyed relative freedom, lots of spare time and access to liquor, it made for a daring mix for men who had been starved of female company for years.

He thought better of the counselling now; it may be patronising if she didn't see his advice as big brotherly. As it was, the nurse seemed confident and smart; he was sure the matrons had made all their charges aware of the complexities of the role they performed. 'Yes, of course,' he answered.

'It's a pity you're not singing tonight. I did check the program.' Jerome gave her a shrug. 'But I gather there's a special treat on tonight of raclette. Do you know this in France?'

'The cheese?' He frowned. 'I thought Switzerland was on rations? Two and a half thousand calories per internee, I am assured,' he said in a lighthearted tone to show how grateful he was for every one of them.

'Not when it comes to our favourite cheese, it seems.' She winked.

'I might have tasted it in my childhood when we visited.'

She smiled, impressed. 'Have you tasted it served properly though . . . the Swiss way?'

He shook his head. 'I can't recall.'

'You wouldn't forget. It's not made for eating raw. The wheel of cheese is heated, and as it melts it is scraped off onto plates and we enjoy it with some vegetables. I can remember my grandmother serving it with cherry brandy on special occasions,' she said, eyes widening with pleasure at the memory. 'Either way, you are in for a treat, Lieutenant.' She smiled and sighed slightly as she continued with her ministrations. 'So, what is special to your part of France?'

He knew she was keeping him talking because the liquid medicine she was about to drop in his eye was going to sting roundly. He obliged; after all of the pain of his war, the eye drops were a mercy.

He couldn't help but enjoy the feel of her soft hands as they touched his face, gently tipping his head back.

'Well, now,' he began, trying to ignore the hint of perfume he could sense rising above the general smell of antiseptic as she hovered above him. 'We have our own special cheese in the Marne region. It's soft with a bright white rind and, like yours, made from cow's milk.' The first drop went in and hurt like merry hell and although he winced he kept talking. 'It's creamy and crumbly and it has a mushroomy smell. It can be dated back to medieval times when the monks of the Champagne region used to make it.'

'One more,' she warned. 'Go on, what else is special in that region?'

He grinned. 'Well, apart from the champagne, there are truffles.'

'Ooh,' she cooed. 'I have only tasted these once. Aren't they supposed to be an aphrodisiac? Little sting,' she cautioned.

The cold liquid pain arrived once again to make him blink and close his eyes. He chose to ignore her query and changed topics again.

'If it's dead, why are we doing this?'

'I am assured it will retain the eye. You don't want it removed, surely?'

He shrugged. 'It's ugly.'

'Yes, but you are not . . . not by a long way,' she admitted. He could hear her romantic youth in the remark and deliberately dropped his chin out of her grip, not so fast that she might be offended but firmly enough that she might believe he wasn't registering her soft tone and intent. 'It will change your face to have your eyelids stitched closed and flat. We don't want that. Besides, when you wear a well-fitted patch, you're going to look even more dashing, Lieutenant.'

'And then there are the pink biscuits,' he finished, determined to stop her flirting, if she was.

She frowned as she put the stopper back in the bottle.

'Roses de Reims, they're called. Crunchy, flavoured with vanilla and very light in texture – they are a very old tradition.' A thought struck. 'My wife makes them.'

She looked surprised. 'I was told you had no family.' He could hear her disappointment.

'The notes will say so because a mistake was made with me years ago,' Jerome explained quickly. 'Will you help me, Agatha?'

'In what way are you asking?' She sounded instantly suspicious, and that reminded him he was a prisoner and she unhappily one of his keepers.

He smiled. 'I'm not trying to escape. I need to reach my family.'

Relief relaxed her features. 'Oh,' she said, smiling. 'Well, there's a whole team of —'

'No, I don't wish to go via that team.'

Those smiling features, fresh and not wearied by war, tightened into a frown again. Grey-blue eyes narrowed. 'I don't understand, Lieutenant. They can make contact faster than —'

'I know this,' he interrupted, smiling his apology for doing so again. 'Their hands are tied.' He gave a gesture to reinforce this as she looked at him, perplexed. 'You see, I'm not Jacques Bouchon – I never was.'

'I am lost, Lieutenant,' she admitted, pushing back a stray curl of blonde hair.

'I understand, but you see I didn't know who I was when I was imprisoned, because I had lost my memory.'

It was dawning on her now, lightening her expression, but she was also backing away, just a single step. It was obvious she knew what he wanted from her. 'No, Lieutenant, I can't help you.'

'Agatha, I'm pleading with you – a letter, that's all,' he begged. 'How can that hurt?'

Agatha shook her head, all flirtatiousness having seeped away. Her pretty doll's face looked deeply hesitant. 'There are rules. They are very strict.'

All he could do now was appeal to Agatha's romantic heart. 'I know you like me, Agatha, and I feel blessed to have you take care of me. If only all the soldiers had you to look forward to when they have to have painful drops put in their eyes.' He bent to catch her downward gaze and won the twitch of a smile he needed. 'I am very, very grateful to be here – and grateful to you for being so kind to me.'

Now she looked coy. 'That's my job, Lieutenant.'

'Which I'm guessing you do better than most because you're so cheerful and, if you don't mind me saying so, heartbreakingly pretty.' Agatha trembled slightly at his compliment.

'I don't mind.' She shrugged, her voice breathy.

'My wife is beautiful like you. The day we married we learned about the war and I joined up the same day.' He watched her mouth open in silent shock as she absorbed this. 'She wanted a baby so much but we didn't have time . . . we only had twenty-seven days together before I marched away in uniform, making her promises that I would be back by Christmas. Three Christmas days have come and gone since then, and although Sophie is my everything, I'd forgotten who I was for most of the war and she will have been told I'm dead. Can you imagine what that has done to her?' Jerome stepped forward to fill the space between them. 'I'd like to hear from my wife, just one more time, before I die.'

'Die?'

'Did you know I was gassed? My lungs catch fire sometimes. I fret I will die before she learns I have been trying to get back to her for more than three years.'

'Oh, Lieutenant, no, don't say that.'

'The thing is, Agatha,' he said with a soft smile, 'if to die soon is my fate, I will accept it calmly if I could just reach her and let her know one more time how much I love her, how her very existence made mine ten times brighter than before I met her.' He heard Agatha sigh gently. 'I want her to know I remembered her, us, our love, before I leave her for the final time.'

Agatha's eyes were moist, touched by his romantic words. 'You must not speak like this, Lieutenant. Let me ask the family unit as a matter of urgency.'

'I am assured that the team *is* looking into this matter,' he said, trying not to sound frustrated. 'But I might be dead before all the protocols that need to be followed have been adhered to.'

She nodded. 'Everything does seem to take a very long time.'

He brightened, an idea striking him. 'Agatha, I'll tell you what. I have a brother in Paris. If you could make a telephone call for me, that's all it would take.'

'I'm not sure I —'

'Just a quick call,' he pressed, not allowing her to resist. 'You can remain anonymous. All I need is for you to tell him Jerome is alive and where I am. He will do the rest. You can forget I ever asked this favour after that simple two-minute call.'

'And then what?' She frowned.

'Louis will be like a cat after a mouse. He will not rest. And his senior connections mean that he might be able to speed up procedures so I can be put in touch with Sophie before . . . well, before it's too late.' He took Agatha's hand and kissed the pale skin. It was intimate and even wicked but he kept it brisk so it couldn't be considered amorous; his only intention was gratitude and pushing her to action. 'Will you do this for me? A phone call? I will repay whatever is required.' He raised his gaze to her and hoped she really did find him handsome and dashing because he was relying on his charm alone now. 'And then we can go dancing and celebrate.'

'Dancing?'

'Yes! Ignore my limp and I shall take pleasure in twirling you around the dance hall at the next opportunity. My happiness will have no bounds when I know I may see or even just speak to my wife one more time. I shall dance until you're exhausted.'

She giggled as he reached around her waist and whirled her in a full revolution, careful to let go immediately so no impropriety could be read into the action.

Agatha gave a sigh of resignation. 'I can try, Lieutenant, but I must not contravene the rules for prisoners.'

His heart felt like it was leaping around in his chest with excitement but he had to convey calm. 'Try is all I ask. Here is his number – see, I can even remember all of this now. It's incredible.' He needed to keep her talking so he didn't spook her, as he quickly scribbled the address of Louis's apartment and his telephone number on a piece of paper. 'This is my brother, Louis Méa.'

Her features became serious. 'All I am prepared to say is that Lieutenant Jerome Méa is in the care of this hospital in Lausanne and is a patient under the name of Jacques Bouchon. I will not give my name.'

'That's it!' he urged her, thrilled. 'Thank you, Agatha.' He took a risk and quickly kissed both of her rosy cheeks. 'I hope to see you at the concert tonight.'

Now her entire face flushed pink. 'I do too. Don't touch your eye – let the medicine work, no matter how it itches.'

He grinned, blew her a kiss as she departed and sighed his intense relief, feeling exhausted from the tension. Maybe, just maybe, his darling Sophie was a step closer to being in his arms again.

Jerome moved to the small window of his attic room, his eye still stinging from the treatment but now covered with a bandage. He cast his gaze down to the shoreline of Lake Geneva. It was a picture of pleasure with no indication that a massive, destructive, traumatic war continued to unfold across its border. The summer sun encouraged plenty of people to play on the small sandy beach, and the waters twinkled an inviting sapphire as bathers enjoyed the warmth. Many of them would be internees, he suspected. Perhaps he should take a swim, no longer be self-conscious of his hollow frame – such a far cry from the strapping man he'd been when he asked Sophie to marry him. He imagined she would be past the shock of grief, living now with the knowledge that he was gone and she must make her own future. She would. Sophie was the most independent woman he'd ever met. She was strong of will. She would meet someone else; she was young enough to start again, start a family too . . . and if he could just speak with her one more time, he would tell her all of this. He would make sure she understood that he wanted her to have a good life, a happy one that searched for joy through a new marriage and family with his blessing. But he also wanted her to know how everything in his heart right now during his incarceration was selfishly only about them and how much he regretted leaving her – and especially that she'd been forced to live with no letters from him. It would be a shock for her to know he was a prisoner. His mind was racing to consider all the possible angles from which the news that he was alive could be viewed. He calmed himself and made a promise to be patient now and hope that Agatha could get through to Louis and that his brother would make all the pieces fall into place.

He focused on the happy scenes below. The Swiss, bless them, were trying to find normality. Lausanne had everything from musical recitals to theatrical presentations, put on by the soldiers to keep them engaged, help them feel uplifted and reconnect them to something more akin to civilian life. Even he had been drawn into helping out with concerts, like the one this evening. Many a time during his incarceration he had been called upon to use his baritone to keep spirits up; now he had been asked to use it to entertain internees and Swiss concertgoers alike. He felt helplessly chuffed to see his photograph in the concert programs.

There was a knock at the door. It was Dr Müller.

'Ah, good afternoon, Jacques. How are you feeling?'

He grinned. 'Better than I have in a long time,' he admitted.

'Truly?' The doctor beamed his pleasure. 'That's wonderful to hear.' He scanned the notes at the end of Jerome's bed, comparing them to the file he was carrying. 'So, you've had your drops?'

Jerome nodded. 'Just a few minutes ago.'

'Good, good. You have excellent colour too,' the doctor observed. 'That's very heartening. I heard you sing last week, Jacques. I do enjoy light opera.'

He nodded. 'I sang that for my wife. She loves opera.' He hoped his wording might encourage the doctor to do more to help him reach her.

'That is why you put so much emotion into it. I understand your impatience, Jacques —'

'Jerome,' he corrected.

The doctor nodded, slightly awkwardly. 'We are making all the right enquiries. Now,' he said, keen to move away from that troublesome topic, 'are you receiving all your rations?' He was looking in Jerome's ears as he asked this.

'Most generously. I receive chocolate, tobacco, real coffee, real milk.'

The doctor chuckled. 'Say *aah*,' he encouraged, feeling around the glands of Jerome's throat. Jerome obliged. 'Good. Very good. I see Nurse Agatha has changed that dressing on your eye. How is it feeling? No pain?'

Jerome nodded. 'None. To all intents dead and blind. No complaints but she did say she might try to find a proper patch for me to wear.'

'Yes, indeed. I can organise that for you. May I listen to your chest, please?'

Jerome enjoyed the Swiss. Now that he was moving among them daily, he'd begun to see them for the lonely yet generous people they were. They had a singsong way of speaking that was peppered with smiles. Despite this he sensed an unease – a sort of melancholy, as if collectively they were always ready for bad news. Perhaps that came from being neutral, surrounded by belligerents, or maybe from centuries of making a living off the mountains, always wondering what was happening over in the next valley. Such a different landscape to his own birthplace. He began undoing his shirt. 'Do you know there's music and dancing in the ballroom of this hotel?'

'Yes. My wife and I attended one a couple of weeks ago. They trialled it and now I believe it will happen more often. The internees have formed a wonderful dance orchestra, haven't they?'

Jerome shook his head. 'I think the English love performing.'

'Oh, if I'm honest I think all the internees do after so long in captivity but yes, you might be right – the British are more openly . . . er, shall I say, theatrically inclined.'

After a pause while the doctor asked him to breathe deeply in and out a few times, he gestured for Jerome to dress again.

'Hmmm, slight wheeze. Have you been coughing?'

'Yes, a few moments ago.' He desperately did not want the bad news today.

'Isn't it marvellous that when you sing you never cough?'

Jerome blinked, then grinned. 'I'd never considered that but you're right, Dr Müller.'

'That's because you're healing.'

'But just now I was —'

Dr Müller waved away his concern. 'More to the point, how are you actually feeling in here, Lieutenant Bouchon?' Müller said, touching his own temple.

Jerome shrugged, perplexed. 'Better.'

'Excellent. Nightmares?'

'Some. Nothing I can't rationalise by morning.'

'Good. Not bored?'

'No,' he scoffed, looking appalled.

'Many are, you know, now that the novelty of being removed from prison in Germany has worn off. I'm glad you're not.'

'I'd gladly work if that —'

'No, no . . . that's not what I meant, son. I'm just seeing boredom creeping in to some of the internees' lives and it tends to equate to them drinking more liquor, and that leads to more indulgence. But you live a healthy life all round and I'm glad to see you've put on some weight, got some colour back into your complexion.'

He had to ask. No point in remaining cowardly. 'So how am I doing, Doctor?'

'Well, this is it, you see, Jacques . . . er, Lieutenant. I actually think you're improving, and rather swiftly at that.'

'Improving?' he repeated. He realised that he sounded appalled.

The doctor nodded. 'Your limp is less pronounced, so your muscles are getting stronger in that leg from the long walks you take, and I want to congratulate you on that. Those hikes will be demanding on your lungs but obviously you are coping so very well. Your eye, well, that's not going to change in terms of regaining sight, but you are clearly adjusting and compensating with the remaining sight you do have, which I note is sharp. The point at which your arm was amputated is healing so much better since we did that second small surgery. There's no pain?'

'It's numb,' he admitted. 'But, Dr Müller, what about tuberculosis?'

'That's the best news of all.' The doctor sounded jaunty. 'Not everyone who has been a victim of the poison gas is condemned to die of TB. I know that was the popular opinion when the first cases came through. So many did die from gas complications and yes, there have been many deaths after long suffering and contraction of the disease. But we've since noticed a large group of men, such as you, who don't necessarily succumb. Your lungs are compromised, this is true, but they will function more than adequately. They already do. And perhaps they can get stronger still.'

'What are you saying, Doctor?' Jerome felt a tingling around his neck as a fresh tension gripped him with impossible optimism.

The doctor looked delighted. 'There is no sign of tuberculosis in you, Lieutenant. I believe it is all about healing from now on. Onwards, my boy – to repatriation, if this war would only end. One day very soon I hope I shall be waving you on your way home.'

# 25

If only Louis hadn't picked up the telephone. His was one of the few private homes in France that had embraced the device; most of his high-society friends still believed their close-knit lifestyle and position within a select part of Paris meant there was no need for the modern appliance that was overtaking their London circle like a plague.

Louis, however, considered himself influential and one of the urban elite, so he'd had one installed as soon as it became available, in spite of the fact that telephoning the majority of his friends was still impossible. For business, though, it felt like an advance as important as the industrial revolution. He rather delighted in the loud jangling, hoping all his neighbours had been disturbed by it and were right now wondering who could be on the other end of that telephone call.

It was from Switzerland, much to his surprise.

'I apologise, I didn't hear your name clearly,' he said, frowning, trying to recall anyone he knew who hailed from Switzerland. 'Did you say Lausanne?'

The woman on the other end, who sounded young, cleared her throat and tried again, louder. 'I said I am a nurse based in

Lausanne . . .' and again he didn't hear a name spoken, which seemed odd, but he gathered she was calling from a hospital. 'Is this Monsieur Louis Méa?'

'It is,' he replied, wondering how on earth anyone in a Lausanne hospital could know him. 'How can I help you, made-moiselle?' He chanced that she was unmarried. What was this all about?

'I have a message for you, sir.'

'Oh, yes?' He was intrigued now.

'It is from a gentleman – a patient – called Jacques Bouchon.'

'I think you have the wrong number,' he said. 'I don't know anyone of that name. I'm sorry.'

'He is an internee . . . a French prisoner from Germany.'

Louis blinked with bewilderment. 'Again, my apologies. You surely have the wrong person.'

'You are Louis Méa, sir?'

'I am, but —'

'I am calling on behalf of your brother, Lieutenant Jerome Méa. He is registered with us under the wrong name, he assures us. He wishes you to contact the hospital in Lausanne immediately. Let me give you the number.'

Louis imagined his skin had suddenly turned as white as the glass of milk he had just poured for himself in an effort to quell the acid of last night's drinking. Bile began to rise, but it was nothing to do with his night at the pleasure palace of the Moulin Rouge. 'I beg your pardon?'

'Please write this number down, sir. I do not have much time and I am not officially authorised to pass on this information.' She began reciting a telephone number, and although he reflexively wrote down the number she gave him, he did so with no concen-tration. It was as though his thoughts had been launched from a catapult and scattered in all directions.

'Are you there, monsieur?'

'You're sure he calls himself Jerome Méa?' His voice sounded dislocated from his thoughts, and higher than normal.

'Yes, sir. He tells me he is a grower of grapes from a place called Avize in Champagne. He asked me —'

Louis replaced the handset, not slamming it but quietly returning it to its cradle and cutting off the young nurse from Lausanne, his mind racing to gather up those careening thoughts because his next decision was going to be vital.

———

Sophie had been invited to Louis's apartment in Paris and found herself privately astonished at how close he lived to the famous opera house. She could swear that if she got herself to the top storey she would be able to see her favourite building's glimmering rooftop. It struck her that although Haussmann's elegant avenues were within an easy stroll, Louis was embedded in the city's narrow, run-down and notorious playtime district of Pigalle. She'd never been allowed to roam this neighbourhood while her parents were alive but she knew about it.

In getting to know Louis better, she had come to realise that everything he did was by careful choice. They were opposites, these brothers: Jerome was as impetuous and spontaneous as Louis was considered and shrewd. The elder calculated his risks, whereas she didn't think Jerome had stopped to consider any, which is how he had so easily rushed off to war. And Sophie imagined that Louis had chosen this district, this street, this very apartment so he could be near his beloved opera but also partake in the more lascivious side of Paris. His suggestion that they live their married life apart was not out of generosity to her, she now realised, or even a polite sensitivity towards Jerome. No, Sophie decided that Louis wished to keep his life separate from hers so that he could continue to live as he always had and not feel in any way answerable for the debauched lifestyle she sensed he enjoyed.

'Where are you staying in Paris?' he called from the kitchenette, which she suspected saw little activity.

'There's a small hotel near the opera,' she called, taking off her hat.

He was busy making a pot of coffee and he appeared now looking flustered; in fact, for the first time since she'd met him, Louis appeared slightly nervous. She believed it might be because she was standing in his most private of spaces. Perhaps he desperately wanted her to like it and thus like him more.

'Are you sure you wouldn't rather go to a café? It's a beautiful day,' he offered.

It was obvious he would. 'All right,' she acquiesced, keen to please, especially as she was here on a mission.

Within minutes, Sophie had her hat back on and they were seated at a pavement table outside a small café.

'There,' he said. 'Now, isn't this splendid?' He turned his round face to the sun and sighed. 'Better than being cramped in my apartment.'

There was nothing small about his apartment and she already spent plenty of time in the sunshine, but his pale skin suggested he rarely did. It even occurred to her that Louis would prefer to be inside the café, out of the sun, and that this sidewalk table out in the open was for her benefit. He was putting on a show of casual breeziness she couldn't fathom.

Until she could work out what was going on, Sophie decided, she would remain neutral. 'It's perfect,' she agreed as the waiter arrived.

'Monsieur Méa, welcome,' he said. 'Madame,' he acknowledged, thin moustache twitching above a brief attempt at a smile. 'Coffee?'

'Two, please, André,' Louis replied, once again not bothering to check with Sophie, she noted. 'And I'll have a small Byrrh.' He finally consulted her. 'My dear, an aperitif for you?'

'No, coffee is fine, thank you.'

The waiter nodded crisply and departed.

'I've never favoured quinine,' she remarked, pulling off her cotton gloves.

'Don't like its bitterness?'

'I quite like that quality, if I'm honest. No, it's more the medicinal taste that I don't enjoy.'

'I think that's the point, my dear, and they certainly promote it as a health drink. The mistelle they add is simply to mask the flavour,' he said, chuckling. 'But in truth we're all enjoying it for the alcohol.'

She joined in his amusement, which didn't sound in any way mirthful, as two small cups of coffee appeared alongside a tiny triangular glass of syrupy liquor.

'To your good health,' he said, not wasting any time and tipping half of it into his mouth.

Sophie nodded and sipped the rich coffee as she watched him lick his lips and tried not to imagine them ever having freedom over her body.

---

Louis sucked his lips, not wishing to waste a drop of the Byrrh, and wondered if it was revulsion he saw darting across Sophie's face like a crack of lightning or whether she was suddenly frightened. He rather hoped that he did scare her; he needed her to feel cornered. The telephone call three days before had rattled him, and it took plenty for Louis to admit to that. He kept reminding himself that all his high-level contacts at the Red Cross had assured him that Jerome was as 'good as dead'. He'd even taken the precaution of menacing his friend Jean at the French Red Cross that he was, under no circumstances, to give Sophie even the remotest hope. All he was waiting on now was the army to confirm his brother's death with a certificate. He hoped a call from a stranger in another country out of the blue was something he could easily dispel.

He'd tried ignoring the nurse's phone call, and when that hadn't succeeded, he'd deliberately got drunk, hoping distraction would help him to forget. But yesterday morning he had woken to a riot of nausea and a pounding headache, both fuelled by the knowledge that his brother might be alive and living under a different name. His memory remained intact, sadly, and the Lausanne-based nurse's words continued to haunt him.

The news, if it was true, couldn't have been more ill-timed. His financiers were beginning to lose patience. Louis needed the instant security offered by his brother's vineyards, not to mention the Delancré estates.

The bank's recommendation that he move from the Pigalle apartment to one in a less desirable arrondissement was ludicrous . . . and the whispered suggestion from his personal banker that he consider selling up in Paris, perhaps moving back to Avize for a while, consolidating his funds, was heinous.

All he needed was time. And time equated to Sophie. To be engaged, to give him even the sense of access to his brother's property, would likely be enough to send the bank hounds scarpering back to their kennels. And if it turned out that Jerome was indeed alive and languishing in some Swiss hospital – he couldn't imagine how or why – then nothing would be truly lost.

His brother could return, Louis would magnanimously let Sophie off the hook, take back his mother's ring, celebrate the reunion of the happy couple, look forward to the children that would no doubt come forth in a few years and keep the name going, but in the meantime, his skin would be saved. He just needed a little time to shore up the investments that had taken such a beating during the war. Nothing that time and a little additional funding couldn't fix. It all sounded so reasonable in his now calm, calculated thoughts.

He needed that ring on Sophie's finger and some sort of little soirée to celebrate a formal agreement between them – to which he would invite a senior financier who had the ability to influence those who wished to foreclose on him. As to the call from Switzerland, he would deny it. Who could prove it? Who would bother to try? If Jerome really was alive, he would surely be repatriated when the war ended. Until then, Louis had no intention of following up the stranger's call. That was that.

He looked at beautiful Sophie sipping her coffee and imagined how pleasant it would be to sire a child with her . . . or at least attempt to. All of the fun was in the attempt, anyway.

'Louis, it sounded urgent. Do you have more news?'

*None that I'd like to tell you about, Sophie*, he thought. 'Not urgent so much as important. I wanted you to know that I changed my mind – I tried one last time,' he lied, feeling almost sad at the way her eyes widened with hope. 'Unfortunately, even at the highest level all I received was a reiteration from the Ministry that it will not change Jerome's status as having died in Flanders,' he said, shaking his head sadly, watching as the light in her expression was extinguished by the news. 'They require no further proof than his bloodstained jacket and a presumption of gassing and then death, lost to no-man's-land in Ypres. That is how it was firmly described to me two days ago. It's proof, Sophie. It's the best we are going to get under the circumstances, and all we can do now is move on with our lives in the most practical of ways.'

They both knew what he meant. He enjoyed the look of despair on her face. She wanted – needed – his pity and that took the form of sugar. He was keen to provide that kindness but it had a price . . . like everything.

'So, this sugar,' he began carefully, watching her take a shallow breath. She'd known this was coming; he didn't have to tread carefully. 'Am I to have it sent to Épernay?' It sounded so reasonable even he was surprised. 'You must be very close to making a decision for this year's champagne, surely?' He made that second statement sound innocent enough, as though it had no agenda.

'I have but days,' she answered in a flat tone, putting down her cup carefully. 'I need that sugar.'

'I know, my dear,' he said, draining the Byrrh and reaching into his pocket to pull out the familiar ring box. 'Shall we?'

––––––––

Sophie was once again confronted by the powerfully loathsome sight of the ring box. Louis didn't open it this time; he simply sat it on the table near his empty glass.

'Louis, do you feel it in your heart – in your very soul – that Jerome is dead?' She didn't wait for him to answer. 'Because I don't —' She watched Louis blanch before he coughed and reached inside his jacket for a handkerchief. 'Oh, are you all right, Louis?' she asked as she was interrupted by his explosive cough.

'Yes, yes, my dear,' he said in a slightly croaky voice. He swallowed his cold coffee. 'Er . . . sorry. To answer your heartfelt question, yes, I do with every ounce of my soul believe that my beloved brother has given his life for France. The proof is irrefutable; the army has a bloodstained tunic, his documents, together with witnesses who saw him fall during that awful gas attack. That's a trio of conclusive clues to his demise and it's enough for our ministry, my dear. The general I spoke to said that the army would move swiftly under the circumstances to hold the necessary enquiry, issue the death certificate and finally release you from your prison of not knowing.'

He broke eye contact with her, glancing towards the thin traffic of passers-by. His gaze flicked back and there was something distracted in it.

'And what if he isn't dead?'

'Turns up suddenly?' He sounded awkward.

'Let's say he did. What then?'

'You are only wearing the ring. You can give it back.'

'And just like that I am free?' she said, both appalled and intrigued at once.

She watched Louis shrug. 'If some miracle that you alone believe in comes to pass, and Jerome walks back into our lives, then you are still married, are you not?'

She nodded.

He shrugged again. 'Wear my ring for one year after peace is formally declared. That's more than sufficient time for my brother to rise from the dead and return. If he doesn't, then you follow through on our agreement and we marry.'

If she looked at this purely as a business deal, she had to privately admit that Louis was not being unreasonable; actually, it was generous. He was the one making all the adjustments while she was the one presumably getting everything she needed out of it in the short term.

'Louis, can't I just pay for the sugar?' she tried, grinning hopefully.

He returned the smile. 'It does sound feasible but you see, my dear, while I have something you want so badly, you also have what I want just as badly. While I hate to reduce someone as beautiful and intelligent as you to a commodity alongside sugar, a bargain is a bargain.'

'The devil's bargain,' she quipped, keeping the amusement in her tone even though she wanted to fling the dregs of her coffee at him. 'One year from the date of peace being formally declared?'

'That's what I will agree to today if you take the ring home with you.' He lifted a hand. 'As soon as the sugar has been delivered, we shall host an evening in Épernay and another in Paris to declare our intentions to be betrothed.'

'And what if I can get my own supplies of sugar or perhaps do not use it, between peace and the formal announcement of our engagement?'

He laughed softly and it sounded cruel. 'Oh, my dear, you are priceless . . . I know your wine is finishing its second fermentation and awaiting that special ingredient of the sugar after disgorgement of the lees, but if you can get sugar for *dosage* within that time frame, then you may return my ring – but I'm confident you will not be able to achieve such magic.'

The word made her think of Charlie: how she'd slapped him . . . how he wanted to bring magic into her life. Sophie was truly sickened as she felt herself being cornered into taking the calculated and repulsive gamble she'd imagined she would never have to take. Yet Jerome had admired her rebellious nature, her ability to take risks.

Sophie reached for the ring box. 'Deliver the sugar,' she said and watched the smile of satisfaction curl slowly into the curve of a well-baked croissant.

# 26

He had riddled more bottles than he could count and the smell of yeast in the air from the fermentation now struck him as being a permanent companion.

The sting of Sophie's slap had disappeared quickly but the memory of it hadn't. He was still angry but was wise enough to realise that he wasn't sure why. Was he angry at himself for stepping into another man's shoes, at Sophie for rejecting him . . . or at Louis for taking advantage of a vulnerable woman in the worst possible way? The cowardice of the blackmail seemed to trump all other grievances and he'd spent days in the dark of the cellar pondering this as he riddled, avoiding any contact with Sophie, not that she hunted for him. Charlie decided she was probably wise enough, or perhaps embarrassed enough by her emotional outburst, not to seek him out until he wanted to be found.

He had decided on just a few more days and then he would go: out of her life forever. Even so, Charlie knew that at any moment the liquor in the bottles would complete its second fermentation and Sophie would need to disgorge the lees that the riddling had brought into the necks of those bottles. But her team could not disgorge without the *liqueur d'expédition* to replace what was lost and that special dosage needed sugar so that all of her fruit's personality would be shown at its finest.

Setting their quarrel aside – if he could term it that way – Charlie fully appreciated how vital this vintage, above all others, was to her. Her first from the wedding vineyard and perhaps, more importantly, her first all-chardonnay vintage. Even Charlie wanted this to work for Sophie because it spoke of who she was: a rebellious female champagne maker, wanting to follow in the footsteps of those other proud women at the helm of their champagne houses who had innovated and taken the beverage to new heights. She needed sugar to achieve her aim. It felt important to him to help her make this happen. Maybe that would be his private legacy that spoke of his love for her, something to leave behind that couldn't be obliterated by others because it was cerebral . . . a notion. Could his novel idea work? His chemist's intellect told him it was not only plausible but that nature's chemistry would embrace it. Would Sophie permit it, though? He would argue it was a solution: one that was expedient, an answer to her problem, which meant she would not have to deliver herself to Louis in some sort of dark exchange.

Charlie had been staring at the bottles that contained the juice, where the yeast had been busy consuming the sugars, and thinking long and hard about the idea he'd had that could mark the finish of hell's reign on earth with a bright new champagne vintage.

It was only now that he looked up to see Sophie had arrived; he had no idea how long she might have been in the cellar. He noticed she was deep in conversation, consulting Étienne over something; their heads were bent close. She looked thinner since he'd seen her and still she managed to make her dark, slimly crafted, fuss-free work clothes look like they were being modelled at an atelier. She'd resisted the urge to don trousers as he knew so many women had during the war, simply because it was easier, given the men's work they were tackling.

He wished he could see her in a gown and finery, off to the opera . . . or perhaps in a négligé with her hair unravelling from a loose, low-rolled chignon at her nape. He dismissed the daydream, remembering their heated words and how those had ended. She seemed to sense he was watching and looked over and trapped his gaze. He had been caught staring when he most wanted to appear unaffected by her presence. Who was he trying to hoodwink? She nodded and lifted a hand in a gentle wave but he didn't return it; it was his last moment of churlish resilience. She bent her head to the old man, who grinned as she kissed the top of his head, before she moved around her cellar giving a word of encouragement here and there to each. Charlie admired the gentle way in which she managed her team; she trusted them and they loved her.

And then she was moving towards him in that way of hers that made it look like as though she was gliding beneath her long skirt.

'Charlie,' she murmured. 'May we talk?'

'Is there anything more to say?' How petulant he sounded.

She gave him a look that a mother might give a peevish child. 'Please, Charlie. I must apologise. I haven't been able to sleep for how badly I behaved.'

'Forget it.' He sounded just plain crabby now.

'I can't forget what occurred. I won't. You must let me make amends.'

He tried to sound exasperated, as though it mattered little. And yet it was so obvious in his tight body language that he felt the opposite. 'Let's agree we brought that, um, episode, shall we say, upon each other. Besides, I will be on my way next week: various trains to Calais and then onto the ship to England.'

She looked shocked by his plans but pressed on. 'I was not brought up to raise my hand to anyone.'

'Then why me, Sophie?'

She blinked, willing but perhaps not ready at this moment to answer. 'There is a saying, isn't there, that you always hurt those you most love?'

'It's a convenient one.' He smiled with no joy in it, hating himself for making her squirm.

'But true, no?' Eyes that shifted between the colour of forest and that of the open meadow fixed him where he stood. 'And I do love you, Charlie. I'm just not permitting myself to explore that feeling.'

He held her gaze defiantly and nodded slowly. 'I accept your apology.'

'Thank you,' she said, sounding earnest. 'Tell me, when you reach England, then what?'

He shrugged. 'I'm unsure myself. I have to go through the repatriation process but there may be an opportunity for me not to leave France immediately.' She cut him a sharp glance. Charlie explained. 'They've set up clearing parties – units of Allied soldiers who are making sure France is clear of the retreating German soldiers. There is also a role for reclaiming our dead.' She winced at this. He shook his head sadly. 'There are so many families waiting for news of their loved and lost.'

'Like me?'

'Exactly. In fact, it's because of your situation that I'd like to offer my services. There's nothing for me to hurry home to, and I could do some good for the fallen soldiers. Find them, make sure we contact their wives, mothers, all who wait on news.'

'That sounds as though it could suit you.'

He nodded, glad she saw it that way. 'Anyway, before I go, I do have an idea I'd like to share with you,' he said, keeping it casual.

'I hope it is the magic I yearn for?'

'It might be,' he answered cryptically.

She regarded him and he saw a flicker of amusement . . . only just there, but a spark nonetheless. There was hope they would part as friends. 'Do you wish to tell me now?'

He nodded. 'Actually, will you accompany me to my accommodation in the sheds?'

'Now there's an invitation,' she quipped.

He gusted a laugh, long overdue. He had seriously wondered if he could again. 'I dare you to accept,' he risked.

Her smoky chuckle made his spirits lift and his heart felt as though it were inflating from its warmth.

'No one has ever called me a coward,' she said, one eyebrow lifting in challenge.

The dormitory was deserted when they arrived.

'It's so neat,' she remarked, looking around the room.

Dust motes flipped around her like tiny gnats drawn to the light. Her hair shone in a shaft of light arcing through one of the small windows of the shed he had called home recently. He had to look away as the desire to reach for her threatened to tear open what felt like a freshly scabbed wound.

He turned away and bent down, deliberately busying himself by rummaging in a cupboard. 'Soldiers live here,' he replied, as if that explained everything.

'I shall miss you.' She sounded wistful.

An awkward silence wrapped around them.

'Anyway . . .' he began, but she accidentally spoke over him.

'So, what's this burning information, Charlie?' She sounded overly bright. 'Sorry, I . . . you go ahead.'

'All right.' He straightened, an unlabelled bottle of champagne in his hand. 'About your vintage for this year.'

She frowned. 'Not this year. As I told you, not without sugar . . . or Louis, and I haven't made up my mind about that yet.' She looked momentarily concerned even to mention it.

Charlie lifted a hand to stop her. 'Well, don't confirm any

arrangement. I think you can still go ahead and make this year's champagne, if you're prepared to be flexible . . . daring, even.' He imagined his eyes glittering with excitement. 'Sophie, I think I may have solved your sugar crisis.'

He enjoyed seeing the shock moving across her expression.

'That's the 1917,' she noted, nodding towards the bottle he held. 'The first juice from the wedding vines.'

'It is. Awaiting disgorgement and then dosage of the final sugar liquor, if I'm not mistaken?' He paused and she shifted her weight to one hip as though he'd intrigued her.

'Go on,' she said.

'I've had this chilling in the stream behind here all night. Now, Sophie, it's pretty rough, all right?'

'My champagne is not rough,' she assured him in an amused tone, sounding genuinely fascinated.

'No, I mean what I've done to it is a bit rough —' he shook his head as if helpless — 'with none of your skills. It needs time to settle, for the flavours to blend properly. So for now it's just a gauge of what might be achieved with your wisdom and experience. Étienne helped.' He struggled to uncork it with only one working hand but was glad she didn't offer to do it, which would have made him feel inadequate. 'Ah, there,' he said when the cork released with a satisfying popping sound. He reached for two small glasses readied in the cupboard for this moment and poured out two fizzing bowls of her unfinished champagne.

'Charlie, what have you added to my champagne?'

He grinned. 'Something extremely close to your heart. I've added Delancré ratafia.'

She opened her mouth to speak but her surprise seemed to take over and no words came.

'It could work, couldn't it? Your sugar-laden ratafia, a by-product of your very grapes, has to be the solution. You're not adding anything that shouldn't be there anyway, or at least couldn't tiptoe into your champagne and not flatten those chiselled bubbles or do damage to the flavours. The chemist in me assures me this can work.' He handed her a glass and was heartened to see her expression was still one of stunned surprise.

'*Quelle folie!*' she began in a shocked whisper and there was a slightly breathless quality to her voice as she tested the theory.

'It is daring,' he said over her thoughts, 'but I promise you it is not crazy, do you agree?'

'No, not crazy.' She shook her head. 'It is creative and inspired.'

'You know it can work, Sophie. And using ratafia keeps it pure, keeps it all about Épernay, keeps you true to your champagne because this is from the grapes of that same vineyard, that same harvest. I'm not suggesting you do this every year but don't miss out on your supply for 1918 . . . I think if anything, this is an absolute triumph for Reims, for House Delancré, for the champagne makers of the region, and above all, for the women of Épernay – who stayed strong, who kept the grapes growing and the champagne flowing.' He warmed to his excitement, all crabbiness forgotten. 'That's how you can be remembered through this period. You didn't capitulate to the enemy's oppression – and I personally include your loathsome brother-in-law in that.'

She smiled ruefully at his words.

'You made champagne in 1918 despite broken people, battered vineyards, no sugar. As France triumphed and banished her enemy, House Delancré will triumph alongside her. You'll have the bottles to prove your courage, and sales to capitalise on that bravery.'

His eyes were sparkling with the power of the notion, and he suspected her spirits were as elated by his rousing words.

'I will drink to that, Charlie. *Santé.*' She clinked his glass.

'Here's mud in your eye,' he said in English.

'Whatever that means.' She laughed.

'No one's sure. Some say it's from the Bible, others from the mud that horses kick up as they gallop down the winning straight,' he began and then waved a hand. 'And there are other stories, I'm sure. But it's habit.'

They shared a smile and sipped in tandem. He waited for several heartbeats, holding his excited breath until after a long pause a smile curled on Sophie's face in a spiral of pleasure – finding her dimples, reaching her eyes and fuelling her voice, which sounded as breathless as he felt.

'Oh, Charlie.' She sipped again, savouring it. 'If only you knew how much more this means now than it did a few days ago. You clever, clever chemist.'

'How so?'

'It's a miracle,' she admitted, shaking her head in awe. 'I dared you to work magic and you have. And you might just have saved me from my fate.'

'Louis?'

She nodded and he could sense the excitement rising within her, and also relief – they were like twin columns suddenly supporting her. 'If we can pull this off, I can return his sugar . . . and his ring.'

'Then do both, because I promise we can make this work,' he said, all grievances set aside. 'Tell me what you're tasting. I need to understand from the winemaker's perspective.'

She lifted a shoulder in a small shrug. 'It is highly personal, of course. This wine is a deity, don't forget.' His expression eased into a smile as he leaned against the wall of the shed and relaxed into her description. 'She is sinuous in her flavour and that gives her sensuality on my tongue. I'm tasting a complex, sophisticated and suave aroma of acacia with notes of lime tree flowers – bright and lively. But after a moment or two that vividness calms to give an impression of mirabelle.' At Charlie's slight frown, she explained.

'These are tiny yellow plums, and that quality provides a smooth, velvety flavour.' Sophie took another sip. 'Mmm, my beautiful goddess is here – there's a superb finish to this, with a full flavour of fresh citrussy fruit. The ratafia has added a beautiful depth.'

'Now encapsulate all of that into a few words,' Charlie encouraged her, 'because that's how you'll sell it.'

She paused, eyes still closed, allowing the memory of her sip of the champagne to resonate. 'This champagne when it's matured and rounded off holds for the drinker the last days of summer and the warmth of her flavours.'

He smiled. 'Now name it.'

'It can only be called "The Immortal".' She gazed at him tenderly. 'I don't know what to say . . . how to thank —'

He shook his head. 'Let this solution be *my* thank you,' he said, becoming serious. 'For looking after me. For rescuing me.'

'Rescuing you?'

'From myself. I feel there's a life ahead of me now. I wish it could be with you but I've made my peace with that, Sophie. Perhaps in a year or two you may wish to see me again if . . . well, you know. What I do care about more than anything is that you do not have to capitulate to Louis, and you can now follow your heart and achieve this special vintage and honour your husband . . . honour those who have fallen, and celebrate the war's end. I know he would be very proud of you. I'm thrilled you can make your champagne this year and that in a tiny way I have contributed to it.' He could see her eyes glistening with tears and couldn't bear to make her sad when they should be celebrating. 'Come on,' he urged, hoping to rally her. 'Tell me again how clever I am.'

It was the right strategy. She grinned and turned away to taste again. 'Well, the alcohol is a bit high . . . we need to adjust, but yes, yes, the sugar from the ratafia will do the work I need to produce this year's vintage. It has a slightly different flavour but I don't think that matters; its fruit was harvested in wartime but it delivered itself to us in peace. This will be corked properly, labelled and sold in peacetime. I can't think of a more emotionally charged vintage.'

They stared at each other in wonder at the achievement. Sophie let out a small screech of happiness and Charlie laughed; he was not expecting her to put down her glass and, without warning, fling her arms around him.

'Sophie . . .'

'Be quiet.' She shook her head as if not permitting herself to question her motives.

Charlie was too shocked, though. 'What are you doing?'

'What does it look like?'

He frowned. 'I thought . . .'

'So did I. But Charlie, I realise that I can't spend the rest of my life being faithful to someone who is no longer in my life. He didn't choose to die. I didn't choose for him to go to war. Life chose our pathway. No one's to blame. But everyone has been so sad for four years. Now it's time for peace and a chance for all of us to start new journeys. Why is remaining unhappy and lonely the best course? You're leaving in a few days because I'm insisting on remaining dutiful. Well, I'm tired of being dutiful. I'm suddenly excited beyond all belief . . . I can start my life again and it's not with Louis, it's with a man I love. That's what my darling Jerome would want from me . . . to love again. I was about to let go of the best thing that's happened to me in a long time – over a sense of duty. No. Standing here, unable to say goodbye, I demand of myself to be happy again. And I'm always happy when I'm with you.'

'Except when you're slapping me.'

'Charlie . . .'

'I'm joking.' He searched her face, unsure of what to say. He felt a sense of disbelief at her shift in thinking, but also despair. 'I have to go, you understand this, yes?'

She nodded. 'I know. But you will come back to me, won't you?'

Was this really happening? She was in his arms again; he wasn't imagining it. They'd both followed the right course, the respectful one, the responsible one, but Sophie was right – they were acting entirely out of respect for the past rather than looking towards the joy of a future. 'Sophie, are you sure?'

She let her darkly golden lashes close and kissed him lightly, waiting . . . letting him decide now. Charlie felt the lightly scabbed wound over his heart reopening. It was a chasm but he let himself fall fully into it. It was a dizzying feeling but he pulled her tighter and their kiss deepened and lingered until all questions of hesitation were fully answered.

# 27

Jerome stood at the shoreline of Lake Geneva and stared towards France, and the commune of Évian-les-Bains, a spa town that lured wealthy holiday-makers, including his own family. When he was a boy, Jerome's mother had brought him and his brother to visit an aunt of hers who lived among other villas near the lakeshore. Until now he'd not permitted himself to let France sit in his thoughts for any length of time, particularly as it had not occurred to him that he would return. He had thought Death's cool arms were waiting for him in Switzerland and yet today he would leave on the train to be repatriated as a hero of France, returning triumphantly home. Except, as far as the authorities were concerned, he was not Jerome Méa returning, but a man called Jacques Bouchon.

He looked at the pamphlet that he'd been handed moments ago by his nurse. It carried a farewell from his Swiss hosts, wishing him a happy life and no doubt a full heart at returning to his homeland.

'Tell me again what you said,' he urged. 'Please, Agatha.'

She sighed and repeated the telephone conversation she'd had with Louis, for the third time.

'And you say the line went dead?'

339

'Yes, quite strange as we had a surprisingly clear line to speak on.'

'It was definitely my brother?'

'He confirmed twice that his name was Louis Méa.'

'Couldn't have been a friend?'

She shook her head. 'Well, unless that friend lied . . . twice.'

'No, no, you're right. Well, the war might be coming to an end but that doesn't mean the telephone lines are any better. Perhaps more crowded than ever,' he said, and her gaze suggested he was being hopeful. But that's all he had, and he would cling to that. 'Thank you, Agatha. I owe you a dance if you don't mind a twirl with a one-armed, one-eyed, limping prisoner.'

Her radiant smile told him she didn't mind at all. One day soon he was going to ask the woman he loved the same question. For now, he would think on his brother's pleasure at hearing the news and Sophie's disbelieving joy when he passed it on. That was going to be his new daydream – imagining the scene as Louis passed on the revelation; the tears, the smiles, the squeals as they hugged each other with joy.

———

Sophie believed that her heart, for the first time in an age, felt the lightest she could remember. It wasn't just the war imploding on itself now as the Allies ran rampant over German forces; the darkest hour, as it was coming to be known, was past them. And her darkest hour was past her. Jerome was gone. He was dead. Finally, she felt ready to accept it and prepared to begin the slow but steady steps that would move her on. And while she would always privately grieve his loss, the rest of her life stretched out far ahead. Deliberately remaining lonely in memory of someone was pointless. She was reminded of Veuve Clicquot, whom many cherished as the first woman of Champagne. Her husband had died when she was about the same age as Sophie, but she had a daughter to love and raise . . . to live for. The other person who inspired her, Louise Pommery, lost her husband and took over his business when she was forty-one. Sophie thought if she were a dozen years older, she might not be thinking about remarriage and starting a family either.

No, her situation was individual and she was making a decision based on her circumstances, rather than how others might perhaps think she should lead her life. She did not view it as romantic to cut herself off from life's joys simply to be seen as a righteous widow.

She broke free of Charlie's kiss, relaxing into his arms, and sighed herself free of her rambling thoughts. This felt right.

'Sophie,' he whispered, his voice croaky with desire. 'Can I see you tonight?' She knew what that would mean.

She nodded. She wasn't going to analyse this but simply respond to her feelings. 'Yes. I want to see you too. Come to the house. There are only a couple of people remaining on the ground floor. I'll give my housekeeper the night off.'

'May I stay? I daren't let you go.'

She smiled. 'I want you to stay, and then I can let you go and do whatever you have to do before you come back to me for good.'

'This is real, isn't it?' he said, and pinched himself to make her smile.

'Yes, Charlie – as real as the war ending. I don't know how long it will take but we must all work hard to put back the structure in our lives that we all had. Reims will have to be rebuilt and that will take many years, but the notion of having shops reopening and people being able to move around freely, without fear, will be a novelty. I'm imagining the pleasure of schools welcoming back pupils, and soon the banks will reopen and we will no longer have to use emergency banknotes. We have so much work ahead of us here in Épernay too, rebuilding the vineyards that have been destroyed. And remind me to smash down the fake wall that Gaston suggested I build behind the parlour.' His eyes widened. 'There's another in one of the animal sheds, to house Delancré's most prized collection.' She smiled, recalling how Gaston had shown her how to mislabel the bottles to protect her most precious vintages and cuvees. 'And I have a life to look forward to again . . . with you.'

He hugged her and she felt him bury his face in her neck and they stood like that, in silence, for a full minute, savouring what those words meant for both of them.

'I love you, Sophie,' Charlie said, finally breaking the embrace. 'I have never said that to anyone, unless you include a pet snail that I kept outside beneath the window next to my bed. I admit, I really did love Ermintrude but that love pales in comparison to how I feel about you.'

'I'm honoured,' she admitted, laughing, stroking his face. 'Beautiful, funny, clever Charlie. What a lucky girl I am to have found you. I think you've just saved my life.'

'You saved your own. The ratafia was always yours.'

'But it took a soldier and former chemist to make that clever connection. Thank you for saving my life, Charlie. I can't wait to tell Louis I don't need his sugar.'

'Or his ring. Wear my ring, Sophie. Marry me if you're going to marry anyone again.'

She kissed him, slow and tender. 'Only you, Charlie. Tonight I'll prove it.' She gave him a look of wickedness that didn't need a verbal response for her to know how that made him feel. The throb of desire against her made her giggle helplessly. What a power it was that women held over men.

'Can I even make it to tonight?' he groaned.

'You have to,' she said, delighting in teasing him by deliberately pulling away from his body.

Charlie gave a small roar as though having to test the warrior within. 'All right, then. I need distraction. Now is the moment that Sophie Delancré makes her dream come true. Let's begin making the new champagne with the ratafia using only chardonnay.'

She gave a sobering swallow. 'You know I will be risking my most precious chardonnay wine?'

It was rhetorical but he answered anyway. 'Of course I do but risk it, Sophie. You have everything to gain. It will work, I promise.'

Their gazes met and held as she grappled with the idea that had been in her heart for so long now it was a part of her. It was her secret, her private treasure that she took out to admire from time to time. But she'd always put it back, locked it away, left it alone – until the next time. Charlie was making it sound so real, so achievable . . . so terrifying. What if it was a disaster? What if the ratafia and the all-chardonnay champagne was a failure, a complete misjudgement? Would her abortive effort make her the butt of laughter in champagne circles? Would the men of champagne be able to nod in her direction and make remarks about why they don't like women meddling in their business?

*Well, to hell with that!* came sharper voices – women's voices. It was Veuve Clicquot and Madame Pommery, laughing at her lack of nerve. And she knew they were right to scorn her. 'We took risks,' they chorused. 'You must be brave to achieve surprise in this industry – to gain more respect. It's harder for a woman but you have our shoulders to stand on.'

Heavens! She was going to do this. It felt so suddenly right, and besides, all those men were busy struggling with how to make their champagnes without sugar. She was the fortunate one.

'Tell me how an all-chardonnay champagne might taste,' Charlie said, taking her hand, entwining fingers, no doubt aware of the internal battle raging, wanting to help deflect her fear.

It was the right question.

'Ah,' she sighed in a tone as if she'd just slipped into a warm bath. She let go of his gentle hold as an indulgent smile creased her expression and she closed her eyes to imagine for him. 'Bright on the palate, a sense of dazzling lightness but not quite that specific. She will give up her gifts gradually. First a hint of brioche that comes through as a buttery quality, which eases away to deliver a flavour of dried fruit, and then just as you're being seduced by that richness, you'll be surprised by the crisp pleasure of citrus. It will feel supple in your mouth – there's no better way to describe the sensation – it could go anywhere, depending on her mood, and most importantly, on yours.'

'What does that mean?'

She opened her eyes briefly to regard him. 'Well, Charlie, if you were feeling low, she would give a different taste sensation than if you were in love, for instance. It is individual, as well – your gloom and my gloom might make her taste differently on our palates.'

'I'm betting our love might taste the same, though?'

She gave him a lazy smile and closed her eyes again. 'But my chardonnay champagne will always finish on a mineral note because that's her strength. The goddess knows from where she's come . . . she respects the chalk soils and the limestone caves that have nurtured her. And then she will finish lively on your tongue in a refreshing spritz.'

'I want to taste that,' he pleaded and made her laugh.

'I haven't told you about her bubbles yet.'

He reached around her waist but Sophie twisted away playfully, more strands coming loose from her chignon, giving her such a wanton look she suspected Charlie wanted to make love to her right now. How close she was to losing herself entirely to his love: feeling their whole bodies against one another, all of their skin touching, Charlie inside her, and moving together in a way that made everything else in life seem irrelevant for a while.

'The bubbles are petite and so finely chiselled they are like ballerinas on the palate, rising elegantly through the wine, linking hands at the surface to take a bow.'

He applauded her description, clapping awkwardly, able only to make the motion but no sound because of his sling, but nonetheless with genuine pleasure at how well she had described her imaginary wine. 'We are going to make this wine,' he insisted, and this time she let him encircle her waist and pull her close to kiss her with longing. 'Make it, Sophie. Follow your dream.'

'We shall do it together, Charlie. We shall make love tonight and tomorrow we shall make champagne.'

Crazily but hilariously, they began to sway in a dance to music they alone heard. It felt dizzily romantic and as he gently spun her, Sophie's gaze landed on some war gazettes stacked neatly in an open cupboard. 'Charlie,' she murmured, intrigued. 'What are those?'

They stopped moving and he followed her gaze.

'They're gazettes. Do you remember I told you I met someone who said he was going to help with the clearing parties that are making France safe, reclaiming our boys?' He shrugged. 'I was thinking about joining him in that important work . . . if he made it.' He nodded at the newspaper she'd picked up. 'I scan for his name each week.'

Sophie left his arms to reach for one of the gazettes, looking confused. 'I've not seen this one before.'

'Probably because it's published out of Switzerland. I have it sent to me.'

'For what?'

'Prisoners. Since 1916 Switzerland has been taking internees. Surely you know this?'

She shook her head, perplexed, flicking through more pages. 'What do you mean, internees?'

Charlie gave her a look of surprise. 'I know you read the German prison gazettes.'

'Yes, of course, religiously.'

'Right, right. Well, a few years back the Swiss negotiated a special humanitarian effort that permitted seriously injured or ailing soldiers who were being held in poor conditions in German prisons to travel to Switzerland.'

She looked up at him in astonishment. 'I did not know that.'

'Well, they're still prisoners, bound by a strict code that was agreed upon, but they live in various camps, hostels and hotels in Switzerland in peace, with proper nourishment, medical care and every facility to recuperate as best they can. The conditions are unimaginable compared to where they've been. I mean, look at this.' He picked up one of the newspapers. 'This is from, er, let me see, last February. Now . . . where is it?' He flicked through the pages. 'Ah, yes, look, they always publish photographs in the middle pages. Here are the internees enjoying winter sports. Look – they're learning to ski! And these ones are doing some sledding . . . or tobogganing, as they call it. And there's loads of other stuff.' He reached for another issue. 'This is the most recent one, from a couple of weeks ago. Look, they're swimming – that's Lake Geneva in Lausanne. And they've had concerts and recitals, including a series of light operas put on by the soldiers.'

She blinked in consternation. 'I had no idea. Charlie, may I take a couple of those?'

'By all means. Take them all if you wish. Harry Blake is not there.' Then added, his tone cautious, 'I haven't seen Jerome's name either. I do check for it.'

'No, no, I don't expect to find it . . . but I'm thrilled you have looked for him, thank you. I'm curious about these; it's remiss of me not to know – and I may find some names for other people. There are still so many women holding out for news of missing loved ones. Thank you, I will take a stack.' She shook her head as if shaking herself free of that topic. 'Now, Charlie, have you been invited to the feast in the vineyards? It's our farewell to the vines before they sleep their well-earned rest.'

'I have, and I shall see you there this evening, but I'm looking forward to later.'

She waggled a finger at him in warning and they both laughed.

# 28

Sophie was in the cellars with Étienne and Charlie, collecting all the ratafia they had available. They planned to measure the volume of the sweet liquor for the *dégorgement*, which involved removing the dead yeast cells. During this process some wine was inevitably lost, to be topped up with the ratafia, which would then be corked to finalise the 1918 vintage.

She noted that Charlie was happy to fetch and carry as best he could. He looked over at her regularly and smiled, and she imagined he was watching how the laughing girl could shift to become the serious business owner, and in a heartbeat transform into the articulate and emotional champagne maker. Perhaps he was realising that she was many people encased in one, and she hoped that made her intriguing to be with rather than confusing.

Her thoughts bubbled like the champagne she intended to make. She was happy. It was the first time in four harvests she had felt such positivity that it was an almost childlike joy. She reflected on the silence of all guns in France, a successful vintage, the people of Reims returning to their streets to rebuild, the people of Épernay losing that twisted tension that had lived in their bellies for far too long . . . and especially the making of this most special of all champagnes. It was her daydream becoming reality, but it was also her way to honour Jerome and their love, to mark his passing and the peace he'd fought for. She was filled with effervescence that life's wheel had finally turned.

And so it was with some dismay that she found herself being called up from the cellar to be confronted by Louis leaning against a car, in front of which stood a full wagonload of sugar.

He beamed as she emerged, still wiping her hands on her apron. 'I wasted no time, my dear.'

'Louis, I —'

'No, I know you don't know what to say,' he said with delight, unable to hear his own condescension. 'But it's my pleasure to take you by surprise and deliver on my promise. Sugar for my lady, as asked.' Louis swept a triumphant hand towards the wagon, as if she were unable to see for herself what it carried. 'And now, my darling girl,' he said, taking her by the elbow and walking her away from anyone who might overhear, 'it is time for you to deliver on your promise.'

All Sophie's billowing optimism was deflating at the sight of him, but this was her mess and now she had to face clearing it up. She straightened herself and took a slow breath for the confrontation that was surely coming.

Louis was gesturing again at the sugar sacks. 'Get that unloaded,' he snapped to the two men from the wagon, who were awaiting instructions. Now he turned back to her. 'Where do you want the sacks stored, Madame Delancré?'

She shifted her gaze from Louis to the men clambering down from the wagon and shielded her eyes from the sun. 'Gentlemen, I'll arrange some cool drinks and food for you.' She pointed to the side of the house. 'Head down there to the parlour but drive the wagon around to the back of the house first, please.' She saw

Charlie arrive, walking up to them with an expression that told her he was sizing up the situation.

'Ah, Captain Nash, still here?'

Charlie's face split into a smile. She knew him well enough to know he was enjoying the secret that only she shared. 'Good day to you, Monsieur Méa. Did you have a pleasant journey?'

'I did. I wonder, Captain, would you be kind enough – as I gather you now seem to work for Madame Delancré – to show these men where they can store the sugar I've brought? Someone needs to supervise the unloading. Sophie, I'm sure that's —'

'That's not the captain's role, Louis, thank you. I run things around here, in case you'd forgotten?' She said it sweetly and accompanied it with a smile as though it were a lighthearted remark, but no one could mistake it for anything but the cautionary note that was intended.

'Oh, my, my, not at all. I was just speeding things along, my dear.'

She nodded, still smiling, and returned her attention to the patient driver and his companion. 'Drive around to the back of the house so you don't block the street. Please do not unload the wagon. Go to the parlour and take some refreshment,' she instructed them, glancing briefly at Charlie.

Charlie grinned. 'Madame, I would be more than happy to show them where to unhitch the horse and feed and water it?' He was clearly enjoying himself, knowing a surprise was coming the way of the brother-in-law he detested.

'All right, thank you, Captain.'

He even leapt up onto the cart and began guiding the driver.

Sophie looked back at Louis, whose face expressed only confusion.

'My dear, what is going on?'

'I'll explain. Join me for a coffee, Louis? Perhaps even a cognac?' *I think you may need it*, she thought.

The makeshift hospital had been all but emptied of its patients. Her main reception room once again held elegant furniture and decorative items, and Louis sighed his pleasure to see its status restored.

'Can't quite rid it of its smell of disinfectant,' he remarked as she returned from the parlour, no longer wearing her apron and her hair reconfined in its chignon. 'But what a welcome relief it is, my dear, to see normality reappearing.' She watched him take in the paintings now rehung, some of them priceless. All the Limoges porcelain was laid out in its cabinet, the bookshelves were crammed again, the gold leaf on the spines glinting as the sunlight struck it. Louis was in the love seat near the window; she knew he wanted her to join him, but instead she walked around the walnut dining table that seated twelve with ease, and twenty-four if they opened up its leaves. It gladdened her to see it dusted and polished, carrying the familiar silver platter that she was going to enjoy filling again with fruit. Silver candelabras shone – the household team had been busy, she thought.

'Yes,' she agreed wholeheartedly. 'Even the change to this one part of the house is affirmation of the world coming to its senses. We have only two remaining patients now, and they've been moved to a small space near the kitchen. I'd forgotten just how beautiful this room is in late summer.' Was she babbling? Perhaps, yes, she was. It was time to confront him, to return his ring and his sugar and send him back to Paris. It sounded simple, but instead it felt like a mountain that was hers alone to climb.

'Louis —'

Jeanette came in with coffee and some freshly made biscuits as a treat. Sophie smiled benignly as the coffee was served and thanked Jeanette as she left, feeling the coil of tension tighten in her belly.

'Perhaps now, my dear, you will tell me why you did not wish for my wagon of sugar to be unloaded?' Louis spoke evenly but there was such a keen edge riding beneath his words that she could have sworn he'd just sliced her open.

She poured his coffee and handed it to him, not bothering to offer a biscuit, given his mood. She watched Louis carelessly place the cup and saucer on a prettily carved demilune table nearby, its half-crescent sitting neatly against the papered wall. Sophie absently thought that her mother would have preferred Louis not to place the china directly onto the soft wood of that beloved table, but her thoughts refocused quickly as the man in question cleared his throat. 'Well?'

'Would you like a cognac, Louis?' she offered.

'No, I would like an answer.'

She sat opposite him and placed her hands in her lap. *Just say it.* 'Louis, this is awkward, I realise, but I have to tell you that I no longer require the sugar you've brought.'

Small eyes blinked, dark and cunning, as he listened to her hesitant beginning. He said nothing so she had no choice but to continue.

'I've solved my crisis, or at least Captain Nash has.'

'And by that you mean . . .?'

She breathed out. 'Captain Nash, as you know, is a chemist, and he has some novel ideas with regard to champagne making.'

'Because he's had so much experience?' Louis enquired facetiously.

'No, Louis,' she said, tiring of this careful dance. 'Captain Nash simply applied his knowledge of chemistry to the chemical process that is taking place within the champagne bottle. The yeast is —'

'Please,' he said, already tired, it seemed, of the conversation. 'I don't want a tutorial on champagne making.'

'Well, then, you have to just accept my word that he has found a way to give me the sugar we need for the final stage, without having to resort to the unfair bargain that you were offering.'

'I see.'

'Do you?'

'I see that you've ignored my best advice and you are now taking your instruction from a charlatan soldier who wants nothing more than to take advantage of a wealthy widow.'

She inhaled silently, deeply. 'He is far from a charlatan, although I readily admit that Charlie has worked magic.'

'Charlie, now, is it? My, my, you two are familiar. Didn't I warn you about him, Sophie, my dear? Didn't I caution you that spending too much time with the English soldier would put you on dangerous ground?'

Finally, her bristling emotions showed through in her sharper tone. 'You see, Louis, I don't set much store by your counsel. I trust my own instincts. And my instincts tell me that Charlie – who has become a good friend – has been rather selfless in his endeavours to return kindness, to help wherever he can and contribute to solving a problem that I felt had no solution but misery. You, by contrast, have been feeding that misery, even preying upon it. Louis, how proud do you feel to have blackmailed your brother's widow? How tall do you walk knowing you have done your utmost to coerce me into your bed while still enjoying what I suspect – but you must correct me if I'm wrong – is a perverse secret lifestyle? I know this sugar you've brought is not available through regular means, so to me that suggests you've blackmailed someone else to get it. You're not a good person, Louis. You are a selfish soul and I will not let you lay a finger on me, on my property, on Jerome's property, or on my family's wealth – and I fear that is what's really behind all this supposed generosity.' She watched him falter, knowing she'd hit the mark, and wondered why it had taken her so long to achieve clarity. 'I cannot for a moment believe that your endeavours on my behalf are not rooted in self-advancement – or worse, Louis,' she said, as a new idea occurred to her. 'Are you in trouble? The whole business of wearing your ring without any serious commitment from either of us never sat comfortably in my mind. It felt contrived, but only now is it making some sense to me. I believe you are using me to make it appear that you are financially sound.'

'How dare you!' he sneered, hauling himself to his feet, but she waited, remaining seated, glad the worst of it was said and she could cool the burn in her cheeks. He advanced on her. 'You wicked, spoilt temptress. You use your sex to get what you need.' She opened her mouth in shock but no words came. 'I suppose you've convinced the English wretch to do your bidding with promises of your affections, have you?'

Hating herself for allowing him to enrage her, she still couldn't help but act on it. 'Oh, you're as beastly as I recall, Louis. It's been nothing but pretence, hasn't it? Just faking that you cared. But first impressions don't always lie. The day I met you I felt only repulsion, and that was heightened by the arrival of your brother, who eclipsed you in every respect – and that's part of your life's problem, isn't it? Jerome was better than you, Louis. He was kinder, smarter, stronger, more courageous, more talented, more generous . . . I could keep going but I don't want to waste any more breath on you. And yes, the captain and I are fond of one another,' she admitted, unable to resist one final barb to puncture her visitor's swollen rage. 'And perhaps one day we might marry.' She watched the shock flash in his eyes. 'As for you, Louis, I hope I never have to look upon you again. Take your sugar,' she said, 'leave my house, leave my life. I don't know what is going on in yours, but I don't wish for it to be entangled with mine. We share Jerome, that's all. And with him no longer between us, we have nothing in common.'

He smiled and it was cruel. 'You're right to some degree, Sophie. I am in need of an injection of cash, but —'

She was not going dance around him any longer. 'How much?' she interrupted.

He hesitated, and she could picture the cogs of his well-oiled mind spinning and connecting. He was shameless, happy to blithely move past her accusations and onto the topic of money at the root of them. 'I will sell the house in Avize; it is not your concern.'

'Your childhood home!' She sounded helplessly wounded. 'Jerome's too.' She knew she was being baited but fell for it all the same.

'Jerome hardly needs it.'

She refused to bargain with him. 'What is it worth?'

He laughed. 'Why? Are you going to purchase it?'

'Give me a figure, Louis.'

He did and she knew it was vastly inflated but she was pleased not to blink or show any sign of shock.

'I will instruct my accountant in Paris to have that money transferred to your account. I will expect the deed of the house in Avize to be delivered to my lawyers. The accountant will provide you with that address.'

Louis regarded her now with a mixture of what she took to be white fury combined with loathing. She no longer cared what he thought.

'Why would you do this?'

'To get you far from my life. I never had any intention of marrying you, Louis, although I suspect you had every intention of marrying me. I feel somehow dirty for being engaged in such skulduggery. I lied. I pretended. I used you for what I needed. So consider this reparation for that poor behaviour. But I mean what I say: once you leave, I never wish to look upon you again.' She was breathing heavily. He still looked shocked, as though searching for the trap. 'How's that for a devil's bargain, Louis? And you can live your debauched life and end up homeless – penniless, for all I care after this – but you will never cross my threshold here or in Avize again. That house will belong to Delancré by law. Is that clear?

Do we have a deal?' She said the final word as though it were filthy in her mouth.

His small eyes grew darker still. 'We do.'

'Good.' She pointed to the ring, which she had placed on a small table near her chair. 'That is yours – take it. Do you want me to buy the sugar from you, too?'

He smiled lazily. 'Well, it does save more inconvenience.'

She nodded, disgusted. 'I know the price of sugar, Louis, so I won't be allowing you to inflate it as you have the sale of the house. I will pay you the going rate plus twenty-five per cent for your trouble and that more than covers what you can no doubt get on the black market. Or you can take it back to Paris with you today. I really do not care.'

'No, I'll accept your terms,' he said, sneering again and reaching for the ring box, his coffee untouched.

'Then I shall put my accountant and my lawyers in touch. I believe there is nothing more to say.'

'Oh, there is one more thing to say, my dear, and that is that I think your Captain Nash is a sad idiot to fall for your wiles, and maybe he has a terrible surprise coming his way.'

'Get out!' she said, angry that he could hurt her still, with no idea what he meant other than to inflict emotional damage. 'I never want to see you again.'

'You never shall. Who'd have thought that sweet girl who walked down the aisle with my brother was a slut? I think I got away lucky in not having to marry you, my dear.'

Louis turned on his heel and left her biting her lip so she wouldn't say another word to him and to prevent the tears that so desperately wanted to spill.

# 29

As autumn was gathering itself to take over from summer, Sophie held her traditional picnic in the nearby vineyards for her workers. The talk around the table was the rebuilding of Reims.

Charlie sat back quietly to let the conversation flow around him; this was not really his place, although curiously he had never felt more at home than here in Épernay. Sophie was finally his. What a delicious notion – not just belonging at long, long last, but looking forward to being married in the future and belonging to her. He suddenly wanted it so badly he had to look away from her happy expression as she held court. He'd not heard how the meeting with Louis went because they'd had no time to discuss it, but his enquiry had been met with a wan smile.

'It was unpleasant, as I expected, but it is done,' she'd said and it seemed she wished it to be left at that.

He heard her soft rebuke from the other end of the table as she responded to someone's remark. He hated being so far away from her but to be closer would be to risk reaching under the table and squeezing her hand or offering to pour her a drink to find a reason to touch her fingers. No, he must not let her down in front of her workers until she was ready to tell them and so he kept his distance.

'Marie, we must not complain. We have all lost people close to our hearts so we are allowed to be melancholy, but we must not set our pain above the pain of others. I heard about a town only a few days ago that had been taken, lost, and retaken by the Germans over and again since 1914. It's been ravaged. The women have lost everyone: husbands, sons, lovers, brothers, fathers, uncles, and even sisters and mothers. They are so alone, their town destroyed. And those few women, caring for their children with so little, are talking about rebuilding. We must bear up. We grieve, yes, but we will rebuild our town, our lives, our hopes and the future for our children.'

Nods and murmurs of assent followed this.

Charlie looked around the makeshift table that had been set up haphazardly among the rowdy vines, now strewn with the remains of the picnic.

'I wonder now what the Ministry of Food will do?' he said to lighten the topic. 'Their members are surely redundant.'

'They've taxed everything they can,' someone said.

'We are starting again,' Sophie said. 'I heard on a recent visit to Reims that France has lost up to half of her agricultural land that she had before the war – it is ruined.'

'Mainly in our parts,' one of the old men said.

'Certainly north,' Charlie agreed, remembering that traumatised landscape. 'It will take some years for it to recover,' he said, grateful for the cheese and fruits they'd managed to scrounge. There was no meat at this picnic but Sophie's workers had produced a thick, savoury broth that tasted meaty in its intensity from local mushrooms and dense beans. He had been astonished to see loaves of bread, which everyone had greedily shared, and he'd had to presume that Sophie had somehow exercised her incredible powers of persuasion within her network to find flour for those loaves. They wouldn't taste such largesse again for a while, Charlie was sure. Their gaze met across the table, lit by a golden light from the last of the summer sun on its downward journey.

The shadows of bottles and tall pottery jugs on the table were long as the sun sat low in the sky. He had not taken off his jacket and he couldn't be sure whether it was because he felt the chill or because he wore it properly now, not with one empty sleeve. He flexed his hand, feeling so much stronger now. The women sensed autumn's arrival, beginning to pull their shawls more tightly around them. The canopy of crispy golden and red leaves in the vineyards would soon fall like an imperial cloak. The vines would know the right time to say farewell . . . and it was as though they were urging him to do the same. Time for their sleep. Time for the romance of summer to end. Not for him, though, because he was in love and the woman he adored loved him in return . . . so why did he feel melancholy?

Sophie surprised him out of his thoughts by tapping her glass. The sound tinkled across the vineyard and the conversations dried up quickly until all gazes were on her, including his.

'Thank you, everyone. I'm sure we have all enjoyed this special treat in the vineyards.' She paused while hands banged on the table and her guests smiled back indulgently. 'Next time we gather like this, I hope I can put on a spread that harks back to the 1912 autumn feast that to date has had no equal.' Charlie smiled to hear the cheers erupt – obviously, it had been a memorable celebration. Someone remarked about missing her annual charlotte cake. He looked over at Sophie and saw her blush at this. He wouldn't have thought much of it, but the glance she cut towards him at those words and the way she looked back at the woman who'd spoken them to hush her caught his attention. What was that undercurrent around the table? Why was this cake so significant that Sophie didn't want it elaborated upon? Was it Jerome? Was his ghost circling the table where they feasted?

Sophie continued quickly. 'But now, as our vineyards become peaceful – and I mean that in every possible way . . .' She paused as everyone applauded loudly for the end of the war. 'I have something very important —' she shrugged — 'something exciting that I'd like to share with all of you because you share my life and the champagne house with me.'

People fell quiet again and she waited until there were no more murmurings.

'Our single English soldier, who has become a familiar face and a good friend to us,' she said, nodding his way, 'opened a doorway for me today that previously I couldn't see.'

Charlie blinked as the gazes now slid his way. He looked down, surprised at his self-consciousness but mostly by how much their approval mattered to him.

'You all know our problem with not being able to make a champagne this year. I know you share the sorrow and feel it as deeply as I do that in this of all years, when we should be celebrating peace, we feel unable to produce a vintage. It is what our lives revolve around and what we've worked so hard for through such difficult times.' There were nods and fresh murmurs of assent. Once again, she waited for silence. 'Well, our own Captain Charlie Nash has come up with an idea that may – no, *will* – solve our dilemma for the daring all-chardonnay wine that is ready to be finally corked for sale.'

The stares intensified and there were soft noises of surprise and urgings for her to continue. Sophie wasted no time in telling them that their generous stocks of ratafia would replace the sugar they lacked for this year's production.

Étienne smiled benignly, already in on the secret and impressed by its daring, but the quiet around the table was complete, its diners almost forming a still-life painting. Charlie could hear distant birdsong. That in itself was so special he wanted to home in on that delicious sound, which had been absent from the battlefield. Birdsong was taken too much for granted, he thought – it was only noticed when it was gone. He recognised a robin's familiar series of whistles, which could sound particularly cheerful or just as equally plaintive. The bird's welcome sound only magnified the stiffening silence of the people around the table.

It was Sophie who broke it. 'Well?'

Voices exploded into the peace, drowning out the bird. Large, gnarled hands of old men smacked him on the back and women sighed and clapped modestly, smiling at him.

Sophie beamed. 'Captain Nash, that sounds like unanimous approval.'

He cleared his throat; they couldn't know how much their praise meant. 'Blimey, the silence before was frightening, though.'

More laughter.

'No one has thought of this before. It is a unique idea, Charlie, so everyone was surprised,' Sophie explained unnecessarily but it made everyone cheer again. 'It is such an inspirational idea that I plan to waste no time – our wine is ready and calls to us. I have tasted the trial sample he made with Étienne – thank you,' she said, raising a glass to her elder. 'And I plan to disgorge tomorrow. Instead of topping up the wine with sugar, I shall add only the ratafia. Everyone, please pray this works, for all of us.'

The catcalls and cheers intensified, glasses were raised and approving glances shifted his way.

Yes, this was the life he wanted. Nothing could stop it now.

———————

Night was falling faster now. Soon winter would be nipping in the air. She could feel its threat against the windowpane, as the coolness drifted across the landscape she loved. The negativity of her life was retreating – it was feeling easier somehow to accept that Jerome was gone; meanwhile it was a plain relief to know that Louis was gone too, and she didn't care how much his absence would cost her. The war was fading, peace was surely imminent, and now she was permitting herself to be in love. What a release it was to cast off the shackles of grief to allow herself the thrill of anticipation. Sophie had bathed, brushed out her hair, perfumed her skin and was contemplating the wonder of allowing a man to touch her in a way she hadn't felt in years. She was both terrified and excited.

She expected Charlie late. He had decided to go back into the cellars with Étienne to assist on a final count of the wine and ratafia bottles for tomorrow. He would be gone in a few days and then she didn't know how long it might be before they saw each other again, so tonight was important to both of them. It would consummate their love and their intentions. They might even begin to let others know of their desire to be a couple.

Sophie looked around the attic, her private space for so many years now; it was probably time to start thinking about moving back down into the main house, although leaving here would be poignant. She'd grown used to bending beneath its rafters, the smell of the timber and the beautiful light that seemed to shimmer just for her through the dormers. Her gaze scanned the sparse furniture – not that much to move, really – and fell on the Swiss gazettes that she'd brought from Charlie's dormitory. They were the only unfamiliar items. She switched on the single light overhead and settled back into her mother's chair, still feeling a sense of astonishment that she had not known about the internment camps. Why? Had she become so distracted that she hadn't paid attention, or had this news somehow escaped her?

She read through several, feeling a sense of wonder at the life these men had been allowed to enjoy as prisoners. They looked so happy in the photographs. Some had lost limbs, others wore bandages across their faces, some stood with the help of crutches, and still others appeared healthy, although she knew they likely were not. Life in the neutral zone was surely improving their health but perhaps those smiles, now that she studied them, covered the true feelings of being isolated, cut off from the soldiers with whom they'd begun the war, and confronting the reality of their personal losses.

Two of her workers – strong, wonderful women, both with children to care for – were waiting on news of lost husbands. Like Jerome, they'd simply disappeared: injured, killed, taken prisoner, no one knew any more than she did of her husband. Sophie had diligently read the prisoner gazettes published out of Germany for their names with no success. But here was a new hope, perhaps. Charlie had already confirmed Jerome was not among the internees so she was scanning only for the other men. What joy she might bring if she could find a single name. *Remuer ciel et terre*. It was her father's favourite saying and she would practise it now – she would indeed move heaven and earth if it meant bringing one of her town's lost soldiers home to his family.

She checked the date of the gazette in her hand; it was from last month, and contained photos of concerts put on by the internees. She was amused at the thought of the men in costume with brightly made-up faces. Such jollity must be healing in its own way.

Sophie found a spread of photographs from an opera and smiled to realise it was *Mirette* they'd chosen – a comic opera that had originally been written in French but was ultimately recast for Britain's Savoy Theatre. Clearly the soldiers had put on a good show for everyone – and unlike the German prison concerts, she noted, plenty of women had participated, so the men hadn't had to dress up as women. She wondered if they were nurses or Swiss hotel employees. What fun amateur productions could be.

She gave a wistful sigh and checked the time. It was nearing nine. Charlie wouldn't be far away. After tonight she couldn't have a change of heart. He'd been strong because she'd demanded that of him but her relenting had now weakened his resolve to the point where there was no turning back. Spending the night together and getting to know each other so intimately would change their lives irrevocably. *Are you ready for this, Sophie?* Earlier in the day she'd felt sure, her confidence and passion overwhelming them both. Now, looking at these gazettes, she felt heartsore again – guilt had crept back and was tapping her on the shoulder. Or perhaps it was just the ugly confrontation with Louis and his horrible threat at the end. She still didn't know what it meant and she assured herself that frankly, she didn't want to know.

Sophie flapped the newspaper with disgust and was about to fold it up and set it aside when her gaze snagged on a photo of one of the players. The caption read: *Jacques Bouchon's rousing baritone amused and entertained a large crowd who enjoyed his rendition of the gypsy character, Bobinet.*

Sophie stared at the eyes looking back at her. The man was in full stage make-up and garbed with loose sleeves. His breeches were tucked into his boots and he wore a waistcoat that tied with thongs. One arm was missing. He also wore an eye patch. Despite the costume and the unruly hair, she knew that searching gaze viewed the world with eyes the colour of the night sky, that deepest of dark blues. She couldn't swallow, even though her mouth was dry. Sophie read the caption again. Jacques Bouchon. How could it be when this man was surely Jerome Méa!

Sophie's breath finally let itself out in a gasp. She stood up and began to pace, habit reminding her to step only on the rafters. She reached for the roof rafter above her and held it tight until her knuckles whitened to match her lips, which were clamped to prevent her from screaming. It couldn't be, could it? Is that what Louis meant? Louis knew! But how? Had the Red Cross told him? No, because Jean had reassured her.

Her thoughts took off like a flight of swallows swooping and turning back on themselves as one. If Louis knew Jerome was alive, why hadn't he told her? Why? Because he needed her money, that's why. Sophie could feel herself shivering as if the window had been opened to let that cool air in. She pulled a knitted shawl from the mirrored dressing screen, whirled it across her shoulders and tucked it around her arms, lost in her thoughts.

She picked up the gazette again. She had no doubt now. That was Jerome in the photograph: a baritone, a French soldier, with identical features.

He was also an internee in Switzerland.

She would start making phone calls immediately. The alarm racing through her body added to the tremble but sharpened her thoughts. She moved towards the door, and as she reached for the handle there was a soft knock.

'Sophie?'

*Charlie!* Horror and guilt overwhelmed her. Only honesty could work now. She dragged the door open to see him staring up at her from the stepladder. His flushed face was creased with a bright smile and he was puffing slightly from running up the stairs to reach her as quickly as he could. He looked a little drunk, no doubt after a sip or three with Étienne.

'I'm sorry I'm a bit late. I was held up with —' He stopped and frowned, noticing her shock, no doubt. 'Sophie . . .?'

She forced him back, clambering down behind him, and he helped her onto the landing. Sophie stared at him, momentarily unable to speak. She was hungrily committing his beautiful face to her memory, because she understood now she would lose him forever. Those plump lips pursed in confusion and the firm brow knitted and drew his features into a grave expression. His happy tipsiness had disappeared.

'What's wrong?'

'It's Jerome.'

He blinked but his expression didn't shift. He didn't say anything, so she had to fill the tense silence. She lifted the crumpled gazette and shook it in front of Charlie. 'He's one of the internees.' Her voice was breathless. 'Singing opera!' She sounded even more horrified by that, although she hadn't meant to.

'Calm down.'

'Here, you look. You've seen photographs of him.' She struggled to turn the pages and he took the newspaper from her.

'Let me.' He flicked to the centre section with the photographs.

'There!' She jabbed a finger at Bobinet.

After only a heartbeat he looked back at her. 'This says it's a man called Jacques B—'

'I know what it says. But that is Jerome, I swear it.'

His gaze landed tenderly on her, full of sympathy, and she wanted to yell, beat him, take out her frustration that she couldn't have the man she loved now because the man she'd loved back then was still alive. Even to her it sounded like the storyline of a comic operetta of mistaken identity. But it was not fiction. This was her life.

'I have to go to Switzerland,' she said, pushing past him.

'Sophie —'

'Charlie, I'm so sorry. But this is my husband. *Remuer ciel et terre.*' She watched him take a low breath as he took in her full meaning.

He nodded sadly.

'I'm not asking you to wait.'

'And yet I will. Because I feel the same way about you. If it takes heaven and earth, I'll give it.'

She touched his cheek, freshly shaven, she noted, and he covered her hand with his. She wanted to kiss him, knew he wanted to kiss her, but she couldn't . . . not now with Jerome's image so large in her mind. It seemed that Charlie, as much as he loved her, sensed that shift. Her pain on his behalf was exquisite, even though she knew she was the cause.

Sophie leaned her forehead against his. 'I wish I could take it back.'

'No, it's all I have of you. I need the memory.'

'Forgive me, Charlie.'

She knew he was being heroic for her when he dredged up a crooked grin. 'If I was your husband, I'd be very proud to know you fought for me like this.'

His words were so touching she couldn't hold back the tears any longer. They swept out in a torrent and he gently kissed each cheek. His lips were damp when she pulled back.

'Go find him, Sophie.'

She grazed her lips against his, tasting her own tears, and then she was moving fast, her footsteps fleet down the stairs, barely acknowledging the flights as she descended.

# 30

*September 1918*

The man stood and took his salute.

'Good morning, Lieutenant. I am Colonel Sheridan. Have a seat, please.' He smiled, warmer than the fire that was burning in the grate. 'You'll have to forgive me. I'm afraid my French is rusty.' He extended his hand in the friendliest of greetings now that the formalities had been dispensed with.

'My English is reliable,' Jerome replied with a grin as they shook hands.

'Thank heavens for that. I've ordered some tea. Would you . . .?'

Jerome nodded. He didn't particularly like tea, but he understood the English drank such copious quantities of the black leaf that to decline would be like spitting in the colonel's eye. 'Thank you.'

'These last four years we've been drinking stuff not much short of warmed mud but finally, finally, I've got my hands on a caddy of Darjeeling. And only the best – Vickery's, if you please. My wife had it sent over so I could celebrate. Thank the stars for Fortnum's, eh?'

Jerome frowned in a friendly way. He understood the words but didn't grasp much of the meaning.

'Sorry, old chap. I'm probably speaking gibberish to you. Too much excitement that this filthy war is ending and the Hun's on the run.' Sheridan smiled broadly.

Jerome had always liked the English but they were truly a quaint and rather curious lot.

A man arrived with a tea tray.

'I carry my own tea cosy,' Sheridan said somewhat proudly, not at all self-conscious at how ridiculous this sounded. Jerome liked him even more for that as the moustachioed senior officer pointed to what could only be described as a hat sitting on the teapot, pompom tassels hanging jauntily from the top of it.

'The wife knitted it for me. Can't bear cold tea.'

'Charming.' Jerome refrained from saying anything more regarding the teapot hat.

The tea was poured and handed over.

'Marvellous brew, eh?' the colonel wondered, smacking his lips with pleasure.

The steaming golden tea was indeed refreshing with a bright, almost floral flavour; it was surprisingly delicious. Jerome nodded genuine admiration and smiled.

'Couldn't find a wretched tea strainer so watch the leaves, old chap.'

'It's delicious, thank you. I'm wondering why I'm not meeting with French authorities?' he said, trying to refocus his companion onto matters at hand.

'Well, you're a bit of a conundrum, old chap. You were trans-ferred with British prisoners and just to keep the paperwork all neat and tidy, we feel it's best to sign you off here before you move to your company and they do whatever they have to,' Sheridan said, looking like he hoped his simple explanation of an otherwise highly complicated process would help. 'However, I gather there's a little snag.'

'Yes, sir.'

'Care to put it in your own words?'

'Thank you, Colonel.' He began his long tale, leaving out no detail. He'd rehearsed it a dozen times in his mind since leaving the hospital team and arriving in Paris. It had been surprisingly poignant to bid farewell to the Swiss, who had been so generous – particularly Nurse Agatha, who had fought back tears when he placed a gentle kiss on each cheek, looked her firmly in the eye and thanked her for being so good to him. They had not shared their secret, so only they knew what it meant, and he wondered if poor Agatha might take some ribbing over the meaning of his cryptic words.

'I'm distraught, but I've had time to get used to my situation. Now all I want is to see my wife, return to my home, hug my family.' He stared at the colonel. 'Something's not quite right, is it?'

'Well, old boy, I have to tell you that I did receive some information to this end yesterday and I took the liberty of calling a Monsieur Louis Méa —'

'That's my brother. Excellent, he —'

The colonel held up a hand, his moustache twitching. 'And this Monsieur Méa denied that he had ever received a call from Switzerland.'

'But that can't be right. The nurse is well known to me, I trusted her and . . .' His words petered out. 'What did you tell him – did you give him all the details, sir?'

'Well, I said a Swiss hospital. I didn't say its name or exactly where it was because I never had the chance. He denied the call ever occurred and he was rather abrupt about it, as I recall.' He gave a sad shrug. 'Look here, can you prove what you claim?'

So they had come full circle. 'Bring my brother here,' Jerome said, as if it were obvious.

'I would if I could. Monsieur Méa has been called away, I'm afraid.' Again, he put up a hand. 'Please don't ask me where, I have no idea. He didn't give me the details, but I know he was on government business. Now, I do understand your plight but can you understand it from our perspective?'

Jerome wanted to suggest that if they couldn't bring Louis in immediately, then they should urge Sophie to come to Paris but he knew they'd make excuses about not wishing to upset an already heartbroken and grieving widow. He could hear the excuses and placations now.

When Jerome stared at him, seemingly lost for what to say next, the colonel gave a tight smile. 'Anyway, look lively, old chap. Let's not panic. There's a solution here – we simply have to find it. You won't be the last misplaced, misnamed soldier we have to find a fit for, eh? At least we have you back in Paris.'

'It's good to smell France again,' he admitted carefully, not entirely sure what he meant by that. He knew it probably sounded strange but the unmistakable fragrance of strong coffee at local cafés told him enough about being home. The ash of smelly French cigarettes was in the air but he loved it and only now realised how much he'd missed France all these years.

Sheridan nodded. 'All right. Let's start building a picture so I can hear it directly from you. Where is home, Lieutenant?'

'Épernay.'

'Good. Perhaps you could give me your full name and the full name of your wife.'

He did so without hesitation.

'Excellent,' the colonel said, his nib scratching across a form. Jerome watched the older man take in his injuries in one all-over steely glance. 'So, what was it, Lieutenant?'

He knew exactly what the man wanted. 'An incendiary, sir, following a gas attack at Ypres in 1915.'

'Date?'

He gave it without hesitation.

'Your exact position, as best as you recall?'

Jerome obliged.

'Now tell me what you remember.'

Jerome dutifully walked the colonel through the most painful episode of his life.

'I'm sorry for you.'

'Don't be. I'm assured by the nurses that a man wearing a patch over his eye is intriguing.' The man twitched a sympathetic smile at the dark jest. 'I manage, Colonel Sheridan,' Jerome assured him.

'Another cup? We're just waiting on someone,' Sheridan said with a bright smile.

_____

The building in the 10th arrondissement she had arrived at was emblematic of the Third Republic, built in a neo-Renaissance manner with richly carved pale grey stone topped by steeply pitched, charcoal-slated rooftops. Its symmetrical design was high-lighted by a lantern chime of three bells for the clock at its centre. Sophie had entered the doors of the enormous town hall promptly, as asked, and was escorted down various corridors. She supposed a similar business of repatriation was already underway in town halls around the city's districts, although the guns were yet to be entirely silenced. Her belly felt as though a whole team of acrobats were twisting and tumbling, turning somersaults and leaping around her insides. She'd fully anticipated using every ounce of influence she might wield in order to enter Switzerland. Her last resort was to claim to be a long-lost relative of Jacques Bouchon, as the Red Cross had insisted during half-a-dozen urgent telephone calls that this soldier had no living family. But she had managed to find out where this internee was being housed and ultimately identified the clinical team that looked after him. She'd spoken first to a gently spoken doctor, who assured her that although he had not expressly taken care of this patient, his notes told him that the man she sought was now on his way to Paris, and that he was a widower from Brittany. She still didn't believe it, but her heart leapt at the mention of Paris. Sophie had to know more before she made her final move. Could she talk to some of the other people who had looked after him? The kindly doctor obliged – he was unable to secure anyone who had taken care of Lieutenant Bouchon directly but he found a matron.

'This is Matron.' She listened to Sophie's introduction.

'. . . and I was wondering did he ever reveal much about himself?'

'Not to me, although I know he confided in Nurse Agatha. He liked to talk about food,' she chortled. 'A soft cheese, some pink-coloured biscuits that were originally dyed with beetroot . . . that sort of thing.'

'Roses de Reims,' she murmured, chills creeping over her body.

'That's it. That's what he called them.'

'Anything else?'

She imagined the older woman in Lausanne shaking her head. 'Nurse Agatha is not here but I recall he had a lovely voice and liked to sing. He refused a crutch but his limp was better and he did a lot of hiking to get strong. He was polite, amusing, very well-liked. His arm healed well after the second operation and we were hoping to save his eye so it didn't change colour.' Sophie felt ill – could this be him or was she clutching at a desperate straw? 'Oh yes, he always carried around a cork. It was a champagne cork.'

Sophie's breath caught in a gasp.

'Madame?'

'I'm here. A champagne cork, you say?'

'He spent a large part of his imprisonment without his memory. I'm sorry, you really need to speak with the people who dealt with him daily. I shouldn't be giving you this information – much of it is second-hand.'

'Please, madame – what about the cork?'

'Nothing really. I remember remarking that perhaps he had held on to the cork in order to hang on to who he was.'

No, Sophie thought. He kept that cork because it reminded him he had a wife waiting for him. She knew the very cork, knew it had the name Delancré burned into it. It was all Jerome had of her.

And just as she was ready to cast all protocol aside and start making demands of the Swiss, she had received a call from a British colonel based in Paris who was helping to return a French internee who had found himself bundled in with soldiers from Britain.

'How can that be?' she'd asked.

'Oh, it's chaos, despite the tight Swiss organisation,' he'd told her. 'I've been called in because my wife is French and I have a better handle on the language than most, although I would hardly call it good. We have lots of troops to repatriate so they sent me here to help out because I can probably make faster sense of the British troops and names on our lists.' He gave a groan. 'I shan't bore you.' She'd smiled at his kind voice. 'Now, I gather you might be hunting a French fellow who has somehow found his way onto the British lists . . . a soldier called Jacques Bouchon, is that right?'

'I am. Please tell me that you have news?'

'Well, yes, as a matter of fact, I do.'

She caught her breath.

'Madame Delancré, are you there?'

'Yes . . . yes, forgive me. I am listening.'

'I think we have your man. He arrived here yesterday morning and he's on my list for tomorrow. I'm wondering how hard it might be for you to travel to Paris?'

'I shall be there,' she said, not giving him the chance to offer any other option.

He gave her the address. 'Ask for me at the front desk that we've set up. We'll have someone bring you up. May I ask, Madame Delancré, what relation are you to this soldier, please?'

'I believe this man is my husband.'

She didn't think she could have shocked the poor colonel any further if she'd tried.

He stammered and blustered but she finally explained that she thought her husband must have lost his memory because she was certain that it was him – she had photographs to prove it, which she would bring. By the end of the conversation the colonel was as intrigued as he was eager to help.

'No, I won't say anything – that would be too much of a shock – but, madame, if you'll forgive me, I do need to test his bona fides. Why don't you arrive at eleven-thirty and we shall take it from there, Madame Delancré?'

'I don't like the idea of tricking this man, especially if he is my husband, Colonel.'

'No tricks, I assure you. These men have seen hell; they've lived it and survived it, but returning to their former lives is going to be an enormous challenge. This is especially so for someone like Jacques Bouchon, if he is your husband and he has somehow lost his connection to his past. He may require patience and understanding. He might also turn out to be an impostor, for all I know.' He sighed. 'I'm just being cautious, you understand?'

'I'll prepare for that, Colonel Sheridan.'

'It would be wise. I shall see you tomorrow, madame.'

And so now she sat, nervously wringing the handle of her handbag, waiting to be summoned into the office behind her, where she hoped her husband sat.

The colonel's aide sidled up. 'Madame Delancré?' She startled but kept her features calm as she nodded again to the man who had greeted her earlier in the reception. 'Would you care to follow me, please?'

She stood, smoothed her lightweight wool jacket and touched the neat cloche hat, which was perched at an angle. She'd wrestled with what to wear today and had settled on a sombre but elegant suit of deep plum, which was as far from the colours of Épernay as she could manage. She didn't want to frighten Jerome, if this was him. In her matching oxblood leather gloves she clutched a velvet handbag; she clicked it shut before making sure her taupe satin blouse was neatly closed at her neck. She wore only the barest hint of a soft rose lipstick. She was half the size she was when she'd last hugged her husband – if this was Jerome, would he even recognise this bronzed, thin woman as his wife?

The truth was that they were strangers to each other.

'Thank you.' She smiled at the man by her side before he knocked on the door.

---

Jerome felt the gentle touch of the man's smile but despite its generosity he had the feeling that something was afoot – that he'd passed some sort of test. He heard a knock on the door.

The colonel gave a nod as if expecting it. 'Come in.'

Jerome swung around to see the colonel's batman leading in a slim, elegant woman dressed in the rich colour of burgundy wine. A ringing in his ears began as soon as the colonel said, 'Good morning, Madame Delancré.'

He didn't hear another word after that. He was struggling to his feet, his one good eye watering to blur the features of the only woman he had ever loved with all of his heart. How could he have ever forgotten her? He heard her speak in a voice that cracked as she uttered his name.

The intensity of his shock and the eruption of his emotions were so brightly disturbing he wanted to yell his despair. He watched what he hoped was sympathy and not dread marching across the familiar features of the dark blonde woman he knew to be his wife, all the more hauntingly beautiful for the hollowness of her frame.

'Jerome . . .' was all she could say before he fell back heavily into his chair and groaned out loud with four years' worth of anguish.

———

Sophie had to hide the shock mixed with devastating sorrow she felt at seeing Jerome again. She had thought she was ready but nothing could have fully prepared her for the emotions buffeting her now. She could swear a gale was pulling at her hair, whistling in her ears and making her squint. Yet the room was still. Her memory of the man she had kissed goodbye did not match this wasted version collapsed into a chair. He was trying to hide the damaged part of his face, one sleeve hung loose below the elbow, and she swallowed hard as she realised that Jerome would never prune his beloved vines again.

She looked at the colonel, whose moustache twitched. The senior man coughed gently. His gaze over the top of his glasses asked the question: *Is this your husband?*

Sophie nodded.

The colonel cleared his throat peremptorily. 'Er, well, I shall leave the two of you for a while.'

'Thank you,' Sophie murmured and waited until the man had vacated the room. She moved on feet that felt weighted, reached for the flask of water on the desk and poured some into a glass. She handed it to him.

'Jerome.'

'I'm so sorry for leaving you.'

Her breath felt trapped. An apology? It was the last response she could have imagined, especially after all her thoughts of kissing Charlie, loving Charlie . . . The fact that she'd come so close to tumbling into bed with Charlie to consummate their desire was feeding the tornado of emotion whirling around her. She spoke what was in her heart. 'But you've come home to me – that's all that matters.' It sounded more useful to him than *I love you* or *I've missed you*.

Jerome took the water with a shaky hand and drank it in one draught before he sighed and finally lifted his gaze to her. 'Sophie,' he began, more composed, and drew from his pocket the champagne cork he had carried since their wedding day. 'I'm home because you lit the way . . . even when I was lost. I always had this and I knew it was important – I just had to remember why.' The voice was the same but it had lost that wonderful lightness of humour that she recalled. They were yet to touch each other, both feeling awkward. 'Did I find you or did you find me?'

She unclipped her bag and removed the crumpled gazette that she'd carried to Paris, unfolding it. He stared at the picture before he sighed again. 'I was very good that night,' he quipped.

And that's all it took for a wonderfully familiar shared laughter to wrap itself around them again and fill her with all the joy that had leaked away over his years of absence. Sophie bent to crouch alongside him, placed her hand over his and felt a trill of excitement to remember the shape of those fingers, the ridges of his knuckles, the silvery trace of a scar that she recalled from a wound he'd received falling from the same tree in the vineyard that she had sat beneath with Charlie. And his voice. That rich voice that had always excited her was back in her life . . . and he was still capable of using it for levity.

'Do you know I can feel my other hand and it wants to cover yours . . . it wants so much to caress you,' he said.

Her throat tightened with all the emotion it was trying to wrangle into composure. 'Then use your beautiful mouth, Jerome, and kiss me.'

He didn't hesitate, and the familiarity of everything she had loved and had felt safe about before the war returned in a cascade of pleasure as the first lips she had ever loved upon her found their spiritual pair and joined to speak of love found. They cried as they kissed and there was no shame in that and they kissed until Sophie could feel her crouching limbs pinging with the need to stretch. She admitted as much, laughing out of his embrace.

Sniffing and smiling at once, she urged him to talk. 'Tell me everything, Jerome. I want to know it all.'

Without a care for protocol, she curled up in his lap and let him talk, allowing his voice and sad story to enter her and fill in the missing years since his last letter.

'So you're Jacques Bouchon? I mean, can they officially change it now?'

'Immediately. You are the proof they seek.'

'I'm your proof,' she repeated, smiling. 'I like that.' She kissed him again.

There was a knock at the door and a sensible pause, which gave Sophie time to leap from Jerome's lap as if stung and straighten herself. He stood too, presumably tired of allowing himself to look disabled. She walked to the door and opened it, expecting to see the colonel. He was there all right, beaming, but he had someone else with him.

'Louis,' she said, trying not to load any emotion into her voice.

'Is it really him? Is he here?' He sounded stunned, awe-struck, and he all but pushed past her into the room. 'I cancelled everything to come. Jerome? It *is* you!'

'Louis, oh dear brother, hello! I thought you were out of Paris.'

She heard Louis making an excuse, watched the brothers kiss and glanced at the colonel, who was finding the reunion jolly, it seemed.

'So glad he came. Grand to have a happy ending,' he whispered to her. 'I'm so used to passing on only bad news to families. I'm thrilled for you, madame.'

She smiled with all the grace she could muster, trying not to feel the bile rise again at the sight of Louis. 'I shall have to return to my married name,' she said, unable to think of anything else to say.

'Well, now, Lieutenant, this is wonderful,' the colonel said aloud for everyone's benefit. 'I think we can safely say you have been reunited with your family and that you most certainly are Jerome Méa.' Jerome looked fit to burst with pleasure, and Sophie realised she must not be the one to prick that happiness. 'I'm going to organise all the relevant paperwork. Sound good?'

'Thank you, sir.' Jerome nodded, returning his attention to Louis as the colonel departed. 'Louis, I have to ask about the telephone call.'

'Which telephone call, brother?' He looked perplexed but Sophie sensed the guile that Jerome either overlooked or could never fully grasp.

'There was a nurse called Agatha Huber and I begged her to call you. She had your number, told me she'd spoken to you.'

'Yes, the colonel mentioned this – I have no detail, simply that a man claiming to be Jerome Méa was an internee in Switzerland, but I had absolutely no idea what he was talking about then, or what you are talking about now.' He sounded horrified, as though he couldn't believe it. 'She said this?'

'According to Agatha, she rang the number I gave her and the man on the other end agreed he was Louis Méa and then confirmed it.'

'Then she is lying! Or a stranger is impersonating me,' Louis said, sounding affronted now. 'My brother, when did this supposedly occur?'

Jerome shrugged. 'Not long before I left Switzerland . . . a fortnight ago, perhaps.'

'It is a shock. I have taken no phone call from anyone in Switzerland. Do you think I would have left you languishing in Lausanne had I known?'

'No, no, of course not, but . . .' Jerome looked baffled. 'She didn't strike me as someone who would lie.'

'You are home, brother, isn't that all that matters?' He looked at Sophie. 'You must be so thrilled, Sophie, my dear.'

'You can't even guess, Louis,' she said, so only he could hear the barb in her words.

The colonel was back with a staff member in tow. 'Right, let's get you all signed off, Lieutenant Méa. Er, perhaps Monsieur and Madame wouldn't mind waiting for you in our reception room? Tea is being served.'

Sophie sensed it wasn't a suggestion. 'Of course. Louis, shall we? I'll just be down the hall, Jerome,' she said, still in awe that it was him standing there.

'Don't disappear,' he said with a wink.

They walked politely enough into the reception room into which the colonel's batman guided them.

'Help yourselves,' he said, gesturing at the silver tea tray. 'Shan't be long.'

When the door was closed, Louis rounded on her. 'Well, well . . . all that faith you had in him has been borne out.'

'I'm glad you see it that way,' she remarked.

'I wonder how he'll feel about his unfaithful wife when he hears of the English captain who has been worming his way into her heart.'

'He won't have anything to worry about, Louis, because he isn't going to hear about Charlie.'

'Oh, is that so? And how will you prevent that?'

'By warning you that if you so much as mention Captain Nash in any more than a formal way, I will tell Jerome of your intentions towards me and how you've blackmailed me.'

Louis flicked carelessly at some lint on his jacket collar. 'I'd deny it. You have no proof,' he said, his tone breezy, assured.

Her gaze narrowed. 'How about the money you've accepted? I have proof of that being transferred.'

'A gift, my dear. I came to you with my financial situation and in your incredible kindness and care for your brother-in-law you offered to cover my debt. It's marvellous and I'm ever grateful.' He smiled with cunning and licked his lips. 'You are no match for me, Sophie, my dear. You do not scare me. And Avize will be mine again once I speak with my brother.'

Sophie stared at him and decided on one final threat. 'Then let me just say this, Louis.' He stepped forward as if to say, *There's nothing you can say that can hurt me*. He even opened his palms to her to invite her try. 'If you received no call from Switzerland and if the colonel gave you no detail, how did you know that Jerome was, as you put it, languishing in Lausanne?'

She watched as her brother-in-law's expression clouded. All his amusement fell away as though the load were too heavy for his face; his cheeks suddenly drooped, turning the sneering curl of his plump, rosy lips into a frightened scowl. He blinked rapidly.

'You slipped up there, Louis. We all heard your denial but we also heard you mention Lausanne. Now, while Jerome only thinks the best of you and in his confusion may not have made the link, I have. And I will not forget it and I will not permit Jerome to forget it if you don't walk away from our lives once and for all. I want your toxic presence nowhere near me. The best you can hope for,

Louis, is that Jerome never knows what a snake you truly are and that he will always think kindly of you and simply wonder why we don't see more of you. Go away. Slither back to your den of iniquity in Pigalle, and don't let your shadow darken Épernay again. If we meet by chance, we can be polite – pleasant, even – but we both know we'll be pretending, and if you wish your brother's love to continue and perhaps his largesse – that is his business to negotiate and not mine – then I suggest you keep our secret.' *Say it*, she said to herself. 'Quid pro quo, Louis.'

'Rot in hell, Sophie,' he snarled, starting towards the door.

Relief flooded through her but she refused to let it show in her voice. 'Farewell, Louis. Oh, and one more thing.'

He turned, scowling at her.

In spite of all his hideous behaviour, Sophie found a moment of clarity that convinced her not to mirror his behaviour – she was better than that. She took a breath of calm. 'Louis, I mean this sincerely when I say that even though we don't like one another, and what's happened between us will keep it that way, I have to say that blackmail aside, you are enjoyable company.'

He looked back at her, stunned in a different way now. 'Pardon?'

'No, I mean it. You're fun, you're witty, you're elegant, you have poise and education. You read, you enjoy art, you love music. You appreciate all the finer things in life . . .' She shrugged. 'I found you engaging.'

'What is this?' he demanded in consternation.

'It's me trying to tell you that you have plenty to offer the right woman. There are so many single women after this war who would be thrilled to have your company, not to mention your name in marriage. Find her, marry her, have that child or even children and discover love, Louis. It's what's been missing in your life. It will change you. You will see the world through a different lens when you find someone who falls in love with you – in love with Louis Méa, exactly as he is, with all of his faults and all of his good traits. This isn't an apology, but I do say let's call a truce. We have no reason to hurt one another. I know you did what you did to Jerome out of fear about money, about your future, and you didn't mean it to harm him. You said you love him in your own way. So keep doing that. You have the money you need to start afresh; I won't begrudge you it any more. So start again. Live a good life in Paris as you choose but maybe stay open to finding a woman to love who loves you back.'

He searched her face as if looking for the sort of cunning that was second nature to him. He failed to find it. Finally, he nodded. 'A truce, then . . . because we both love Jerome.'

'We do.'

'Farewell, Sophie.'

'And Louis?'

He turned back.

'I've let you off lightly. Don't cross me again.'

'I'm not scared of you, Sophie,' he said, more amused than condescending. 'I'm impressed by your nerve and your ability to look past my transgressions and, in fact, help my cause.' He gave a tight chuckle. 'But no, I do not feel intimidated.'

'Well, as you journey home, congratulating yourself on how clever you've been, please think on this – the money I am providing is not as simple as you imagine.'

He blinked.

'It is not a straightforward gift.'

'More strings?' he said, still sounding careless.

'One more. The money I'm providing will be to pay off your immediate debt, but I have acquired your loan.'

He frowned. 'Why?'

'Let's call it added security. I now own the loan on your most glorious apartment in Pigalle, Louis, and should you default, or should you decide to turn even nastier than you have been and think enough time has passed for you to reveal information to Jerome that could hurt our marriage, I will foreclose on the loan and I will bring all of my considerable wealth and connections towards bankrupting you.' She smiled. 'Are we very clear on where the line is that you will not cross?'

'Perfectly.' He sniffed.

'Good luck,' she said as she opened the door. 'Close it behind you, Louis, and don't look back.'

# 31

Sophie nestled close to Jerome as they made their way to the train that would take them back to Reims. 'Thank you for coming home.'

'Are you sure?'

She frowned. 'About what?'

'Being happy that I'm back?'

Sophie sat back, aghast.

'It's just that I've struggled to imagine my beautiful wife by my side while I hobble around as a cripple with half my features gone, one arm missing and —'

She couldn't have been more shocked if he'd slapped her. 'Jerome, you've lost an eye, not your features. And do you think so little of me that you believe how you look is the reason I married you? Can you not come to terms with the fact that you remain one of the luckiest men who walk this earth – that you are alive, that you are loved? You have a whole town that will welcome you home as a hero. You have a life you can return to. You have survived what millions of your fellow men have not.'

'You're right, I'm sorry . . . truly. I have had nightmares since my memory came back of someone else taking my place.'

Guilt twisted like the bottles being riddled in one of her pupitres. 'Leave Jacques Bouchon behind. I fell in love with what lives in here,' she said, prodding his thin chest, wondering how to build him back up to the robust, burly man he'd been. 'Not because you had two eyes that could see and a right leg in perfect working order, or two arms. I think your eye patch makes you look heroic,' she said, leaning in to kiss it. 'And I think this scar here where your hair doesn't want to grow will tell people that you've been through battles and survived.' She kissed the scar. She touched where his arm should be. 'You gave this to protect France. How could I not admire you all the more? And your limp. I'm proud to walk along-side you.'

'I'm half a person,' he said.

'And I'm your other half,' she answered. 'And I know I didn't marry a coward. No more self-pity, my love. Let me take you home. Let me show you your brave vineyards that have remained strong, waiting for you.'

'Can you forgive me for forgetting you for so long?'

She didn't hesitate so much as pause to search his face as she considered telling her truth. 'Yes,' Sophie answered firmly so he had no doubt. She was going to add that he might need to forgive her too, but that secret would only serve to hurt them and this simply had to be a time of healing. Only she and Charlie – and Louis – knew. That was how it must remain, she decided.

Her romance with Captain Charlie Nash had effervesced with all the joy and enthusiasm of a newly opened bottle of champagne, but just as her bubbles had to die almost as soon as they'd lived, that was the reality of her love for Charlie. It was real, it erupted brightly, but now it must fade and their worlds must separate as hers realigned with its former trajectory.

She could smell soap and the English Vaseline Jerome had used to comb his hair neatly this morning.

'I don't enjoy you looking this tame.' She pushed away thoughts of Charlie, knowing she had to find a place to store him that could never be found. 'I like you wild and tousled,' she said, ruffling his hair.

He stood straighter and she remembered now just how tall her husband was. He was still broad, and his voice hadn't changed from that low, mellow burr.

'I want to kiss you.'

'You don't need permission.' She smiled, grief for Charlie fluttering like a trapped bird, and then she opened her heart so it could escape. The beautiful bird that had offered so much promise for her in its sad song understood it was free. And it flew . . . as it knew it must.

Jerome closed his eyes and touched his lips to hers. More memories flooded back. Their bodies recognised each other. As if invisible hands pushed them together, they leaned into each other intuitively and the kiss deepened, neither of them prepared to let the other go again.

The riddling was Charlie's favourite; the repetitive work was good for his healing arm, wrist and especially fingers. He'd learned fast how to do it properly, swiftly, allowing the wine and its lees to instruct him, although he'd had patient tutors in Sophie and Étienne. Charlie now believed he was an asset to the riddling team, rather than someone they all had to keep an eye on. He enjoyed listening to the low chatter of the women, trying not to blush when they made a saucy remark deliberately spoken to shock him. Those who were not widows had an extra spring in their step and a lightness in their voices as more news filtered in of Allied victories. He prayed they would all get their men home.

All except Sophie? No. That was cruel.

But he couldn't avoid his private joy. Her change of heart had felt like the morphine they'd administered when he was in the field hospital. Like the drug, it took all the pain away. For those few brief hours last week Charlie Nash had known he was where he belonged, where he had always been headed . . . he was home. And yet something in his heart where Sophie resided told him she was not to be his. She never had been. Did she love him? Yes – but that wasn't where his doubts lay. His uncertainty sat with the other man she loved, the one who had been there first, the rightful love of her life. Charlie understood that their romance, under any other circumstances, would never have occurred. Random decisions – from him running in the wrong direction when the apocalypse of the spring had occurred, to an Arab soldier fishing him half-dead from the river, to a French commandant tiring of not being able to make sense of him and sending him to the Reims hospital underground, and Sophie Delancré happening to be on shift as he was brought in. In a confluence of tricks by whichever forces were amusing themselves at his expense, they had been pushed together to discover a pair of broken souls that knew how to mend one another.

How sad then, he thought as he twisted the bottles in the pupitres, that while his heart wanted to believe otherwise, his intuition was telling him that there would always be three people in their relationship, even if Jerome was dead.

Summer was finished.

And she'd gone to find Jerome.

She'd sounded so convinced it was him that Charlie believed she was right.

Sophie would return with her soldier husband.

Even so, to leave at this moment would be cowardly. And he wasn't about to be accused of cowardice as the war ended. No, he would see her one last time – see that radiance and give her a brave smile back.

If that was Jerome in the photograph, why had he kept his silence and anonymity? Charlie believed there would be many men who might never want to face 'normality' again, might not even know how to be 'normal' after all that they'd seen and experienced of the dark side of humanity. Perhaps it was hard to trust again. Perhaps it was hard to hear laughter or singing again. It might feel impossible to dance or simply to allow oneself to be happy. It could feel like a betrayal of the men who hadn't survived. He understood all of this because he'd fought his way back from that same place, but it was because of Sophie. Everyone needed something to come back for; that was perhaps the great adjuster.

———————

Sophie was grateful that Gaston had arranged to pick them up from the station in Reims. She let the two men talk around her in an excited reunion. They had plenty to discuss.

Gaston explained that he'd kept up with the news from across the Swiss border but had never seen Jerome's name published and so presumed he had never been captured, never interned. 'I'm so sorry. I'm just amazed we both survived Ypres, to be honest.'

Deserted trenches crisscrossed the chalky plains of the Champagne region. Sophie had become accustomed to it, but she could tell that the landscape was a shock to Jerome. It was pock-marked with craters and littered with the junk of war: barbed wire, shells, broken machinery, twisted metal. The battlefields of Marne looked no different, she was sure, to any of the others in Europe, but this was their homeland and it no doubt hurt her husband to see for himself just how bad it had become.

'My beautiful Champagne looks like me,' Jerome said absently, staring out the window. 'Ruined.'

'Be assured, Épernay is not as devastated.' Sophie said.

In a few days it would be her birthday. Surely this was best present any wife in France could dream of, but she suspected this year she would know only tears, although she would need to keep them private. If only he'd been able to make contact from the German prison, she would never have opened up her heart to another man.

Guilt had begun to corrode her from within. Much as she demanded candour in their lives, she couldn't tell Jerome the truth – such honesty was destined to destroy their fragile reunion. There was guilt at encouraging Charlie and then still more at not letting him leave when he'd found the courage. She had been weak. She had been selfish, wanting them to share a life together. Sophie knew the corrosion was hers alone to bear.

'Do you remember all of this?' Gaston asked, over his shoulder.

Jerome shook his head in awe. From this side, he looked whole and she wondered about the demons that belonged to the other side of that face. She refocused on what Jerome was saying. 'I held this like a picture in my mind that could never tarnish, never blur. Do you know, my love, not even when I was lost in my mind could I forget these fields,' he said, twisting the cork he habitually carried. 'They lured me back to reality. Prison wasn't the reality I expected or wanted, but I was alive once again.'

'Do you regret it?' she couldn't help asking.

'Being alive, do you mean?'

Sophie nodded, wondering if that was pushing him too far.

'I did, often. Yes, of course. Daily at the beginning, frequently after the first year. More recently I simply accepted that returning to the life I'd enjoyed was impossible . . . it's hard to explain why it felt so unattainable but I was an impostor by 1916, I'd lost who I was, who I'd been.'

'And now?'

'Seeing you again was like a drug that cleared away doubt and despair. The fact that you want me like this —' he waved his hand at his wounds — 'makes me the luckiest man in France.' He looked past her, out of the window. 'I can feel my soul reaching out to these fields. We can plant again. Everything responds to kindness, doesn't it? These vineyards . . . and me – if we receive care and affection, we can come back to a new version of what we once were.' He took her hand and kissed it. 'I owe you my life, Sophie. Thank you for believing in me . . . for finding me.'

'She never gave up on you, Jerome,' Gaston said, and Sophie had to look away.

———————

Étienne looked confident; their anticipation felt like another person dancing around them in the low light of the cellars. 'Let's drink a toast with ratafia to new beginnings with our new champagne.' The lines of Étienne's craggy face folded in on each other to form a wide grin. He held up his penknife and flicked it open, reaching for one of the bottles of the syrupy wine. 'You are a clever chemist, Captain Charlie.'

'I'm pleased to leave something of myself behind in Épernay,' he replied, glad to say it aloud, to reassure himself that he was going – and he would not be back.

Étienne handed him a small glass and prodded a stubby finger at Charlie's chest. 'You leave more than your cunning science, no? A bit of what sits beneath here, perhaps?' he said, prodding gently again.

All Charlie could do was stare at the man. Why did he think they'd kept it such a clever secret?

'Don't be ashamed.'

'She rescued me.'

'And you rescued her back. She hasn't smiled like she's smiling now in four years. And it's not her husband who has brought that sunshine . . . it's you.'

'Does anyone else know?'

The old man shook his head.

'I have to go, Étienne.'

'I know. And it is right that you do. If she has found him, they must rediscover all that they once had. We were very proud of this couple here in Épernay.'

Charlie nodded.

'To have them reunited is part of Épernay's healing too. The earth has been hurt for four years. It doesn't matter that we are far from the main battlefields. It's all connected. I'm sure Épernay knows what's been happening in Reims, across eastern France – even further afield into Belgium. It knows the landscape's sorrows. This wine you've made it possible for her to make will be one of sorrow as much as celebration, especially important as we uncork it in peacetime after years of war, but maybe this vintage holds the memory of battle and grief. It will also hold you . . . and her memory of you.'

'Thank you for being my friend,' Charlie said, raising his glass.

'To peace at last and to friendship. You will always find friends here, Captain.'

---

'Why here?' Jerome cut a look of dismay towards Sophie.

'It's important. You are a returning hero,' Gaston insisted.

'Sophie, I . . .' he began in a voice rimmed with fear.

'Listen to me!' she insisted. 'You're never going to look different, so hiding will not change anything. You went to war, and everyone still standing knows they're safe because of men like you.' She tapped the window. 'Most of theirs aren't coming back. Your injuries are testimony to the punishment you took on behalf of your nation – on behalf of the people of this town. Stand proud: for them . . . for me . . . for us.'

393

Gaston joined in. 'Wear your injuries – don't let them wear you. Honour the uniform. Honour yourself. France asks no more of you. Now walk through your town alongside your wife.'

She had no doubt in her mind that Jerome would look as dashing to the townsfolk as he did to her. The eye patch hid his injury, and despite the scarring at the top of his lovely face, a proper haircut and an excellent shave had worked wonders. Neither of them was ready to rediscover the lively and passionate affections of their marriage but they'd shared a bath at their hotel, enjoying the feeling of familiar skin on skin. She'd shown him she was not scared by his wounds and that one arm was enough to hold her. They'd had to replenish the warm water twice as they talked through the lost years, and then they'd slept in each other's embrace, touching but not exploring. Not yet.

Sophie thought Jerome's limp was somehow fitting and she encouraged him now to walk proudly in spite of it. It didn't take long for people to notice. It began as a nudge, then a murmur; people began to whistle and clap.

'It's for you,' Jerome remarked modestly, looking as though he dared not believe what was happening.

'They see me around here often enough. No, this is for you – a son of Épernay returned.'

A ball of emotion began to rise in Sophie's throat as more and more women, older men and a straggle of returned soldiers began to cluster by the roadside. Soon they had put down their baskets or moved a small child to a hip so they could wave and cheer.

'You doubt us all too much. Come on, walk with me the length of this street to your home.'

Since Jerome had last been here, the familiar street had become an avenue where the major champagne makers kept their front of house. Many from Reims had relocated to Épernay during the war. His eyes widened to see his hometown so greatly expanded.

'I can't believe it,' he said, sounding awed.

Word had spread as fast as fire. More and more people began to appear on the long street that would lead Jerome home. The applause changed to a cheer. They knew him.

'They recognise me.' Jerome sounded shocked and emotional. He looked at his wife and in that glance she saw the genuine stirrings of the man she had married. Not yet that spark in his eye, but definitely something was being ignited. 'I love you, Sophie.'

She nodded. 'I know. I've always known.'

# 32

Below ground, where no cheering could be heard, Charlie held his breath for a second as Étienne picked up his glass. He'd selected formal champagne bowls for the old winemaker to taste the precious brew for the first time.

'It's still very rough, Étienne —'

'Hush, Captain. I know. Let me concentrate.'

'All right but talk to me. I want to understand what you're tasting.'

The older man nodded. 'As I pour, I get my first mineral bouquet, which we all hope will be present. I'm relieved that the sweetened liquor of the ratafia has not chased that beautiful fragrance from Madame's wine.' He shrugged and sniffed the air above the glass. 'It has added a new warm note that came with that tiny addition of the syrupy pinot.'

Now Charlie held up his glass to observe it as the old man continued, 'The bubbles remain small and lively.' Charlie watched them launch into a twisting column to break the surface and swim gamely to the edge to form their ringlet. They were perfect – like a disciplined troupe of ballerinas, each knowing where it must be and at which moment. He knew now those ballerinas were yet to give their flourish, which would be felt on the drinker's tongue in their finale, to give the champagne its excitement and applause.

'To you, Captain Charlie, for your idea.'

'To you, Étienne, for believing,' Charlie replied, holding his glass out to touch it against Étienne's.

'*Santé!*' they said together and tipped their glasses to take a first sip.

'Madame, as always, has shown restraint, keeping that dosage to just three grams of sugar per litre.'

'I thought she might double it,' Charlie admitted.

'That is always the temptation for other champenois. Not Madame Sophie. She has a helpless leaning towards using as little added sugar as possible. Together you have delivered a remarkable champagne, I believe.'

'I was worried it might come out tasting like a champagne cocktail,' Charlie began, but Étienne was already shaking his head at the notion.

'No. It has its own special flavour but it is still firmly a champagne. Actually . . .' The old man didn't finish his thought. They both heard it at the same moment.

It was distant but penetrating, racing its way down into the muted cellars. It was persistent too. Étienne sighed and put his half-finished glass of 'The Immortal' down onto a barrel.

'Sophie?' Charlie wondered aloud, knowing the answer.

'I think so. Come with me, Captain Charlie. You need to be brave just one more time.'

With a heavy tread, each step feeling like he was walking further from Sophie rather than towards her, Charlie followed Étienne and together they emerged from the cellars into the soft sunlight of a late autumn afternoon. Side by side they walked up the pathway that led around the side of the Delancré mansion to its impressive face, which looked out onto the main street of Épernay. Charlie fell back slightly but reluctantly followed Étienne to the pillars that supported the gates, which were flung open onto what resembled a parade.

It was brisk after the temperate cellars. The cool wind blowing across the vineyards pricked at his cheeks like stinging nettles as he stood in shirtsleeves at the gates. He wasn't straining to see like some of the others around him; he already knew who was approaching. He felt the clench of his belly.

*Let her go, Charlie*, whispered the stinging nettle wind.

He watched the only woman he could truthfully say he had ever loved approach, holding the arm of a returning French soldier. She moved so close to him that there wasn't even a thread's breadth to separate them. She'd lost him once and she was never going to let him go again – that's what this image told him.

Charlie could see the wounds, what the war had taken from this man of Épernay, but he stood taller than Charlie had expected. As they arrived and Étienne offered them a fond greeting with a wobbling chin and misty eyes, Charlie watched Jerome lower his chin to kiss the top of his wife's bent head. He looked every inch the hero with his eye patch, one empty sleeve folded neatly and pinned up. Charlie was sure women were swooning when Jerome shifted his weight to the stronger leg so he could fully embrace his wife, feel the full length of her body against him . . . just like Charlie wanted to. As Charlie now never would.

As others watched her husband, Charlie saw Sophie lift her gaze to look at him while Jerome was distracted by the cheering crowd. Her look was filled with apology. *If I could be two people*, it said, *I would live two lives with two men I love.*

Charlie couldn't watch any longer. He looked towards Gaston, who was watching him in return. *Time to go, Captain*, the French commandant's expression said.

And Charlie knew the sentiment was right. He wished he could let the commandant know just how close he and Sophie had come to belonging to each other, but there was nothing to be gained by it.

'I'll grab my things,' he said, turning quickly away.

'Captain Nash?'

He pretended he hadn't heard and kept moving towards the house.

'Charlie?' He couldn't deny her. He paused and turned, knowing she would understand his misery. 'Charlie,' she repeated, her eyes tearing up, and everything she felt was in her expression. Sophie had broken free of the cluster of people who were personally congratulating the French lieutenant, shaking his good hand and kissing him on both cheeks.

'Don't,' he said softly. 'Nothing anyone says can make this any easier.' He was pleased that Gaston had dropped back to stand with Jerome.

She nodded, swallowing the tears, drying her eyes with a handkerchief. 'I meant every word I said.'

'But that's all changed now.'

Now she shook her head. 'No, it hasn't. But that's my burden to carry, the villain in my life to make peace with. I love two men but you must forgive me for being a loyal wife. I never got the chance to be the best wife I can and I want that chance now.'

He dredged up a smile for her because he understood her impossible position. 'Sophie, I know you never stopped loving Jerome.'

'I didn't. I had to give myself permission to love you. I'm sorry that you suffer our happiness to be reunited.'

Charlie smiled wider, not enjoying her bruised features. The French men were coming closer, with Gaston generously holding Jerome off for as long as he could while these important words were exchanged.

'Don't be. You've let me glimpse what it is to be happy. I've experienced it with you.' He grinned.

'You'll find it again, Charlie.'

He shook his head. 'No, don't do that. My heart isn't that robust, Sophie. This loss needs time. Let me keep loving you. I can't forget you that easily.'

Before she could say more, he stepped forward and kissed both her cheeks. It looked polite but no one could see how he squeezed her hands or how she covered his and squeezed them back.

'I love you, Charlie,' she whispered.

'I know.' He smiled and turned his gaze to welcome Jerome.

'And you are the Captain Nash I've heard about from my wife. Apparently you've been working hard in our cellars.'

'I tried to stay useful, yes. Welcome home, Lieutenant.'

'It's cold. Shall we all go inside?'

The crowd began to disperse. Jerome and Sophie waved their thanks for such a rousing welcome.

'Sophie?' It was Gaston. 'Er, Captain Nash and I thought we'd get away shortly. He is eager to get to his unit, and as I'm here it's best I help him get as far along that journey as possible.'

'Today?' She looked distraught.

'Now, in fact. I've been away from my men for long enough getting this husband of yours back safe under his own roof,' he said as though it was settled. 'Are you packed, Charlie?'

'Yes. I was going tomorrow anyway, Sophie, so this is a boon. I've got good company to travel with,' he said, finding that smile again, knowing it was contrived now for the two men standing between them. But he had been making up smiles all his life – he knew how to fake it.

'Darling,' she said to her husband, 'just before I left for Paris, do you know what we were doing?'

Jerome's smile was genuine. 'I can't guess, my love.'

She told him about the new champagne.

'Ratafia,' Jerome repeated.

'Er, the twenty-year-old pinot,' Charlie said, sounding as though he was fully across all their wines.

'It's very exciting,' Sophie said. 'You go in. I'm just dashing down to the cellars to see that Étienne and his team are set up to produce it just as I insist.'

Jerome grinned. 'You never change. I've been gone four years and still I take second place.' Charlie couldn't help but note how Sophie looked down briefly at the remark. 'It's dangerous to fall in love with this woman, Captain Nash. She's like her grapes – unpredictable!'

Sophie gave a chuckle for him. 'Have a bath and a soak, my love. I shall be up in a minute to help. And I will not leave your side again.'

'Promise?'

'I promise,' she said before she pulled herself away. 'Gaston, will you help Jerome upstairs, please?' She didn't wait for an answer. 'Charlie, back to the cellars for us – we need to finalise what we were discussing.' She even pulled his sleeve as though she was anxious that he might not follow.

'Give me five minutes, Gaston,' he promised.

'Five minutes,' Gaston agreed in a brisk tone, and Charlie could tell that not for a second did Gaston believe they had anything important to discuss about wine.

---

She led him back to the private area where Étienne had set up the tasting. In the distance they could hear voices as women resumed their work after the excitement of Jerome's arrival. In the working part of the cellars, Étienne and his crew would be busy degorging the wine and dosing it with the ratafia. Her mind was reaching towards the labels that would need to be printed, perhaps with a new styling so the bottles could be clearly branded as something special – a limited release of champagne with a higher alcohol content to celebrate the new world peace.

She'd walked ahead of Charlie as she thought this, unable to face him, but now she had to. She turned, words failing her. He knew it too.

'There's nothing to say,' he said gently. 'There is no blame to be laid. And importantly,' he said, giving her a half attempt at a sad smile, 'I'm happy in my way for you both.'

'Do you regret it?'

He looked back at her as if bruised, and shook his head. 'No, how could I?' He lifted a shoulder in a half shrug. 'You brought me back from the wilderness in so many ways. I am grateful even though right now I don't think I've ever known such pain, and I suspect it has to get worse for a while as I learn how to miss you . . . to live without you.'

'Oh, Charlie.' She couldn't help herself – she moved towards him and wrapped her arms around him. 'I am so, so sorry.'

They leaned their foreheads together and she was grateful he didn't press their intimacy any further, but then she shouldn't be surprised, she reminded herself, that Charlie had never overstepped that line. His one reckless move had been to kiss her the first time up in the gods of the house, and she could never regret that.

'I don't know how to do this either. I am feeling sickened and frightened. I don't want to let you go but —'

'But you must. Neither of us could foresee this and I know you'll bring him fully back from all those demons that have their hold on him. He needs time and your love.' He sighed, let go of her and nodded, running a hand through his thick hair. It was not unlike Jerome's, but she knew Charlie's hair better than her husband's these days – knew its texture, its smell, how it curled at his ears and liked to drop over an eye when he bent down to work.

Sophie looked at him. Charlie was right. It couldn't go back to how it had been. She and Jerome would have to start afresh, work out a new way of living alongside each other and hope the old love was enough to build on . . . enough to push aside this new love that had bloomed through her. 'Will I ever see you again?' Even to her it sounded like a bleat.

'You want to keep breaking my heart open?' He laughed with no mirth. 'No. I must in the next minute walk away and for good.'

'What will you do?' She touched his cheek, needing to kiss him one last time, but she didn't know how to make that move without it feeling awkward or somehow desperate.

He smiled. 'I'll work it out, Sophie. I've always been alone. Caring for someone is the novelty. I'll find Harry Blake, as I told you, and when this war is fully over I will travel to Germany to find a man in Bavaria called Willi, who was my enemy but also my friend when we saved each other's lives in the bowels of a barge.'

She felt the emotion brim, choking at her throat. Her eyes stung as they watered. 'I can't bear the thought of never seeing you again.'

'But you will bear it because you have immense strength, as you've demonstrated throughout the war.' They both heard approaching footsteps in the distance. 'But I do want to thank you for being the most extraordinary woman I've had the privilege to know. And when you sip the 1918, think of me. I am going to look for its arrival on British shores, and I'm going to buy as many bottles as I can afford so that I taste you in the wine.'

Her tears spilled over. 'We're both in there, Charlie.'

Charlie took out his handkerchief and dabbed her cheeks dry. 'Yes, dancing with the bubbles, making love in the depths of all that glorious summery juice, kissing each other as we rise to break the surface and laugh. I will taste you in all the Delancré champagne I plan to buy in coming years.'

'And I will taste you with every bottle of ratafia I make forever.'

He grinned and she felt her smile returning. 'Each time it touches your lips, that's me kissing you from afar.'

She nodded. 'And while I will love my Jerome up close, you need to know that I will love you from afar forever, Charlie.'

He stared at her and she could feel all of their shared agony linking tendrils of pain and looping them around to clutch each other close, to soften the blow of the only decision they could make, to hold each other's torment in an invisible, unbreakable embrace.

The footsteps were close.

'Goodbye, Sophie.'

The commandant arrived, emerging from the darkness of the tunnels.

'Are my five minutes up?' asked Charlie.

'About two minutes ago.'

Sophie held Charlie's face in both hands now, committing the feel of his jaw to her memory, filing away the tactile sense of the stubble of his unshaven face, fixing the melancholy of that look in his eyes as they regarded her for the last time. She knew she would never see this man again, so memory was everything. She leaned in to kiss both of his cheeks, letting the roughness of that stubble graze her lips. And then in a moment she would hold in her mind forever, she left a fleeting touch of her lips against his. 'Goodbye, Captain Nash.'

And without letting either man respond, she pulled away and hurried into the cellars, deep into the womb of darkness where no tears would be seen but they would be absorbed and be held in trust by the chalk walls that had known her down the years since birth. They remembered her every tear. And they would comfort her when she returned to cry tears again as she surely would over Charlie.

But for now, it was to Jerome she fled and with whom she must rediscover her love and bring him fully back from among the dead where he had surely been living. They had time now, a long winter to rediscover one another as the three women slept in their fields and would not wake until spring to greet a peaceful France.

# EPILOGUE

Jerome had planned an evening picnic in the chardonnay vineyard he had planted almost five years earlier to celebrate their union and Sophie could not imagine anything more healing than to walk the rows of the now quiet vines. It would be their last chance to enjoy such a romantic pause before it turned too cold. Sophie had considered it a wonderful idea and had prepared the food herself.

'What have we got?' he asked, full of anticipation, peeking into her basket being readied in the parlour.

She tapped away the hand that wanted to steal one of the plums. 'We have our bread,' she said, brandishing a crusty baguette that had been baked only hours earlier. 'We have ham, chutney, some cheese.' He gave a happy sound. 'Some plums, if you leave them alone . . . and I have made the very last of our peaches into a clafoutis that is still warm.'

'Cream?'

'Of course.' She smiled.

'Champagne?'

'Ah!' Sophie gusted surprise. 'I'll get glasses. How could I forget?'

He kissed her from behind, nuzzling into her neck. 'Well, I'm ahead of you. I've had some chilling in the river. I shall fetch it and meet you at the bottom of the garden. Give me ten minutes.'

She noted Jerome carried two blankets under his arm.

'One to lay on the ground,' he'd said at her query.

'And the other?'

'To cover our naked bodies.' He winked. 'I have plans.'

To see him behaving mischievously again, no longer self-conscious of his injuries, was balm to her soul. He moved more easily, his limp improving, and he was already impressively dexterous with one arm. The eye patch gave him the appearance of a swashbuckling pirate, and every time she thought of this it gave her a small jolt of anguish because it reminded her of that painfully exquisite private moment in the attic room when Charlie Nash had brandished his pirate hook and captured her heart.

That heart still hurt from being torn, from having to choose; she'd not questioned her decision but it didn't make the loss any easier. As Jerome left with a grin, she moved through to her favourite room, which contained her parents' dining table and china. She retrieved from her pocket the letter that had arrived for her a few days ago. She'd already read it repeatedly and she swore this would be the final time before she put it away for good.

The single page unfolded easily from its creases.

*Darling Sophie,*

*Destroy this if you must but I had to write after my hasty departure with little more than my uniform and your silken scarf that I treasure. Your perfume is still with me and I'll keep feeling you close as long as that scent lasts.*

Sophie had to swallow again.

> *You may remember me mentioning Captain Harry Blake*
> *of the 20th London? Anyway, in case you don't, we met by*
> *chance at a basilica when we were both stationed close to*
> *Albert. We were admiring a statue of the Virgin Mary and*
> *Child. A legend had grown up around the golden Madonna*
> *that when it fell, the war would end. We all wished it would.*
> *Allies and enemy tried to knock it over with their artillery, and*
> *when that didn't work, a superstition erupted that whichever*
> *army knocked it down would lose the war. I think we were*
> *both intrigued to see it on a rare day off from our respective*
> *units. We got friendly over a couple of beers and he wrote to*
> *me while I was still at Épernay to tell me of his plans – like*
> *me, he was in no hurry to return to England. He'd accepted a*
> *role to lead clearing parties and suggested I do the same as they*
> *needed more men on the ground. So here I am, writing to you*
> *from Fromelles.*

When she'd first read that, she sucked back a gulping breath.
Charlie was just hours away from Épernay, but he might as well be
on the other side of the world because they could never see each
other again.

She continued reading the familiar words.

> *I'm leading one of the groups that is moving through*
> *eastern France, facing minor resistance from the retreating*
> *enemy now scattered, undisciplined and frankly desperate*
> *to get back to Germany. We are marking any fallen we find,*
> *recording details, making sure we gather up their belongings*
> *to return to families. Harry found a British soldier the other*
> *day and there was something particularly sad about the fact*

*that he hadn't opened his tin of chocolate sent by our Majesties and Rowntree's back in 1915. I think I ate mine the first day – I now use the tin to keep some wildflowers I pressed in Épernay and one of the Delancré foils from the special ratafia champagne we were bottling before I left. They give me happy memories when I look upon them.*

Sophie covered her mouth to stop the sob escaping. She checked her watch . . . just a few minutes and then she must go. Through tear-filled eyes she read the rest.

*So I'm helping families, hoping to bring them some peace regarding their loved ones. It feels good to be doing this, especially after knowing what you went through. I keep wondering how I survived . . . and why? But that's a question no one can answer so rather than wrestle with it, my darling Sophie, I want you to know that I am trying to make plans for a future. I don't wish to return to industrial chemistry, and inspired by you I think I shall likely head north into Scotland – somewhere windswept and lonely where the water runs pure and the barley grows strong – and learn how to make whisky . . . perhaps open my own distillery.*

Sophie turned the page, knowing what was coming, but needing to hear it again quickly in her mind.

*I listened to Harry talking to the fellow with the untouched chocolate tin, which contained a note from his sweetheart called Kitty. It was as though he was having a conversation with this soldier and I felt moved. This is where I've gone wrong over the course of my life in keeping my emotions tightly held down, and it's why I felt reborn around you, Sophie. I thank my lucky stars for knowing you, for having a short time to know what loving someone – and being loved – feels like.*

*I'll miss you every day of my life but I know I must now try to build a new life that doesn't include you. I have a high hope one day to find a German soldier called Willi Becker. I hope he survived too. I think we both saved each other's life on that terrible morning of battle in May, and I want him to know I took his advice, opened up my heart, and despite the pain I'm feeling I cannot regret falling in love.*

*So here's to you, Sophie, and here's to love . . . to being with the one that you have always loved and always will. Be happy, think of me now and then and know that you've brought laughter into my life, and hope. Both gifts. I am wishing you and the goddess a long and fruitful time together too – I can't wait to see the 1918 vintage on shelves in England. I will buy some and drink to your health, tasting you in that effervescence and in that sweetness we found together.*

*I love you, Sophie. I always will. C x*

She had to wipe away the stream of tears, dabbing at her cheeks. Sophie hid Charlie's letter in one of the Limoges tureens in the dining room, with the intention of giving it a proper hiding place later. Standing in the middle of the room where she'd had her confrontation with Louis, she looked past the love seat, out of the window towards the vineyards. The sun had swooped low to lick a golden tongue across the vines and autumn was heralding herself. Summer had ended – life as she'd known it was going to sleep and it felt right that when the vines woke to a new spring Charlie would be gone from France, fully gone from her life. It was in this moment that Sophie accepted she must let him go entirely . . . now. Without allowing herself to hesitate, she retrieved the letter, grabbed a matchbox and threw it into the picnic basket.

She marched out of the house and into the garden, where she paused in the private space away from the stables and the entrance to the cellars. Striking a match, she touched the flame to the corner of Charlie's letter and watched with a feeling of half despair, half relief as the letter singed and then caught aflame. It occurred to her that these were the flames of passion that had burned brightly in the short time they'd had the freedom to love each other.

The flame, well-lit now, curled the page and burned through his heartfelt words. Sophie held the paper until she risked scorching herself and then she dropped it to watch it burn out among the fallen leaves, not yet dry enough to burn with it. She bent and dug a small hole with one of the spoons from the basket, before pushing in the ashes of Charlie's letter and covering them with the earth and rusted leaves of Épernay.

Sophie stood and sighed. She wouldn't forget him, but she did feel a sense of release.

'Sophie?' She looked up and Jerome waved.

'Sorry, I got caught up.'

He grinned, not offended, and held up a bottle triumphantly; in that moment of happiness, she saw all the promise of their future. There he stood, tall and ridiculously handsome despite his missing limb and eye; the grin was as carefree and crooked as the one she remembered falling in love with. His clothes were shabby favourites that she'd not had the courage to part with and now felt only glad for that selfishness.

Perhaps her soul had known what her heart couldn't?

Looking at him now she could see a bright future. She could almost hear the voices of the babbling brood of little Méa-Delancrés he planned to have with her. Her world was idyllic in comparison to so many others and it was important she return to that world now with all of her heart. Jerome decided to sing his pleasure loudly as she walked towards him; she began to laugh knowing she could let

Charlie go at this moment and she would embrace all that Jerome promised for her.

The sun was slipping below the horizon, leaving a sky that looked like someone had splashed coloured ink across it. Blues bled into lilacs that gave way to pinks, which in turn bowed to the brilliance of cerise and orange that curtsied to amber and a final brilliant last gasp of shimmering gold as the day bid her farewell.

And as they walked the rows of the vineyard Sophie felt the goddess beginning to settle into her slumber with a contented smile that Sophie realised she wore too. They were as one . . . at peace . . . and they were happy.

# ACKNOWLEDGEMENTS

This story has many people's fingerprints on it and it couldn't have been written without their generous involvement.

All but bumping into Sophie Signolle on the avenue de Champagne, while admiring her beautiful French mansion and home to House Gonet, was beyond serendipitous. I was walking the avenue, waiting for inspiration to find me . . . and I found Sophie, who invited us in and poured us a flute of her finest, and we began talking. Within that hour we had made a promise to return and she had made a promise to help me with my story, especially as her life matched my fictional heroine's so closely. 'Make sure I have a wonderful affair,' she quipped as we hugged farewell. I met Sophie in Épernay on three more occasions and on the final visit we stayed as guests in her beautiful home, so I feel I know the house in this story. We have used a photo of House Gonet in the inside cover to show you from where I drew my inspiration, and in the story this is Charlie's first glimpse of the house as the character Sophie accompanies him into Épernay. As I finished my research, House Gonet was throwing open its doors to take overnight guests for the first time, so do visit if you have the chance to travel to the Champagne region.

Sophie Signolle lost her father not long after I lost mine, so we were both grieving through the crafting of this novel, which lent an additional emotional thread to tie us together.

I learned from Sophie's network of contacts but especially from her daughter, Diane, who works for Chateau Vieux Landat, the estate inherited from her father close to Bordeaux. She spent a full day with me in the cellars. Also Benjamin Dagot was tirelessly helpful with translation and hunting down historical information for me. Thank you, Nicolas Signolle, Chloé Delaporte at House Gonet, and Sophie's Aunty Marie-Claire for her lovely food. As I write this, Marie-Claire is arriving at the house featured in the novel because it's cherry jam–making time. I have tasted no finer jam than hers, when I was a guest in this home.

I must acknowledge Isabelle Rousseaux, who runs private guided trips around Reims and Épernay, for her time and for introducing me to Michel Jolyet, a photographer, who through his library could take me directly back to images of WWI and the region. It was invaluable. Michel also organised for me to take a wholly private walk through the Veuve Clicquot crayères in Reims, and without the usual crowds of tourists I was able to build my mental pictures of the subterranean life of the people of Reims during the war. Thank you to the team at Veuve Clicquot for its generous help too.

Without the help of Bloomsbury Press and the academic work of historian Susan Barton in her brilliant book *Internment in Switzerland during the First World War*, I would never have found out as much as I did about this aspect of WWI. In fact, I didn't know that Swiss internment existed, and it offered a marvellous solution to a vexing corner I'd written myself into.

There is of course the usual cavalry that circles my books. When it comes to WWI and the French battlefields, I'd be hard pressed to find anyone as knowledgeable or determined for me to stay authentic when it comes to military matters as historian Simon Godly. He guides me over former bogs and trenches, walks me over No Man's Land and does his absolute best to make sense for me of the landscape of those four terrible years that today looks so different. Simon kept me on the straight and narrow throughout this novel with his copious notes and with all things army, from the right uniforms to how people should be addressed, to the language they'd use, and *tsk-tsk*ing at any liberties I took for the sake of story. That does happen and I apologise for those occasions – any errors are all mine – including taking licence such as putting Sophie's vineyard so close to the frontline in Reims. Anyone who needs private guiding around the battlefields of France, look no further than Simon. A former British policeman, he's brilliant . . . and fun.

And Alex Hutchinson, archivist and history buff, busy with her own writing projects and on her third novel, still takes time to accompany me on my jaunts around England. There was to be a section about England in this book and we did the research together, but when it came to writing it I realised the story had to remain in France with a brief detour into Germany and Switzerland. So our efforts never made it to the final cut but that doesn't mean I didn't appreciate her sterling help that never loses energy, enthusiasm or inspiration. And she'll be back stomping around Yorkshire with me in the next novel. Look out for her Quality Street series.

Heartfelt thanks to Ali Watts, my publisher and friend, who sat through four hard drafts before we finally hit on the one that made us all sigh with pleasure. This book was hard won because it was written through a time of grieving for me – no doubt why it took so many drafts to get it right. I applaud Ali's determination to keep pushing me, keep searching for the right recipe, and it came because of a casual comment made by my lovely editor Amanda Martin, who frowned and said something that lit fireworks in my mind and was responsible for that fifth draft we all were thrilled to see delivered safely to copyedit. And thanks to Penelope Goodes for her efforts during that edit and Saskia Adams for the tight proofread.

Louisa Maggio . . . another sensational cover and perhaps our best yet. Excited to take this book to market looking so lush and inviting. Thank you for your fine work.

Love all round to my family, especially Ian, Will and Jack, who provide so much support and good times, and even in the tough times making me laugh. Laughter really is healing and while this book is not a lighthearted one, I do hope you'll find a smile at the end and know Sophie made the right decision.

Fx

# RECIPES

*Sabayon*

In *The Champagne War*, Sophie Delancré is taken to the famous Hôtel de Crillon in Paris by her brother in law, Louis Méa, for lunch. As Louis explains, tradition goes back a long way in this hotel and after a meal of fish, he orders a sabayon, memorable from the childhood of the two Méa brothers.

Sabayon itself is the simplest of sweet dishes and the building block of many desserts like custard or ice cream. At its most refined it requires three ingredients, which are egg yolks, sugar and your choice of flavour: anything from orange zest or vanilla, through to coffee or alcohol. For the latter, think amaretto, coffee liqueur, Moscato . . . whatever pleases you.

Many of you may recognise this as the Italian zabaglione, claimed to date back to the court of the Medici in medieval Florence and made with sweet marsala wine. The French have their own version using champagne, which I felt was most necessary to go with this book.

This beautiful, elegant custard is the perfect accompaniment to poached fruits, warmed cake or thin, crunchy biscuits like the popular French Langues de Chat – or Cat's Tongues as we know them.

417

I have not offered a stabilising factor, so this requires your speed, determination and patience – it will work! However, you can stabilise if you wish with whipped cream, turned gently through the silken foam and then chilled in the fridge to spoon over whatever takes your fancy (or straight into your mouth when no one else is looking!).

All you need, apart from those three ingredients mentioned, are heat, a stainless-steel bowl, a saucepan of water on a low simmer and a big balloon whisk, plenty of stamina and your promise that you'll keep beating until it rewards you with ribbony traces through a pillowy custard.

This recipe will easily provide four small glass dishes of sabayon, more than enough to serve over berries or stewed autumn fruits, or simply to dip into with biscuits with a bowl or flute of champagne nearby. If you do stabilise with cream then the threat of separation is removed and you can make it ahead.

Choose a lovely dry sparkling wine, such as Taylor's from the Clare Valley, or your favourite bubbles.

**Ingredients**
3 extra-large egg yolks
115 g caster sugar
180 ml sparkling wine

**Method**
Get a saucepan of water on to simmer. You don't want ferocious heat or you're going to end up with scrambled egg. And you don't want any steam getting into your mix.

In your stainless-steel bowl, whisk the egg yolks and sugar together until the mixture is pale.

Add the sparkling wine and mix it all in.

Now, it's off to the stove. Put the bowl over the simmering water and start whisking. A figure of eight motion works best.

You are not trying to achieve bubbles, but a fluffy cloud of pale microfoam.

Have some back-up handy – your arm might not be up to it! I kept swapping hands and nearly asked the dogs to help out. Grit your teeth and keep going. The mixture will thicken, stabilise and start to lose its frothy appearance and look plump, like a big cumulus cloud.

When you can see a ribbony pathway through the custard as you make your figure eight, then you are probably there.

The wonderful part of this small but elegant sweet finish to any meal is that you can serve it chilled, warm from the bowl, cooled to room temperature, or throw in some cream and freeze it. The alcohol will never let it freeze fully, of course, but it would be lovely as a firmer semifreddo-style topping on a hot tart.

We have so many apples falling off our tree as I sign off this book at the start of winter 2020 that I served mine with stewed apples and lightly toasted almonds. Heavenly!

# *Fiona's champagne truffles*

Sometimes you don't want dessert after a meal . . . you may feel like cheese and its accompaniments or a cleansing flute of champagne but, honestly, doesn't everyone want some little sweetish treat? I have to admit I feel roundly cheated when asked to someone's house for dinner and you get the main meal and then a piece of camembert to gnaw on – I want to say, 'Blimey, what about pudding?' So, how about a treat that is every bit as elegant and simple as the sabayon featured in *The Champagne War* – and made with champagne, of course? I defy anyone to say no to a small cocoa-dusted, dark chocolate champagne truffle.

With only three main ingredients, you will be rewarded if you work with only the highest quality chocolate and cream.

If you don't like rolling truffles and all that mess – I don't either – then it's quite elegant to serve them as cubes, or square pastilles as I prefer to call them. Either way, I like to dust them with bitter cocoa or you may want to decorate in your own way. I faffed around with edible gold leaf – more trouble than it's worth, but the shiny glimmer does make it all look expensive and celebratory! If you are using gold leaf, you'll need a small, clean, dry paintbrush and to make sure the area on the truffle where you're going to add it is free of cocoa, or it won't cling.

Your champagne can be fizzy or flat as you prefer. I used a freshly popped bottle but since you're only using 50 ml, please don't open it just for these unless you plan to enjoy a flute alongside these treats.

These are super rich but will melt in your mouth in a blink from their deliciously firm texture . . . and just beneath all that deep chocolatiness, you will definitely get the hit of acidic freshness from the champagne – it's a lovely combination.

### Ingredients
280g dark chocolate (at least 70% is ideal), chopped
    (or just broken, if you're lazy like me!)
½ cup heavy, rich cream
Pinch of salt
50 ml champagne
High-quality cocoa powder, sifted

### Method
Very lightly butter and then line a small square cake tin with baking paper (15 × 15 cm or smaller). Cut the paper so it's taller than the sides, forming a hammock so you can lift out the set truffle mix.

Combine the chocolate with the cream and salt in a bowl. Now, sensible people will use a bowl over simmering water, but I'm a big fan of the slow microwave method – I have the patience to work with 30% power and go in 30 second increments until I have a beautifully smooth mix. But you go ahead and melt the chocolate in your preferred manner.

Remove from the heat and whisk in the champagne.

Scrape the silken melted chocolate into the prepared tin and chill this overnight.

It should lift out easily since you lined the tin with paper, but if it needs encouragement, a blunt knife dipped in hot water and dried will loosen the edges.

To form your truffles, warm a knife in boiling water, trim the edges and then cut the truffle mix into cubes. If you want to, then roll each cube into a ball.

Toss in the sifted cocoa (avoiding any areas where you may wish to decorate further with gold leaf). Apply gold leaf if using.

Store in the fridge until serving, but take them out for a few minutes before you want to enjoy. They'll keep for a few days in an airtight container in the fridge.

Serve with flutes of champagne . . . or just eat them all yourself, with a flute of champagne as you read this book again!

# BOOK CLUB NOTES

1. 'Épernay must survive – the champagne must keep flowing.' Sophie is determined to continue making her champagne throughout the war. Why is this so important to her?

2. Charlie joins the war effort as a soldier rather than using his skills as a chemist in chemical warfare. Do you understand his choice?

3. At one point, Charlie feels closer to Willi, his enemy, than to any other person alive. Why do you think that is?

4. Would the strong women of Champagne who had gone before Sophie – like Veuve Clicquot and Madame Pommery – have approved of her determination not to conform, and of her choice in a husband?

5. Sophie believes that 'everything responds to kindness'. In what ways does she display her own kindness in the novel?

6. Who really holds the power in the relationship between Louis and Sophie? Would you be as forgiving of him as she is?

7. Jerome believes he is likely to die from the gas attacks, and yet he strives to get a message to France. What is his motivation?

8. What does Charlie mean when he says home is an emotion? Why is this an important revelation for him?

9. If you were Sophie, would you have chosen Charlie or Jerome?

10. Sophie tells Charlie: 'It's a great pity the world cannot behave like a good champagne. Harmony, peace, pleasure – every grape giving its utmost, its very best to the champagne experience.' What parallels can we draw between life during the war and modern times?

11. What connections does the author make between champagne itself and the themes and issues explored in her novel?

12. *The Champagne War* features many real events in history. What new or surprising things about France or World War I did you learn while reading this book?